Praise for Shelly Laurenston's
Hunting Season

"I loved how Ms. Laurenston makes a scene come alive to the point where I can picture what is happening around me... The Hunting Season reminds me why I love Ms. Laurenston's writings and also what a recommended read should be."

~ *Joyfully Reviewed Recommended Read*

"Hunting Season will endear you towards these hardened warriors quickly. I laughed, I worried, and I was in desperate need of a fan during some of the more scorching hot scenes."

~ *ParaNormal Romance*

"Hooray for Shelly Laurenston, who has just renewed my faith in a genre I have found to be sorely lacking in originality lately... The world Ms. Laurenston has so cleverly crafted is completely different from anything else out there. Viking gods, valkyries, psychotic zealots and a motley group of fierce winged warriors that will have you laughing out loud...[And] Wilhelm Yager has to be the hottest hero to grace the pages of paranormal romance in a long time. He's a vicious fighter, blindingly gorgeous, carnally skilled and a bit of a geek. I fell in love."

~ *Fallen Reviews Recommended Read*

Look for these titles by
Shelly Laurenston

Now Available:

Here, Kitty Kitty

Go Fetch!

Pack Challenge

About a Dragon (Writing as G.A. Aiken)

Hunting Season

Shelly Laurenston

A Samhain Publishing, Ltd. publication.

Samhain Publishing, Ltd.
577 Mulberry Street, Suite 1520
Macon, GA 31201
www.samhainpublishing.com

Hunting Season
Copyright © 2010 by Shelly Laurenston
Print ISBN: 978-1-60504-788-1
Digital ISBN: 978-1-60504-672-3

Editing by Jennifer Miller
Cover by Scott Carpenter

This book has been previously published.
First Samhain Publishing, Ltd. electronic publication: October 2009
First Samhain Publishing, Ltd. print publication: August 2010

Dedication

To my CPs. You helped me during a difficult transitional period and I will be forever grateful. Thanks for your continuing support, your faith in me, your feedback, and your invaluable time.

To my Magnus Pack Groupies. As you read this book, you'll realize what an inspiration you crazy females have been to me. Every day you make me laugh and keep me sane. Yeah, you're all pains in my ass, but I wouldn't have you any other way. This book is dedicated to each of you. Enjoy.

Shel.

Prologue

"Find her!"

They chased her into the woods. A dark beauty, with dark eyes and hair. Haakon and his men had plans for her, but as soon as they hit the clearing, she disappeared.

He silenced his men with a slash of his hand. She probably hid right in front of them. Haakon smiled. He could already imagine her taste, her cries, her screams for mercy. Willing or otherwise, he'd have the tiny female. Then his men would have her.

A noise behind them had the entire group turning.

Haakon relaxed the hand on his sword and chuckled. "It's just a raven, you fools."

"She's a crow."

As one, they turned at the sound of the girl's voice. She stood before them in worn, ripped clothes and dirty hair. Brown-skinned, she must be from one of the raided lands. Dragged here for breeding. Still, none of that could take from her beauty. Perhaps Haakon would keep this one. Perhaps he wouldn't share her as he'd planned. He didn't have to. Not with the power he now possessed.

He held his hand out to her, feeling that power surge from the weapon he'd recently taken from the cave they'd discovered near the river. The power made him bold and confident. The power made him strong. "Come to me, little girl."

She stared at him and he no longer saw any fear from her. Perhaps she wanted him. Perhaps she realized what fun they could have together.

"Look," one of his men barked. But Haakon ignored him, too focused on the woman in front of him.

"Look!" his second-in-command insisted. With a sigh, Haakon followed his men's line of sight...to the trees. There were more birds there. More crows and maybe some ravens, hundreds of them, silently watching. He didn't care.

Still staring into the trees, Haakon snapped, "They're just birds, you fool. Get hold of yourself."

He heard the men gasp and his gaze dropped to them and then to the woman. He took an involuntary step back as giant black wings slowly extended from her. Almost as big as her, they looked just like the wings of a crow.

She grinned. "Don't you still want me, sweet Haakon?" The girl knew his name. How did she know his name? He'd never seen her before this day.

"Don't toy with your prey." Haakon and his men turned yet again at the sound of another female voice behind them. This time, however, they drew their weapons. It was a slightly older woman. Another set of wings. "It is...unseemly," this woman chastised.

"Why should we be fair?" the girl barked. "Do you think he would have been kind to me?"

He wouldn't have been. He could assure her of that.

"Ach!" another one snapped, stepping out of the shadows of the trees. "You waste our time! Odin's warriors arrive tonight and I have plans of much drinking and at least one of them warming my bed. So hurry up so we can go."

"Oooh!" another cheered, stepping into the clearing. "The Ravens are coming?"

The females laughed. "If I have my way," one of them promised.

The old women of his village had warned him about this many days past. They'd ordered him to return the jeweled dagger to the cave where he'd found it. But he'd laughed at them. How could they expect him to give up something that had given him so much power, so much strength, and had given it all so quickly? Within days, he'd ruled his village and had plans to own the surrounding ones. "But they'll come for you," they whispered to him. "And when they do, no one will help you. For nothing comes between a Crow and her prey."

Like most of the men in his village, he'd never believed the old stories about a goddess' brutal warriors. True, the bloodthirsty Valkyries were frightening, but they were the daughters of gods and fought on the side of the mighty Odin. Yet, according to legend, the females staring at him with such coldness were very much human, and they fought for a goddess with little patience for men and their ways.

These...women, if you could call them that, were known as The Gathering, and they were the winged warriors for the goddess Skuld. Warriors who had already died once who Skuld returned to the living. They were still human, although slightly...changed.

As he stared at their mighty wings, the small one he'd chased struck first, slamming her small fist into his face. Haakon quickly realized her tiny size hid a mighty strength as he grabbed his shattered nose. Before he could recover, she had him on the ground, her kicks and fists having much more impact than any male he'd fought.

The dying screams of his men filled his ears, but he was unable to help them. Unable to stop The Gathering from ripping them apart.

It didn't take them long to wipe out his men. Hard men who'd fought many wars for many years. Some he even considered friends. And these relatively young women killed them all in mere seconds.

Yet they kept him for last.

The one he'd chased had her tiny bare foot shoved against his throat. One of them pulled the magically charged dagger from the sheath at his side. The dagger had given him so much power, but just as quickly, these females were snatching his power away. Now he was paying a mighty price for taking—and using—what belonged to Skuld.

"Here." The woman expertly flipped the blade over so the girl could grasp the handle. "Make it quick. Make it clean. Then Hella can deal with him and we can spend our night teaching Odin's Ravens how to beg."

The girl nodded. "As you wish." She straddled him, lowering her body until she sat on his chest. She was warm and naked under her clothes. He could smell her lust but it wasn't for him...it was for the kill.

"You should have listened to the old women in your village, Haakon—and returned the blade to our goddess. Now you must pay the price."

"No Valhalla for you," another one of them sneered, already heading toward the village and the Ravens they all spoke fondly of. She acted as if the loss of his place at Odin's table in Asgaard meant nothing to a warrior such as himself, adding, "No Valkyries to take you home."

The girl shook her head sadly. "No. There'll be no Valhalla for you."

Then she slashed his throat.

Chapter One

New Jersey
One thousand years later...

Glass shattered as a grown man threw himself out of a fifth-story window. Will Yager closed his eyes and turned his head to protect himself from the spray of glass. He knew the man threw himself out that window because that's what any sane person would do in a similar situation.

"You can run, David," a female voice from the man's apartment taunted as the man landed hard at Yager's feet. "But we'll find you."

"Don't leave, sweetness! I wasn't nearly done!" another female voice laughingly added.

The man at his feet—"David", Yager guessed—struggled to crawl away. The only reason the man's back hadn't snapped like a twig when he landed was due to the little item he'd recently stolen. Which was the only reason Yager and his team were even here on a Saturday night.

Why people insisted on stealing from gods, Yager would never know.

Reaching down, he grabbed David by the neck and lifted him to his feet. "Where exactly are you crawling away to, little man?"

"Trust me." Yager's protégé, Mike, chuckled behind him. "We're much nicer than the women you just ran from."

That was true. The Gathering didn't do rescue missions or help those in need or involve themselves in the politics of gods. In fact, The Gathering only answered to one god. A Fate called Skuld, the Veiled One. A goddess who once rode with the Valkyries when she got bored, Skuld knew the future, could bring the dead back to life, and believed in wisdom. She'd created The Gathering more than a thousand years ago when Yager's people still raided monasteries for sport. Like Odin, she wanted her own warriors, but unlike Odin, Skuld didn't choose from the finest Nordic stock. Instead she chose from the descedents of the girls his people had stolen. Girls thrown over warriors' shoulders and carried away to a cold and foreign land they knew nothing about. Mike probably put it best when he observed of the two groups, "The Ravens look like an ad for Hitler Youth while the Crows look like a big box of crayons."

In the early days, when Skuld rode with the Valkyries, she would choose among the slain who would go to Valhalla. And now that she chose her own warriors, nothing had changed. For those who wanted to commit their lives to her service and to The Gathering...they had to be taking their last breath.

"Give it up, little man," Yager ordered as he took firm hold of David's hair and held him in place like he used to hold his childhood teddy bear. Yager hated chasing anybody. "With us you'll get a quick death. But I can promise you won't get that from them."

David shook his head but didn't speak.

"I'm not even going to ask why you're here, Yager," a female voice calmly stated.

David squealed as strong female hands gripped the man's shoulders and yanked him away from the dubious safety of Yager's men. Of the Ravens.

Yager winced in sympathy when he realized David definitely lost hair and some of his scalp in that little transfer.

"This one is ours, Yager."

Odin help him. The delectable Neecy Lawrence. Second-in-command to the Jersey Crows, Neecy was lethal with a blade and her talons. She was also stubborn, tough, brutally honest, and the hottest piece of ass on the East Coast. Neecy also made his life a living hell because she wouldn't admit the truth—they were perfect together.

"I didn't say he wasn't yours, Neecy. We're just here to help...and to get Odin's rune. Which I believe is somewhere on him." Yager snatched David back.

"We're not doing this again," Neecy promised.

As always, she and her team wore the requisite Crow fighting gear: black jeans, black steel-toe boots, white racerback tanks so their wings were unencumbered, and the brand of their goddess burned deep and black onto their necks. And because it was the middle of

January, tightly fitted wool sleeves that went from the palms of their hands to their upper biceps.

The Ravens' fighting clothes were similar except for the sleeves. Viking males just had to deal with the freezing Northeast coast cold. Otherwise the Elder Ravens called them pussies.

"Besides, he's already used the rune and given a sacrifice," Neecy continued. "His tongue specifically. And you know the rules—once they use it, the prey belongs to us. And Skuld gave me orders to bring that rune to her, so I guess you're shit out of luck, huh?" She again yanked the man to her.

"Actually you are, baby." Yager grabbed hold of David by the neck and pulled him back. "I don't care if he's already used the damn rune. I'm returning it to Odin. You can have the carcass for all I care."

"And Odin can go to hell for all *I* care. And stop calling me baby." Neecy took David back, ignoring the whimpering sound he made.

"Why do you always have to be so difficult?" he asked, because really...couldn't they just get married and work the rest of it out in bed?

Neecy gave that tight smile of hers. The one that told him she was losing her patience. "You haven't seen difficult, Yager. But trust me when I say I can get difficult." She wasn't bragging or uselessly threatening either. Neecy Lawrence didn't need to. Her reputation preceded her.

She'd come to Skuld early. Only sixteen when she woke up at the Bird House, the name for the Jersey safe house many of the Crows called home. She woke up from dying. The last thing she probably remembered was her drug-dealer boyfriend pulling the trigger. Six bullets to the chest—a gift for warning two undercover cops they'd been made.

Fifteen years later and she ruled the Jersey Crows. In fact, only one woman stood between Neecy and Skuld. Didi handled the politics while Neecy handled everything else. Always so serious, always so determined, Neecy never took her oath to her goddess lightly and she demanded the best from all the Crows. A ball-buster she may be, but a fair one.

He took a step toward her. "Neecy."

"Back off, Yager." Her wings, glistening blue-black from the streetlight, spread dangerously away from her body even as she remained outwardly calm.

Shelly Laurenston

Man, he'd never known a woman more beautiful than Neecy. Short, short straight black hair she'd lately let grow long in the front. So long, her bangs nearly covered her gorgeous black eyes. Neecy was brown-skinned and tall, but no one really knew what she was. Even Neecy. Rumor was someone found her in a Dumpster when she was barely a day old. She could be black, Brazilian, Cuban, or a mix of all three or a mix of something completely different. Yager didn't know or care. He only cared about one thing when it came to Neecy Lawrence. Making her his.

Sighing, he said, "I don't want to fight you."

"I know, Yager," she responded softly. "I know." Then she punched him in the face.

Dammit! He should have seen it coming. The calmer she got, the worse the damage. She only managed to snap his head to one side, but that gave her enough time to use her wings to lift her body into the air so she could slam both her feet into his chest, sending him slamming into his men. The momentum of her attack sent her body flipping back in midair. But when she landed, she did it silently and firmly on two feet.

"Katie," she barked.

"Got him." Katie Clark. A vicious little redhead, who'd died when she'd tried to stop a knife fight between two friends, took firm hold of poor, growing-balder-by-the-moment David. Talons burst from Katie's hand and she ripped his side open with one swipe. Then she dug her hand into his open flesh, snorting at his unintelligible screams of pain.

"Oh, quit whining, ya big baby," she snapped. "You brought this shit on yourself."

She pulled her hand out of his body, the rune he'd given up parts of himself for held tightly in her bloody fist. Katie dropped him to the ground like old garbage. Now that the rune was gone, Yager knew that David felt every ache, every pain...he felt it all.

"Got it!" Katie cheered.

"Good," Neecy barked. "Go!"

Katie spread her wings and her feet left the ground. But Mike charged past all of them, grabbed her around the legs, and slammed her back down.

A second of stunned silence followed. Yager never expected him to do that. Actually, none of the Ravens expected Mike to do that. They watched as he reached down and snatched the rune from Katie's hand. Mike shrugged. "What did you expect me to do?"

Quick to recover, Katie slammed her foot into his knee. She didn't use her heel—a six-inch metal spike—so Yager could only guess she didn't want to permanently damage him. Mike still dropped to one knee, though, with an angry grunt of pain.

Katie rolled back and out of his way, quickly coming to her feet.

"You're going to get your ass kicked, little boy," she growled.

"Oooh. A chick threat," Mike mocked, still kneeling in front of her. "I love those." The kid never knew when not to push it, did he?

Mike waited for Katie to make her move and that was his mistake. He didn't see Connie Vega, who'd died when a drunk driver hit her bicycle, standing behind him. She kicked him between his shoulder blades, slamming his big body to the ground. She put her knee against his back while she wrapped a chain around his neck and pulled.

Mike gritted his teeth and tossed the rune to Yager, who caught it easily and stared down at Neecy.

She held her hand out. "Give it, Yager."

"Nope."

"I'll let Connie have fun with him if you don't give it to me now."

He rolled his eyes. "You wouldn't hurt Mike and we both know it." Believe it or not, the Ravens and the Crows were on the same side.

"That's where you're wrong. I wouldn't *kill* Mike, but I wouldn't think twice about hurting him."

He couldn't help but smile. Mike drove everyone crazy, but the Crows still treated the twenty-seven-year-old like their baby brother. "Neecy, come on..."

"Exactly how many times do you think I've had that conversation with one of my young sisters, explaining to her that the reason Mike didn't call was because he'd already fucked her and was done?"

Yager winced. Goddamn horny Mike. Out of principal, he should leave Mike Molinski to the not-so-tender mercies of the Crows.

"Trust me when I say I'd have fun making him cry... So, give it." She still had her hand out and now she wiggled her fingers.

He shrugged. "Okay."

He placed the rune in her palm. As she started to close her hand around it, Yager caught hold of her wrist, quickly turned Neecy around, and dragged her against his body, both his arms holding her tight.

"Get Mike!" he barked at his team.

Now Neecy was pissed and she showed it. She struggled to get out of his arms. *"You son of a bitch!"*

17

"You've never even met my mother." How come the angrier she got the calmer he got?

The Crows and Ravens all dived at Mike and Connie at the same time, creating a rather interesting "pile on" while Neecy struggled in Yager's arms. She moved one way, then another. And that's when they both froze.

Through gritted teeth, she said, "Yager, get your damn hands off my tits!"

"I'm sorry...I'm grabbing your tits? I didn't even notice." Liar! But he just couldn't resist. Calm, cool Neecy angry? A rare moment and one he planned to savor.

What he didn't love...her slamming her booted foot against his instep while yanking her arm away and bringing her elbow back to his chin hard. Yager's head snapped back as she turned to face him.

Neecy's wings lifted her a bit, and she brought her leg up to kick him in the chest. He caught her foot before it could touch him, spun her over, and slammed her down onto the pavement.

Yager struggled to ignore her yelp of pain, but he still wasn't about to let her up.

When she couldn't get him to release her leg, she looked up at the sky, and he knew exactly what she planned. Man, he was starting to know this woman better than himself.

"Don't you dare, Neecy Lawrence!" he ordered.

"*Come to me,*" she bellowed, her voice ricocheting off the alley walls.

Both sides froze in midattack, immediately looking up at the sky. Silence descended because now they were waiting for something worse than all of them put together.

"Goddammit, Neecy!"

"Don't yell at me, Yager. You started this shit." She yanked her foot away and stood. Her team pulled themselves out of the body pile and moved behind Neecy while the Ravens helped Mike up.

Neecy folded her arms across her chest, calm and cool once again. "Guess you better get your men out of here, Yager. I'd hate for anything to happen to them."

"Fine," he snapped. "Ravens...go." His men stared at him. "Now!"

Three took off, but Mike wouldn't leave. Pulling the chain from around his throat, he walked up to Yager. "Bro, let's go."

Neecy grinned. "You heard him, Yager. You better go."

But he didn't go. He simply stared at her.

Mike again looked up at the sky. "Yager. I hear them. We have to go."

Yager heard them too, but he wasn't going anywhere. "Then go."

"Without you? No way."

"I said go."

Sighing in annoyance and resignation, Mike spread his wings and took off. Leaving Yager, the Crows, and poor dying David.

At the moment, Neecy looked bored, but he knew better. "Yager, I'm not kidding. They're coming."

"I know," he said simply.

Her smug smile wavered a bit. "Look, you've got Odin's rune...so go."

He continued staring at her, his arms folded in front of his chest, mimicking her stance.

"Yager," she pushed, the tiniest hint of panic finally easing into her tone.

He took a step toward her. "Ask me nice."

The other Crows passed surprised glances, but Neecy shook her head. "Are you high? I will not!"

He shrugged and stood there.

"Yager, I'm not calling them off."

Still, he didn't move, even though he could see David trying to drag himself away. The guy shouldn't bother. He'd never leave the alley alive.

"Yager!"

What had been distant was now clear—the flapping of wings. Many, many wings.

"Neecy," Janelle McKenna, another one shot to death at an early age, muttered softly as she stared up at the sky.

"Seriously, Yager. Go. They won't hurt my girls, but you..." Neecy tried to keep her usual calm demeanor, but it wasn't working. He could see right through it.

Something black sailed by him and he felt pain rip across his neck. He knew there'd be blood. He didn't care. Another came by, tearing past his cheek. Another line of blood, he bet.

"Jesus, Yager," Neecy whispered.

"Ask me nice, Neecy," he ordered. "Ask me nice or I'm staying right here until they're done."

Through gritted teeth, she barked, "Fine. Go." This time another emotion crossed her face. The emotion of annoyance. "Please," she spit out.

Yager smiled. A grin that had Neecy Lawrence glaring at him. "I knew it," he sighed happily. "I knew you liked me."

Then he unfurled his own wings and took off.

He pushed through the flock of real crows—and even some ravens—that Neecy commanded. They were heading toward David and would leave nothing remaining of the man but his shredded clothes.

And, as Yager headed back to the Ravens' Jersey safe house, he could hear Neecy yelling at him from that alley.

"I hate you, Will Yager! *And the longboat your ancestors rowed in on!*"

Chapter Two

Denise "Neecy" Lawrence landed on the club's roof. The Gathering booked the place for the night, so she knew the roof doors would be unlocked so those flying in would have a handy entrance.

"Do it again, Connie!" Katie begged. "Do it again!"

Neecy stifled her growl as Connie stared up at the sky and shook her fist in the air. "I hate you, Will Yager. I *hate* you!"

That performance prompted fresh howling laughter from the rest of her team, and she wondered how bad it would look if she kicked their collective asses...probably really bad.

"Okay. Let it go," she told them, knowing that if she showed them how very angry she truly was, she'd never hear the end of it.

To be honest, it would help if she knew what the fuck was going on. Yager had always flirted with her. Had always shown her some interest over the many years they'd known each other. But in the last twelve months or so he'd suddenly become relentless. She could only guess he was looking to slum it a bit. Unlike Yager, Neecy didn't have a fine Nordic-American family upbringing. Mostly because she never had a family.

Some homeless guy found her in a Dumpster over on 118th Street. A sickly brown baby who, in the end, no one wanted. She was in a Catholic orphanage until she turned nine and then she started making the foster-home rounds. Smart and quiet, she didn't last very long with any of her foster families. She'd made them paranoid. They'd always thought she was plotting—and that was probably because she was.

Growing up, Neecy always knew there was better out there and she'd become obsessed with finding it. When she turned fifteen, she thought she found her way out. A nineteen-year-old drug dealer who was thoroughly impressed with how well she managed the pothead college kids who came his way. Her brutal honesty and directness made her a surprisingly well-respected dealer in her own right. In the end, though, it was that same honesty that got her blown away. The bastard didn't even blink when he pulled the trigger.

And she didn't blink when she testified against him in court. The best part was when he first saw her alive. He knew he'd killed her. With the tiny tank top she'd been wearing that day, she couldn't have been wearing a vest. Plus all that blood spouting from her arteries and chest had been kind of a giveaway, too. And yet there she was...turning state's evidence against his evil ass.

He'd really wanted her dead then. From Rikers, he sent his boys on the outside to take her down. They had found out she was living in Jersey with some women. Not hard to discover since she'd refused protective custody, to the utter bewilderment of the cops. The night before she would finish her testimony, twenty of her old boyfriend's guys showed up, armed to the teeth and ready to shoot, gut, and rape everything and anything they'd found in that house with Neecy.

That was also the night Neecy called on her crows for the first time...but only for the remains.

His screams in court the next day were like music to her ears as she calmly walked up to the stand. To this day he still lived in the mental ward of the little Alabama prison the authorities had transferred him to.

Ever since then Neecy had worked hard to make up for the person she once was. Worked hard to prove to Skuld, her sisters, and, most importantly, herself that she was better than that little drug-dealing piece of trash she once was, hanging out at college parties and raves.

She would never stop working to prove that.

Which meant that Wilhelm Yager was nothing more than an unnecessary distraction to her goal. Because the one thing Neecy could say about all her second-life boyfriends...they always knew better than to get in her way. And they always knew she'd never love them.

There was only one thing she truly loved these days...and man could those bitches get on her nerves!

"Why don't you just go out with him and get it over with?" Janelle asked as she headed toward the rooftop entrance, her dark blonde curls bouncing around her face. That sweet, dimpled face and those big, fat blonde curls hid one of Neecy's best and most vicious fighters. Like the Ravens, Janelle preferred using her bare hands more than the blades all Crows learned to use. And neither Clan used guns. Not Neecy's choice, but an edict from their gods. Whatever.

"Once he finds out how truly unpleasant you are, he'll definitely leave you alone."

"I am not going to date Will Yager. End of subject. And I am not unpleasant. I just don't gush, and…"

"Act like a girl?"

"Yes. Exactly."

"Well it may be end of subject for you, maybe…but definitely not for him."

Neecy pushed past Janelle and pulled open the roof door. "I am not talking about this anymore. Let it go or I'll make you wish you'd let it go," she promised. Calmly.

Neecy didn't yell. In fact, only one person ever got her to yell and, if she could, she'd rip the wings from his back.

The team headed down the stairs leading into the main part of the club. This was one of The Gathering's favorite hangouts. Owned by Shifters, beings that could change from human to animal in a heartbeat, it was the one place the Crows could go and unfurl their wings in peace.

Still, they didn't come here unless they rented out the place. The Shifters hated them.

"Abominations." "Acts against the gods." "Freaks." Just some of the terms tossed their way by the holier-than-thou dogs, cats, and whatevers that roamed the tri-state area.

The Shifters tolerated the Ravens, but barely. Yet they outright hated the Crows. Not surprising. As direct descendants of Odin's elite guard, the Ravens were born with their wings.

The Crows, however, only got their wings after they pledged their allegiance to the Viking goddess Skuld…and died.

Skuld only chose from the dying.

The music was pumping hard by the time the women got to the main floor, but Neecy could still hear the Crows over it. They were loud bitches. Loud, annoying bitches—and she couldn't imagine her life without them.

Stripping off her wool sleeves and dumping them on the pile by the exit door, Neecy passed two Shifter bouncers. Wolves, probably. She didn't know or care. To her they were all cranky dogs and cats with attitude. Like show animals. She patted them on their big chests as she walked by, loving how they flinched.

Janelle wasn't as kind. Another street kid like Neecy, Janelle waited until she was between the two big bruisers before she extended her nearly six-foot wings, slapping both men in the face.

The women's laughing became hysterical at that point. Man, the Shifters really hated when they were around.

Neecy walked out into the main area and the entire room exploded into cheers. It wasn't just the Jersey Crows present tonight. The Alabama Crows were passing through town, heading toward Philly. Hence the party.

Although Crows didn't actually need a reason to party, they loved coming up with them.

Once they'd thrown a party for Neecy when she got a B in geometry. Math being her worst subject, it seemed only right.

"Well, well, well," Neecy said, laughing. "The country cousins have come to town."

Serena, leader of the 'Bama Crows, tackled her from behind. A bottle of tequila in one hand and a beer chaser in the other, Serena lived to party—and she had a thing about using hacksaws on her prey.

"Darlin' little girl! How are you?"

Neecy turned around, reached down, and embraced the woman. Because Neecy was six-one, she had to reach down to embrace almost everybody.

"Serena. I'm so glad you guys could come tonight." She hated the need to shout over the loud music. Clearly she was inching up in age. Her desire to party lessened with each passing day.

"If there's one thing in this life that I've learned, darlin', it's to never pass up a Jersey Crows party."

"Yeah. But I'm just sorry you guys can't stay longer."

Serena hooked her arm through Neecy's and dragged her toward the bar. "I wish we could, too. But those Philly gals are waitin' on us. And they are a cranky bunch of bitches, let me tell you."

Pushing Neecy into the bar, Serena slammed her bottles down. "Barkeep! A bottle of Russian vodka for this little lady right'chere."

"No. No. No." Neecy shook her head at the bartender. "Bottle of beer. That's it."

"What kind of drink is that?"

"One that will hopefully keep me out of the gutter...unlike the last time you guys came to town."

✧

Yager gritted his teeth as one of the Valkyries, Shawna somebody, gently worked the salve into his battered flesh.

Damn woman and her big feet of fury. She had no qualms about kicking the shit out of him. Or calling down those goddamn birds of hers. According to legend, Skuld endowed all her warriors with several things: strength, speed, wings, and talons. But some of them received a special skill on top of all that, which belonged only to them.

For Neecy, it was the ability to call flocks of real crows and ravens to do her bidding. Feared throughout the tri-state area by the Norse Clans, her birds were relentless, brutal, and loyal to her beyond anything Yager had ever seen. No flying south for these birds. They endured the cold just so they could be near her. Kind of like Yager himself.

"Is it me or does that woman really detest you?"

He looked at Mike Molinski, who had somehow become the baby brother he never had...and started to realize, he never wanted. "Why do we keep having this conversation?"

"Because you insist on being the one to deal with her. I can do it."

No way would he let Mike anywhere near her. One, because Neecy really would squash the idiot into the ground. Mike was still learning it wasn't all about strength. He may be stronger than most Crows, but The Gathering—and Neecy in particular—went beyond strength with downright craftiness and evil. And the second reason...well, he didn't want anybody else touching her. At least anybody with an actual penis.

It wouldn't be the first time a Crow and a Raven got together. Some did it for fun. One-night stands or light dating. Others married, had kids. It wasn't that big a deal. In fact, it made sense. Both groups had big black wings. Both groups were the warriors of Norse gods. True, Odin didn't like it much. He liked his warriors "undiluted". Pure Norse blood. Yager's god could be as bad as the Sicilian Mafia.

"I can handle her."

"Not unless you really start hurting her. I don't see her pulling any punches. Unlike you."

He did pull punches. He couldn't help himself. Besides, The Gathering wasn't their enemy. Every once in a while they may end up on opposite sides, but that was down to the gods. Releasing his aggression on Neecy would only have her responding in kind, which meant all bets would be off. That would be an ugly and brutal fight he'd like to avoid.

Especially when fighting was the last thing he had in mind when it came to her.

Tussling maybe, but never fighting.

Chuckling to himself, Yager pushed the woman's hands off his ribs. What's-her-name had stopped handling his wounds and now simply handled him. But he had no interest in her. Lately, he had very little interest in any woman but Neecy Lawrence.

Yager remembered when he first saw her. They were both sixteen, and Skuld had just called Neecy to The Gathering. He'd accompanied one of the Elder Ravens to the Bird House to meet with their leader at the time. A strange little woman called Mitzy. When the conversation touched on things they believed Yager too young for, they sent him off to explore the house. He stumbled upon Neecy in the backyard.

Since Neecy wasn't born with wings she had absolutely no idea what to do with them. He watched her jump up over and over again trying to take off. Getting more and more frustrated in the process. Then she sneezed, her wings extended and caught a breeze, and the next thing he knew she had trapped herself on the roof. When he went up there to get her, Yager thought for sure she'd be grateful for his help...she wasn't. He made the mistake of suddenly "appearing" on the roof beside her—the Ravens could sometimes move so fast people often didn't even see them until they were right in front of them.

That's what happened with Neecy. All he got out was "Hi" when she screamed and kicked him in the face. She broke his nose and sent him right off the roof. He landed in front of the Elder he'd accompanied, bleeding and trying hard not to cry. Unless you really wanted to suffer, you never cried in front of the Elders.

Since then, Yager had never stopped thinking about her. But with him going off to Caltech and MIT for his degrees, he only saw her a few times a year at joint Raven-Crow-Valkyrie functions, but to be honest, she never seemed too interested, and he was too young to care.

Yet it wasn't until he'd moved into his position as head of the New York-New Jersey Ravens when his mentor and leader died suddenly that everything had changed. Because it was around that time that Neecy Lawrence went from the occasional wet dream to full-on sex goddess.

Receiving the mantle of Raven leader meant receiving Odin's rune branded to the back of his neck in front of an audience filled with Ravens from all over the world, as well as Valkyries and Crows. The branding wasn't pleasant, but Yager showed no signs of pain. He didn't even flinch. If he were to lead the Ravens, he needed to show them and Odin he could take pain. That he, in fact, welcomed it. It was the typical Viking bullshit, and it hadn't changed over the last thousand years.

Once they completed his branding, one of the Original Seven—the original immortal Valkyries who called Odin "Dad"—presented Yager to the audience as the new leader of the Tri-State Ravens.

He'd been standing before the warrior representatives of all three Tri-State Clans, giving a speech that had taken him hours to craft and even more hours to rehearse, when he saw her.

Leaning against a wall, staring out over the crowd and bored beyond tears, Neecy wore a little black dress with three-inch-heel sandals. In the middle of his speech about the changing face of the Odin warrior, Yager stopped talking. He couldn't take his eyes off her. It became so bad Mike had to slam him with his wing to get Yager to focus on the rest of his speech.

He couldn't help himself, though. A vision came to him. As clear as anything he'd seen before. A vision of Neecy Lawrence naked and tangled up in the white sheets on his bed. Well-fucked and beautiful, she sighed his name in her sleep.

That simple vision was, by far, the most erotic thing he'd ever seen in his life and he was determined to make it his reality as well as hers. The only problem? Neecy treated him like some rich white trash she couldn't get away from fast enough. It drove him crazy. *She* drove him crazy.

Those small, pale hands returned to now rub his shoulders. Yager gently removed them. "Thanks, uh, Shawna." Or whatever...

"Anytime." She gave an alluring smile and walked out of the room.

Mike shook his head. "And what's wrong with her?"

"Nothing. She's perfect. Exquisite." Not surprising. Odin, known for his lusty ways, never picked ugly mortal Valkyries. He liked his women beautiful and big-chested. But since that bad night a bunch of them took Odin to a local strip club, Mountain Creek—the Ravens' tri-state safe house—had turned into the set of a Russ Meyer film.

Still, Yager could care less about Shawna's big tits. Not when he could still feel Neecy's adorable breasts in the palms of his hands. An accidental grab he'd fully enjoyed.

He stood, allowing his wings to once again unfurl. He stretched them out, shook them and pulled them back into his body. For now they'd sit hidden behind flesh and muscle. The only telltale sign his wings were there at all were two long scars racing down his back, next to his spine.

"I'm going home."

Mike watched him pull on a fresh T-shirt. "Look, if you're trying to slum it a little, I can hook you up with some very accommodating girls from my old neighborhood."

Yager sighed. "It's like you want me to hurt you."

"No. But I'm the only one who will be honest with you. You've got Valkyries falling over themselves to get to you. And you're concentrating on a Crow. The same bird used in the *Omen* movies."

"Actually those were ravens, you idiot."

Before Yager could leave, or twist Mike into a pretzel, his second-in-command walked into the room. "Just got an interesting call."

Tye Ulrich was his best friend and a man of few words, which was why he was Yager's best friend. Yager got enough chatter from Mike.

"Yeah?"

"Yeah. We've been invited to a party downtown."

Yager shrugged on his leather jacket. "Not in the mood... What the fuck are these?"

He pulled the condoms from his jacket pocket, then looked at Mike.

"What? I'm being a good friend and hoping you get laid before the end of the next millennium."

Sighing, Yager shoved the condoms back in his pocket. Tye raised an eyebrow. "If I toss them away, he'll just put more back in."

Mike nodded. "He's right."

"Whatever." Tye crossed his arms over his massive chest. "Anyway, seems the 'Bama Crows are in town and our girls are throwing them a party at some Shifter club."

Yager's head snapped up as Mike let out a moan of annoyance.

"And I was thinking," Tye continued, "that we really shouldn't let our country cousins come to town and not give them a nice Raven greeting."

Shrugging, a huge grin on his face, Yager quickly agreed. "It would be downright rude."

"Exactly."

Neecy sat at the bar and looked out over her girls. One thing would always be true...Crows could throw a mean party.

Glancing to her left, Neecy spotted two seventeen-year-old Crows ordering a beer. The stupid Shifter bastard didn't even card them. She slammed her fist down on the bar, causing the two girls to jump. "Don't even think about it, ladies."

Rolling their eyes and groaning, they headed back to the dance floor. She motioned to one of the older Crows heading out for the night. "Take them home."

Chuckling, "You got it."

The few young ones that came to The Gathering soon learned Neecy kept a tight leash on them until they turned eighteen. But no drinking until twenty-one. And no drugs ever. Since there was no leaving the Crows except by death, the other alternative when the young ones got out of hand was one of those brutal Raven Elder–type beatings. Since the Crows hated even the thought of something like that happening, they followed orders or hid their antics real well.

"Okay, Neece. Talk to me." Neecy turned around to find Janelle sitting next to her. "Arri Chang."

"What about her?"

"Explain to me again why I'm wasting my time trying to train that pipsqueak?"

"Because I told you to."

If Janelle was lucky, she may become second-in-command one day. But she'd never lead the Crows. Not because she asked questions, but because she asked them like she already knew the right answer. Skuld hated that.

"Give me a break, Neece. She's terrified of me and she couldn't fight her way out of a paper bag."

"She's not terrified of you."

"She hides from me. When I do finally track her down and take her to the training room, she cowers." Janelle sighed, her blonde curls falling in her face. "It's starting to give me a complex. I feel like this giant ogre."

Janelle wasn't quite as tall as Neecy, but she was bigger and stronger. She was a lot of woman and Neecy knew it made her self-conscious.

"You're not a giant ogre. She's just new."

"She's been with us for two years now."

Neecy winced. Janelle was right, and she didn't even know the whole story yet. Things were about to get much stranger because of Arri. That, however, was not a discussion to have during a Crow party.

"Look, I'm not talking about this tonight. Now you can sit here and freak out..." Neecy slid off her stool. "Or you can try and live in that fantasy world of yours where you out-dance me."

Janelle stood up slowly. "I *know* you didn't just issue a direct challenge...to me."

"Bring it on, baby." Neecy could always hold her own on a dance floor, but Janelle used to street dance for money before Skuld took her. In fact, in some old rap and reggae videos, you could see Janelle in the background. Sometimes she was the only white girl in the entire video. Still, it was fun to fuck with her about it.

"Oh, that's it, Lawrence. Your ass is mine."

Katie sauntered up, a drink with an umbrella in it gripped in her hand. "What's going on?"

"Neece just challenged me."

"What?" Katie suddenly scrambled up onto the bar.

"Hey!" Her loud voice reached the DJ across the room. The music immediately cut out. "We have a challenge, ladies!"

Neecy shook her head as the Crows cheered and opened up a space on the dance floor for her and Janelle.

Stepping away from her, Janelle turned and walked backward to the dance floor. She gestured for Neecy to follow with both her hands.

"Come on, bitch. You're talking shit. Let's see what you really got."

Rolling her eyes, Neecy followed. Honestly, the shit she endured in order to distract her team from the potential nightmare of Arri Chang.

Derrick hated working Crow parties. These bitches creeped him out. They creeped out all the Shifters. These women died and some goddess brought them back. And she brought them back...altered.

Shifters, and even the freaky Ravens, were born the way they were. Although the Ravens couldn't shift into shit, they did have those stupid wings.

The Crows, however, weren't born with their wings. Instead they woke up from dying and suddenly had them. They weren't immortal or the undead or anything. They were just a bunch of broads with wings, enhanced strength and immune systems, and a really unhealthy bloodlust. Like Shifters, the Crows were still human...sort of. They could breed, get old, and die. But none of that made them right.

Still, the tips were good and some of them weren't too bad to look at.

One of the cuter ones waved a twenty in his face. "Another one of these." She held up the bottle of pricey imported beer. Derrick went to grab one from the fridge behind the bar, but found it empty. Less than five minutes ago, he'd had at least thirty bottles in there because the Crows really liked it.

He sniffed the air, but all he smelled were humans. Another reason Shifters didn't like the Crows and the Ravens—they didn't smell any different from normal humans. They simply smelled like humans who slept on down pillows.

He looked out over the dance floor, but the Crows were still grooving to another disco favorite. Then his eyes caught movement and Derrick's head snapped up. That's when he spotted them, on the balcony that ringed the dance floor. The Ravens, their purple-black wings shimmering in the club's strobe lights, silently watched the Crows, each male holding one of the missing beers. How the Ravens got past Derrick to get the damn beers, he'd never know.

And, to be honest, he never *wanted* to know.

"I do love watching women dance." In surprise, Yager and Tye looked at Mike who stood between them. It was such a nice, clean thing for him to say. Until he added, "It makes their tits shake."

Rolling their eyes, Yager and Tye looked back at the dancing females.

Yup. Yager liked watching Neecy dance. He also liked how she acted when alone with The Gathering. She actually smiled and laughed. She let herself go with her sisters. He wanted to see that side of her. He wanted her to smile at him the way she smiled at her friends.

"So are we going to go down there and dance with 'em? Or just sit here and watch like a bunch of stalkers?" Mike asked.

Tye shrugged. "I like watching."

"Yeah. He's got a thing for that big girl," Mike offered.

Yager raised an eyebrow in surprise. "Which girl?"

Mike answered for Tye. "My fellow hoodrat, Janelle." As long as it wasn't Neecy, Yager really didn't give a shit.

"I find her...interesting." Tye didn't say much, and often what he did say sounded innocuous. But Yager had known the man long enough to know "interesting" was simply another way to say "a piece of ass I can't wait to hit".

"I understand that. Especially after seeing her dance. She's amazing."

"Yeah. Dancing. Whatever."

Mike sighed. "I don't get you two. There are much better-looking women out there. And if not better looking, then definitely less mean. I saw Janelle rip out a man's heart once...and that didn't seem to bother her."

Mike put his arms around both men. "Gentlemen, you guys should hang with me some night. I'd get you hooked up with some very hot and extremely accommodating supermodels."

Even though Mike was about six-two, both Yager and Tye still towered over him as they towered over pretty much everybody. They looked at each other, smiled, and slammed the man with their wings, flipping him over the balcony. The Crows, like the birds whose wings they possessed, sensed the kid and quickly moved out of the way as Mike hit the floor. The women looked down at him and then their gazes drifted up.

For several long seconds, they merely stared at the Ravens who merely stared back. After they got bored with that, the Crows went back to dancing.

Except Neecy. She glared up at Yager, her hands on her hips. He smiled down at her and winked.

Snarling, she strode off the dance floor.

"All right. Which one of you dumb bitches invited the Ravens tonight?"

Janelle, Connie, and Katie looked at each other and shrugged.

"I asked you a question."

"We didn't invite anybody."

"Did you *tell* someone to invite them?" Their responding smirks said it all. "And this is why you bitches piss me off."

Katie held up her hands in mock fear. "Geez, Neece. Control the rage!"

Connie laughed and Janelle shrugged, adding, "So the Ravens are here. It's always a good idea to keep them on our side."

"Which isn't easy when you keep trying to kill their leader," Connie muttered.

Katie giggled. "I couldn't believe you called those goddamn birds of yours."

Neecy walked away from the three women before she really did lose her temper. She'd already put in a couple of hours at the party and had kept her drinking down to two beers and a tequila shot, so clearly it was time to go.

Plus, she needed to check in with Didi and let her know they'd lost the rune to the Idiot Brigade.

Coming around the corner, she slammed into a solid slab of concrete. Also known as Yager's chest.

"Hey, Neecy."

Neecy looked up at Yager. And kept looking up. There were very few men on the planet that made her feel small, but Yager was definitely one of them.

And he was "looking" at her again.

Not like people always looked at her, including her past boyfriends. With that little bit of fear mixed in with awe. No. He looked at her like he'd never seen anything so beautiful or amazing before.

She hated that look. It completely confused her and made her all sweaty.

And Neecy Lawrence didn't sweat.

"Yager."

She moved to step around him, but he stepped, too. A small one, but the man was so huge, he easily blocked her.

"So what are you up to tonight?"

Sometimes the man asked her the dumbest questions. "Nothing."

Christ, Yager was gorgeous. Really. Just plain gorgeous. His light brown hair reached past his shoulders and looked as if he never combed it. Ever. His searing grey eyes made her seriously uncomfortable and horny. Those stark Nordic features blended well with his chiseled cheekbones and painfully hard jaw, as her fists could attest to. His shoulders completely dwarfed her, but he needed them that size to support his long, thick neck. His entire body was one sheet of pure rippling muscle, and he had to be at least six-seven. For once, a man actually taller than her.

"Wanna drink?"

Neecy sucked in a breath, about to tell him no she didn't want a drink—*and get those goddamn gorgeous eyes off me*—when she heard giggling behind her. She knew it was her team. In battle they followed her every command without question. But during their off hours they truly were her family...and she realized now she never wanted siblings. Mostly because they were a pain in the ass.

She raised her knee, giving her access to the weapons she kept holstered to her calf, turned, and threw one of the deadly blades. The women dived out of the way, the sharp steel planting itself in the wall behind where they'd all been standing.

Clearing his throat, Yager slowly walked around her. He pulled the blade from the wall and handed it back to Neecy.

"A little tense, Lawrence?" he teasingly asked.

"Quiet, Yager." She slid the blade back in its holster, keeping her head down to hide her smile, but unable to stop her chuckle.

"Do you really have to go?" That voice! She'd had wet dreams about that voice alone. Especially when it got all husky and yearning-like.

"Yeah. I gotta tell Didi you got what Skuld sent us out for. Then Skuld can duke it out with Odin." She looked up at him. "Unless you want to give it back to me."

He grinned and her toes curled inside her boots. "Dammit. If only I were the kind of guy who would use *that* request to my advantage."

Yeah, but Yager was too nice. A true nice person—probably one of the last on the planet. A big, dumb, gorgeous nice guy.

Whereas Neecy was too smart for her own good and used to deal drugs before she took six bullets to the chest. She was once one of those scumbags she now went about eradicating from the universe. She wasn't nice. She wasn't good. And she'd gotten exactly what she deserved when she'd died.

Yet she thanked Skuld every day for giving her a second chance to make it right. And she would make it right, if it took her the rest of her second-life.

"Well, you're not. Might as well get used to it. And stop staring at me like that."

Frowning in confusion, "Like what?"

Neecy shook her head. "Forget it."

She walked around him and headed to the roof and home.

Chapter Three

Many people were lucky enough to find themselves gently awakened on Sunday mornings by a sweet kiss on the cheek or a soft pat on the shoulder.

Neecy, however, got her ass rolled out of bed by the leader of The Jersey Gathering.

"Wakey, wakey, sunshine."

Neecy knew she should have returned to her own apartment last night instead of the Bird House. But, stupidly, she'd hoped to catch Didi before she went to bed—she didn't—and she wanted one of those wonderful brunches The Gathering had every Sunday afternoon.

She thought maybe she'd overslept until she glanced up at the clock on the night table. It was barely ten...*on a Sunday*!

"What the hell was that?" she demanded.

"Where is it?"

Neecy looked up into Didi Gowan's smirking face. More than ten years older than Neecy, the woman still looked great. People barely noticed the jagged scar on Didi's neck anymore. A remnant from her first husband's dirty dealings and what brought her to Skuld. He didn't cut her himself, but the men who wanted him to pay off his gambling debt sure did.

Didi was the first person Neecy saw when she woke up after dying. It wasn't often a person finds a black woman with black crow's wings extending from her back standing at the end of her bed.

"Welcome to the party, kid," she'd said with a smile.

Seventeen years later and Didi still called her "kid".

"Where's the rune?"

Neecy sat up and sighed, pushing her too-long bangs out of her eyes. She really needed to get them cut, but she kept putting it off. Sitting in a beauty salon always ranked low on her list of things to do.

"Yager got it."

"Again? You must be losing your touch, kid."

"I am not." She was losing her mind. At least that was how it felt every time she was around Wilhelm Pain-in-her-ass Yager.

Didi walked to a straight-back chair, spun it around, and sat down. She was in her requisite all-black jeans and T-shirt. That ensemble and her second husband, Harry, were the only "New York things" Didi allowed herself. Everybody knew Didi hated the East Coast. She was born in one of those states Neecy would never go to because she was sure there weren't enough minorities to make her feel comfortable. Didi only came to New York because of the first husband. But since she'd died here, she ended up with The Jersey Gathering. Although Didi didn't mind. Everyone knew that with her attitude, the Southern and Midwestern Crows would have run her ass out of town.

She could be a mouthy little thing.

"Okay," Didi said. "Tell me what happened."

"What's there to tell? We were dealing with our prey, and the Ravens showed up."

"And?"

"There is no 'and'." Neecy stood up and flopped back on her bed. "One second I had it and the next second I didn't. End of story."

"*You* let Yager get between you and your prey?"

"No. I let Yager get between me and that stupid rune. I got my prey." Neecy always got her prey. Always.

"Did Yager say why he wanted it?"

"No. He only said Odin sent him to get it. Which is becoming pretty common."

"What do you mean?"

"I mean Ravens keep showing up and none of us know why. Sometimes they want whatever we came for, but mostly they're just there to 'help'." She made air quotes around the word. "It's been going on for like a year now."

"Interesting." Didi was quiet for a moment and Neecy allowed her eyes to close. She almost fell back to sleep, when Didi's next statement nearly had her falling out of bed again.

"I think it's time for you to have a conversation with Yager about what's going on."

Neecy forced herself to remain her usual calm self outside, even though her insides screamed bloody murder. "Excuse me?"

"Did I start speaking in tongues? Exactly what part of that sentence did you not grasp?"

Was there any time in their relationship when sarcasm didn't play some part? Neecy didn't think so.

"Why should I talk to Yager? Isn't he more your level, politically?"

"That's an inventive load of crap, Lawrence."

Well, she was desperate.

"What I mean is that he's leader of the Ravens. You're leader of the Crows. Shouldn't you two be talking to each other as opposed to getting me in the middle of it?"

Didi stared at her for a long moment and Neecy thought for sure she'd say something mighty profound. Instead, she shook her head. "Get the fuck over it, Lawrence. You need to start dealing with him."

Frustrated but without any room to argue, "Fine. Just write down his office address for me. I'll go there tomorrow after my morning class."

"He doesn't have an office. Well, he does, but it's in his apartment."

Neecy sat up so fast, Didi's entire body reared back and almost fell off the chair.

"His apartment? *Have you lost your goddamn mind?*"

Neecy didn't yell. She didn't scream. She didn't lose her temper. She didn't do anything but hunt and destroy her prey. But lately, when it came to Yager, she'd been feeling something she hadn't felt in a very long time...rage.

And Didi's shrewd ass didn't miss a second of it. "Little tense aren't ya, Neece?"

Neecy cleared her throat. "I mean...I'm not sure it's a good idea to go to his apartment."

"'Fraid you'll fuck him right there in the hallway, Lawrence?"

"No!"

Didi smiled as Neecy dropped back on the bed.

"Then deal with it. I need you to step up to the plate a little, Neece."

Didi had been looking tired lately, and Neecy didn't relish the idea of being second-in-command for anyone else. Even Serena, who loved her but would most likely turn Neecy into a raging alcoholic.

Neecy nodded. "Fine. Whatever."

"Now, now, Lawrence. Don't blow me away with your enthusiasm."

"Wakey, wakey, sunshines!"

Yager forced his eyes open only to realize the heavy weight on his face was a foot. Tye's, specifically.

Never again would he drink with the 'Bama Crows. Those were some hardcore ladies.

Pushing Tye's big foot off his face, Yager sat up and looked out over the living room floor of the Mountain Creek house—safe house and property of the Tri-State Ravens.

Thirty hungover Ravens littered the floor. All except Mike. Molinski's father was a raging alcoholic so Mike never touched the stuff. But he took great delight in making sure to remind those who did drink of all the stupid shit they did the night before.

"Morning, my brothers!" Mike cheerily announced. "Guess what I did?"

Uh-oh.

"Made breakfast! Eggs Benedict and bacon and hash browns and fried eggs...the runny kind..." Before he could finish, three of the Ravens were up and running from the room heading for the bathrooms. Some of the others moaned and turned over or buried their heads into couch cushions.

"Stop it, Mike," Yager ordered quietly.

"I'm just trying to feed my brothers."

"You're an asshole," Tye muttered and turned over.

"Bro, that's harsh!"

Mike ducked as pillows and couch cushions flew at him.

Yager slowly shook his head. *What an idiot.* Of course, Mike didn't drink at the party. And Yager? Well, Yager drank. A lot. He barely remembered the drunken flight home.

But it worked out in the end. He got to see Neecy move that gorgeous ass to music and spend time with the rest of The Gathering. Getting them on his side was half the battle as far as he was concerned. But apparently a battle he'd already won. As soon as Neecy bailed, five of the Crows dragged him off to a corner. They plied him with liquor and then proceeded to talk about how amazing Neecy was, but also how stubborn.

Janelle probably put it best: "She'll make your life a living hell. But trust me, in the end...it'll be worth it." Then she gave him her number and told him to use it if he had any problems. If a Valkyrie had done that, she would have been hitting on him. He knew better with the Crows. Their loyalty to one another was legendary among the Clans.

When he only smiled at Janelle's pronouncement about Neecy being worth it—'cause that's all he really heard—the other Crows seemed impressed. They wanted what was best for Neecy and, like him, they all thought Yager was best for Neecy.

Of course, now he only had to convince Neecy of that fact. But a more stubborn female he'd never met. Even if he couldn't see the Viking in her blood merely from looking at her, it was obvious to Yager it was there. The woman could have been captain of her own war party. Oh, wait...she was.

Mike walked over to the big picture windows and threw the curtains back. The groans and blood oaths for his death were loud and vicious.

"Come on, guys! Look at this beautiful day! Let's enjoy it!"

Yager dropped back to the floor. "Take him down, gentlemen."

Using his forearm to cover his eyes against the bright light, he smiled as he heard Mike tackled to the floor. He was willing to bet there were some brutal kicks thrown in for good measure, too.

Janelle McKenna stared at her team leader across the breakfast table. "Are you nuts?"

Neecy gave her that "stare". She learned it from Didi and she learned it well. But she had to be kidding. Right? *Right?*

"Look, Neece, ya can't be serious."

"Serious as a heart attack."

"But that's a really bad idea."

"It wasn't mine. But the decision's a done deal. Not up for discussion. The next time we go out on a hunt, we're bringing Arri."

Arri was a cute little thing with constantly changing hair color and extremely quirky mannerisms. And she couldn't fight a teacup poodle if her life depended on it.

Really, the girl was a mess.

"Is Skuld trying to get us killed?"

Neecy glared at Janelle over her orange juice glass. Unlike Janelle, Neecy didn't question Skuld's orders, which could be why she was second-in-command and Janelle so...wasn't.

Katie walked into the kitchen. "Morning, ladies." Janelle loved the fact that if you didn't know Katie at all, you'd have no idea the woman lived with two big cops who did whatever she told them to. She was into that dominant-sub thing and hid it well. Personally, Janelle found the whole thing a little bit creepy, but the threesome had an eight-year relationship that seemed to keep them all happy. Which was more than Janelle had. Most men couldn't handle a woman who could probably kick their ass. And the ones who thought of her as a challenge were usually criminals or bikers. She'd already dealt with the criminal side of life. Her father had been an Irish mobster. A Westie, specifically. His career choices got her entire family gunned down...including her.

But Skuld came for her, and although Janelle often missed her parents and especially her two older brothers, she refused to wallow in the past.

"Did you hear this?"

Katie filled a mug with coffee and walked over to the table. "Hear what?" she asked as she pulled out a chair and daintily sat down. Well, it seemed "daintily" to Janelle because she was never dainty about shit.

Her father used to call her his Little Baby Mack Truck.

"Next hunt...Arri comes."

Katie blinked and turned those big blue eyes to Neecy. "Oh?"

"Yeah. So get over it."

"Does Connie know?"

"Yeah. I told her this morning before she went out with Fran." Another solid couple, Connie and Fran had been together since they were both sixteen. Even the lesbians had Janelle beat.

"And we're sure that's wise?"

"Skuld does. And we're all here because of Her blessing. She has faith in Arri. So we give Arri a chance."

Katie sighed. "Look, don't get us wrong. We all think Arri is very sweet in a weird sorta way. But the girl can't fight for shit."

Poor Neecy. Janelle knew she wanted to argue that point, but she couldn't. Arri was a creampuff in comparison to most of The Gathering. They all knew it. And at twenty-five, the woman had never been out on a hunt for anything but good coffee cake for Sunday brunch. Whereas Janelle started hunting six months after she arrived. Neecy started after three. Neither one had even turned seventeen yet.

Janelle pushed her empty plate away from her. "And if she can't fight, we'll spend most of our time trying to protect her." Because Crows always protected their own—even the messes.

Neecy took a deep breath. "Look, we'll take her out and we'll see how it goes. That's all we have to do. But she'll be my responsibility."

Janelle almost said, "Just like always," but stopped herself. Neecy had taken little Arri under her wing from the time the girl arrived. Pretty much what she did with Janelle even though Neecy was barely a year older than her. Her team leader sure did love the underdogs.

"Okay?" She stared intently at both women. "I've already got Connie's buy-in on this. But I want yours."

Janelle and Katie glanced at each other. They knew they could argue this point until the cows came home, but why bother? Skuld was loyal to her warriors, but you fucked with her at your own risk. Their goddess could be mean. Really, really mean.

"Okay," Janelle sighed. "I'm in."

Katie shrugged. "Yeah, okay."

Neecy pushed herself away from the table. "Great. Thanks, you guys. I have to head back to the City. Gotta get some class work done for tomorrow. Oh! And don't say a word to Arri. I'll tell her myself." Good. Such a squirrelly little thing, you never knew what Arri would say or do next.

Really, she was a weird little girl.

Once they were alone, Janelle turned to Katie. "So...what do ya really think?"

Katie shook her head. "We are so fucked."

Karl Waldgrave felt the power of his goddess flow through him. Felt it like a caress, like a loving lick across his cock. She'd come for him a year ago. Invaded his dreams. She knew what he was and she spoke his language. The language of the Hunter. She'd given him a target. A Hunt to make him proud. A Hunt he could tell his grandchildren about.

He accepted her offer without hesitation. She liked that. She gave him whatever he needed. He already had money, so she gave him disciples. Hunters like himself. The best of the best.

"You are ready," she whispered seductively in his ear. "You will make me proud."

He felt her hand slide over his cock, squeeze his balls. He gasped.

"Don't stop until you kill them all. But bring me the one I want alive."

"I will. And I won't stop. I won't."

Her lips kissed his neck; her sharp teeth nipped his ear. "Make it easy on yourself. Go for the one they look to as leader. Kill her and the rest will be so easy."

He nodded as her hand stroked his cock over and over again.

"But don't underestimate them. They have loyalty to only one, and she has chosen them well. Understand?"

He nodded again as she brought him closer to orgasm.

"Good. Now make me proud."

He came hard at her words. Like he always did. And, seconds later, he awoke on the altar, still crouching over the sacrifice. Its blood covered him as did his own come, his hand still gripping his cock.

He looked at the disciples surrounding him. "It's time."

Chapter Four

Yager snatched up the phone, knowing it was the doorman. Without waiting to hear what he had to say, he barked into the phone, "Send him up." He slammed the receiver down and went back to the bathroom to grab a towel.

Mike wasn't normally early for anything, especially on a Monday. But Yager always knew there could be a first time. He wrapped the towel around his waist and finished shaving. When the doorbell rang, he frowned. Mike had a key. *Bonehead probably lost it...again.*

He wiped off the rest of the shaving cream and walked to his front door. "I can't believe you lost that goddamn key again, Molinski." He yanked the door open and froze.

Standing in his doorway, wearing a fur-lined denim jacket, jeans, a black T-shirt, and a black leather backpack was the woman he'd spent a good hour in the shower masturbating to.

"Neecy?"

She stared at him, her mouth slightly open. Then her eyes slid down his body and as soon as they got to his towel she bolted.

"I'll come back later!"

It took him at least thirty seconds before he realized he hadn't been hallucinating. That *was* Neecy Lawrence at his front door. He ran after her, catching up with her at the elevator pummeling the poor call button.

"Neecy, wait."

"I'll take the stairs."

"I'm on the thirtieth floor."

"Okay, I'll go to the roof and fly."

No way. She wasn't getting away from him that easy. She'd just gotten through the fire-escape door when he grabbed hold of her wrist.

"You know as well as I do that you can't fly in the middle of the day in New York. They'll just shoot your ass down." Their gods would only cloak them at night. During the day, they were on their own.

Yager headed back to his apartment, forced to drag the woman behind him. She didn't exactly kick and scream, but he got the feeling it wouldn't take much to push her over that edge.

He did manage to get her back inside, though. He closed the door and locked it, although for a wild minute there he thought for sure she'd try to bolt for the windows.

He tightened his grip on her and dragged her to the kitchen. "How about some coffee?"

"No. I don't drink coffee."

"Bottled water? Coke? Pepsi?" *Vodka? Tequila? An entire brewing plant?* Anything to get her to relax. Anything to keep her right there.

"I don't want anything. And feel free to let me go."

Yager stopped in the middle of his kitchen and took a deep breath. He turned around without releasing her.

"I don't want to let you go."

She stared up at him for a moment, then tried again to pull away. To run from him. "I gotta go."

"You came all the way from Jersey to tell me you gotta go?"

She sighed and stopped struggling. At least for the moment. "No. I came to find out when we ended up on opposite sides."

"I didn't know we were."

She tried to yank her arm back. "When you get between me and my prey, you can damn well bet that we're on opposite sides. And would you let me go!"

He did, and she slapped herself in the face.

Yager winced. "Sorry."

She rubbed her slightly wounded eye and sighed again. "Look, I know you guys aren't gunning for us or anything..."

"See, that's where you're wrong."

Bright black eyes narrowed. "What?"

"Maybe we should make a few things clear, Lawrence."

Could she kill him? Could she possibly get away with it? Nah. The doorman could I.D. her. "Such as?"

"What I feel for you has nothing to do with Odin or Skuld or anybody but you and me."

"You and me?" *What in hell was going on?* "Have you lost your mind?"

He took a step toward her, but she refused to move away from him. She didn't back away from anything. Never had, never would...unless, of course, it was Will Yager answering his door in a towel, but there was only so much a girl could take in a day.

"I like you, Neecy. A lot."

He liked her? What? Was she back in high school? Next the man would ask her to the prom.

"That's great and all, but I don't know what that has to do with me."

Yager sighed. "You are such a difficult woman."

"No. Just a confused one. I don't get you, Yager."

"Yeah. I noticed."

She ignored him and kept right on talking. "I mean, I don't exactly see why one of the Odin Chosen would have any interest in a Daughter of Skuld."

"Did that hurt?"

She blinked in confusion. "Did what hurt?" She sounded frustrated even to her own ears. Neecy didn't get frustrated. Damn him! He kept bringing out all these weird emotions from her and she didn't like it one goddamn bit.

"On your throat." Instinctively her fingers reached out and touched the brand on the left side of her neck. Once you agreed to join her, Skuld marked you as one of The Gathering. From a distance, her brand resembled a tattoo. But up close, you could see the *Naudhiz* rune for what it was. A five-inch, pitch-black burn mark resembling a slightly askew cross, placed on her flesh by a god.

"Yes. It hurt. Just like yours did." She remembered that day better than any other. Yager, all big and half-dressed, looking unbelievably hot—kind of like now. Neecy could see every one of the Valkyries creaming over him, hoping once the Elders completed the ceremony, Yager would take one of them somewhere and fuck her brains out.

While Neecy was making bets with herself on which slutty Valkyrie Yager would pick, an evil-looking Raven Elder pulled a brand out of a pit fire not five feet from where Yager stood. Pushing his head down, the Elder brutally slammed it against Yager's neck.

She waited for it...a cry of pain. A sob of pure torture. Something. But Yager didn't do anything. He didn't flinch. He didn't cry out. He didn't ball up his fists or plant his feet firmly. The son of a bitch didn't even blink. He just stood his ground and took it.

Suddenly she was no longer at the Call of the Leader rite, watching Yager get marked like an animal. Instead, she was waking up in bed with Yager next to her, on his stomach. That damn unruly hair of his partially covering his face. White sheets wrapped low around his narrow hips and what she automatically knew as her little bite marks all over his shoulder and neck. Those long scratches down his back were hers, too. As she stared at him, he opened his eyes, looked at her with a smile and sighed her name.

Then, like that, Neecy brutally snapped out of her little daydream and found herself back at the ceremony with her panties soaked, her nipples hard as rocks, her heart beating like she'd just run fifty miles in thirty seconds and Wilhelm Yager staring at her. For a moment, she thought she zipped out during the rest of his boring speech and he busted her over it, but then Mike Molinski shoved him and he turned away from her. She realized he'd gone somewhere himself and, to be honest, she was too afraid to ask where that was.

Never before or since had Neecy been so turned on by anything and it terrified her.

A year later, and Neecy now watched Yager's hand reach out, his big fingers sliding across her jaw, settling on her cheek. His thumb dragging across her bottom lip. He did it so casually. Like they'd been lovers for years.

"Christ, what is with you?" She wished she'd put more force behind that statement. Instead her voice broke and she couldn't stop staring into his steel grey eyes. His unruly shoulder-length golden brown hair fell across his face as he bent down. She always wanted to comb that hair and never understood why he didn't. Especially since his out-of-control hair made her absolutely insane. She saw it and her nipples got hard.

Staring, mesmerized, Neecy watched as those delicious lips of his came nearer, finally settling across her mouth.

Her body jerked at the contact. She'd kissed quite a few guys, but no one had ever kissed her like this. Slow. Sure. Like he had all the time in the world.

Yager's tongue swept across her top lip, then her bottom. Neecy opened her mouth just a bit and in usual Norse fashion, he grabbed the advantage, his tongue sliding in between her teeth. She stared straight ahead, debating how much his kitchen cabinets cost, as the tip of Yager's tongue rubbed the roof of her mouth.

She really had no idea what to do with the man. When she came here today, she had it all planned out. She'd mentally prepared herself to deal with him like she would deal with any Raven. She would be in charge, confident, and determined. She wouldn't let him put her off by calling her "baby" or asking her out on another goddamn date. She'd been so ready to deal with him and his bullshit.

But she never expected to see him in his way-too-small white towel. All wet and delicious from the shower.

Damn. Damn. Damn.

Both his hands framed her jaw as he tipped his head to the other side, his lips slowly taking her, claiming her. She held her tongue back. But he didn't seem to care. Instead, he used it as an excuse to delve farther.

She knew she could pull away. She knew she *should*. He wouldn't stop her. Not slow-witted, nice-guy Yager with his amazing sense of honor. But the man really knew what he was doing. His tongue curled around hers, coaxing it to join in. That's when it all changed. They both groaned at the contact and her eyes slid closed as his grip tightened on her jaw, pulling her closer.

Part of her knew she should be ripping herself away from this man. Ripping herself away and beating the living hell out of him with his very fine Calphalon pots and pans.

Instead, one hand grabbed his shoulder while the other wrapped around his waist.

The man felt so good under her hands. All hard muscle and smooth skin. She slid her hand across his ribs, her fingers brushing against the ridges where her talons once tore and ripped into his flesh during a fight. A complete accident, but she couldn't help but feel Yager somehow now belonged to her.

She had to stop this. He had to let her go. She had to let *him* go. But dammit, she wasn't made of stone. Her last boyfriend had ended their relationship four months ago. He'd turned to her one day and suddenly announced, "You don't love me at all, do you?" She'd shaken her head and replied, "No."

Of course, it wasn't that big a loss. The entire Jersey Gathering didn't call him Mr. Tiny Penis Man for nothing.

Yager, however...well, he was one of Odin's finest. Every Valkyrie in the tri-state area would give their left tit to be in this man's bed. Yager was a true warrior and Neecy had seen him grind men into dust at his feet. She'd also seen him save those who couldn't fight for themselves.

47

Now here she stood, in his really nice kitchen, letting him kiss her. And, Jesus Christ, what a kiss.

Yager leaned into her body as he sucked her tongue into his mouth. As soon as he'd seen her at his front door, he'd been fighting a mighty hard-on. But now he couldn't hold it back any longer. Not with her soft and pliant in his arms.

Her tongue slid around the tip of his, then rubbed under it. He thought about her doing that to his cock and he almost exploded.

He pulled his mouth away from her, but kept his hands on her face. Christ, he never wanted to let this woman go.

"Stay with me, Neecy."

"What? When?"

He smiled. Neecy Lawrence was a stone-cold killer and yet she could be such a bubblehead at times. "Now, woman."

"I can't."

"Why?"

She glared at him. "Because I can't. I got shit to do."

"Oh, really? Besides me, what else have you got to do?"

Neecy turned her head, but not fast enough to hide her smile. "I hate you, Yager."

"Liar."

He let his hands slip down to her neck, then down her body to her hips. He leaned in and kissed her throat, bit the same spot. She moaned and his cock hardened even more at the sound.

"Stay, Neecy. Stay with me."

"Not on your life, Yager."

Rubbing his nose against her neck, "Why?"

"You know why. Because it will be messy and complicated, and I don't do messy and complicated. I've got priorities and they don't involve you."

A more brutally honest female he'd never met. Still, she made that little speech while grinding her hips against his.

Yeah. Neecy Lawrence was a difficult woman, but the woman he wanted. He'd have to play this very differently from anything he'd done in the past.

Because he knew what he wanted. Maybe what he'd always wanted.

He straightened up and growled, "Twenty-four hours."

Frowning, she asked, "Twenty-four hours...what?"

"I want you for twenty-four hours." He pulled her hips tight against his; otherwise her constant grinding would have him coming all over her. "I want your adorable body under me, over me, whatever way I can think of, for the next twenty-four hours. Just you and me. Anything I want."

Maybe, just maybe if he could come a few thousand times in the next few hours, he could actually focus on something other than those scrumptious tits and that luscious mouth. He'd actually be able to figure out how to *keep* this woman. Still, he absolutely had to get this out of the way first or both his heads would explode.

She tried to step away from him, but he held her tight. He didn't want her to bolt again... Besides, he wasn't sure he'd closed the window in his bedroom.

"Anything you want, huh? That must be nice," she sneered. "And what do I get?"

"Anything *you* want. *Anything.*"

She looked away, an expression of intense thought on her face. It suddenly hit him that he'd actually gotten her to consider it. He worked hard not to let his surprise show. He didn't want anything spooking her at this point. So, he waited...and prayed.

Finally, she looked up at him, her eyes clear...and determined.

"Twenty-four hours, just to get it out of our systems. Nothing else. Then I go."

Holy shit! Okay. Breathe, Yager. Breathe!

Yager offered his hand to shake. "Deal."

She stared at his hand and Yager feared she may have changed her mind, but instead she grabbed hold and gave a firm, determined handshake.

"Deal." He released her hand and she continued. "So after this we never discuss this again. I want you never to look at me the way you're looking at me right now again. This ends here. Now."

That wasn't the agreement they just shook on. But why bog down the moment with little details?

He shrugged, hoping she wouldn't push for a verbal yes. He never gave his word unless he meant it. And as far as he was concerned, this wasn't the end of anything. It was just the beginning.

Chapter Five

Christ, what did she just get herself into? What bargain with the devil did she just make?

All this time Neecy thought Yager was sweet but kind of dumb, as only big Vikings can be. But the grey eyes staring at her this very moment looked far from dumb. More like shrewd and calculating.

Well, it didn't matter. She was going to do this because she really wanted to do this. Neecy didn't let herself "go". She left that to rich debutantes with trust funds. Where Neecy came from, you let yourself go...bad things happened. But for once, Neecy was going to do something she really wanted to do. And, at the moment, she really wanted to *do* Yager.

So she wouldn't worry about anything long-term or the ripple effects it may have on The Gathering. She didn't need to worry about any of that. Because after twenty-four hours, it would be over. She'd have gotten Will Yager out of her system for good.

She smiled at the thought and Yager groaned.

"That smile of yours gets me every time, Neecy."

Startled, Neecy looked up at him. He watched her with that delicious intensity, which immediately made her all hot and jittery. Oh, man, she was in trouble.

His phone rang, yanking her out of her near-panic, but nothing seemed to be able to make him stop staring at her face.

"Don't move." He reached over and grabbed the phone from its cradle. "Yeah?" The fingers of his free hand caressed her throat and jaw as he stared at her.

"No. Don't send him up. Tell Mr. Molinski I'm not feeling well today. Tell him to come by tomorrow around this time. Okay...thanks."

He replaced the phone and turned all his attention back to Neecy.

Neecy shrugged as she glanced around his big kitchen. "So now what?" Good. That sounded confident and almost bored. She would need to stay in charge of this so it didn't get out of hand. And she would, too. This was "nice guy" Yager—he was no match for her.

"I need you naked. Now."

Uh-oh.

"Here?"

He didn't answer her. Instead, he started pushing her jacket off her shoulders, the backpack going with it.

"Look, Yager, maybe we should..."

He kissed her and she realized she'd completely forgotten what she was going to say. How could she think anyway? With his tongue in her mouth and his hands on her breasts.

Yager pushed up her T-shirt and unhooked her bra in record time. And as soon as those big hands of his grabbed hold of her tits, she was lost. Possibly for good.

There was a desperation to Yager's actions that for some unknown reason didn't turn her off. Maybe it was because she'd seen the man in battle. Yager didn't get desperate. So if he was feeling desperate, it was because of her.

Whatever he was feeling now was forcing its way into her. She wanted him inside her. She had to have him inside her. Now. This second.

Yager knew he should slow down, but he couldn't. Not when he finally had her. Her skin felt so amazing under his hands. And he had no idea if she knew it or not, but she'd begun moaning softly as he stroked her breasts, the nipples turning hard under his fingers.

Determined to get her naked as quickly as possible, Yager dropped to his knees in front of her. He unzipped her jeans, pulling them down with her panties. Leaning in, he rested his head against her stomach while he maneuvered off her boots and jeans. He could already smell her arousal and the scent almost made him slam her to the floor. He wanted inside her so bad, he didn't know what to do.

Glancing around his kitchen, he realized she stood in front of his butcher block. He easily lifted her up and laid her out on the cold marble.

"Yager! Yager...wait!"

He closed his eyes. Goddammit, she was bailing on him.

"Get this fucking T-shirt off me. It's strangling me to death."

51

Yager's eyes popped open and he saw that her T-shirt had somehow twisted tightly around her neck. Leaning over, he pulled it up and off. That's when he felt her mouth against his neck.

She leaned up, her teeth grazing his throat as she kissed him. Her hands desperately clutching his shoulders, her legs wrapped around his chest, holding him tightly in place. And that's when he knew. All these months, he hadn't been wrong. The vision that rocked his world hadn't been wrong either.

Neecy Lawrence wanted him. Based on the way her short nails cut deep into his shoulder, she wanted him bad.

Growling, he pulled away from her only to settle his face comfortably between her legs. He'd spent so many lonely nights dreaming about this. Of course, in his dreams they were on satin sheets in a bed at the Ritz Carlton. But hell, his mighty butcher block would do.

Yager slid his tongue into her hot pussy. She was already so wet, he was shocked he didn't drown. As soon as he started licking her, her hands grasped his head, her fingers digging into his scalp. He licked the lips of her pussy, teasing them with the tip of his tongue. Her back arched, so he flicked her clit and she almost shot off the butcher block.

A lot of the Ravens figured Neecy was an unresponsive, cold bitch. Taking bets on whether she simply lay there during sex, waiting for it to be over, or if she did her best to get the guy off and out so she could sleep or go hunt. Well, he was going to let them keep those delusions. Because all of this, all of her, was his. Not anyone else's. This woman whose hips continued to surge against his face as she responded to his exploring tongue would always belong to him.

He went lower, pushing his tongue deep inside her and she groaned, deep and low, making him shudder. Did she even know what she was doing to him? Did she care?

"*God, Yager.*"

No, no. That wouldn't do. He pulled away, replacing his tongue with a finger. "It's Will."

"Wha..." She stopped to grunt as a second finger joined the first, her eyes closed and her head thrown back. "What?"

"My name's Will," he told her as he steadily fucked her with his fingers. "People I work with call me Yager. For the next twenty-four hours, you call me Will."

Her hips surged forward again, now riding his fingers as they'd ridden his tongue. "Whatever," she gasped out.

"No. Not whatever." With his other hand he grasped her clit between thumb and forefinger. "Will. Say it."

Neecy tightened her fingers in his hair, unwilling to let him go. "Will. Fine. Will. Just don't stop. God, please don't stop!"

He didn't. Instead he returned his tongue to her clit as he kept his fingers pumping away inside her. Her groans became louder and louder as her body began to shake. When he knew she was close, he gently grasped her clit between his lips and sucked hard. Her soft groans became a hoarse shout as she came on his face, every muscle in her body tight.

Leaning away from Neecy long enough to reach into the pocket of his bomber jacket thrown over the back of one of the kitchen chairs, he pulled out a long line of condom packets.

Neecy focused on them and turned questioning eyes to Yager. He shrugged. "Mike."

"Oh." For many, that was really the only explanation they ever needed.

In seconds, he'd sheathed his cock and yanked Neecy off the butcher block. Once again, not exactly how he'd dreamed their first time together would be. But he'd run out of patience months ago. The only thing the Norse male in him knew was that she was wet, willing, and whimpering.

Up to this point, Neecy really hadn't had a chance to look at Yager's cock. He'd kept the towel on and, although she felt his hard-on through the thick cotton, actual dimensions were lost on her. And once he threw her up on his butcher block she'd forgotten everything with that damn tongue of his getting her to make noises she didn't think possible. Still, she didn't get a chance to get a good look at it as Yager quickly pulled her down, immediately shoving his cock inside her.

And holy shit, but the man was *huge!*

Neecy yelped as he settled himself inside her. As wet as she truly was, he still stretched her. And, don't forget, last boyfriend...Mr. Tiny Penis Man.

Yager turned and pushed her up against the much sturdier, nailed-to-the-floor island that stood proud and stainless steel–like in his kitchen.

"Are you okay?" he panted desperately in her ear.

It took her a moment, but Neecy suddenly realized Yager wasn't moving. He was waiting for her. Making sure she was okay. She knew it was killing him. Every muscle on his body was rigid and sweat dripped from every pore. Still, as much as it hurt him, he didn't want to hurt her.

Neecy wrapped her arms around Yager's neck while one leg wrapped around his waist and the other around his calf. She leaned in and growled into his ear, "Fuck me, Will. Fuck. *Me.*"

She winced as his hands tightened around her body, his big fingers digging into her back. Then he pinned her to the island and fucked her like he'd just been let out of prison, holding her tight as he mercilessly powered into her.

She couldn't move, even if she wanted to. Even the trace of pain only enhanced the pleasure. So she held on tight to Will Yager and let him fuck her. And she may never say it out loud, but Jesus Christ, it was the best fuck she'd ever had.

Each hard thrust pushed her closer to the edge. Each rough pant made her hold him tighter. But when he whispered her name like he was praying at church and not coming like an out-of-control bus, she lost it, flying over that edge with him.

It took several whole minutes before Yager could actually focus his eyes or remember his name. And the entire time, he never let Neecy go. Nor did she pull away. How he got her to come, though...he'd never know. He stopped thinking about anything once she told him to fuck her. His mind completely shut off and his cock took over.

He actually felt embarrassed. He had more self-control than that. At least he did with everyone else but Neecy. Slowly, Yager pulled away from her, letting her legs drop to the floor. She almost fell, though, when he tried to release her.

"God, are you okay?"

"Yeah." She smiled. "Just a little shaky."

"Here." He grabbed her by the waist and placed her back on the kitchen block. "Wait here. I'll be right back."

Yager went to his hallway bathroom and quickly stripped off the spent condom. He moved to the sink and turned on the tap. He splashed cold water on his face and told himself to remain calm.

True, he had Neecy Lawrence sitting in his kitchen. A naked Neecy Lawrence whom he'd just had the most amazing sex he'd ever had in his entire lifetime with. And he now had twenty-four hours to do that over and over and over again.

But fucking her wasn't the prize. Keeping her was.

✧

Neecy glanced at her watch. Damn. It wasn't even eleven yet. She came from her eight a.m. class to here and never expected to do more than to again tell Yager she would not go out with him.

Somehow, though, she'd ended up naked on his butcher block.

Taking a deep breath, Neecy glanced around Yager's kitchen. Clearly the man had money. You didn't get an apartment like this in Manhattan without a few million to your name.

He also seemed to have a thing about stainless steel and marble. At least in his kitchen.

Neecy glanced down at herself. She had two Japanese sleeve tats on both her shoulders and upper biceps. Plus one on her right forearm. She got them to cover up her gang tattoos. She still had scars from the gunshots to her chest since Skuld liked to leave little reminders to her Daughters of where they'd come from. And she still had bruises from a brutal fight she'd had several days earlier with some idiot who'd sacrificed his own sister to activate one of Odin's swords.

Christ, what the hell am I doing here?

"Thirsty?"

Her head snapped up to find Yager standing in front of her. She never even heard him come back in the room. For a very large man, he was awfully stealthy.

"A little."

"Bottled water okay?"

"Perfect." She should tell him she wanted to go. She should tell him this was a mistake.

Before she had a chance, Yager slipped one big arm around her waist and easily lifted her off his defiled butcher block. He held her next to his body. "Wrap your legs around my waist." She did. "Arms on neck, Lawrence." She did that, too.

He walked them over to his stainless-steel fridge and pulled open the door. "Can you get the water?" She could and she did, grabbing the neck of two water bottles in between the fingers of one hand. Once she had them secure, Yager closed the fridge door and headed out of the kitchen.

"Where are we going?"

"The bedroom. We can't stay in the kitchen for the next twenty-four hours, now can we?"

"Twenty-three hours."

"What?"

"The next twenty-three hours and ten minutes to be exact."

"You Crows are such sticklers for the details."

"We sure are, but you should know that by now."

Yager walked down the very long hallway of his very big apartment until he reached the master bedroom. Like the rest of the place, it was enormous. Had to be, though...so it could fit that bed.

Slowly, he put her down on the bed and grasped one of the waters she held out to him. In silence, they opened the bottles and drank. While doing so, Neecy, feeling a little bit insecure suddenly, examined Yager's room. Very little steel here except for the bed frame. Instead, he had lots of manly wood furniture. Mahogany being the wood of choice. Plus a couple of plush leather chairs scattered around the room, both filled with piles of clothes Yager must have tossed off before heading to the shower. He also had a laptop on the dresser and what looked like a PC game paused on-screen. He had only a couple of pictures of his Raven buddies and his old mentor. No other family shots or girlfriend pictures she could see. And five framed posters on his walls...three from the first *Star Wars* movies, one from *War Games,* and one from the original *Heavy Metal* movie.

She didn't know what she expected to find in Yager's apartment, but for some reason these posters weren't it. They seemed kind of...well, geeky. She never thought of Yager as geeky. Of course, a few hours ago, she did think of him as dumb. Quickly, however, she was realizing Yager wasn't stupid at all.

"You gonna look at me, baby?"

Neecy sighed. "You really have to stop calling me that." She brought the bottle back to her lips and took a healthy drink, turning to face him. Bad move, since she almost choked on her water.

Yager stood in front of her. Completely naked and completely gorgeous. No towel or anything else for that matter between them. And, to her surprise, he'd gotten hard again. Seriously, take-down-a-door-with-that-thing hard. Her last couple of boyfriends were lucky to bang it out twice in a night and that was usually only after some liquor and porn were involved. She'd heard Odin endowed his Ravens with his sexual resilience, but she thought that was a myth.

Lowering the bottle of water, she slowly licked her lips.

"Uh...Lawrence? My eyes are up here."

"So?"

Yager laughed. "God, I love your honesty."

Well, why bother lying? When a man sports a cock that big and it was all yours for the next twenty-three hours, why waste time with bullshit?

Stretching out her hand, Neecy grasped Yager's cock tight. He took in a startled breath as she gently pulled him toward her.

"When you took off the condom, did you wipe yourself off?"

She heard him swallow before he answered. "Yeah."

"Good. I hate the taste of spermicide." Then she wrapped her lips around him and sucked.

As soon as her mouth glided over his cock, Yager realized how far gone he really was. He could spend the rest of his life with his cock trapped in this woman's mouth and be so okay with that. And she took her time. He didn't sense for a second that she was trying to get him off just so she could get it over with. Instead, it seemed like she enjoyed running her tongue over every vein, every ridge. Exploring him. Tasting him. Testing him. Testing how much he could take.

Not much. As soon as the tip of her tongue began playing around his slit, he almost lost it. He pushed her off before he shot a load down her throat.

"What?" Wow, she sounded annoyed he stopped her. Could he actually have found male nirvana? A woman who *liked* giving blowjobs?

Taking deep breaths and thinking about ice hockey, "Not yet, baby." He'd promised himself to make this round last.

Yager pushed her back on the bed as he stretched out beside her. "Trust me when I say we'll get back to that, but right now I wanna—" using one arm to prop his head up, he slid the fingers of his free hand across her stomach and around her breasts, "—savor."

Frowning in confusion, she asked, "Savor what?"

"You, Neecy."

"Why?"

"I find it amazing you even have to ask that."

"We're on a schedule here, Yager." She slapped the back of one hand into the palm of the other several times to emphasize her point. "So don't start fucking it up with 'savoring' and meaningful looks. We don't have time for that."

57

Yager laughed so hard he almost fell off the bed. After about two minutes, he heard Neecy growl. He grabbed hold of her arm before she could take two steps away from the bed. He yanked her back down and stretched out on top of her, holding her still with his weight.

"Don't even think about leaving, Lawrence."

"Well you seemed to be having so much fun without me," she snapped.

"I just really irritate the living shit out of you sometimes, don't I?"

"As a matter of fact, yes you do."

"Now that doesn't seem right, does it?" He nuzzled her under the chin. "I really should make up for that." He licked the skin between her breasts and brushed the sides with the tip of his nose.

Her breathing changed, becoming deeper. Her body trembled slightly as he used the tip of his tongue to lightly tease her nipples. Long fingers dug into his hair as even longer legs wrapped tight around him.

Pulling himself up a bit, he spoke softly against her ear. "But don't forget, Neecy Lawrence—" slowly thrusting his hips so his hard cock rubbed against her, he heard her moan, "—you're mine until tomorrow. That means I can savor, pamper, spoil, or play with this body until our time is up." He thrust again and Neecy moaned. "And you're gonna let me, aren't you, baby?" He thrust against her, harder this time, making sure to hit her clit in the process. "Aren't you?"

"Yes," she hissed, gripping him tighter, burying her face in his neck. "God, yes."

Yager smiled, feeling like one of the triumphant warriors he was a descendent of. "Good, baby. Now lean back, get comfortable, and enjoy the ride."

Chapter Six

Will pushed her hair out of her face, but her eyes didn't open. "You okay, baby?"

She yanked the covers over her head. "Go away!"

Poor thing. He'd ridden her pretty hard most of the day. She went to get more water from the kitchen and he fucked her up against the fridge. She went to the bathroom and he nailed her on the sink. She walked down the hallway and he fucked her on the hallway floor. And none of that included what he did to her in his bed...again and again and again. He should feel bad...but he didn't. Not when he felt so damn good. And he wasn't remotely done with her. Not yet.

Not ever.

"Aren't you hungry, baby?"

"This is another one of those trick questions, isn't it?"

He grinned as he fought with her to pull the covers back. He always knew he'd enjoy tusslin' with Neecy Lawrence. "Don't be ridiculous." He snatched the covers out of her hands. "Besides, what else could I mean when I say, 'So, do you like protein in your diet?'"

"I thought you were talking about that diet where you only eat meat."

Laughing, he slipped his arms under her neck and legs, easily lifting her off the bed. "In a way...I was."

He carried her into his living room where he already had the food laid out on the floor. He even had a reason to use his fireplace. The whole crackling-fire thing...that was romantic, right?

He placed her on top of the flannel blanket he'd already put down.

"Chinese food." She smiled. "Very creative."

"Can you think of anything better for sustaining bouts of serious sex than takeout Chinese?"

Stretching out, stomach down, she took the chopsticks he offered her. "Good point."

He stretched out next to her. "I didn't know what you liked, so I got a little bit of everything."

"I'm not finicky about food." She snagged a piece of barbeque pork and popped it into her mouth. "Especially when I'm actually allowed to eat."

"Don't give me that look. I gave you time for lunch."

"Letting me eat soup while you lick me out is not really conducive to getting in a full meal."

"But it was chicken noodle. It had everything necessary to get back to sex."

She shook her head and sipped the red wine he put out.

"I hope the wine's okay. I've got soda and water if you want that instead."

"Nope. This is fine."

They ate in silence for a good ten minutes, and Yager really liked that she didn't feel the need to talk while she was eating. When he ate, he just wanted to eat. Basic conversation came before and after. Never during.

He also liked that she didn't seem to mind sitting around his living room naked. Yeah. He could easily see spending the rest of his life naked with Neecy.

When they'd polished off most of the food, he decided it was time to get a little information out of her. She seemed so relaxed and there was so much about her he wanted to know. For once, she didn't seem closed off to him, and she was actually letting him be nice to her. "Can I ask you a question?"

Neecy took a bamboo shoot out of his nearly empty bowl. "How did I die, right?"

Yager shook his head. He didn't need to ask about her death. He already knew. It was the first question every Raven asked when they brought in a new Crow to The Gathering: "So, bro, how'd this one buy it?"

"Actually, I was going to ask about your tattoos."

"Oh." She glanced down at the tattoos covering both of her biceps and one on her forearm. They were amazing workmanship and something about them seemed to fit Neecy perfectly. "I got these from an Okinawa Crow. She's also a tattoo artist and came to the States to visit for a couple of weeks. Didi knew I wanted to cover up my old tats,

60

so she asked the woman to swing by and meet with me. I thought for sure I wouldn't be able to afford her. I mean, she's world-famous. But she did these for free."

"Why?" Yager didn't know much about tattoos. He went through his life avoiding needles as much as possible. His doctor cringed every time he realized he had to give him a shot for something. Still, Yager knew tattoos could be expensive based on what Mike told him. The better the artist, the more expensive the tat.

Neecy gave a small smile. "She talked to me for hours the first night she was here. When she was about to go back to her hotel, she said she'd do my cover-ups. She'd be back in a couple of days."

"Just like that?"

"I think she felt sorry for me. And she knew I wanted to get rid of the gang tats."

"Felt sorry for you or admired you? There is a difference." He ran his finger down one of her tats, tracing the soaring black crow within the intricate design. "This isn't the tat of someone I should feel sorry for. It's about power and strength."

She finished off her wine and shrugged self-consciously. "Yeah. I guess. Maybe." Quickly, Neecy moved on from the topic of herself. Seemed she didn't feel too comfortable with that.

"Can I ask you a question?"

"Anything."

She blinked at that, before barreling ahead. "When did Odin come for you?"

"When I was thirteen."

"Wow. You were young."

"It's the standard age for the Ravens."

"Crows don't have a standard age." He knew that. Crows came whenever their deaths came. "So, how did that work?"

"What do you mean?"

"How did Odin come for you? I mean, Skuld waits until you're on that last breath before she makes an appearance. Then she offers you fruit—although none of us figured out why yet. Anyway, I wondered how Odin handled it."

Will took his fist and lightly tapped Neecy on her forehead. "Knock. Knock. Mrs. Yager, we're Raven Elders and we're here for your son."

Neecy frowned. "Just like that?"

"Yup. Just like that, and no Odin. I met him by accident three years later. I ran over his foot with one of the Elder's Ferraris. That's when I learned drinking and driving...very bad."

Neecy's head was down, but her entire body shook from laughter.

"Oh, sure. Laugh. But let me tell ya...for a god, he was awfully asshole-y about the whole thing."

Clearing her throat, Neecy continued with her questions. "And your parents didn't freak out about any of this?"

"Not at all. I come from a very long line of Vikings. And a few from our line had been called by Odin before."

"So they just...handed you over? To some strangers?"

"Yup. They were honored."

"And you?"

"Me?" He shrugged. "I'm good at what I do."

Neecy nodded in agreement. "Yeah. Me, too."

They both stared into the fire crackling in his fireplace. Both of them had started down these paths so early in life, but he couldn't say that if anything had been different, their lives would have necessarily been better. He found himself damn grateful to Skuld. If she hadn't taken Neecy, she wouldn't be here now. Right where she belonged, as far as Yager was concerned.

Her soft lips brushed against his throat and he closed his eyes, enjoying the feel of her mouth on his body. As the day wore on, Neecy became more and more affectionate and he loved every minute of it.

She kissed her way up his neck. Her arm stretched across his shoulders as she breathed into his ear, "Fuck me, Will. You feel so good inside me."

He melted at her words, leaning down to kiss her. The woman had no idea what she did to him. How much she made him want to chain her to the bed so that she could never leave him.

She had no idea when he unfurled his wings, but nothing felt as cool as having those wings sweep across her naked back. She pulled out of their kiss, gasping in surprise.

"Oh, my God!" She twisted her body a bit so she could watch the feathers glide along her skin. "That feels amazing."

"You've never done this before?" A mischievous grin spread across his face. "Even with the other Crows?"

Smirking, "You guys have a whole lesbian-fantasy thing going on over there at that Mountain Ridge, Mountain Creek, Mountain Cock...whatever ya call it."

"Just a little one. All those tough women alone...wearing leather. There's gotta be some wrestling going on that involves oil, right?"

She bumped her shoulder into his. "I find that such a sad, pitiful, all-male statement."

"Even the Warriors of Odin have their sad, pitiful, all-male moments."

She stretched, her back arching as the tip of his wing kept up its steady movement against her flesh. She especially loved when the feathers swept across the scar tissue that hid her own wings. They'd always been kind of sensitive, but this was mind-blowing.

Who knew she'd enjoy spending time around Wilhelm Yager? Up to now, she just thought he was another dumb rich guy looking to slum it a bit with the Crows. She'd quickly found out he was anything but dumb and not once the entire day had Yager made her feel different or low class or less than anything else in the world. He actually made her feel...well, kinda special.

Neecy's body jolted as Will's feathers slipped between her legs. Her head dropping to rest on her folded arms. "What are you doing?"

"Amusing myself." His wing stroked her pussy lips. "Mine for twenty-four hours. Remember?"

How the hell could she forget? She was already dreading the end of this. But it would end. It's not like she could live like this forever...right?

"Spread your legs, baby."

She looked up at his smiling face through her too-long tangled bangs. She really needed to get them cut. "Must you call me that?"

"I like calling you that. Now spread 'em."

She did and he glided the tip of his wing against her clit, flicking it with a twist of his feathers.

Neecy's body jerked again. She'd heard about getting a feather-tease, but this was ridiculous. And delicious. "You have got to be kidding me." No way would she let him get her off with his wing, but she seemed unable to stop him. It felt too good. He felt too good.

"Nice, huh?"

She nodded and moaned, but kept her head down. For some reason, she felt acute embarrassment the man could get her off so easily and had been doing it all day. It didn't take her long to realize there would be no controlling Wilhelm Yager—in bed or out.

"You want me to stop?"

She shook her head.

"Are you avoiding me, baby?"

She nodded.

"Why?"

"I'm embarrassed by my weakness."

"Why? Because I can make you come whenever I want?"

Her head snapped up, an angry glare etched across her beautiful face. But before she could start ripping the feathers off his wings, he flicked her clit again. Her body stiffened, her eyes slammed shut, then her entire body clenched and she came hard and fast. He kept the pressure up, enjoying just watching her body writhe in release.

After a few moments, it seemed she couldn't take it anymore. "Stop, stop, stop!" She pulled away, panting hard, and rolled onto her side. "Well, that was freakin' amazing."

"Thank you."

She rolled onto her back and stared up at him. "Can I ask you something else?"

"What part of 'ask me anything' are we not grasping here?"

She rolled her eyes at his tone as her cheeks turned red. It took him a second to realize she was embarrassed and not by what he'd said either.

"I can't believe I'm asking this, but—" she took a huge breath, "—could you really not tell you were holding onto my tits the other night?"

He snorted. "Of course I knew." He brushed his cheek against her forehead, marveling at the realization that Neecy had let him see a side of her he knew she'd never show anyone else. "And, to quote you, they felt freakin' amazing."

Reaching up and punching him lightly in the chest, she teased, "That's sexual harassment in the workplace. I could complain to Odin, ya know?"

"Odin *is* sexual harassment in the workplace."

"I have noticed an even bigger increase in the jiggle factor with the newest crop of Valkyries."

She watched as Yager retracted his wings and stretched out next to her on the floor, the two of them staring up at the ceiling. "Well, you've met some of the older Valkyries. They're exceptionally cool. Very kick-ass. Brutal. But Odin met that stripper a few years back and it's been downhill ever since."

Had it ever. And Neecy was the one who decked their leader, Clarissa. Or as all the Jersey Crows liked to call her, "That Valkyrie bitch Clarissa." It was during the infamous Valkyrie-Crow bar fight in Yonkers. And every second she spent in jail that night...totally worth it.

The pair grinned as Yager suddenly took hold of her hand and intertwined their fingers together. Part of her wanted to snatch her hand back. Not that it didn't feel good. It felt great. Too great. The act itself seemed so intimate to her. Almost more than the two of them fucking.

"Okay. Another question for you," Yager said as he continued to stare up at the ceiling. "If you hadn't...uh..."

She knew where this was going. "Died? If I hadn't died?"

"Man, you guys deal with that really well."

She smiled. "Well, we've already done the hard part."

"True. Okay, so if you hadn't died, would you still be dealing drugs?"

"Oh, no. No, not at all."

"Really?"

"Oh, yeah. I was planning on moving into gun-running. I hated dealing with addicts and the asshole kept pushing me to deal the harder shit, which meant the scarier addicts. So, I thought...gun-running. My whole goal was simple..."

"Money?"

She shook her head. "College. I didn't care what I had to do. I was going to college. I used to watch TV and I'd see all these people with good lives and they all seemed to have college educations." She finally pulled her hand away from his, put both her arms over her head and stretched. "The Gathering was actually perfect for me. They didn't care if you hunted every night, all night, for ten weeks in a row. Your grades better be A's or high B's, and your SAT scores better be high. If your grades slipped because you were screwing around, you got what we refer to as a Raven Elder–type beating."

Grimacing, Yager said, "That's brutal."

"Yup. Needless to say we all work to keep our grades up. The other option's just too scary. But they pay for all your education right through master's and doctorate work, so it balances out."

"And you seem relatively unscathed."

"'Cause I'm really, really smart."

He laughed and she decided to change the subject, hoping to get them back to safer, non-Neecy-related ground.

"Will...what exactly do you do?"

"You mean besides save the world from evil?"

"Well, shit. *I* do that. What else do you do?"

"I don't wanna tell ya."

"Oh, come on. Admit it. The Ravens don't have to work, do they?"

"What gave you that idea?"

"You guys always seem to be lounging around with your incredibly hot cars. I mean, all of you have offices, but we just figured none of you actually worked in them."

"We do work. All of us."

"Then what do you do?"

He sighed. "Me, Tye, and Mike design game software."

"No. Seriously."

"I am serious."

She snorted a laugh. "My God. You're a geek!"

"Shut up."

"A big, giant geek." She laughed harder and suddenly he was straddling her hips. The man was so enormous and she realized he may not take too kindly to her laughing at him. Most guys didn't. The drug-dealer boyfriend sure didn't.

"You know, I actually take what I do quite seriously. It's an art."

"An...art?"

Fresh round of laughter from that. Man, she really hoped this guy had a sense of humor because she was practically hysterical at this point with a naked giant sitting on her.

"You're making fun of me."

"Well, yeah. I mean, come on! Computer games? What are you? Twelve?"

"What do you think paid for this apartment? And my house out on the Island? And Tye's Lamborghini? And the lawyer for Mike during that whole paternity mess? So, we're not geeks."

Neecy choked back the laughter. "Okay, then...where did you go to school?"

"MIT and Caltech."

She pushed herself up on her elbows, staring straight into his eyes. "Geek. Geek. Geek. With some nerd thrown in for flavor."

Yager leaned down, their faces inches apart. "Yeah. And this geek has been getting you to scream his name. All. Day. Long."

Damn right he had. And she'd been enjoying every goddamn minute of it.

"Pure luck," she smirked. "But I bet you can't do it again."

"Neecy Lawrence, you know a Raven can never turn down a direct challenge."

"Really?" she asked in mock innocence. "I've never heard that before. It must be a Viking thing. You know with my girl brain, I'd never understand any of that."

"You know, Lawrence," he began as he settled himself comfortably against her hips, his naked ass rubbing against her pelvis, his big hands framing her face. For such a big guy, he knew how to handle his size well. And nothing was more delicious than having Will Yager's hard body at her disposal. "You really do talk some shit."

"Oh?"

"Yeah. And I think it's time we find something else for your mouth to do..."

Rachel lost sight of her prey as he went over a fence. She spread her wings and followed. As she moved something flashed past her, slamming into her wing and yanking her back, nailing her to a wall.

Screeching in rage, Rachel stared at the all-metal spear jutting from her body. Covered in Nordic runes and infused with powerful magic, it pinned her to the red brick. Her feet didn't even touch the ground.

Again she screeched in pain and rage. She reached for the spear as men stepped out from the shadows. Human men. Hunters. They were dressed like they were hunting deer in the mountains. She didn't understand. How the hell did they see her? It was dark—cloaking time. Once her wings came out at night, only her prey, some Norse-descendent Shifters, and other Clans could see Crows when they were on the hunt. But these men were looking straight at her.

"Bastards!" she spat in Russian. She only used her father's language when she was really pissed off. "I've already been killed by better than you."

"Is it her?"

"No. Waste her."

One of the men raised a rifle and aimed it at her. So focused on her, they never saw her sisters coming. Crows never fought alone. They'd been moving toward her from her first screech. Now her team leader, Delia, landed behind the one with the gun. Snatching his head back, she dragged her blade over his throat while another sister grabbed the gun from his hands before he could fire. They both moved so fast, the man didn't even have a chance to whimper.

The other Hunters realized females surrounded them, so they went for their weapons. But they'd never be fast enough. Not against Crows.

Rachel gritted her teeth and yanked the spear out of her wing. She dropped to the ground and gutted the first Hunter who crossed her path. She liked this spear. She planned to keep it and use it for future hunts.

"You gonna stand there bleedin' or you gonna kick a little ass, Rach?"

Rachel looked up at her team leader, and smiled.

Karl Waldgrave watched as the team of women ripped apart his men. He knew when he sent them out, they wouldn't come back alive. They were necessary sacrifices to give him and the other Hunters an idea of how these females fought.

And even Waldgrave had to admit, as legendary a Hunter as he was, his goddess had given him a true challenge.

He offered up a silent thanks to Her as he planned his next move.

Chapter Seven

Neecy picked up her crumpled jeans from off the floor and dug her cell phone out of the back pocket. She flipped it open. "Yeah." She cringed at the croak she wanted to pass off as a voice.

"Am I interrupting anything?"

"What is it, Didi?"

"Get your ass back to the house. But feel free to stop at your place and shower first. It's not that big a rush." Didi hung up.

Flipping the phone closed, Neecy slid it back into her jeans. She shook her head, trying to clear her brain. She couldn't remember the last time she was this exhausted. Her entire body sore and sticky.

A big hand gripped her jeans and pulled them away, dropping them back to the floor.

"Yager, I gotta go."

"I've got an hour left." He kissed her neck, his lips sliding down to her breasts.

"Didi wants me back at the house and I need to go home and get some clothes, catch a shower...ah!" He sucked her nipple hard into his mouth and Neecy couldn't help but squirm in response. How did the man keep doing this to her? Damn him! She needed to get out of here or she may never leave.

"Shower here. I'll give you one of my sweaters."

"Sweaters? What happened to my—"

"It got dirty on the butcher's block."

"Yeah, but—"

"No buts. My time. Didi can fuckin' wait unless she said it was an emergency."

True, she could lie to him. But Neecy didn't lie. Didi didn't tell her it was an emergency. Otherwise, she would have ordered her back to the house immediately.

"I'll take your silence to mean it's not an emergency." Yager pulled himself up until he hovered over her, his arms braced on either side of her shoulders. "I still have an hour. Which means this sweet body still belongs to me."

Her body may belong to him at this moment, but once she walked out of his apartment that would be it. She'd allowed herself this indulgence, but never again. At least not with Yager. It would be way too easy to lose herself to this man. Way too easy.

But, hell, what was one time? And it was just one time. She and Yager had an agreement.

Neecy looked up into his gorgeous face and smiled. "Tick-tock, Raven."

Yager pushed her up against the wall, his mouth fastened to hers. Her hand reached out, fumbling for the door handle. He grabbed it and her other hand and pinned them both above her head.

She pulled her mouth away from his. "I've gotta go," she gasped.

Leaning his body into hers, "Stay."·

"I can't... No, no, no! Not the neck! Not the neck!" He gripped the flesh of her throat between his teeth. Once he found out how much nipping her neck turned her on, he did it all night long. Of course, he didn't bother telling her he'd riddled her poor neck with hickeys and he kept her away from mirrors as he got her showered and put her in his turtleneck sweater.

"Off! Off! Off!" She pulled her wrists out of his grasp and pushed against his chest. "We agreed to twenty-four hours. We are now past that." Way past...he'd kept her busy for another two hours after Didi called.

"When will I see you again?"

"You won't...unless we're at one of those hideous Valkyrie parties or I'm kicking your ass." She pulled away from him and snatched his front door open, stumbling out into the hallway.

Neecy turned around and glared at him. "And remember our agreement, Yager."

"Right. Twenty-four hours and you go. That was our agreement."

"*And* we never discuss this again, we never meet again, and you stop looking at me that way you have...which you're doing right now!"

"I didn't agree to that."

Neecy stared at him. "Yes you did."

"No. I didn't. We shook on the twenty-four hours. You mentioned those bullshit rules *after* we shook hands. All I did was shrug. I didn't agree to anything. It's not my fault you didn't confirm the terms of our agreement."

He wasn't sure, but it looked like Neecy's head just might blow off her body at any moment. Man, he'd pissed her off good, now hadn't he? A woman who didn't get angry was suddenly seething. And dammit if she wasn't cute even pissed.

"You lying sack of motherfuckin' shit!" she bit out between clenched teeth. Of course, he could do without the name-calling.

Yager glanced over his shoulder when his phone rang. "That must be Molinski. I gotta go." He looked down into Neecy's pretty face. "I'll call you tonight, baby."

"No! You will not call me tonight!"

Yager closed his front door. He couldn't stop smiling. Because the woman had absolutely no idea what she'd gotten herself into.

Neecy stared at the closed door. *That tricky, Odin-loving bastard!* If he thought he could walk all over her, he was insane.

Neecy banged her fist against the door. "Open up, you lying prick!"

This wasn't over.

Mike Molinski heard the yelling before the elevator doors opened. Although he would be eternally surprised to see who was behind it.

"Open this door, you lying sack of shit!"

Nice mouth on this one. Mike shook his head as he ambled down the hallway. He'd known girls like the Crows in his old neighborhood. Girls he learned never to turn his back on.

Although Neecy Lawrence seemed much more dangerous than that. The quiet ones always were. While other neighborhood girls screamed and announced their plans, giving a person time to make a run for it, Neecy was all about the silent attack. Like one of those drug dealer–owned pit bulls with their vocal cords cut.

As he got closer, she finally kicked the door, turned, and stormed past him. He watched her walk by, fascinated by a grown woman muttering to herself like a psychiatric patient.

He wasn't even sure she actually saw him until she got right next to him. Then those black eyes nailed him with one look. *"What the fuck you lookin' at?"*

Mike learned a long time ago never to answer *that* question.

Instead he went to Yager's door and stuck the key in the lock. As he opened it, he saw Neecy Lawrence step inside the elevator. As the doors slid closed, he could see her kicking the elevator walls.

Stepping into Yager's apartment, "Hey, Yager. You here?"

"Bathroom."

Mike walked into Yager's master bathroom to find his mentor soaking in a steaming-hot tub of water. "Feelin' better?"

"Much."

The man did look better. Calmer. Kind of happy. Yager never really looked happy. Polite. Friendly. When motivated, charming. But never happy. Until now.

And he definitely looked satisfied.

"I see you pissed Neecy Lawrence off."

Yager, his head back against the rim of the enormous tub, shrugged those massive shoulders. "Probably."

"That's a major coup, pissing that cold female off." Mike scratched his neck, walking back toward the door. "Of course, that's what I was thinking before I noticed she was wearing the sweater I gave you two Christmases ago. You've been fucking her since yesterday, haven't you?"

Not bothering to wait for an answer, he headed toward the kitchen and a glass of orange juice as Yager angrily questioned Mr. and Mrs. Molinski's marriage status when Mike was born.

Chapter Eight

Neecy pulled off her helmet and headed toward the house. She usually only used her sport bike in the summertime, but it hadn't started snowing yet, and she needed the cold January air to control her almost overwhelming rage.

He'd tricked her...but why? What exactly did he want from her? A repeat of last night? *No way.*

Of course, as quickly as she thought "no way", she remembered the feel of his mouth on her pussy and her entire body clenched with need.

Damn him! He did this to her, and she would never, ever forgive him!

She reached to open the front door, but someone snatched it open from the inside.

Neecy looked into the sweet but always-expecting-the-worst face of Arri Chang—one of the most nervous Crows Neecy had ever known. Arri had already died once. What could she be worrying about now?

"Hey, Arri."

"Where have you been?"

To heaven. "In hell. Why?"

"I'm just glad you're here," she sighed.

Poor Arri. No matter what she did, she was having the hardest time fitting in with the other Crows. Neecy did her best to make her feel at home, but the rest was up to Arri and the girl was really struggling. Of course, it might help if her hair wasn't fuchsia. She dyed that shoulder-length mess the oddest colors.

"Lawrence," Didi called from the living room. "Is that you?"

"Yeah."

"Well get your big ass in here."

Big ass? Bitch.

Neecy looked at Arri. "When we're done here, I wanna talk to you for a few minutes."

"Why? What did I do?"

Rubbing Arri's shoulder, she chuckled. "Nothing. Calm down."

Arri braved a little smile as Neecy put her arm around her shoulders and walked with the kid into the living room. All the Jersey Crows were there and well into the middle of Didi's meeting. *Gee, nothing like waiting for their second-in-command.*

"So what did they look like?" Didi asked as Neecy dropped her backpack and shrugged out of her jacket.

Delia's crew looked at each other. "They were white guys," Delia offered. "Just average white guys."

"How is that helpful to me?"

Neecy looked around and suddenly noticed Rachel's tightly bandaged shoulder; her pretty but pale face. The bandage not only locked her arm against her body, it covered her back. Which meant only one thing. Someone or something had wounded her wing. The only way to get a wing to heal on one of them or the Ravens was to keep it tucked inside their body for several days. Usually a few rune spells were enlisted as well, depending on how bad the wound. "What's going on?"

Didi nodded toward Rachel. "Hunters."

At that moment, Neecy felt raw, almost overwhelming hate well up in her system. "You've gotta be fucking kidding me," she spit out between clenched teeth.

"Hunters that hunt us...right?" Arri squeaked out.

Didi glanced at Arri. Of all the Crows, for some unknown reason, Didi had very little patience for the pint-sized girl. But she answered her nonetheless. "Pretty much. Every few decades some asshole Hunters find out about our existence and decide to come after us. Usually the very wealthy and the very well-connected looking for new and more exciting prey."

"It must be something about having Crows wings over their fireplace that really gives these idiots hard-ons," Janelle added.

"Yeah." Katie grinned. "Then they're so shocked when we retaliate."

"I've heard some Crows from centuries ago would destroy whole villages and castles to prove they were not to be fucked with," Didi finished.

"Nice," Janelle stated before biting into the apple she held in her hand.

It seemed only Arri could sense Neecy's rage based on the way she carefully inched away from her. Neecy hadn't spoken because she couldn't see straight. She felt like dog shit. She spent hours fucking Yager while one of her own was almost killed. Nope. She was lower than dog shit... Cat shit. She was cat shit.

And she'd make the ones who did this to one of her sisters pay.

Neecy stared at Rachel. "Are you gonna be okay?"

"Yeah. One of the older Valkyries patched me up." When the Original Seven were the only Valkyries, healing anything was the last thing on their minds, being brutal warriors in their own right. But when they grew bored after centuries of duty to their father, he began choosing mortal females to carry on the Valkyrie role. Not a problem, except they could get hurt and die. They taught themselves to heal, and when the Ravens and Crows came on the scene, they helped out when they could. Lately, though, it seemed only the older, less nubile Valkyries were the ones with actual healing skills. The newest crop could barely put on bandages. And some of them outright passed out at the sight of blood. Losers.

"Did they say anything to you, Rach?" Didi questioned.

"Yeah. One of 'em said, 'Is it her?'"

The Crows glanced at each other as Didi frowned and looked at Neecy. "Are you sure that's what he said?" Didi pushed.

"Yeah. That's what he said."

"So." Didi took over the room in that effortless way she had. "From now until we find out what's going on, y'all fight in full teams. No pairs 'cause a few of your teammates are out gettin' a mani-pedi. Make sure y'all have your cells and please make sure they're charged." Some of the females looked embarrassed, knowing Didi spoke directly to them. "No fucking around on this, ladies. For some unknown reason they can see us. Maybe other gods are involved. I don't know. But clearly this wasn't a random attack. Until we know exactly what's going on, I want all of you to play it smart and safe. Am I making myself clear?"

Smiling and in unison, "Yes, Miss Didi."

That eyebrow peaked. "Smartasses."

Yager slammed Mike into the garage wall next to the training area. "You know what really pisses me off, though?"

Tye swung at Mike, barely missing his head. "What?"

"That after the great night we had, she walked away." Mike tried to move but Yager grabbed him by the throat and shoved him back. "I mean...she is the most difficult woman I've ever dealt with."

Slamming his knee into Mike's stomach, Tye muttered, "She's a Crow. What do you expect?"

"I expect her to admit she's crazy about me so that we can move on to living together."

"Living together? With a Crow?" Grabbing Mike by the neck, Tye slammed him against the wall and then shoved him to the ground. "I guess it could work."

"It'll work. I just don't wanna wait twenty years for her to frickin' figure it out."

A foot firmly planted against the back of Mike's neck, Yager looked at the ten fourteen-year-old boys standing and watching them.

Addressing the boys, he said, "And that's how you push somebody in a corner and beat the shit out of 'em. Any questions?" When no one answered, "Great. Break. Then we'll get in a little weapons training."

The boys cheered as Tye turned to Yager. "Look, you knew going in that Neecy was kind of...ya know..."

"Cold and unpleasant?" Mike asked from his spot under Yager's big foot.

In answer, Tye and Yager kicked him. "Shut up!"

"That's the thing, Tye," Yager continued, ignoring Mike's yelp of pain. "She's not cold and unpleasant. Not really. She's just cautious."

"Then you need to get past that. Any way you can. Be persistent."

"Yeah, but when does persistence turn to stalking?"

"I think you're already there, bro...ow!" Mike grabbed his kicked-in, bleeding nose and glared up at Tye. "You son of a bitch!"

Ignoring him, Tye said, "Trust me. You're not there yet. If you were, you'd have every Crow in a hundred-mile radius coming down on your head."

"They like me."

"Then use that to your advantage. Use them. They'd use us, if we let 'em."

Yager chuckled. "We do let 'em use us."

Tye shrugged. "Yeah, we do. But they're all so fuckin' cute. We can't help ourselves."

Mike punched Yager's boot. "Excuse me, Men With No Penises, but can I get up now?"

"No!" they barked, then looked at each other and grinned.

Didi sat behind her desk and stared at her second-in-command. "So, what exactly did you find out from Yager?"

"Yager? Oh, yeah...um..."

Didi rolled her eyes. Good goddess, she fucked him. The flushed cheeks, the stammering, the hickeys...you didn't have to be Columbo to figure out the girl had spent most of the night with her ankles for earrings.

"He said he didn't know anything. You know those Ravens...just following orders."

"Did he tell you that before or after the first time he went down on you?"

"Oh, it was before—" Neecy's head snapped around and she glared at Didi. *Lawrence, you dumbass.* "We are so not having this conversation."

"Oh, we so are, Lawrence. Now spill."

"There's nothing to tell."

Oh, really? "You do know that turtleneck is *not* covering up those hickeys."

Based on how big her eyes got, Didi guessed she was, in fact, unaware of that.

Reaching into her drawer, Didi chastised, "I swear, Neecy, I don't know how you get yourself into this shit." She pulled out a hand mirror and shoved it across the desk.

Neecy stared at her reflection, her mouth open in horror. Yager had bitten so high up on her neck, the turtleneck sweater he gave her to wear did nothing to hide them. Really, the woman would have to be in a burka for anyone not to see those marks. And Didi bet Yager knew exactly what he was doing.

Apparently, Neecy felt the same way. "I'll kill him! That motherfuckin' son of a bitch..."

Didi let her second-in-command rant. She couldn't remember the last time Neecy allowed herself a good rant. It was good for her. Healthy.

"I hate him! I absolutely hate him!" Those scary black eyes looked up at Didi. "And I blame *you* for this!"

"Me? How am I at fault here? I send you over there to get information and you go down on the man like you're on the Titanic."

"I did not!"

"If I check your knees will I find rug burn?" The fact Neecy had to think about it gave Didi her answer. "Jesus, Neecy!"

"What?"

Giving her best mock glare, "Is this how I can expect you to handle political shit when I'm on vacation? By blowing Odin?"

All at once, calm, collected Neecy returned. "That is not funny. And it wasn't like that."

Didi shook her head. Poor Neecy. Always so serious. "I know, dumbass. I just don't understand why you're all upset. We're Crows. Not nuns. There's absolutely nothing wrong with a healthy sexual appetite. If it were me, I would have walked through the front door doin' the rumba."

"Wouldn't Harry be upset if you slept with Yager?"

"First off, I would never cheat on my husband...especially since he never got me killed because of his gambling problem."

"Ah. Well that's a recommendation."

"And second, you uptight heifer, the last thing I would be doing with Wilhelm Yager is sleeping. Now let's go. I want details...the more specific the better."

"I'm not giving you any details."

Didi leaned back in her chair. "I bet you can suck a golf ball out of a hose."

"Oh, that's lovely."

Didi just couldn't help herself. Neecy was the most fun of all the Crows to torture. Always so serious. Always so determined to fulfill her obligation to Skuld. Didi felt pretty confident the girl never had any fun whatsoever. Which wasn't fair. Neecy had been through a lot in her past. It seemed only right she should get a chance to relax and have a good time just like the rest of them.

And if that meant her friend needed to spend some quality time with one gorgeous hunk of winged male...well, dammit, that would just have to be.

Neecy's eyes narrowed. "Why are you looking at me that way?"

"What way?"

"Like you're up to something."

"Don't be ridiculous. What the hell would I be up to?"

Neecy pushed the chair away from the desk. "I'm out of here. I've gotta figure out who the hell is hunting us."

"Sit that ass down, missy."

Sighing, Neecy sat her ass down. "I'm not in the mood for this, Didi."

"Let's make this clear, you will *not* be dealing with our current Hunter situation."

"Why the hell not?"

"Because I said so." Didi leaned back in her leather chair, putting her bare feet up on the highly polished wood of her desk. "Now—" she sighed, putting her hands behind her head, "—I want details. Start at the first kiss and work your way to the very last shudder."

"I am *not* having this conversation with you. So let it go."

A knock at the office door almost had Neecy breaking out in a jig. "Thank God...*come in!*"

Arri stuck her head in. Her eyes locked with Neecy's. "You said you wanted to see me."

"Yeah. Come on in, hon."

Arri glanced at Didi before moving into the room. Neecy gave Didi her hardest glare, which simply said, "Be nice to Arri or I kick your ass." Didi really had a hard time with anyone that couldn't keep up. And in her mind, poor little Arri couldn't keep up.

"Sit."

Arri sat down in the chair next to Neecy, glancing between her and Didi.

Then, out of nowhere, Arri volunteered, "You're throwing me out, aren't you?"

Neecy blinked. "What? No! Of course not."

"Not that it hasn't crossed my mind, though."

Without taking her eyes off Arri, Neecy grabbed a box of tissues from Didi's desk and chucked it at her.

"Hon, it doesn't work that way around here," Neecy explained.

"But I don't contribute anything. I've been here two years and I'm not sure why...and no one else is either."

"Well, that's about to change."

"It is?"

"It is?" Didi barked. She sounded like a startled poodle.

Focusing on Arri, Neecy said, "Skuld wants me to take you on our next hunt."

Arri's frown was so deep, it looked painful. Add in the way she chewed on her bottom lip and you could almost smell the panic coming off her.

Didi, however, was much more verbal. *"Has she lost her ever-loving mind?"*

Unlike most goddesses, Skuld didn't have a problem with her Daughters questioning her. She was the Goddess of Wisdom, among other things, after all. And she seemed quite happy when questions were asked, concerns raised. However, she didn't appreciate out-and-out rudeness.

But, for some reason, Didi was one of the few who could get away with it. Skuld liked Didi. No one was quite sure why, though. Other than Didi was naturally charming. But Skuld seemed to hate charming since very few of the women she chose for her army were what one would call friendly, much less charming.

Neecy stood up. "Come on, Arri."

Didi's feet dropped to the floor with a dangerous thud. "Wait a minute. We're not done."

"We are so done." Neecy pushed Arri toward the door. "Go out back and meet me outside. I'll be there in five."

"O-okay." Christ, the girl sounded terrified.

Once Arri was gone, Neecy turned back to Didi. "Could you at least try and be nice to her?" she snapped.

"I am nice to her. I just don't know why she's here. And I seriously don't know why you're taking her out on a hunt."

To be honest, Neecy didn't know either. But Skuld made it clear this was what she wanted.

"Skuld has asked me to do this...I'm doing it. And you're going to back off and let me—"

"Get yourself killed protecting her?" she cut in.

Sighing, Neecy headed toward the door. There was no talking to Didi once she'd made her mind up.

"And what about Yager?" Didi demanded as Neecy pulled the door open.

Neecy glanced at her from the doorway. "It was just sex, Didi. You of all people should understand *that* concept."

Yelling through the door as Neecy closed it, "*Just sex my ass, Lawrence!*"

This was bad. Really, really bad. How was she supposed to do this? Everyone knew she was a mess. She could get Neecy killed and she'd never be able to live with herself if she did. Neecy cared about her. She knew that for a fact.

Arri rubbed her arms as Neecy came to stand beside her in the back garden. "I don't want you to panic about this, sweetie. It'll be okay."

"I see auras."

Neecy didn't say anything right away. Instead, she scratched her head and stared off into the enormous backyard. Only a small part of the many acres of The Gathering's land in the tri-state area.

"You can do what?"

"I can see auras."

Neecy nodded. "Um...so?"

Arri smiled. That's why she loved Neecy. Direct and to the point. And a really funky purple she'd love to paint all over her bedroom wall.

"I'm not making fun of you, Arri," she rushed to add.

"I know. I just think that's why Skuld brought me here."

"Why does it matter? So you can see auras. So?"

Arri'd been holding onto this for so long, it seemed only right to tell Neecy first. So she did. In one big rush: "I can tell if someone's sick. If they're dying. If they're lying. If they're about to kill. If they already have. I can see if they're plotting to take over the Kremlin. I can tell Didi doesn't like me, but I don't need to see her aura for that. But I knew Misty needed to see a doctor a few months ago. So I convinced her and they caught that infection before it got really bad. And I knew Olivia was pregnant with a boy the day she conceived."

Neecy took a step and Arri knew it was simply to steady herself.

"You're serious."

"Very."

"Why didn't you say anything before?"

Arri walked off the patio and onto the hard, ice-covered ground. During the summer it was a beautiful lawn. "It's a thing I've always had. It's why my father..." She stopped, hating even mentioning the man.

Neecy took a deep breath. "It was why he killed you."

A family adopted her and took her from her homeland when she was barely three. Weird enough being Korean among a bunch of Anglos, but the fact that her father was a religious zealot added to the bizarreness of her life. How many times had the kids in school called her "Carrie"? Heck, how many times had she felt like her?

When her father found out about her abilities, he'd drugged her breakfast, put her in his car, turned on the motor, and closed up the garage. He was doing fifteen to life for attempted murder. Funny thing was...he *did* murder her. There was nothing attempted about it. But Skuld came for her and she took her hand gladly.

The best part was the look on the bastard's face when the cops came to the house a few days later to arrest him and she was with them. Alive, well, and marked by a goddess.

"Yeah. He said I was evil. Everything about me was evil and unholy."

"He's a religious zealot, Arri. He doesn't matter. We're your sisters. *We're* you're family."

She remembered when she met Neecy. One second she was taking Skuld's hand and the next she woke up in a big bed to find Neecy looking down at her. "Welcome to the party, kid," she'd said with a pretty smile. And her colors were so honest, so pure, Arri felt an immediate kinship to her.

"But you're the only one that's accepted me."

"That's not true...and Didi doesn't count."

"Yes she does. She leads the Crows. What she feels affects the rest of them."

Neecy stood in front of her. "Then prove that you're worth having here. Skuld would have never sent you here if we didn't need you. She wouldn't waste her time or ours. We both know that."

As always, Neecy was right. And so soothing and calming. She always made Arri feel like she could do anything.

"Go on one hunt with me and the team. Just one. If it doesn't work, we'll never go there again and I'll tell that to Skuld myself."

Arri chewed her lip. A really bad habit she had, and Neecy picked up on it immediately.

Smiling, she teased, "You going to answer me, shithead, or just chew your lip off?"

Neecy was the only one who treated her like family. She joked with her. Teased her relentlessly. And Arri loved every minute of it.

Arri giggled. "Okay. You evil heifer."

"Evil heifer, huh?" Neecy laughed. "Those are some mighty fightin' words there, Arri." Neecy hugged her and Arri felt her warmth and caring. It flowed around her like soft rain. She knew those outside The Gathering saw Neecy as cold and unapproachable. They were wrong. She was anything but cold and unapproachable.

"I wanna show you something. Look up."

Arri pulled away from her mentor and looked up into the bare trees towering over them. That's where they were. Where they always were when Neecy was at the house. There were hundreds. At least. They lurked constantly. Always at the ready for Neecy.

"They're not going to dive-bomb us or anything, are they?"

"Don't be silly."

Neecy motioned to one and a huge crow glided down from the trees and landed on her shoulder. The bird rubbed her head against Neecy's cheek, and the incredibly tall woman smiled.

"They're my friends. They wouldn't hurt anybody I cared about."

Arri hid her smile. She didn't want Neecy to know how much what she said meant to her. "She's beautiful."

"Yep."

"When did you know?"

"Know what?"

"That you could call the crows?"

"About a week after I got here." Neecy grinned at the memory. "I was back here and suddenly looked up and saw all these freakin' birds in the trees. There had just been an Alfred Hitchcock marathon on channel nine or something the night before, so you know I freaked out big time. Anyway, I screeched like a banshee and they suddenly flew at me. I was only sixteen, so it never occurred to me to run. So I covered my head and screamed 'stop'. And they did."

"And then you knew?"

"Pretty much."

"It's very cool. Your Gift."

"So is yours." Although Arri's ability to see auras was not the Gift from Skuld. Her ability to read people had been there since birth. The problem was...she had no idea what Skuld had given her as a Gift or if she'd given her one at all.

Still, she had no intention of telling that to Neecy. Instead, Arri would go out on the hunt. Get her Korean ass kicked and that would be it. Her only concern was not getting any of them killed in the process. If she could manage that, she'd be damn happy.

"It's just weird," Arri admitted. "Knowing more about people than I feel comfortable with. Probably the way Kerri feels about seeing glimpses of the future all the time. It can get overwhelming."

"I understand." Neecy put her arm around Arri's shoulder. "But it's still cool. And you should be proud of it. Use it to your advantage."

Arri nodded as she looked up at the trees. With all the birds that hung around, Arri thought there would be more bird droppings. But their cars, the backyard, the windows...none of them *ever* had any messes on their stuff. Like all the birds in the world knew who The Gathering was and respected the sisterhood for it.

"So...you and Yager, huh?"

Neecy stiffened next to her. "How did you..."

"Anytime he's around, you get these big fat swirls of pink in your color. And they're all over you right now. It's really cute. They're all extra swirly, too."

"That's bullshit, Arrianna. And we both know it."

Smiling, she told Neecy, "He's crazy about you."

"Shut up."

"His colors change as soon as he sees you."

"Shut. Up."

"Not a little either. Big, fat swirls of color as soon as he knows you're in the room."

Growling, Neecy yanked her arm off Arri's shoulders, causing her little bird friend to head back to the safety of the trees.

"Don't worry," Arri yelled at the woman's retreating back. "They're pretty colors!"

Didi handed Delia Kim a beer as she sat beside her on the big couch.

"Thanks. So what's up?"

"I want you to track down the Hunters. Track 'em down, so we can wipe 'em out."

Delia opened her bottle of beer using the corner of the coffee table. "No problem. I'll get started tonight."

"Good."

"Although I'm still trying to figure out how they saw us. Has Skuld said anything to you?"

"Not lately." Didi sighed. "I can ask her... Maybe in the next twenty years I'll actually get an answer."

"These Nordic gods sure are difficult."

"That's a nice way of saying bitchy."

Delia stared at her beer bottle. "One question, though."

Didi gulped down a swig of beer. "Shoot."

"Shouldn't Neecy be on this? This is the kind of stuff she lives for."

"I know. That's the problem. The woman has no life."

"It has gotten kind of pathetic, hasn't it? Ever since Mr. Tiny Penis Man dumped her about four months ago."

"Try six months. And I knew that wouldn't last. *She* was calling him Mr. Tiny Penis Man." Didi took another gulp of beer and shook her head. "Right now I want her concentrating on more important things."

Delia grinned. "Like Wilhelm Yager?"

"Exactly."

"For a white boy, he's not bad."

"White, black, brown, or yellow, he's perfect for Neecy. That's all that matters."

"Maybe. But this *is* Neecy we're talking about, Didi. If it's not about The Gathering or school, it doesn't exist for her."

Didi grabbed the remote and turned on the TV. "Trust me. Yager'll make sure she knows he exists."

Neecy stood in the middle of the mom-and-pop video store, staring blankly at the horror section. She already had three DVDs in her hand, but she'd completely forgotten what she was supposed to be doing.

Christ, forget what she was supposed to be doing? How about...*what the fuck have I done?*

To get involved, even for a day, with Yager was such a stupid move on her part. A move she would have never made five or six years ago. But lately she'd been feeling restless and tense, she just didn't know why. Like she was waiting for something.

Clearly what she needed more than anything, though, was a solid slap to the back of the head like the nuns used to give her.

And what made all of this even worse...she still wanted him. Nice-guy Yager. She had no idea what to do with a nice guy. She definitely wasn't a nice person. Far from it. Forget her first-life, Crows were simply not nice beings. When you did hits for gods, the last thing you could afford to be was nice. She'd learned that early on from her mentor Lorraine. She still had the scar from the ceremonial dagger shoved in her back, just missing her kidney. Her mentor saw it coming and didn't stop it because she knew she needed to teach Neecy a lesson. And it was a lesson Neecy never forgot—being nice gets you shanked.

So she protected her own, trusted in her goddess, and went on about her day.

But Yager...Yager confused her. He'd been confusing her for a year now, and the time she'd spent with him the night before sure as hell didn't help. The whole time she was with him, he'd treated her better than anyone had ever treated her, and they never left his apartment.

"Are you just going to stand there or what?"

Neecy looked over at Janelle. "Shut up."

"Yo, Neece." Janelle tugged at her turtleneck sweater that still smelled of Yager. "Are those hickeys? *Ow!*" Janelle grabbed her nose, which Neecy had happily slammed with the DVDs. "What the fuck was that for?"

"For asking too many goddamn questions."

Neecy stopped. Her entire body tensing. Someone was watching her. She spun around, her eyes searching every corner of the small store.

"You feel it, J?"

"Yeah."

Janelle turned and stared off at the back entrance. But Neecy saw something out of the corner of her eye at the front of the store. A man, shorter than her. Grey hair. Enormous muscles over his entire body. She looked in the direction where she knew he stood, but she saw nothing. Still, she wouldn't turn away. She kept staring at the same spot until, finally, she knew he'd left.

"He's gone."

"He?"

"I think I saw him. I'm not sure."

"What do ya wanna do?"

She shrugged. "Rent these movies, then go home, and tell Didi."

Janelle glanced at the movie cases Neecy had in her hand. "No way, Neece. No way! We are *not* watching goddamn *Evil Dead again!*"

"Oh, get the fuck over it."

Yager snuggled down deeper into his covers and smiled. Half-asleep and half-awake, he'd been thinking about Neecy Lawrence's cranky, evil ass all night. He dreamed about her. Thought about her. He thought about her naked body pressed against his, her hard brown nipples burrowing into his chest. That soft little panting noise she made every time he entered her.

He wanted Neecy. All the time in every way possible.

"Having sweet dreams, baby doll?"

That deep male voice rumbled through Yager's consciousness, and he leaped out of bed, his fists up and ready, his back slamming against the far wall.

"Jesus, Odin! I hate when you do that shit!"

Odin, the All-Father of Norse gods laughed as he stared at one of his Raven leaders. His back against the headboard, his long legs reaching to the end of Yager's enormous bed, his big hands comfortably folded over his stomach. *Christ, is the man wearing Armani?*

"Sorry. Did I interrupt passionate dreams of Ms. Lawrence?"

Yager's eyes narrowed as he relaxed his stance, crossing his arms over his chest. "What do you want?"

"Is that any way to greet your god and leader?"

"It's the best you'll get at three in the morning and when you mention Neecy to me."

"You know you can do—"

"If you say I can do better, I'm going to lose my mind."

"I think you already have." Odin gave that indulgent smile he gave all humans. "Foolish boy. Crows are not to be trifled with. They protect their own. If they think for a moment you're merely toying with that girl..."

"But you know I'm not. That's why you're here. Afraid I'll muddy up your Viking gene pool with our kids?"

One pale blue eye turned his way. Odin had given up his other eye centuries ago...eeesh. There had to be an easier way to gain wisdom. Yager found reading quite beneficial.

"I have nothing against the Crows, per se."

"But..."

"But they're not one of us. They're not Vikings. They're mutts. Skuld with her damn sense of humor."

"They're more Viking than any Valkyrie you've brought in here the last five years. Speaking of which...Morgan says she's been trying to get in touch with you. She says you're avoiding her." Morgan was one of the older Valkyries. Very old school and very dear to Yager. She was the mother he never had once the Raven Elders took him from his own family.

"She'll simply complain again."

"You better pray she doesn't call to the Original Seven." Yager smiled. "You know they'll make your life hell."

"The pain a father has to go through." Odin easily pulled himself off the bed and stood. There were not many men in the universe who were taller than Yager. The few who were normally were in carnival sideshows or played starting center for the NBA. But at seven-ten, Odin made Yager feel downright tiny.

"I want you to live your life. But don't forget who you are and what you represent."

"I haven't forgotten anything. And Neecy Lawrence is mine. So you might as well deal with it." Yager grinned. "And if I were you, I wouldn't just show up in our bed once she moves in. I can tell she'd hate that."

Odin growled. "I blame Skuld for this," he muttered as he headed toward the door. He passed by Yager and did what he always did. He playfully slammed Yager's shoulder with his own. The first blow, like always, knocked Yager's shoulder out of joint. But slamming into the wall quickly popped it back into place.

Yager knew one day the bones in his poor shoulder would be nothing but shattered pieces.

"By the way, I've heard rumors that Hunting Season has begun again. A new Hunter this time."

Yager's head snapped around to nail Odin to the spot. "What? I haven't heard anything from the guys."

"You're not the only one with wings, boy."

Rage. Pure, simple, and white hot welled up in him. He didn't move. He simply stared at Odin.

Odin shook his head. "Try and protect the Crows and they'll crush you. I'm only telling you about this because once they start with Crows, they usually move on to the Ravens...if they can get past the Crows, that is. And that's a big if."

Yager didn't respond. Actually, he was unable to respond. He'd clenched his jaw way too hard.

"Foolish boy," Odin muttered again. "Never get between a Crow and her prey. I just hope you know what you're doing, Yager. Sometimes you're way too nice."

The god who could simply leave the room with a mere thought decided to use the door. As he pulled it open, he added, "And Neecy Lawrence isn't anything like she seems."

Chapter Nine

Dr. Denise Lawrence, PhD, scooted back on her desk and looked out over her small room of graduate students. They'd stop giving her any undergrad students who were merely trying to fulfill credits, especially freshman, almost seven years ago. Although her teacher evaluations received high marks from the serious students, the others absolutely hated her. So the university, at the insistence of one of their most important board members—who just happened to be a Raven Elder—gave her only the graduate and senior undergrad classes. They had no real problems after that.

"I don't want to have the Magna Carta discussion ever again."

Her students laughed as Pat Johnson attempted to push his point. "Wait, I'm serious. Really."

"I don't want to have the King John conversation either, Patrick. Not again. Let it go."

Patrick was so cute. Like most of her male students, he liked to flirt with her and she let him as long as it didn't go past a little light banter in the classroom or her office during office hours. Anything beyond that had required her to put one student in a headlock he never forgot.

She heard the doors to the huge auditorium open and she readied herself to rip Jason Benson a new one. The little fucker was always late to her class and she was done.

But when she looked up, she stopped breathing as Will Yager walked a few rows down and then plopped that gorgeous and way-too-big-for-the-chair body in one of the many empty seats. The auditorium was much too large for her small group of students, but she didn't mind. She simply made them all sit up front near her.

Now, however, the room seemed way too small.

He stared down at her and smiled and she felt like someone sucker-punched her. Finally, remembering they weren't alone, she looked back at her class. The girls still stared at Yager, while all the boys stared at her. Pat looked particularly annoyed.

"So...um..."

"Magna Carta," Pat filled in helpfully.

And just like that, Neecy snapped back. "We were *not* discussing the Magna Carta, Mr. Johnson."

He shrugged. "Can't blame a guy for trying."

"Oh, yes, I can." She crossed her legs at her ankles and pushed her glasses back on the bridge of her nose. She felt unexpectedly silly. Yager had never seen her like this. She wore her favorite burgundy plaid skirt, a solid burgundy turtleneck since she still had those damn hickeys, black leather knee-high boots and dark thigh-high wool stockings because of the cold. Plus she'd used a way geeky headband to keep her long bangs off her face. And she knew for a fact, Yager had never seen her in her glasses. She only wore them when she was reading or teaching since she often had to refer to books for information. When she needed to look at her students, she just dropped her head and looked over the frames. A scary but effective move.

"What I'm saying is I want something different from this paper." She slid off the desk and walked over to Cindy Barone. "I don't want the obvious. I don't want to read about the Magna Carta. Or Prince John. Or another debate about whether Robin Hood actually existed."

Neecy rapped her knuckles on Cindy's desk and the girl's head snapped around and away from her obvious adoration of Yager.

"I'm sorry. Am I boring you, Ms. Barone?"

"No, Miss...uh...Dr. Lawrence."

"Good. I really do live my life simply to entertain you." She spun on her heel and walked back to her desk. "So I want ideas by next Wednesday. And once I've approved those, I'll want outlines the following week. And you better hope I approve them. At least partially. Give me the Magna Carta—" she glanced at Pat, "—at your own risk."

The students chuckled again as she motioned for them to leave with a wave of her hand. "Out. I'll see you guys on Friday."

She walked around the desk and began piling her books together to head back to her office. Without looking directly at him, she could see Yager stand. And she could see all her students staring at him as they walked by. The girls looked like they may swoon at any second, while the boys looked truly horrified...and jealous.

Once the last one left, Yager walked down the stairs toward her. "Are you covering Vikings in this class?"

"Nope. I have a separate class for the Vikings. There's so much there to cover."

"You know, I might have gone for my doctorate too if any of my teachers looked as good as you."

Neecy slammed the last book on top of the pile. "Why are you here, Yager?"

"To see you. I tried calling you last night, but it rolled over to voicemail."

"Yeah. For a reason." She grabbed hold of the pile of books and lifted them up. "I don't want to talk to you."

Before she could take a step, Yager took the books from her.

"Hey!"

"I've got 'em. Just go. I'll follow."

Christ, it's gonna be like shaking my shadow.

He had no idea the woman wore glasses. Nothing fancy. Simple square burgundy frames, perfect for her face.

He wanted to fuck her wearing those glasses. Actually, he wanted to fuck her in that outfit, on her desk. He actually pouted a bit when she removed her glasses to leave the classroom. Damn, maybe some other time then.

Odin had been right. Neecy Lawrence wasn't anything like she seemed. Who knew this Neecy even existed? He didn't. He knew she taught, but a PhD? A history professor? And the book on top of the pile he carried...written by her and already a fourth edition.

There was so much about Neecy he knew nothing about. So much he was dying to learn.

He watched her walk toward her office and he almost drooled all over her books. *What an ass on this woman.* The best part, he knew about her "night job". He knew Neecy the predator. The woman who could snap a man's neck with just a twist of her hands. He knew more than anybody besides the other Crows. And even they didn't know she liked to have her clit nibbled.

He followed her down a long hallway and into an alcove. Her office was at the very end. She unlocked the door and pushed it open. It was a small room with books in every corner. Her shelves were filled several rows deep with big tomes. She had them on the floor, on top of her desk...absolutely everywhere.

"You need another office."

"Yeah? Well, tell that to the dean."

She walked to her desk, dropping the keys on top of another stack of books. Yager kicked her door closed and discreetly turned the lock. He didn't want any annoying students walking in on them.

"Where do you want these?"

"Drop 'em on that table."

He did.

"Why are you here, Yager?"

Yager turned to find her grabbing a bottle of water from the shelf behind her desk. She took a long swig while she waited for him to speak.

Finally, "Like I said, I wanted to see you."

Grumbling, she stalked past him, handing the reclosed bottle to him. He smiled at her unconscious actions as she stood in front of the stack of books he just dumped.

"Look, I'm sure those bubbleheaded Valkyries think the dominant-male thing is cute and all, but it really just pisses me the fuck off." She angrily proceeded to shove books back in the shelf behind the table.

Yager looked around her office and drank the water while she lit into him. He wondered if she'd actually read all these books. He wondered how she'd made it this far. He found Neecy Lawrence absolutely amazing. Sure, she was hot and an outstanding lay. But come on—from drug dealer to warrior to PhD. Only Skuld seemed to see the potential in all these women. She didn't waste her time with idiots. Stupid girls need not apply to The Gathering.

"Are you even listening to me?"

Sighing, Yager walked over to her office chair and sat down. He put his feet up on her desk and looked at her.

"Yeah. I'm listening."

She crossed her arms in front of her chest. "Oh, really? Then what did I just say?"

He had to be kidding. Really. When he put his humongous feet up on her desk...she knew he had to be kidding. But he wasn't. He truly *was* that cocky.

"Your exact words? 'This wasn't part of the agreement. And if you think I'll take your shit for two seconds, you are sadly mistaken. Are you even listening to me?' That's what you said."

Bastard. That was *exactly* what she said.

Okay. Forceful wasn't working with him. And the bottom line was she still had to work with this guy.

She growled to herself. *This is why you shouldn't fuck coworkers!*

"Look, Yager, I'm sure that...that... What are you doing?"

Once again, he seemed to have stopped listening to her and instead fiddled with her extremely expensive and self-purchased, ergonomically correct office chair. She watched him push a button and drop the armrests under the seat.

"Excuse me, but I had that chair exactly the way I wanted it."

He looked at her and she wondered why he wouldn't just comb his hair. That tousled, just-rolled-out-of-bed-after-a-night-of-good-fucking hair absolutely killed her.

"I'll fix it." He glanced around her office, and she wondered what the hell he wanted—and why wouldn't he leave her alone? He'd fucked her, what more did he want?

"So, Neecy, any problems at your night job?"

Neecy frowned. "What?"

"Anything the Ravens should know about?"

Aw, shit. "There's nothing you need to worry your big head about."

"Hunting Season is something we don't need to worry about? That's new."

"If it truly is Hunting Season, they're not after you. And the Crows don't need you. But thank you, O Big Great Strong One, for trying to come to our rescue."

Yager grinned. She just snapped at him and he grins at her. What a freak.

"Come here, Neecy."

No, she didn't like the sound of that one bit. He said it all low and husky, causing her nipples to immediately peak under her sports bra and burgundy sweater.

"Uh...no."

He sat up straight, dropping his big feet to the floor and pulling his leather jacket off, tossing it aside. "Come here."

"I don't think—"

"I just don't feel like yelling at you across this office." He smiled at her. "So come here."

She knew this was a bad idea, but she couldn't stop herself. At least, she couldn't stop her body. Her mind tried. It told her to stop walking. It told her to stay away. But her body completely ignored her mind, walking right across the room until she stood in front of Yager.

"What, Yager?"

He took a deep breath and let his eyes glide over her body. Now she had a wet pussy to go with her hard nipples. Plus, she could barely breathe. Which she found a little scary, since breathing was so important.

"Didn't you miss me at all last night?" he asked softly.

"No." Mostly because she spent the night partying with the Crows. Apparently, the opening of Hunting Season by men unknown was just another reason for the Crows to throw a party. Once the party was over, she only had time to run home, shower, and get to her eight a.m. class. Good thing Crows didn't need a lot of sleep.

His big hand gently grabbed the hem of her sweater and tugged. "Not even a little?"

"Yager, I can't—"

But before she could finish, he'd pulled her in between his legs, wrapped his arms around her waist, and rested his cheek against her stomach.

Then he held her.

Neecy didn't know what to do. She'd never had a man hold her like this. Just hold her. And it didn't help it felt kind of nice.

She shook her head. No, she would not allow herself to have those thoughts.

"Yager—"

"You smell so good."

Dammit!

"I've been thinking about your smell since you left yesterday morning."

Yager turned his head and her eyes slid shut in desperation as he kissed her stomach through her sweater.

"It's barely been twenty-four hours since I last saw you and I can't stop thinking about you."

"Yager," she whispered, unable to control her voice.

He pushed her sweater up and out of his way, kissing her bare stomach.

"We...we can't."

He simply growled in response. Then his hands slid down her waist and thighs, only to loop back under her skirt.

She let out a breath and so did he.

"Neecy...these are thigh-highs."

"I—" she cleared her throat, "—I hate pantyhose." She wore them because they were convenient and very comfortable, especially when she rode her bike to school. And only a few places sold thigh-highs for someone her height and build.

Not until this moment, though, had she ever been more grateful for tracking down those stores and buying a big stack of the wool stockings.

Yager slowly pushed up her skirt, watching his own hands move the plaid material out of his way.

"Yeah, this *is* the sexiest thing I've ever seen."

He must be kidding. He saw the Valkyries almost every day and she knew for a fact at least one of them used to be a *Penthouse* Pet. Exactly what about Neecy he found sexy, she had no idea. Unless he simply got turned on by girls who, on more than one occasion, had thrown a knife at his head.

No, this wouldn't do. They had to stop. Right now. Right this second. Right this very moment!

Neecy's head fell back as Yager's hands ran up the inside of her thighs. He kissed the flesh just above where the stockings ended. She dug her hands into his hair as he spread her legs and gently moved her so that she straddled his big thighs, pulling her down until she sat on him.

Now she knew why he moved the armrests out of the way.

"Look at me, Neecy."

Neecy slowly opened her eyes and then almost shut them again. No one should look at her like that. No one. Exactly how was she supposed to think straight when a man as gorgeous as Yager looked at her like that?

"Kiss me, Neecy."

"You promised—"

"No. I didn't. I only promised you anything you wanted for twenty-four hours. You want more than that...you'll have to renegotiate our deal."

Damn business majors. Being nosy after their time together, Neecy discovered the man had an MBA and a master's in computer science. She knew the Magna Carta and Prince John. Clearly outmatched in this particular situation, she gave in and relaxed...sorta.

"Kiss me," he growled again.

Neecy couldn't help herself. The man had the most amazing lips. And she already knew what a great kisser he was. She hated her weakness, but a girl could only take so much. Besides, she still wanted him. Fucking him for twenty-four hours straight hadn't remotely dampened her desire for him. If anything, the whole thing only made it worse. Now she knew exactly what she was missing.

She leaned forward, gently touching her lips to Yager's. He groaned softly and his hands tightened on her ass. He tilted his head to the side and slipped his tongue into her mouth. As soon as his tongue touched hers, she was lost.

Yager gripped Neecy to him, pulling her into his body. Christ, why didn't she see it? Why didn't she see that this was where she belonged? Right here. With him.

Her fingers dug painfully into his scalp and she pulled him closer. Her kiss was desperate. Demanding. She explored his mouth while he slipped his hand between the two of them and brushed against her crotch. She whimpered but didn't pull away. So he moved her panties aside and with unerring aim born of twenty-four hours of practice, he thrust two fingers inside her pussy. She let out a soft squeal, pulling her mouth away from his.

"Yager, wait—"

He pulled his fingers out and thrust them back again, making sure he curled them just right. He couldn't believe how wet she was. Wet for him. She may have all sorts of rational reasons why they shouldn't be together, but clearly her body didn't buy that bullshit either.

She gripped his hair tighter and buried her face in his neck. Then her pussy clenched his fingers and he thought he might explode. Christ, she was so tight. He couldn't wait any longer. Not for her.

He kept finger-fucking with one hand while he unleashed his cock with the other. Thank God for button-fly jeans. If he had a zipper, it would have caught on him and torn the shit out of his cock. Although he was so hard right now, his cock felt like it was made of titanium.

With his free hand he reached into his back pocket and pulled out a condom. He tore the package open with his teeth and quickly removed the latex. In seconds, he sheathed his cock, tore off her panties, and buried himself so far inside her, he was positive he must be choking her to death.

She let out a startled cry, her legs tightening around him and the back of the chair.

"I hate you, Yager," she mumbled into his neck.

"Why?"

She finally pulled back a bit, staring him in the eye. "'Cause you're not playing fair. And you know it."

Yeah. He knew it. And he had no intention of playing fair. Not if it meant she wouldn't be in his bed forever.

"You know me, Neecy. I don't bullshit around." He tightly gripped her waist with both hands. "I want you, Neecy. Not for a mindless fuck. Not just for twenty-four hours. I want *you*. And if you think I'm going to just let you go without a fight, you're nuts."

Just as he knew she would, she tried to pull away from him. He yanked her back hard, bringing her down on his cock, and she moaned in defeat as he held on to her.

"Fuck me, Neecy. Now."

She couldn't resist him. No matter how hard she tried. Not with his big cock buried so damn deep inside her and her entire body screaming for release.

"Fuck me," he ordered again.

Hating herself for being so weak, she rocked her hips back then forward.

Yager shuddered. "Goddamn, Neecy."

Yeah. Her thinking exactly. She didn't know anything could feel so good.

She rode him, her hands gripping his shoulders while he stared at her face. His hands moved off her waist and slid under her sweater, pulling it up above her breasts. He smiled when he saw her sports bra and she rolled her eyes. It's not like she planned on getting laid in her office—what exactly was he expecting?

He pushed the soft cotton over her breasts and leaned forward so that he could grasp one of her nipples between his lips. She barely bit back a cry as she pulled him closer, her arms wrapped around his neck and head. They no longer spoke. Not with him having a mouth full of tit, and she really couldn't think past the cock shoved inside her pussy. Besides, her office was surrounded by other professors' offices and the walls were thin.

And even when someone knocked on her door, they kept going. Their grips tightening on each other like they were afraid the other would bolt.

"Hey, Neecy," came a voice through the door. "It's Delia. You in there?"

Who? Who is this person? "Busy!" Neecy gasped out.

"Okay, but Didi sent me over. She's been trying to call you all morning, but she thinks you're ignoring her."

This is so not happening.

Well, she wasn't about to stop now. Not for anything. The world could crash down around them, and there was no way she was stopping until she came. No way in hell.

"She told me to tell you that she wants to discuss the Arri thing. I think she's hoping to talk you out of it. She wants you at the house tonight."

Yager's hand slid around to squeeze her ass, forcing her harder onto his cock. Her whole body jerked and he chuckled against her neck.

She growled. "Tricky sonofabitch!"

"Hey," Delia barked. "Don't curse at me. You got a problem, talk to Didi. I'm only here 'cause I was the only idiot heading into the City today. And trust me, you didn't want her to come instead. Then she would have been really mad. All she wants is for you to say you'll be there tonight to talk."

Yager moved his mouth to her other breast, sucking her nipple hard.

Her grinding movements became stronger. Harsher. She could feel every inch of his big, hard cock. It stretched her open, forcing her to accommodate its girth. Like its owner, it was a demanding bastard.

"Goddammit!" she burst out as his big fingers dug deep into her cheeks, causing a nice bite of pain.

Delia sighed. "Bitch all you want, Neecy. Just so you know, Didi told me not to leave until you swear that you're coming."

"Yes! God, yes!"

"Don't bullshit me, Neecy Lawrence. Are you comin' or not?"

"I'm coming! I'm coming!" And she did. In big gushing waves.

"Cool. I'll let Didi know she'll see ya tonight."

✧

As soon as her muscles spasmed around him, he came. So hard, he was surprised he hadn't blown her across the room. Instead he held her tight as his cock spurted over and over again.

When her pussy finished milking him dry, Yager leaned back in the chair as they held on to each other for several minutes. He feared she'd immediately pull away from him, but she didn't. She simply rested her head against his neck while he did the same to her. It had to be one of *the most* comfortable positions he'd ever been in with a woman.

"Did someone knock earlier?" she muttered against his neck.

He shrugged. "I have no idea."

"Okay. Probably wasn't that important."

They sat quietly for a few more minutes and then, finally, she pulled back. "Christ," she sighed softly. "I've got another class."

He reached up to pull her sports bra back down, but she grabbed his wrists. They stared at each other. "You are really starting to piss me off, Yager."

"If this is your rage, I can't wait to see what you're like when I make you happy."

She released his hands and pulled her bra and sweater back into place. "This is bullshit and we both know it."

"Really? Is that what we *both* know?"

She stood up and he gritted his teeth at the loss of her heat on his cock. He watched her pull down her skirt. "You better go."

He disposed of the condom in a tissue, tossing it in the trash. He tucked himself back into his boxers and buttoned up his jeans. "Don't shut me out, Neecy."

"Shut you out?" She reached into a cabinet and pulled out a gym bag. "You were never in."

Neecy unzipped her emergency clothes bag and dug through it. Christ, she had to have a pair of panties in here somewhere. She kept it in the office just in case she couldn't make it home after one of her long nights.

"You want it that way...fine."

"Yeah. I want it that way. It's just sex, Yager. Don't make this into any more than it really is." She found another pair, yanked it from the bag, and quickly tugged it on.

As soon as she pulled her skirt down, she realized what an outright bitch she was being. There was no reason to cut the man off at the balls simply because she refused to have a relationship with him. Especially when he kept getting her off in such fabulous fashion.

To be honest, she wouldn't mind a completely sexual relationship with Yager. A regular booty call when they both had an itch that needed a good scratch. Anything more, she could never give. Her life belonged to The Gathering. It always would.

"Look, Yager. I'm not trying to hurt your feelings or anything."

"I know. You're just scared."

Neecy slowly turned around. "Excuse me?"

"Want me to spell it out for you? Or would you prefer I write it in some ancient text? Maybe then it'll be a little less threatening."

"I am *not* threatened by you. I'm just not having a relationship with you...or anyone."

"Fine." He reached down and snatched up his jacket. "Then the war is on."

Fuck. She couldn't afford this shit. Didi would have her ass in a sling if she started some major shit between the Crows and the Ravens. "What war?"

He walked to the door, glancing back to smile at her. "The war for your heart. And in case you're wondering, I never lose."

At first Neecy couldn't move. *The war for her heart?* Was he kidding?

She watched him walk out her office door. Then she charged across the room, wrenching the door open. He sauntered down the hallway of her school like he'd just gotten laid.

"You know," she yelled after him, "only white people come up with that kind of trite bullshit!"

He turned, blew her a kiss, and walked off.

Neecy growled, turning her head as one of the other professor's doors opened. She nodded. "Dean Eggert."

The elderly man who'd recommended her for tenure years before nodded back. "Dr. Lawrence."

Without another word, she went back into her office and slammed her door shut so hard, several books hit the floor. Three of them she'd written herself.

Jesus, Mary, and Joseph! What the fuck did I get myself into now?

Chapter Ten

Arri met them in the backyard and appeared seriously panicked, if her pacing and hand-wringing were any indications.

She did have on the standard Crow fighting outfit—white racerback tank top, black jeans, black steel-toe boots, wool sleeves for her arms—and possessed the minimum amount of weapons. Long, steel blades shoved in the holster wrapped around her right leg. But Arri being Arri had also dyed her hair dark blue for the occasion. It was a good color on her but still couldn't hide the shaking of her hands or the trembling of her small body.

Neecy put her arm around the girl. "It's gonna be okay, Arri. Just remember to stay near me and if things get really bad—find a corner and stay in it."

For two hours Didi had argued with Neecy about this. She didn't want little Arri out with the team. She even tried to call on Skuld herself. Like that was ever a good idea. But it was too late. Neecy received her orders for a hunt while sitting at a traffic light on her bike. One second she was sitting there trying to forget Yager and trying to remember who came to her office door earlier in the day and the next...she knew it was time. That's how it happened for all the team leaders. Skuld simply uploaded them with the information they needed and expected them to take care of it.

In employer terms—she only hired "self-starters".

Arri took a deep, shaky breath. "Okay."

Neecy winced at Arri's squeak. She hated doing this to the poor kid. She really did. If she had her way, she'd let Arri handle everyday admin stuff for The Gathering. There were all sorts of things that needed taking care of that Neecy never had time to handle and Didi never wanted to bother with.

Yet, for some unfathomable reason, Skuld was making Neecy do this instead. Put this poor, defenseless, terrified little girl out in the middle of a Hunt.

Janelle walked up, her tattooed arms crossed in front of her chest. She stared down at Arri, and Neecy wondered if she was going to again voice her complaint that this was a bad idea.

Instead, Janelle said, "Keep your eyes on me and Neecy. Okay? You'll be fine."

Arri nodded. "Yeah, I will."

Neecy was relieved to hear Arri say something other than "okay".

"Then let's go, ladies." Neecy looked at her team. "The quicker we get this over with, the quicker we can get something to eat."

Katie and Connie took off, Janelle right behind them.

She turned to Arri. "You're not going to pee on yourself, are you?"

Arri snorted a laugh. "What?"

"I just wanted to make sure, so I'm not flying behind you or under you."

"Aw, that's disgusting, Neecy!" But she got her to smile.

"Disgusting, perhaps, but possibly a little accurate?"

"No! Ewwww!" She slapped Neecy's shoulder. "I'll be fine. Yuck."

Arri spread her wings and flew. Neecy blew out a sigh of relief. To be honest, she was kind of worried the girl couldn't even fly.

Yager wiped blood from his cheek. The little asshole cut his face. Grabbing him around the throat, Yager lifted him off the floor. "I love it when you guys make it easy for me."

This was what the Ravens did best. Interrupt some weird religious rite usually involving the sacrifice of some poor schlub. Save the "sacrificee" and "manage" everybody else. He liked saying "manage" because that sounded a hell of a lot better than "kill".

It wasn't Yager's favorite part of the job, but at times it was the most fulfilling.

Yager didn't know who these guys were. Maybe Satanists, but he doubted it. They kept their stuff pretty quiet and often the Christians handled them. But anything involving the Norse gods belonged to the Ravens. Unless, of course, that invisible line was crossed and the Crows were called to clean house.

Gripping the man tighter around the throat, Yager slammed him against the wall three times until he stopped wiggling. He dropped him and turned to find the others had been "managed" by the rest of the team.

Tye moved up behind him. "We may have another problem."

Yager turned, facing his friend and saw that he held one of the prey in his big hands. "What?"

Tye shook the man—once. "Tell him."

"We were paid to hold this rite," the man choked out desperately. "Paid to make sure the right people knew about it."

"So that it would get back to me," Tye growled.

It was a well-known fact among the Clans that Tye had some rather...unholy connections. He could find out stuff that no else—absolutely no one—could ever find out through normal mystical means.

"So what does that mean for us?" Yager asked.

"If this is a decoy—" Tye snapped the neck of the man in his hands and let his carcass drop to the ground, "—then they've opened up a doorway somewhere else."

"We need to find that doorway."

"Bet you money it's already been found."

Slamming the door to the Hoboken butcher shop, Janelle pushed her back against it and desperately looked at Neecy.

"Portal to hell! We have a portal to hell!"

Neecy threw the biker up against the alley wall. "How bad?" she yelled over the fighting and the unholy screams coming from the other side of the door Janelle stood in front of.

"Uh...straight to the very pits of hell. So we do have a problem here, ladies."

As Janelle finished her statement, heavy bodies threw themselves against the door from the other side. Pushing on it harder, Janelle gasped out, "If you're going to do something...do it quick!"

Neecy knew how to close mystical doorways leading to alternate dimensions, but portals to hell? That was something different altogether. Way beyond her skill set.

Yeah, this was getting seriously out of control.

"What are you gonna do, little girl?" the scumbag, Lewis, barked at her with a smile. In response, Neecy slashed him with her talons.

Lewis' head snapped to one side, but by the time he turned back to her the wounds had healed.

Uh-oh.

Yeah. He'd activated that necklace all right. No wonder Skuld wanted it back so badly.

Of course, the necklace had been what they originally came for. This should have been an easy "kick ass and grab". But stumbling into the middle of a human sacrifice in the back of a Hoboken bar—so not on the menu. And what was this idiot doing opening portals to hell? Like that was ever a good idea.

Lewis' biker buddies went after the Crows, eagerly hoping to get a piece of them. Five guys against them. Easy. Even with Arri. But the portal to hell was a little distracting. Especially when her strongest warrior was having a hell of a time keeping the door closed.

Then you add in the nine or ten really sweet Harleys pulling in beside them and Neecy was now a little less confident about her team's current situation.

Knowing Lewis could experience pain and serious discomfort, Neecy reached into the back of her jeans and pulled out her stun gun. She pushed it against Lewis' neck and sent one hundred thousand volts through the man.

That's when the rest of the bikers moved on them. "Crows! Get ready!"

They couldn't leave until they got what they came for and until they closed that doorway. They especially had to close that doorway.

Neecy heard a squeal and discovered Arri in a dark corner keeping a scumbag at bay with a well-placed slap to the face. *Who knew a bitchslap could be so effective?*

Then, like a thunderbolt, it suddenly hit her.

"Arri! The portal! Close it!"

"*Me?* Are you insane?"

Neecy started to tell her to get her butt into action or she'd kill her herself, but Lewis had dragged himself to his big feet and she became real busy, real quick.

Arri didn't have much choice. But she also *knew* she could close that portal. The power tingled in her fingertips. This had been the Gift Skuld had given her.

Her only problem at the moment? Fear. Mind-numbing, limbs-unable-to-move, head-about-to-explode fear. But Neecy needed her to do something and, at the moment, her mentor had her hands full.

No. She couldn't let Neecy down. Not Neecy.

Choking back her fear, Arri ran to the door Janelle had placed herself against and dropped to her knees.

"Do something, Arri-girl. Or we're fucked," Janelle ordered as she desperately worked to keep that door closed.

Arri raised her hands, a chant on her lips to seal the door, when Janelle bucked forward from the force of the blow behind her. Janelle quickly moved back into place, but she wouldn't be able to hold whatever was on the other side much longer.

Then they were surrounding Arri, dropping out of the sky. Ravens. Yager's men. She looked up in time to see Liar-Mike, as she liked to call him, land beside her. He walked over to Janelle.

"Move it, sweet cheeks." With his usual arrogance, he grabbed Janelle's arm and pulled her away from the door, quickly replacing her there. "Go kill somethin'. I'll hold the door."

Janelle gave him a look of disgust and then she was ducking the biker chain aimed at her head.

Arri looked up at Mike, his legs on either side of her.

"You know, while you're down there..." He raised an eyebrow and leered.

Biting back her desire to spit in the man's face, Arri went to work calling on the powers of Skuld and the other Fates.

Neecy and Lewis squared off, moving around each other like two wrestlers. Growling, she charged him, but before she got two feet, a brick wall dropped in front of her.

"Hey, baby."

She pulled her blades back just in time. Another few inches, she would have gutted Yager.

"What are you doing?" she demanded. If Yager tried to take Lewis from her, she'd rip out pieces of him he didn't even know existed.

"Came to help."

"What?" Helping was one thing. But Yager was standing in front of her. He was *protecting* her.

She moved around Yager as he tossed a biker against the wall. His usual crew was with him as well. Mike, Tye, and Danny Terleski as well as a few other Ravens.

"Yager, I don't need you protecting me." Well, at least that much was true. She didn't need Yager protecting her. Helping her, however, that was different.

"I know, but these assholes sent us off on some bullshit hunt. I hate that. Behind you, baby."

Neecy spun on her heel, going low, and gutted the biker behind her. Just as quickly, she turned back to Yager.

"Thanks." She motioned to the dying man at her feet.

"No problem. And your scumbag is getting away."

Neecy turned to find Lewis trying to get past Tye. "Dammit!" She flew at him, literally, her talons out. For a big guy he moved fast, backhanding her as soon as she was within reach. He was strong too, knocking Neecy right into the wall.

Okay. Now she was pissed.

Okay. Now Neecy was pissed. Yager could see it on her face. Man, but watching her slam into that wall hurt. He felt it as surely as if it had been him. Who was this guy anyway? Well, he'd have to die. He'd touched Neecy. No one touched his Neecy. No one but him.

Yager, growling low, moved on the biker. But Neecy moved fast when pissed. She charged into the man, her hands around the scumbag's throat, and slammed him into the opposite wall. Her legs up, her feet straddling his waist and planted firmly on the wall behind her prey. Her wings fluttered dangerously, ready to take her airborne in seconds.

Yager almost smiled. She would rip this idiot apart and he couldn't wait.

"Neecy!" Katie yelled. "It's Arri!"

Neecy, her talons digging into Lewis' throat to hold him in place, glanced over to see Arri surrounded by purple light. As rich and vibrant as anything Neecy had ever seen before. But she also saw two bikers moving on her fast. Mike couldn't help her because he was the only thing keeping that door closed. And whatever was on the other side of it in. Still she knew Mike well enough to know he'd leave his post at the door before he let a woman get hurt. If she was going to move, she better do it now.

"Yager! Get Arri!"

Yager didn't waste time with answering her, he just moved, Tye by his side. But four bikers got in their way and Neecy realized she'd have to release Lewis to protect Arri. She couldn't let her get hurt.

Shit. Can this get any worse?

A wet-sounding growl caused Neecy's head to snap around and she realized something was happening to Lewis. He was changing. Shifting. His eyes were a bright yellow. Like a dog's.

He was a motherfuckin' Shifter. *Oh, just great!*

Claws came up and grabbed her around the throat.

Then she heard Arri's squeal and Mike's growl of anger. She tried to pull away from the Shifter, but he had her by the throat and wasn't letting go.

Then Neecy was flying. Actually, they all were. And she had only a moment to wonder "what the hell" when she hit the wall and everything went black.

One second Tye was busy wrapping a chain around some idiot biker's neck and the next he was airborne. He slammed into a pole, which killed his back but luckily didn't touch his head. He watched as one of the Crows flew past him and right into ongoing traffic.

"Shit!" He took off after her, diving on her and rolling them both out of the way of a speeding tractor-trailer.

He landed on top of her and looked down into her very pretty face. Sharp cheekbones, adorable pug nose, and full lips. Eyelids fluttered open and amazing hazel eyes locked onto Tye's. *Whoa.*

Yeah. He'd been right. Janelle was seriously, blindingly hot.

She stared up at him, a slight frown creasing her brows. "Um...what are you doing?"

He smiled. "Daydreaming."

"Huh?"

When did it start raining? Snowing, maybe. It was January. But rain? They didn't forecast rain.

"Oh God, Neecy! Please don't be dead! God, please!"

Neecy forced her eyes open as she heard Yager's soothing voice. "It's okay. She's okay. Just a little stunned."

She saw Yager with his arm around Arri, and Arri hysterically crying into his neck. For the first time ever, Neecy wanted to rip the throat out of a fellow Crow who wasn't Didi.

Oh, my God. I'm jealous. Kill me now.

Using his free hand, Yager ran his hand over Neecy's cheek and smiled when he saw her eyes were open.

"Hey, baby."

"Stop calling me that." Neecy slowly pushed herself up on her elbows. "What happened?"

Yager nodded at the sobbing girl in his arms. "You better ask her."

And then Neecy understood. Arri did this. It seemed like somehow she'd blown everything within a two-mile radius away from her.

Neecy struggled to a sitting position. "Is everybody okay?"

"Yeah. I think so."

"I'm so sorry!" Arri wailed as she threw herself into Neecy's arms, knocking her back on her ass.

Poor Arri, she'd hate herself in the morning over this. Not about what she'd done, but about the crying. Expending that much Magick abruptly led to extreme emotions. Some became mean, violent, loving, horny...and some became emotional messes. Like Arri.

"Check on everybody for me, would ya, Yager?"

"Yeah. Sure."

Neecy squeezed Arri as Yager stood up. "It's okay, kid. Really," she soothed.

"I thought I killed you guys."

"Between you and me...you saved our ass. The one I was fighting was a Shifter. Which meant all his friends were, too. That would have turned real ugly, real quick." Speaking of which, where the hell were those bastards? "Honey, what happened to the bikers?"

Arri cried harder and held on to Neecy tighter. Glancing past the sobbing girl, she saw Janelle. The woman shook her head and made a slashing motion across her throat.

Holy shit. Arri had taken them out. All of them it seemed, since none of the Crows or Ravens showed any sense of urgency or panic.

"Um...let's get you back to the house."

Neecy struggled to her feet, her arms still around Arri. All the girl needed was sleep. To get her energy back. She'd feel better and probably a little awkward come morning.

"Neece, we need to get out of here." Katie stood next to Janelle, one side of her face swollen from a fist.

"Yeah." They were lucky the cops hadn't shown up yet, but that wouldn't last. And Skuld and Odin only cloaked them but so much.

Motioning to Janelle, Neecy ordered, "Check the door."

"Are you insane?" Janelle ran her fingers over her eyebrows. They'd almost been singed off the first time she opened that door. "I'd rather not start drawing these in."

With the tiniest of head moves, Janelle motioned to Mike. Neecy shrugged. *Why not?*

"Mike. Could you check that door for us?"

"Sure!"

A sudden look of panic streaked across Yager's face. "Mike! Wait!"

But it was too late. Mike opened the door and glanced inside. "It's a butcher shop...although I wouldn't actually eat anything from here. I don't think this place is up to code."

Yager let out an enormous breath. "Don't ever do that again," he muttered to her.

Neecy worked hard not to laugh out loud as she hugged the still-crying Arri.

"I'll take her." Janelle looped her arms around Arri's waist, then she was gone. Neecy nodded to Katie and Connie, and the women followed after Janelle.

A quick glance around the alley showed Neecy there were no bodies. Only the Ravens and Crows remained after Arri finished. Weird. There should be bodies. It looked like her birds would have to find dinner somewhere else tonight.

"Here. This is what you wanted in the first place, right?"

Neecy looked at Yager's outstretched hand. Christ, his hands were big. Reaching out, Neecy took the enchanted Rhine Gold necklace from his palm.

"Thanks."

"No problem, Neecy."

She looked up into that oh-so-gorgeous face and steeled herself against the heat in that gaze. The way Yager looked at her—the way he *always* looked at her—drove her absolutely nuts. It made her entire body desperate to feel him against her one more time.

She noticed the blood on his cheek. "Yager...your face."

He frowned and touched the wound on his cheek. "Oh. That. It's nothing."

"Bullshit." She pulled his hand away so that he didn't keep playing with it like a ten-year-old. "You need to get that taken care of before it gets infected."

Smiling, he gripped her hand in his, unwilling to let her go.

Neecy could hear the wail of sirens, but she couldn't move. Couldn't unlock herself from that blistering gaze. And the way he smiled at her. It was such a sweet smile, she couldn't help herself—she ended up smiling back.

"Yager, man," Mike said. "We gotta go."

After another moment, Yager finally released her hand. "Yeah. Okay. See ya, Neecy."

"Yeah. Sure." Afraid of what she might say or do, Neecy closed her eyes, unfurled her wings, and took to the air.

Chapter Eleven

Neecy landed in the backyard and found Didi waiting for her. "You okay, kid?"

Retracting her wings, Neecy took the sweatshirt Didi offered her. "Yeah. I'm fine. Where's Arri?"

"Janelle took her to her room."

"Okay." Neecy pushed open the sliding back door and walked into the house. It was warm and she'd never felt so grateful. "I'm gonna go check on her, then I'll be down to talk to you."

Didi followed behind her until they reached the stairs. "Okay."

"They were Shifters, Didi."

Sighing, Didi shook her head. "Don't worry about it."

Neecy took care of the girls, but Didi had to deal with the political fallout of any fights with certain factions. The Shifters spent most of their time fighting their own, but they were fiercely protective of each other against the outside world. And they considered the Crows as outside as you could get.

Neecy jogged up the stairs, greeting other sisters as she passed. She went to the third floor and stalked down the hall. Katie and Connie sat outside Arri's room, probably waiting for Janelle.

They'd put on warm clothes and Katie had an icepack over her face. Good thing they kept a healthy supply of those in the basement freezer.

Nodding toward the bedroom door, Neecy asked, "Well?"

"Janelle's putting her to bed." Connie didn't whisper but she did keep her voice low.

"You two okay?"

Connie nodded as Connie's girlfriend, Fran, brushed past Neecy. She handed both Katie and Connie hot coffee and sat on the floor next to Connie, putting her head on her girlfriend's shoulder.

"My face hurts and my boys are working late shifts." Katie had the nerve to pout.

"I'm sorry your slaves are busy being cops and helping others when they could be running your bath, rubbing your tiny feet, and following your orders under fear of not being allowed to come."

Connie and Fran burst out laughing as Katie glared at her. "Jealous bitch."

Neecy winked and moved to the door. Gently pushing it open, she stepped inside. Janelle was just pulling the covers over Arri.

"How is she?" Neecy whispered.

"Don't bother whispering. She's out cold."

"Good. She needs the sleep."

Janelle came around the bed. "Well, now we know why Skuld wanted her out there."

"What the fuck happened anyway? I didn't see any bodies."

"You wanna know what happened?" Janelle gave a short laugh that had absolutely no humor in it. "Our little Arri ripped open a doorway, pushed all the Crows and Ravens out of the way, and threw all of those bikers in there. Then she sealed up the hole and shut the doorway to hell. And she pretty much did all that at the same goddamn time."

Neecy looked at Arri, so small under those covers, and back at Janelle. "What?"

"You heard me. I've never seen anything like it, Neece. Never."

After a moment of pure shock, Neecy grinned. She couldn't help herself. "Still worried about her coming out with us now?"

Janelle snorted as she headed toward the door. "What? Are you high? I say we make sure she goes out with us until we all retire."

Walking around the bed, Neecy stared down at Arri. Tears still clung to her long black lashes, but she was definitely asleep. Neecy felt an overwhelming tenderness for her friend. She'd been through so much, and the other Crows had never really accepted her. Maybe now they would. Or at least fear her enough to give her more respect.

Leaning down, Neecy kissed the top of the girl's head.

And if they didn't give Arri more respect, Neecy would start kicking the shit out of people.

✧

Neecy fell face-first onto her bed. She really wanted to go back to her apartment, but she wanted to be here when Arri woke up.

She definitely didn't want Didi getting to her first. Who knew what she'd say to her? What Neecy learned quickly was that Didi had no patience. None. A lovely woman, with delightful Southern values, but you better be able to keep the fuck up or she would leave your ass behind in a New York minute.

And since they had much work to do before Arri would be a truly effective part of the team, she didn't want Didi scaring her with one of her "speeches".

Already naked, Neecy lay there debating whether it was worth reaching over to turn out her light when her cell phone rang.

She rolled her eyes. She had no doubt who the hell was on the other end of that phone. The question was did she answer?

Growling, she reached down and yanked the phone from her jeans.

She flipped it open. "Yeah?"

"Just wanted to make sure you got home okay."

Christ, that voice! "Yes, Yager. I got home just fine."

He chuckled low. "Man, you're testy tonight."

"I don't get testy. I do, however, get annoyed."

"Why?"

"Look, I don't know what you think we're doing, but it's not what you think it is."

There was a pause, and she could easily imagine him with that confused frown he sometimes got when stuff didn't make sense to him. That adorable but misleading frown that originally had her believing Yager was another big, dumb Viking.

Dumb, her ass.

"Please feel free to repeat that, Professor. 'Cause you lost me."

"What I'm saying is, I don't need you checking up on me to make sure I got home okay. That's what boyfriends and husbands do, and you ain't either."

"What if I wanna be?"

"Then I'd say you need to get out there and find yourself a nice girl. I've heard online dating is popular."

"Neecy, you've been in serious relationships before."

"Sure was. How do ya think I got shot?"

Yager sighed in frustration. "Don't pull that shit on me. You've had other relationships since then that didn't end in gun play."

"Yeah. So?"

"So what's the difference? Why do I get the special Lawrence rejection?"

This was where things got complicated. How could she tell him he was the one man who could actually get to her? Make her vulnerable. Sure, she'd had good, steady boyfriends who always remembered anniversaries and birthdays, and knew exactly how to make her come without too much effort.

And she'd never loved one of them.

When those relationships inevitably ended, she shrugged and moved on. Nothing ugly or complicated. Boyfriend of the Moment would go off and find himself a nice girl who actually loved him. Neecy went off and found another good, steady Boyfriend of the Moment. Perfect.

But as Neecy didn't lie to people, she refused to lie to herself. Yager would be messy and complicated. There'd be fights and discussions on money and whether they wanted to see the Joneses on Saturday night.

She'd fall in love with Wilhelm Yager, which meant she'd be vulnerable. And when that asshole pulled the trigger, she'd sworn she would never be that way again.

When Neecy didn't answer his question, Yager growled. "What do you want, Neecy?"

Frowning, Neecy turned over onto her back and stared up at the ceiling. "I want what you'd never be able to give me."

"Which is?"

"A completely sexual relationship void of drama and emotions and the usual bullshit. Just two people getting together on occasion to fuck."

The pause that followed her declaration went on for so long, Neecy thought he'd hung up or the connection lost. She looked at her phone several times to see if she still had him.

Finally, "Are you naked?"

Neecy squeezed her eyes shut. She spoke and it was like the man didn't hear a word she said. "Did you even hear what I said?"

"Yeah. I heard you. Are you naked?"

She sighed. "Yes, Yager. I'm naked. I just got out of the shower."

"Mhhmm. I love how you smell when you're just showered."

Neecy locked her knees together. "Look, Yager, I've gotta—"

"Put your hand between your legs."

Suddenly she wasn't as dead tired as she thought. "No, Yager."

"Why?"

"Because I'm not in my apartment. I'm in a house full of women, a few of them under eighteen, and I'm not doing this here."

"Damn." He sounded so despondent. "Well, are you going home tonight?"

Neecy forced herself to frown to keep from laughing. "No. I've gotta be here for Arri."

"How she doin'?"

"Sleeping. But fine."

"Good. So we really can't have phone sex?"

"No."

"Damn."

She took a deep breath and again forced herself not to laugh. "Look, Yager, I'm not the girl for you. You're looking for someone more—"

"Like you?"

"No."

"Yes." He said it so simply. Like she was his slow-witted cousin or something.

"What is your obsession with me?" If she could find out maybe she could convince him otherwise.

"You mean other than the fact that I think you're hot and sexy and downright amazing?"

She rubbed her eyes with her free hand. "Yes," she sighed. "Other than that."

"You bring me joy."

It was like someone kicked her in the groin. All the air left her lungs and she lay there staring up at the ceiling.

She, Denise Lawrence, bringer of death, brought someone joy? How was that possible? The only joy she'd ever brought anyone was back in her first-life when she handed over the nickel bag of pot.

"I...how do I..."

"Every time you take down some scumbag. Every time you try to make Arri feel welcome and stop Janelle and Mike from fighting. Or when you go out of your way not to show Tye when he's completely freaked you out. And every time you smile. Every time, Neecy Lawrence, you bring me joy."

Neecy blinked. Several times. "Yager..."

"I want to see you tomorrow."

"No. No dating. No relationship."

"Fine. Then just sex."

"Forget it, Yager. You could never do that and we both know it."

"You're not even going to give me a chance?"

"No. I'm not." Because she couldn't afford to.

"You're breakin' my heart."

Neecy rolled her eyes. "I am not."

"Neecy—"

"Goodbye, Yager."

She ended the connection and shut off her phone.

Delia slapped Janelle's leg. "Ow!"

"Oh, stop whining, ya big baby. We go through this every time. You insist I braid your hair and then you freakin' whine and complain the entire time."

"'Cause you make 'em too damn tight. That hair is actually attached to my scalp, ya know!"

"If I don't make 'em tight, they won't even last two days, much less a week."

Janelle went back to braiding Delia's dark brown hair while Katie, curled up in one of Janelle's favorite chairs, quietly read a book on knots. Janelle wasn't going to even ask.

Her cell phone rang and both Katie and Delia smiled.

"J, you actually have 'Danny Boy' as your ringtone?" Delia giggled.

"I like that song." She released Delia's hair and scooped up her cell phone. She frowned at her Caller ID and looked at Katie. "It's Yager."

"Ooh. Neecy problems." She sat up straight in the chair, her book forgotten. "Answer, answer, answer."

Chuckling, Janelle flipped open her phone. "This is Janelle."

"Hey, Janelle. This is Yager."

Working hard not to laugh, she covered the mouthpiece. "Oh, my God. He sounds so depressed."

"That bitch. You know she probably just dogged him." Katie motioned to the phone. "Find out what's going on."

Clearing her throat, she went back to her phone. "Hey, Yager. What's up?"

"Remember at the party, you said you'd help if I needed it?"

She did? Damn Alabama Crows. No more grain alcohol for her. "Um...sure." She shrugged at Katie. "What d'ya need?"

"She's breaking my heart, and she doesn't care."

"Of course she cares. That's why she's breaking your heart."

"She says she doesn't want a relationship."

Janelle frowned. "Then what does she want?"

"Sex, but no relationship."

Janelle snorted. "She's kidding, right? I mean, Neece don't do sex with no relationship."

Although only hearing one side of the conversation, Delia and Katie still covered their mouths to keep their hysterical laughter quiet.

Janelle waved at them, since she could still hear Katie's giggles through her hand.

"Well, she says that's what she wants," he went on.

"Then just tell her that's what you'll do."

"I tried. She saw right through me."

"Christ, youse two are pathetic."

Katie glared at her across the room and whispered, "Be nice! That shitty accent we've tried to beat out of you is making an appearance, which means you're getting testy."

Covering her phone again, Janelle snapped, "Oh, look who's talking! She of the knots!"

"I know we are," Yager continued, unaware of Janelle's multiple conversations. "But she won't let me in. Got any ideas?"

With a sigh, "Hold on a sec." She lowered the phone again, covering the mouthpiece. "She's blockin' him. And he's out of ideas."

Katie threw up her hands. "At this rate, she's going to die a bitter old maid. Just like you."

Janelle nodded, then her head snapped up. "Huh?"

Delia, sitting on Janelle's bedroom floor, with Janelle's legs on either side of her so she could do her hair, patted her on the ankle. "Ask him if he's going to that Valkyrie party tomorrow."

"Yager. You going to that Valkyrie party tomorrow?"

"I'd rather remove my eyelids. I'm sending Mike."

Janelle laughed. "Okay." Covering the phone, "He'd rather remove his eyelids."

Katie grinned. "I'm liking him more and more."

"Tell him to go." Delia turned her head to look at Janelle over her shoulder.

"Are you sure? I'd hate for him to go for no reason."

"Trust me. But you bitches have to go yourselves."

"Are you high?" Katie snapped.

"I'd rather eat glass."

"Hey!" Delia growled. "My team has had to go to those goddamn Valkyrie parties with Didi every year for the last four years because you cunts wouldn't go. Well, now you're fuckin' going!"

"Hey, cunts is a little harsh, ya know?"

"There are speeches, honey. I've sat through Valkyrie speeches and Odin grabbed my tits last year. You're lucky I didn't sneak in and cut your throats in your sleep!"

"Christ, such a drama queen." Janelle went back to her phone. "Yager. Go to the party."

"Really?"

"Trust me. We'll be there and we'll drag her ass with us, if we have to bring her in a garbage bag."

There was a long pause, then, "She'll still be alive, right, Janelle? If you have to do that."

"Of course, she will!" Janelle snapped. "Don't make me crazy, Yager!"

"Okay. Okay." He chuckled. "Thanks a lot, Janelle."

She took a deep breath and smiled. "No problem. But I better be a goddamn bridesmaid at your wedding."

"You got it. And if she fights me on it, you'll move over to my side and hang with Tye and Mike. But no more putting Mike in headlocks."

"We both know the little bastard always deserves them," she joked, even as she felt a little shudder pass through her. Not about Mike. Like siblings, they'd been torturing each other for years. No, it was the mention of Tye that got her. She could still feel Tye's body lying on top of hers and see that glossy black hair spilling over those bright blue eyes...

She shook her head. "Look. Gotta go. See ya tomorrow."

She flipped the phone closed.

"So what's the plan, Dee?"

"It's vicious. And involves Didi."

Katie giggled in a most unholy way as she grabbed her knot book off the floor and again got comfortable in Janelle's chair. "Oh, this is gonna be fun."

Chapter Twelve

"Those Ravens are becoming a problem."

Waldgrave sighed as he stared off into his backyard, his big arms folded over his even bigger chest. "How long did it take them?"

"To take out the decoy and get to the Crows? Less than an hour."

Taking a deep breath to dispel the overwhelming desire to start killing things, he looked at the disciple standing next to him. "I guess we shouldn't be surprised, should we?"

"You didn't think She'd make it easy on us, did you, sir?"

He finally chuckled. "You're right." Still, the Ravens were a serious problem. And, unlike the Crows, their god still cloaked them. They were impossible to track, so he had no idea where the hell any of them lived. Plus, they could be right on top of him and Waldgrave wouldn't know it until they had their hands around his throat.

Besides, he wasn't sure he wanted to face off against Odin himself if he fucked with his pets.

"Sir?"

"Forget them for now. Our prey is The Gathering. Focus on them. We need to get rid of that female, and soon. Understand?"

"Yes, sir."

Waldgrave dismissed his disciple with a quick jerk of his head, leaving him to his thoughts and plans.

He wouldn't fail Her. He would never fail Her.

Neecy opened Arri's door but found her bed empty and made. The girl even made hospital corners. Obsessive-compulsives were so odd.

Charging down the stairs, Neecy desperately searched for her friend. She got up later than she meant to and she had to get into the City, but she wanted to talk to Arri and help her ease into this. She'd be freaked out. Scared. Neecy wanted to help her through that as much as she could.

She pulled her backpack on and checked the living room, the study, the library, and quickly headed toward the kitchen. Neecy pushed open the swinging door and froze in the doorway.

"Okay, okay. Tell 'em. Tell 'em." Katie handed Arri a cup of coffee.

Arri, sitting on the kitchen counter, took the cup and said, "Well, your colors are a dark, dark red. Passionate."

The roomful of Crows laughed and Katie struck a little pose. "That's right. I'm passionate! Now pay up! I told ya bitches I was red!"

Giggling, Arri looked past the women and saw Neecy. She gave her a wide grin. Neecy didn't need to read auras to know her little friend would be fine.

Neecy mouthed, *I gotta go. Talk later.*

Arri nodded as Connie rehashed the story from the previous night's hunt. "Like one second we were just standing there, kicking ass, and the next we were being blown away...literally!"

Neecy left the kitchen and headed toward the front door. Now she was really late. Luckily it still hadn't snowed, so she could ride her bike into the City. Rushing out the door, Didi, who'd abruptly come out of her office, called after her, "And don't forget tonight!"

"Yeah. Sure." Neecy didn't know what Didi meant, but she was in too big a rush to actually give a shit.

Neecy stared at the five women standing in her doorway. They all wore gorgeous black cocktail dresses and had their hair and nails done.

Her hair still wet from a recent shower, Neecy mustered up a calm she didn't feel. "I am not going to a Valkyrie party."

When Neecy arrived in the City that morning, she immediately went to the university to meet with the doctorate and master's students she advised and deal with her classes. After a full day of that, she did a little food shopping and then headed home for a night of *Law & Order* reruns and pasta. As far as she was concerned, that plan had not changed.

"Oh, yes. You are going." Didi took a step toward her and Neecy crossed her arms in front of her chest, her feet braced apart.

"Forget it. This is above and beyond the call of Skuld duty. Besides, I thought Delia and her team go to these things."

"I have her handling the Hunter situation."

"So I heard," Neecy couldn't help but sneer. She should be handling the current Hunter situation. Not that Delia wouldn't do a good job, but Neecy was second-in-command. Not Delia. Hunting down these idiots and using their heads as golf balls should belong to Neecy.

Didi snapped her fingers. "Show her."

Janelle reached into a Macy's bag and pulled out a strapless black cocktail dress.

"What is that for?"

"It's for you to wear."

Neecy shook her head. "Forget it. You ain't gettin' me in that dress. And you ain't gettin' me to that party. So you bitches might as well just keep steppin'."

Ducking her head, Arri stepped back as the other women stepped forward. It was when Janelle cracked her knuckles, though, that Neecy became seriously concerned.

Elder Raven Skellan watched quietly as a small group of women dragged a bound and gagged woman out of a limo.

He'd only come out to take a cigarette break before they served dinner. He never expected a floorshow.

Together, five women hauled the woman out onto the curb and stood her up. She immediately began to struggle, but a really large blonde put her in a headlock while a tiny redhead handled untying the ropes.

He'd been a Boy Scout in his youth and he knew those were good knots.

They kept the gag on the woman, however, and kept her in the headlock as they headed toward the hotel entrance.

A pretty black woman looked at him and waved. "Hi, Skellan!"

Suddenly recognizing her, "Hey, Didi. Everything...okay?"

"Oh, sure!"

"How's Harry?"

"Oh, he's great. I'll see ya inside, hon."

"Sure. See ya inside."

Nope. You just never knew what would happen at a Valkyrie party when Crows were invited. Dropping his unfinished cigarette, Skellan headed toward the entrance. No way would he miss any of this.

"Stop frowning, Neecy."

The crazy bitches finally released her, and Neecy yanked off her gag. "You mother—"

"Don't you dare, Neecy Lawrence!" Didi barked. "Just get over it. You're here for the night."

"I don't want to be here."

"I don't care."

The women all handed over their coats. Neecy refused to take off hers, so Janelle snatched it off her back.

"I'm so gonna get you for this," she snarled at Janelle.

"Blah. Blah. Blah," Janelle said with a smile. Since she was following a Crow leader's orders, there was really nothing to nail her for. But Neecy would find something. If it took her the rest of her second-life, she'd find something!

"All right, ladies. Listen up." Neecy crossed her eyes while the other five Crows turned to face Didi. "Remember what I said. No spitting. No punching. No kicking. No telling anyone you'll cut their throat when they're asleep."

"Hey," Neecy growled. "That was one time."

Didi didn't even glance at her. "We are here, ladies, to represent The Gathering and our goddess." She drew herself up to her mighty five-five height, which Neecy at her cool six-one pretty much laughed at. "So, don't piss me the fuck off tonight. Understood?"

They all nodded except Neecy who glared instead.

Moving like the pack of killers they truly were, the women headed to the grand ballroom. Janelle stayed behind Neecy, prodding her all the way.

The Valkyries had rented out the entire hotel for the night. Must have cost them a pretty penny, she was sure. And the Crows would be seriously outnumbered. Her little group the only ones willing to make the effort to attend.

They reached the doorway and Didi stopped.

She threw back her shoulders, and Neecy knew what was coming. It was the middle of winter, but they all had on strapless cocktail dresses, perfect for what they were.

Chicks with wings.

"Ladies." Didi smiled. "Unfurl."

Mike's head snapped back and he grabbed his nose. "What did I say?"

Yager didn't answer him. Just picked up his scotch and took another sip. He'd broken the boy's nose long ago. Now he took pleasure in messing with the little bit of cartilage left anytime the pissant got out of hand. Like now.

"It's not like I asked if she swallowed."

Yager jerked, just a little, and Mike jumped back away from him. He took another sip of his drink to hide his smile.

"Yager. I'm so glad you came."

Yager looked down at Cassie Bennet, once called Cassie Blue—her stage name. He had to admit, the woman had some talent, but only where stripping was concerned. When it came to being a Valkyrie...well, he knew better.

Glancing down at her, he noted Cassie's sinfully short silver dress. It barely covered her prominent ass. And he knew she probably only wore a thong and not much else under it. Add in the silver fuck-me pumps and Cassie was quite the recipe for hot, dirty fucking. He knew he could take her to the bathroom right now and nail her up against one of the stalls. And when he was fifteen, he would have been all over that like a bad rash.

But at thirty-three, only one woman dominated his thoughts. And it sure as hell wasn't Cassie Bennet.

It sounded like a gunshot and it stopped all the activity in the room. But being a Raven, Yager knew exactly what that sound was— wings unfurling. Crows' wings.

He turned away from the bar slowly and faced the doorway. Didi strutted in first. Like always, classy in her unpretentious way. But he'd known Didi for years. Classy she may be. But when she ripped off that one guy's head a few years back and "free-throwed" it into a basketball hoop...not so classy. Scary, but not classy.

A small group of Crows followed her. Arri, looking much better than she had the night before. As well as Janelle, Katie, and Connie.

Following right behind them all, looking seriously annoyed...

"Goddamn she's beautiful."

It took him a good ten seconds to realize he'd muttered that out loud. Cassie looked at him in surprise, whereas Mike just snorted a laugh. Probably all he could manage since he still held his nose.

No need bullshitting now. Yager shrugged. "Well...she is."

Neecy stopped in the middle of the room and looked to her left. There he was. Lounging against the bar and staring at her.

Looking at her the way she specifically told him *not* to look at her anymore. And, of course, Cassie My-pussy-is-so-well-used-it's-the-size-of-Penn-Station Bennet stood right next to him. Surprising the bitch didn't have a leash around his neck.

"This," she bit out between brutally clenched teeth, "is why you bitches brought me here?"

Didi shrugged. "We don't know what you mean."

Feeling her control slip, Neecy walked off. One more second looking at Didi's smug face, and she would bitchslap the woman all over the room. Still, it took a moment to realize Arri walked right beside her.

"They weren't being mean, Neecy."

"I don't wanna talk about it."

"I'm just saying."

Neecy stopped walking and turned to her friend. "I know. I know. It's just...this is getting complicated. I hate complicated."

Arri opened her mouth to respond, but she stopped and turned away, her eyes closing like she stared into the sun. Then a shadow covered them and Neecy thought for a moment that maybe it was Yager because of its size. Somehow, though, she knew it wasn't because the shadow kept growing.

Could this night suck any more?

"Hello, Odin."

She watched the god's one eye glance at her chest and immediately lose interest. "Denise."

It always surprised her he knew her name. Simply because her tits weren't big enough for him to take any interest. But suddenly, he seemed interested. Not in a good way, though.

127

"Can I help you with something?" Neecy knew she shouldn't get what Didi affectionately referred to as "that tone", but she couldn't help herself. He pissed her off.

"Just wondering if you're enjoying your time uptown?"

Actually they were in midtown at the moment. "What does that mean?"

"You and Yager. You must admit this is quite the step up for a one-time drug dealer."

Neecy sucked in air to spit in Odin's face, but before she got the chance, Arri grabbed the back of her dress and dragged her away.

"Well that was exciting," Arri muttered as she pulled Neecy into a safe corner behind an enormous potted plant. "I know *I* like to get into one-on-one confrontations with gods."

"Oh, stop whining. It's not like he would have wiped you from the face of the earth or anything."

With a sound of pure disgust, Cassie stormed off. Mike watched her go. "I fucked her, ya know."

Of course he did. "Was she any good?"

Mike shrugged. "Stripper sex."

"Stripper sex isn't bad." Especially when you were only twenty-seven.

"Nope. It was fun. I like stripper sex."

"Well, this is a fascinating conversation."

Yager looked down at Didi. "Hey, beautiful." He leaned down and gave her a hug.

"If it isn't my favorite vicious Viking." She reached up and gripped both of his cheeks. "And what a cutie little vicious Viking you are!"

Yager laughed and she patted his shoulder, turning her brown eyes to his friend. "How's it going, Michael?"

"Great, now that you're here."

Didi rolled her eyes. "You have absolutely no shame."

"None."

She leaned back against the bar next to Yager. "So, Yager. What *is* going on between you and my second-in-command?"

"At this very moment? Nothing. But—" he smiled, "—give me time."

"There's that Viking glint I love. And to think some of the Ravens thought you might be too nice for this job?"

"Nice? I'm not nice. Am I nice?"

Didi shrugged, but before she could answer, Yager cut her off. "Does *she* think I'm nice?" He felt uncomfortably panicked at the thought. Women never seemed to want a nice guy. They wanted a biker who couldn't commit. Or the criminal with the heart of gold. Yager never took anything after that bubble-gum incident when he was six, he never rode motorcycles because he liked his skull in one piece, and he would fly Neecy Lawrence to Vegas in a heartbeat if she suddenly walked over and said, "Let's do it!"

Shit. Nice was not good.

"If she thinks I'm nice, then she thinks I'm..."

"Boring?" Mike filled in helpfully.

"Shut up," both Yager and Didi snapped.

Didi touched his arm. "She does think you're nice, but that doesn't matter to Neece. Or the fact that you come from money."

"I don't come from money." Every cent Yager had, he'd earned on his own. And he was damn proud of that fact.

"You're from Long Island."

"From Levittown. Not exactly wealth capital of the world."

"Well, compared to the part of Brooklyn or Harlem or wherever the hell she was raised, you guys live in the Hamptons."

"So what do you suggest I do?"

Didi pushed off from the bar and stepped in front of him. "Do what Vikings do best."

"Invade in our longboats and steal all your women?" Yager and Didi looked at Mike. "What? That's what that means to me."

Didi smiled at Yager as she backed away from him. "*You* know what I mean, Yager. Persistence is key with someone like Neecy Lawrence."

She took another step back and slammed into a seven-foot, ten-inch hard body. She glanced at it over her shoulder and smirked. "Odin."

"Darling girl."

She snorted and walked away.

Odin nodded at Yager and Molinski who nodded back, and then he followed two twenty-year-old Valkyries who giggled past him.

Mike shook his head. "You know, next to that man, I feel damn near saintly."

"Bro, next to *that* man, you're the freakin' pope."

✧

"You know, you can't hide here all night." Arri handed Neecy the beer she'd asked for.

"Why not?"

"It's a potted plant. You're a mighty Daughter of Skuld...have some dignity."

"You know, since we discovered your abilities, you've been awfully mouthy."

Arri smiled in surprise. "Me? I've been mouthy? Cool! No one's ever called me mouthy before."

"Your perkiness is irritating me again."

"Oh. Sorry." Arri stared at her soda. "Ya know, I didn't think they'd be nice when they found out the truth about me. I thought it'd be different."

"Different how?"

"A burning-at-the-stake kind of thing."

Neecy laughed. "Don't flatter yourself, kid."

Arri grinned again and sipped her Diet Coke, leaning against the wall to people-watch. Neecy marveled at how clean Arri lived. No drugs. No drinking. And for a girl from Long Island, she didn't curse much either.

"Oh, my gosh! I don't think that Valkyrie's wearing underwear."

Neecy began laughing and couldn't stop.

"Heck, it's a G-string. Oh, I gotta talk to her. She can't be comfortable in that thing. I'll be back." Arri slipped off.

Neecy laughed harder. She was enjoying the "freer" Arri. She was a nut.

"I like you in that dress, baby."

Forcing herself not to spin around or spontaneously come at the sound of the man's voice, "How the hell did you get back there?" She looked over her shoulder at Yager, lowering her wing a bit so that she didn't block that gorgeous face of his.

"Well?" she pushed. The hidden little corner she'd buried herself in had an enormous potted plant blocking her from everyone's sight and kept anyone from creeping up behind her.

Anyone but Yager.

"Man, you're still testy. Why are you so testy?"

Sighing, "I'm not testy." She turned to face him. "I just don't want to be here, but I wasn't given much choice, now was I?"

"What are you looking at me for?"

"I don't know what you and those bitches have going on, but leave me the hell alone."

She turned to walk away, but Yager slid his arm around her waist and pulled her up against his body. "Why do you always run away from me, Lawrence?"

"Crows don't run. From anything."

"Except me. You run from me."

"Get over yourself, Yager."

She should have moved faster. Normally she would have. But Yager always threw her off. So when he turned her, pushing her into the dark corner behind the giant plant, she didn't even stab him with one of her talons.

"Yager!" She didn't yell it. It was more like a desperate whisper.

Taking the beer out of her hand and dropping it into the potted plant, he whispered back, "I missed you."

"I just talked to you last night." She refused to mention the time in her office. Not when she kept waking up all night thinking about it, her hands between her legs.

Feebly pushing against his shoulders, Neecy did her best to ignore the throbbing heat between her thighs.

"Not good enough, Lawrence."

"Let me go!"

He didn't. Instead he leaned against her and dropped his head into the curve of her neck. "Don't be mad at me, Neecy. I wanted to see you so bad."

Christ, how could she stay mad when he sounded so sincere? Especially when his warm breath against her neck sent pulsing shots of lust to her pussy.

"I'm not mad at you, Yager. My team, however..."

"Don't be mad at them either." His hand gently glided along the front of her dress. "I really like this dress on you, baby. I wasn't kidding."

"I'd like this dress more if I wasn't forced into it."

"Forced?"

"Yeah. Janelle held me down while the rest of 'em put it on me."

Yager stood up straight, his eyes looking off blindly. "My God, woman. The visual. Was there porn music in the background?"

Feeling her anger slide away, Neecy hit his shoulder. "No!"

"Any kind of inappropriate touching?"

"No!" She giggled as he leaned back down and kissed her neck and bare shoulder.

"That's so disappointing."

"You're a pervert, Yager."

"Nope. Just a typical male."

"Clearly."

"Does that really bother you?" He pressed Neecy against the wall with his body, his huge erection rubbing against her thigh. He felt so good against her. Man, she could really get used to this.

Neecy's hands gripped Yager's shoulders. She needed to get control of herself right now or she was going to be in big trouble.

"You look so good tonight, Neecy." She looked up into those steel grey eyes and saw nothing but warmth and caring. What the hell? How could this stay completely unemotional if he kept looking at her like he cared?

See? You can never trust men to do what you need them to do.

His mouth lowered to hers and she panicked, blurting out the first thing that came to mind that didn't involve sex. "What is the deal with your hair?"

Stopping abruptly, Yager gazed at her. "What?"

"Your hair...do you ever comb it?"

There. Now all she needed was to see that knowing little smirk that would tell her it was all a plot to get the girls wet and ready for him. Then she could dismiss him as nothing more than a walking, talking vibrator.

Instead, he looked a little embarrassed. "I keep forgetting."

"What?"

He shrugged. "I keep forgetting. I get out of the shower and I always mean to comb it then I get sidetracked by something else. Like tonight, it hit me what was wrong with the code I'd been working on and I decided to try and fix it before coming here." He grimaced. "Does it look really bad?"

No, no, no! This wasn't fair! He wasn't artfully cute and adorable. He was *cluelessly* cute and adorable. Damn him. Damn him to the very pits of Helheim!

Neecy dug her hands in his hair and pulled his head down until their mouths touched. They both moaned as their tongues connected and teased.

Yager pulled her impossibly closer, his hard cock practically burning a hole in her dress.

Pulling back a bit, Yager rasped against her lips, "Let's get out of here, Neecy. Now."

"No."

"Why? You know we'll have more fun alone."

"Forget it. Remember what I said, no relation—" Before she could finish, he kissed her again. Harder this time. More demanding. It suddenly got dark and she wondered why. She realized her wings had folded around them, shielding them from everybody else.

Christ, even her wings were betraying her.

He leaned back from their kiss and she burst out in a desperate whisper, "Forget it!"

"Damn difficult female," he muttered as he kissed her neck.

"I am not...and those better not be teeth I feel, mister! Another hickey and I'm gonna kick your ass."

So distracted by his teeth, Neecy didn't know Yager's hand had snaked up under her dress until she felt his fingers dip inside her panties.

"God, Yager. Stop!" she cried out in a desperate whisper.

And he did. Although he didn't move his hand away.

Panting, she looked up into his handsome face. "Yager."

"Let me, Neecy." He gave her the warmest smile she'd ever seen and her heart lurched. "I love watching you come."

"We can't. Not here." His thumb grazed her clit and she jerked. "Yager!" She slugged his shoulder.

"I wanna see you tonight."

She shook her head. "No. I can't." She wouldn't. Trouble, trouble, trouble. It oozed out of every one of Yager's goddamn beautiful pores.

His fingers teased her clit and she closed her eyes, working hard to stay in control—and failing miserably. She wanted him. Again.

Could she possibly be a weaker female?

"I wanna see you tonight, Neecy," he persisted. "I wanna fuck you. I wanna slide inside you and feel your tight pussy take hold of me."

Holy shit.

"I need to taste you again. On my fingers. On my tongue. I need to hear you whisper my name when I'm inside you. Then I want you screaming it as I make you come and come."

"I...I..." Desperately she tried to get out the words to tell him to stop. To back off. To go to hell. She couldn't. Not with those big fingers of his stroking her just right.

He leaned in and kissed her forehead. A sweet, innocent kiss. *Heartless bastard!* Why was he doing this to her?

"Yager—"

"Come for me, baby," he whispered against her ear as his fingers circled her clit. "I wanna feel you come."

He kissed her, his mouth hard against hers, which was good. Because she came, all right. Came all over his vibrating hand.

In fact, his mouth on hers was the only thing that stopped her from betraying their little full-body corner clutch to the entire party.

Finally, after she sagged against him, he pulled his mouth away and slid his hands out from between her thighs.

"God, you're amazing, Neecy."

She didn't know why, but she found that statement funny. She chuckled as she leaned into his big body, letting him hold her up. "Thanks, Yager."

"What's so funny?"

"I have no idea...and are you sucking your fingers?"

She looked up to find Yager with two of his fingers in his mouth. He shrugged. "Can't help myself." He grinned. "You taste so good."

Neecy laughed harder. *Only I would get mixed-up with a geeky alpha male.*

He kissed her cheek. "Come home with me tonight."

She finally pulled away from Yager. "I don't know."

"At least think about it."

Think about it? The man gave her a rocking orgasm in the middle of some crappy Valkyrie party, what else exactly would she be thinking about?

"That I can do."

His grin was huge and infectious. "Good."

"Now, go away."

"How easily I'm dismissed. I feel like a gigolo."

"You wish."

"Yeah, I do." From behind, Yager grabbed her around the waist, giving her a hug and quick kiss on the neck. "Later, baby."

"Yeah. Later." Taking a deep, shaky breath, Neecy turned to face Yager and instead found him gone.

"How the fuck does he do that?"

"Ow, Neecy!" Spinning back around, Neecy found Arri behind her, shielding her eyes.

"What?"

"Could you be any pinker?"

Neecy didn't get pink. Red, maybe. But she was too brown for pink anything. Then she realized Arri was in no way talking about her skin color.

Damn aura-reading, Underoo-wearing Crow! "Oh, shut the hell up!"

Delia crouched down in front of the man, his weapon in her hands. "Nice gun."

He turned his face away, but she grabbed his chin and forced him to look at her. They'd secured him to a chair in the back of an autobody shop, using one of Delia's handcuffs from her collection.

"There's a lot of ways this can go." Her grip tightened on his face and he cringed in reaction. "But in the end, you'll give me what I want."

They'd used one of the smaller Crows as a lure. That always worked with men. So gullible. So freakin' stupid. If she didn't like cock and a big muscular ass so much, she'd totally go gay. Or at least make the effort. But, like her mother and her mother's mother, she was cursed to love dick.

"Is this going to take long? I'm so hungry."

"Can you not wait five minutes, Sherri?"

"Not when I'm hungry."

Delia rolled her eyes. "Anyone got a protein bar for Ms. Impatient here?"

"I do," one of her teammates offered.

Delia turned back to her prey. "Where were we? Oh, yeah. You were going to tell me everything you know, or..." Delia glanced down at the other Hunters at her feet. Her girls hadn't left much of them, but what remained was damn impactful. And once she was done with this one, she'd open a mystical doorway and shove their remains through it.

Removing the blade from the sheath strapped to her calf, she pushed the point against his Adam's apple.

"Talk now...or feel pain for hours."

The Hunter stared at her for a long moment, closed his eyes, and dropped as far forward as his bonds allowed. It wasn't far, but it was enough to impale himself on the blade.

Delia blinked, the Hunter's blood dripping down across her hand. "Well this can't be good."

Sherri squatted down beside her, half the protein bar already gone. "Aw, man. I hate zealots."

Yager stared up at the ceiling. This was it. He wasn't coming to these stupid things anymore. He couldn't be more bored if they trapped him alone in a room without a TV and no furniture.

There was only one redeeming value to this seriously sucking event.

His eyes slid over to look at Neecy. She sat at the table with all the other Crows. Originally, their table was near the kitchen. A typical Cassie move. But she should have known better. Didi saw that shit exactly for what it was and took her Gathering over to a table filled with California Valkyries.

"Move or we break out the talons." And they did move, because few were stupid enough to fight with the Crows.

He was very glad they moved, too. He had a nice clear view of Neecy from the dais he grudgingly sat at.

Yager always knew he could fall in love with Neecy Lawrence. He just didn't realize he'd already fallen in love with her. Head-over-heels, can't-imagine-his-life-without-her, no-one-else-will-ever-do in love with her.

Of course she kept fighting him. That's what Neecy did with anyone not a Crow who tried to get too close. Not surprising really. She'd been through a lot. All the Crows had in one way or another. That's what he found so amazing about all of them. They all found such joy in the lives they had now and he admired that.

But Neecy...Neecy amazed him the most. She was everything he'd ever wanted. Now he had to figure out how to get her. Not just sex either. He wanted to come home at night and find her there. He wanted to check in with her before he committed to any weekend offers because she may have already planned something for them. He wanted to get pissed because all her girly shit was overtaking his apartment.

That's what he wanted, and it had been a long time since he hadn't gotten what he wanted.

Staring at Neecy, he found himself thinking about her naked.

Naked and wet and all over him.

"If you stare at her any harder..."

Yager smiled and turned to the older woman next to him. "I don't know what you mean."

Morgan laughed. An old school Valkyrie, the fifty-four-year-old woman practically raised Yager and his generation of Ravens. She taught them everything important. How to throw a good punch, how to set things on fire discreetly, and how to pick up girls.

And Morgan had made him well aware of how much the current Valkyrie situation galled her.

The Valkyries Yager was raised with were mighty in their fierceness. Their sexiness came out of their outright viciousness and Viking-like philosophies. Like the Original Seven, the Valkyries he knew and loved did not play games, try and act cute, or take anyone's crap. Especially Odin's.

"Gorgeous, isn't she?"

"Has someone stolen my little Will's heart?"

"Like a thief in the night."

"Well, all I have to say is, thank the gods it's a Crow. If it were one of these wannabe Valkyrie bitches, I'd be beyond pissed."

The beauty of Morgan...she never really said anything quietly. Typical Jersey Shore female, although she and her family now lived near his Long Island home. Yager didn't have to look to know every young Valkyrie eye on the dais was glowering at Morgan. And Morgan knew it, too—she simply didn't care.

"And you know I like the Crows. I did some work with Didi once. She's fierce." Morgan looked over at the Crow table and Yager knew exactly what the woman would do before she did it.

"Hey, Didi! *Didi! It's me! Morgan!*"

Yager looked down at his plate to hide his grin. Fancy dinner and Morgan yells across the room.

"Very nice, Morgan."

Morgan slammed back her scotch and motioned to a waiter for another. "Was that not subtle?"

Yager laughed.

She tapped his hand. "Are you out on the Island this weekend?"

"Maybe. I'm really hoping to get in some Neecy time."

"Aw, nothing quite like bird love."

"You Valkyries are always so jealous. The only thing that flies around you is your horses."

Morgan smiled as she took the scotch handed to her. "Smartass. Wherever did you get that attitude from?"

"You."

"Oh, yeah." She chuckled. "So, is she coming?"

Yager smiled, and Morgan rolled her eyes in response. "Is she coming to Long Island, you goober."

"I hadn't thought about it. I guess I could ask her."

Morgan stared up at him. "You forgot to comb your hair again, didn't you?"

Yager winced. "Yeah."

She smiled at him in that maternal way she seemed to keep just for him. "You always forget to comb your hair."

"Yeah. I think it bothers Neecy."

Choking out a laugh, Morgan put her scotch down untouched. "Yeah. That's it. She *hates* it."

"What does that mean?"

"Nothing. Nothing." She glanced over again at the table of Crows. "What do you think they're talking about over there? Men, clothes, or shoes?"

"The Crows? I'm sure it's something...scary."

"There is a definite, specific distinction between a psychopath and a sociopath, Connie."

"Yes, Katie, but we're talking about narcissists and I just don't see that they're any different from sociopaths."

"You're wrong. There are definite differences between the two."

Neecy glanced over to see Arri rubbing her eyes and stifling a yawn. Such a cute little thing. Although she should rethink dying her hair that color green. It did not suit her.

Neecy brought her Long Island Iced Tea to her lips as Janelle stared off across the room and quietly stated, "If I were any more bored, I'd set myself on fire."

Spitting out her drink, Neecy burst into a laugh, the other Crows joining in as they helped her wipe up.

Janelle chuckled. "Sorry, hon. You okay?"

Neecy nodded as a waiter swooped in and took her empty glass and cleaned up what he could.

"I'm fine. I'm fine."

"He's staring at you again."

Neecy didn't even turn around this time, knowing Katie meant Yager. Neecy had sensed the moment Yager's eyes were on her. She could feel it like a physical touch. Still, she wanted to check, to see those amazing eyes looking at her like she was the most beautiful woman in the world. But she knew if she did that, she'd end up staring and he'd stare back and then it would get typically embarrassing.

Janelle shook her head. "Hon, he's got it bad."

"That's not my problem."

"I don't *see* a problem."

"Of course you don't. 'Cause it's not *your* problem."

"Forget it, Janelle." Katie, sitting sideways, leaned back in her chair, her arm casually hanging over it. "Until she gets over her past, she's going to continue being this way."

Neecy wasn't sure what pissed her off more. The fact that Katie discussed her like she wasn't in the room. Or the fact that she actually had the balls to bring up her past.

"What the hell does that mean?"

"It means that until you let your past and what you did as a kid to survive go, you'll never think you deserve anything that's not specifically Skuld related."

"Are you done?"

"No." Katie adjusted the latex bustier of her dress. A bit of her tattoo stuck out from under it. There were two cops working the city streets this night wearing that same tattoo. "Yager represents what you consider to be nice, clean, and wholesome."

Neecy laughed suddenly. She couldn't help herself. She'd fucked the man. Wholesome was not a word she'd equate to Wilhelm Yager.

Katie paused for only a moment before continuing. "Too nice for the girl who proudly sported gang tattoos. Too wholesome for the girl who used to deal drugs to college kids. Too clean for the girl who used to steal cars and had to sleep in an alley more than once."

"Well, who hasn't done that?" Janelle asked while staring at her margarita.

"Don't even get me started on you, J. Your throat is just begging for a collar."

Janelle nodded, then her head snapped up. "Huh?"

It galled Neecy how close Katie was to the truth. Closer than she wanted anyone to get. Even her sisters.

"Back off, Katie."

"What's the matter, Neece? Hitting a little too close to home?"

"In a second that won't be the only thing that's hit."

Katie held up her hands. "Fine. But remember, Yager's not the kind of guy who's going to sit around waiting for you to get over your bullshit."

"Didi! *Didi!*" The Crows all turned and stared up at the dais as one of the older Valkyries made her way over to Didi.

"A friend of yours, boss?"

"Don't start, J. Morgan is very good people. Old school Valkyrie."

"You mean the real Valkyries?"

"Pretty much."

Arri leaned over, tapping Neecy's arm. "How much longer?" she whispered.

Glad to be discussing anything besides her past or Yager, Neecy leaned down and whispered, "There's still the speeches, I think."

"Speeches?" Arri looked stricken. The glamour of coming to this little event had worn off for her and like the rest of them, she was ready to go.

"Yeah. I know. And they're really boring."

Appearing on the verge of tears but this time from boredom, Arri stood up. "I'll be right back. Going to the ladies'." She headed out of the big room.

Who said "going to the bathroom" like that anymore, besides Arri?

"Where's she going?" Didi asked as she sipped her martini.

"She's going to the ladies'." When Didi simply stared at her, "She went to hit the head."

"Oh! Why didn't you just say that then?"

Neecy shook her head as Katie and Janelle followed after Arri to the bathroom. When Didi stood up to talk to the Valkyrie who'd yelled at her across the room, Neecy glanced up at the dais hoping to catch a glimpse of Yager, but he was gone.

Damn. He must have gone to hit the head, too.

Katie quickly came back into the room and wound her way over to the table. She crouched down beside Neecy. "You better come quick," she whispered, glancing up at Didi.

"What? What's wrong?" she whispered back.

"I think Arri's having a little bit of a panic attack." Clearly Katie didn't want Didi to hear. Everyone knew she still wasn't ready to give Arri her blessing. Something like this would make her crazy.

"Crap." Neecy pushed her chair out. "Um...I'll be back, Didi. Gotta take care of something."

Didi gave a dismissive wave as she continued her conversation.

Neecy followed Katie out into the main reception area and that's when Katie grabbed one arm and Janelle caught the other.

"Hey!"

The two women dragged her through the hotel reception and out the front doors. Then they tossed her into the back of a limo. She landed face-first into Yager's lap.

Arri leaned in and tossed her jacket at her. "Have fun!" Then they slammed the door closed and the limo pulled out into traffic.

Neecy pushed herself up and glared at Yager.

"You know," he said with a huge grin, "you could have kept your head in my lap."

She sat back into the plush leather seat. "Now you're involving sweet, innocent Arri in your bullshit?"

"What can I say? She likes me."

Neecy pushed her bangs out of her eyes. At some point she would really need a haircut. She glanced out the window. Unable to hide her frustration, she growled, "Why are we heading downtown?"

"I want to see your apartment."

"Why?"

"'Cause I wanna see your bed."

Yager hadn't even moved but she held her hand up anyway. "Stay right where you are, Yager."

"I haven't done anything yet."

"Yeah. But you're giving me that look again. And I don't plan on doing anything in this freakin' limo."

Smiling, Yager settled back in the seat. "You're no fun."

They eyed each other from their respective corners. Finally, Yager asked, "You got condoms, right?"

"Here?"

He sighed. "In your apartment."

"Oh...uh...hmmmm."

He really shouldn't *enjoy* the fact that she couldn't remember if she had condoms or not, but he did. Knowing Neecy as well as he did, he had no doubt the only reason she may not have condoms in her apartment was because she hadn't had a partner in a while. Good. Why should he be the only one suffering since he had that mind-blowing vision?

Yager hit the intercom. "Hey, Chuck. Do me a favor and stop at the drugstore before we get to Dr. Lawrence's apartment."

"You got it."

He looked over at Neecy and found her with her face in her hands. "What's wrong?"

"Are you trying to embarrass the hell out of me?"

"Come on, Neecy. We're all adults. Besides, would you prefer he thought I was going in bareback?"

"Who said you were... I... Oh!" She turned away and stared out the window. But she didn't tell him to stop the limo. *Thank God.*

Yager loved that he could get Neecy all worked up and crazy. In almost every other aspect of her life, Neecy ruled with an iron fist. Always in complete and utter control. Yet for some reason, he made her positively unglued.

"You all wet for me, Lawrence?"

Neecy's head snapped around and immediately her eyes strayed to the intercom.

"Don't worry, baby. It's not on." He looked her in the eye. "I wouldn't do that to you. Ever. You know that, right?"

She stared at him for so long, he thought for sure she was about to say, "Are you fucking kidding?" But instead, she simply nodded her head, turned back to the window, muttering low, "Yeah, Yager. I know."

He watched as her finger came up and drew a small star in the condensation on the window. He decided to leave her alone until they got to her place, since he didn't want her jumping out of a moving limo just to get away from him.

But the next thing she said to him got his cock so hard; he barely managed to stay over on his side. "And I *am* all wet for you."

Keys hitting the floor never sounded so loud. As she quickly crouched down to retrieve them, Yager was already there, scooping them up.

"Which one?"

Pointing at her front door key, "That one."

They both stood up at the same time and Yager reached around her to put the key in the lock. With his free hand, he encircled her waist and brushed his lips against the side of her neck.

She leaned against him, enjoying the feel of his hard chest against her back. Somehow, he managed to kiss her neck while unlocking her front door. He pushed the door open and, while keeping a tight hold on her waist, walked them both into the apartment.

Once inside, with the door closed and locked, Yager stopped and stared. "I was going to ask you where the bedroom is, but..."

She smiled and stepped into her loft apartment.

"Christ, woman. Is that a basketball court?"

"Just a half one."

She took his hand and led him into the enormous room. "Before you wonder if this is from drug money, one of the older Crows hooked me up. The building's rent-controlled. I only pay three-fifty a month."

Again Yager stopped and stared, but this time at her. "You got this place for how much? And I never thought it was from drug money."

She chuckled. Neecy had always loved her apartment. It was, to be blunt, freakin' enormous. It used to be an old warehouse that a Crow, way before Neecy's time, bought and renovated. Since then, only Crows lived in or owned this building. The current owner was a cranky old Crow, so she and Neecy got along just fine.

"You know what I find amazing?"

Neecy pulled off her jacket and threw it over the bed and into the chair filled with a week's worth of dirty clothes. Then she jumped back onto her big bed and bounced there several times before she settled down. "No. What?"

"The fact that you have all this space with your motorcycle over there, a half court over there—" he gestured to bookshelves right behind him, "—and you still have all your books piled into one corner."

Neecy winced. "I keep meaning to get to that."

"Sidetracked with all that saving-the-world stuff?"

Snorting a short laugh, "Give me a break. All we do is keep the balance. That's it. I leave saving the world to the Christians and Greenpeace."

She lay back on her bed and proceeded to kick her shoes off.

"Need some help with the dress?"

For a split second, Neecy almost said, "What the hell for?" Then her dumb ass caught up with the moment and she took a deep breath. She'd given up the fight. At least for tonight. She wanted to fuck Yager. She wanted to fuck him bad.

"Yeah. That'd be great."

Yager pulled off his cashmere coat and laid it across a kitchen chair. He slowly walked to the bed and stood in front of her. "Stand up."

Sliding off the bed, Neecy stood in front of Yager. Gently, he gripped her shoulders and turned her away from him.

His hands slid across her bare shoulders, caressing the skin. Neecy closed her eyes, enjoying the rough feel of Yager's fingers against her flesh.

"I do really like you in this dress."

Working really hard not to squirm, she said, "Thanks. I felt a little ridiculous in it. It's not my thing."

Neecy felt Yager's mouth on her neck at the same time the dress zipper slid down.

"You're not wearing a bra."

When you're an average "A", there was really not much reason. "No."

"So the panties only, huh?"

"Except for the shoes and the thigh-highs, yeah."

Yager buried his face in her neck and groaned. "Don't add anything, Lawrence. You're already killing me."

"Really?" she asked, surprised at the husky tone of her voice. "So I shouldn't tell you how hard it was not to squirm in my seat the whole night? Or how I kept thinking about you naked and between my thighs—"

Yager's hand clamped around her mouth. "You really need to stop talking now." He pulled her back against his body. "At least until we get this first one out of the way."

Neecy pried his fingers off her face while he stripped the dress off her body. "The first what?"

Next thing she knew, she was facedown over her kitchen table. Torn between laughing her ass off and moaning uncontrollably, Neecy realized she'd never been so comfortable with a man before in her entire life. Anyone slamming her down over a table should freak her out royally. Instead, she kept laughing while trying to twist around and find out what Yager was up to, but he laid his hand flat against her back to keep her in place.

Neecy heard his pants drop, the ripping of the condom box then the condom package. She squirmed a bit and Yager growled. "Don't. Move. I'm barely holding on here, baby."

She didn't know what was wrong with her, but she just couldn't help herself. Teasing him was so much fun. Spreading her legs, she looked over her shoulder and said, "Then you better get off your ass and fuck me...*Will.*"

"You," he ground out, "are such a vicious brat."

Yager kicked her legs farther apart as he kept her rooted to the spot with one hand. His other hand slid over her ass and down between her legs. She moaned as two fingers pushed their way into her.

"What am I going to do with this body tonight, Lawrence? How many different ways am I going to make you scream my name?" She panted as his fingers went deeper. "Damn, Neecy. You're drenched. Is all this just for me?"

"Not if you keep making me wait."

Yager leaned over her, his tongue licking across her spine.

"We've got all night, baby."

"*You've* got till dawn."

He paused, his body suddenly tight. "What if I wanna fuck you in the morning?"

"That's not part of the deal."

"There's a deal?"

"There is now."

A long moment of silence followed that declaration and Neecy worried he might leave. Especially when he pulled his fingers from her body.

She didn't want him to leave, but she didn't want Nice-Guy Yager to have any false hopes either. Waking up in his arms would be a huge mistake and they both knew it.

Strong hands gripped her hips, yanking her body back. His latex-covered cock slammed into her, forcing its way past tight muscle. She winced as her body took a moment to adjust to his size. As always it was a snug but delightful fit.

"Then I guess I shouldn't waste a second, huh, Lawrence?" Yager demanded as his hand slipped around to the front of her body and slid between her thighs.

"Nope," she gasped as his fingers found her clit. "You better not."

It was pretty much the last thing she said for the next few hours...

Waldgrave took apart his rifle. He loved the monotony of meticulously cleaning his weapons. It allowed his mind to focus on more interesting things. Like the Hunt. His congregation of Hunters knew they'd been preparing for something, but they had no idea what.

Not surprising. How often does a true test of one's skill come? How often do you truly risk your life while on a hunt?

How often does a goddess put you on this path? He worshipped Her not merely because of her beauty or power, but because her cruel nature spoke to him. She understood him when no one else did. Not his ex-wives. Not his children.

And when she finally gave him a task, it was something as wonderful as this. A true Hunt for the best Hunters.

"What do you want us to do with the body?"

Waldgrave didn't bother looking at the carcass of one of his loyal disciples. They'd caught him, but he'd done his duty. He knew the boy had revealed nothing before dying because no Crows attacked his house. They were not females who waited for anything. If the Crows knew where they were, they'd be breathing down his neck this very moment.

No. They still had time.

"Prepare him for the pyre. We'll offer his body to the flames and his soul to Her."

"No. Stop!"

Yager's cock popped out of her mouth and she glared up at him. "What is it now?"

"You can't keep going down on me every time I try to have a conversation with you."

Wanna bet? Neecy licked her lips and again wrapped her mouth around his hard cock.

"Goddammit, Neecy." She liked when he moaned that. Made her feel kind of powerful.

She deep-throated him and sucked hard. His back arched and she thought for sure he would pop. And if he popped, he sure as hell wouldn't feel like talking. Instead, however, he grabbed her shoulders and hauled her off. Next thing she knew, he'd flipped her on her back and pinned her down with his body.

"I wanna talk."

"Then find a priest...or a therapist." That seemed like a pretty nasty thing to say, but he only smiled at her. Why couldn't she have a normal stalker like everybody else?

"You can't fight me forever, Neecy."

"Really?"

"Yeah. Really."

He sat up, bringing her with him. "Now, let's get you comfortable." She *was* comfortable. With his cock in her mouth. But, no, that wasn't good enough for Will We-have-to-talk Yager.

Yager pulled her up until her back touched the headboard, then he grabbed hold of the sheet and covered her. Sitting down close beside her, Yager fixed the sheet so that it covered his hips and his gorgeous cock. Disappointing.

Once he put them the way he wanted, he turned to her. "So, tell me about yourself."

"No."

"What do you mean no?"

"I mean no. This wasn't part of the deal."

"Actually, we don't have a deal. All you said on the phone was that you wanted no dating and no relationship. At the moment, that's what we have."

Neecy turned her body so she could look Yager in the eye. "What do you mean 'at the moment'?"

"Come on, Neecy. You know I'm not giving up that easy." She really wished he didn't look so cute when he said that.

"Is that right? And if you keep persisting, why should I keep this going? Why shouldn't I throw you out on your ass right this second?"

He didn't answer her. Not verbally anyway. Instead, he reached out and gently grasped her breast through the sheet. One squeeze and he had her. They both knew it. She couldn't even breathe. He toyed with her nipple between thumb and forefinger.

"Tell me to go, and I'll go."

He had to be kidding. She could barely think with his hand playing her so effortlessly.

"Tell me to go, Neecy."

Yager knew she wouldn't, she could see it by the look on his face. Not now. Leaning forward, she tried to kiss him, but he pulled back. He kept his hand on her breast, though.

"No you don't. I wanna talk first."

"About what?" Damn, she'd really have to do something about the whining. What was it about this man that pulled emotions out of her she never allowed herself to have, much less express in public?

"About you. I wanna know about you."

Again? "I died when my boyfriend—"

"Not that. After that."

"After that? You were there for 'after that'. Why do I have to go over it again?"

"I wasn't *there*, Neecy. I was living my life with the Ravens and you were living yours. I didn't even know you were a history professor or that you had your PhD. So I want details."

She didn't get this guy at all. Why did he care?

"I know. Let's make this a reward system."

Neecy's eyes narrowed even as she writhed under his hand. "What does that mean?"

Finally releasing her breast, he grabbed her around the waist and pulled her into his sheet-covered lap. Her legs straddled his hips, as she put her arms around his neck.

"Now, where did you go to college for undergrad?"

"Why do you care where I...oh...oh...shit!" He'd latched on to her breast and happily sucked away at her nipple. Digging her fingers into his scalp, she pulled him tighter to her. But, suddenly, he stopped.

Gritting her teeth in pure rage, Neecy bit out, "I have to talk to get you to keep going, don't I?"

"This is why I love the Crows," he joked around her breast. "You guys are so smart."

"You can't be serious."

"Oh, yeah. I think you guys are brilliant."

"I don't mean that!" Dammit! Emotion.

"Don't over-think this, baby. Just tell me what I wanna know."

Sighing, "Fine. I went to Stanford." As soon as "I" was out of her mouth, he started sucking again, making sure to swirl his tongue around exactly the way she liked it.

"Keep going," he ordered around her breast.

Biting her lip, Neecy forced herself to focus. "They have a really good history prog—" She choked on the word as his sucking became stronger. But as soon as she paused, so did he. She shut her eyes tight. With very little effort, Yager could make her come simply by sucking her breasts, but he was torturing her. The bastard.

"Program. I'd heard some really...uh..." One hand stayed on her ass, pulling her tight against his rock-hard erection. His free hand grabbed her other breast and began kneading it. "Uh..." *Think, girl!* "Some really great things about it. Plus, it allowed me to train with the...the...California Crows." She squeaked out the very last part as his teeth gently nipped her nipple. The bastard knew that drove her insane.

Without releasing her, he asked, "What about grad school?"

Neecy blinked, trying desperately to focus on his questions and her answers. Not easy when her entire body was moments from bursting into a nuclear reaction that would destroy the entire tri-state area. "I went to NYU for my master's. And Columbia for my...my...um..."

"Don't stop," he warned again.

Would sobbing at this point really be out of line? She didn't know. But she couldn't handle much more at this rate. And she gripped him so tight, she wasn't sure she might not be killing him.

"For my...my...*doctorate!*" she screamed as she exploded all around him.

He held her tight as spasms racked through her. When she finally started breathing normally again, he lowered her to the bed.

"Now that wasn't so hard, was it?"

Without opening her eyes, she growled at him. Which only made him chuckle.

Slowly he kissed his way down her chest and stomach. When he kissed the inside of her thigh, Neecy forced her eyes open.

With a strange but thoughtful expression on his face, he stared straight into her snatch. The man was getting stranger and stranger by the minute.

Glancing up at her, he grinned. "Now..." He gave her still-sensitive clit a little lick, forcing Neecy to grab hold of the sheets to stop her body from shooting off the bed. "Tell me what your master's was on, then your doctorate. And I want details. Lots and lots of very specific details."

Really? Would sobbing really be *that bad*?

Yager stretched and enjoyed the smell of Neecy surrounding him.

Well, that had been amazing. One of the most amazing nights he'd had in a very long time. He knew he had her now. There was no way she could walk away from him this time. No way in hell.

Turning over onto his side, Yager reached for her and touched nothing but paper. He forced his eyes open and picked up the slip of paper lying on the pillow next to him.

He read it. Closed his eyes. Rubbed them. Then read it again. No. The words hadn't changed.

"There's orange juice and cereal. When you leave, make sure to pull the door closed so that it'll lock. Thanks for last night. See you around. Neecy."

Sitting up, Yager grunted and ignored his sore, well-used body's protests. Right now he didn't care about any aches or pains.

"See you around?" *Is she fucking kidding?*

Chapter Thirteen

Damon Lewis still couldn't believe it. His brother, Darryl, gone. Half the Pack with him. And these...females behind it. These freaks.

As far as he was concerned, they were like demons or the undead. It was one thing for a goddess to bring someone back to life, but to have changed them somehow... Well, that was something else altogether.

Something evil.

But the black woman behind the desk kept telling him and his father that Darryl brought all this on himself. He'd used some ancient artifact to make himself invulnerable. Damon didn't want to believe it, but he knew it was true. Knew his brother had delved into things he never should have and seriously wasn't smart enough to control.

And because of that Darryl paid the price.

Damon looked at the woman across from him and his father. A true politician, that one, but he couldn't stop staring at her goddamn wings. They...fluttered, or something. It was disturbing.

Not as disturbing, however, as the big scary female standing near the door, blocking his way to freedom.

He glanced at her out of the corner of his eye. She had to be at least six feet tall. At least. With short black hair and cold, coal black eyes. He had no idea if she was also black or something else like Cuban or whatever. She stood off to the side, her arms crossed over her chest, her feet braced apart, and a brutally cold expression on her face. She was a big girl. Not fat. Actually, he didn't think there was an ounce of fat on her. But she had muscles and her frame could clearly carry a lot more. Her eyes slid over to him and he moved his gaze to the floor. She made the She-wolves in his Pack seem weak and girly.

These women with their scary wings and watchful demeanor were downright unholy, and he wanted to go. Preferably now.

Damon knew there'd be no war over what happened to his brother. Wolves didn't waste time with bullshit especially when his brother asked for it. His Pack wasn't about to take on these freaks for a wolf who'd gone bad.

His father nodded at the woman's words and then stood up. The tall female opened the door, allowing them to leave. Damon and his father walked out but froze right in the doorway, too terrified to move.

They were everywhere. Perched on the banister and stairs. On top of the hallway furniture. And if there was nowhere to perch, they stood. Stood and stared. Damon had no idea how long they'd been sitting out here waiting for them. But he felt like it might have been the entire two-hour meeting.

Damon's father snapped out of it first, grabbed his arm, and headed down the hallway toward the exit. He pulled the heavy oak door open and stepped outside, but there were more waiting out there, too. This time, his father ignored them and kept going. Down the front house steps and toward their car.

Their completely shitted-upon car.

The only thing that didn't suffer was the window on the driver's side—so they could leave. Damon looked up and saw hundreds of actual crows in the trees. They didn't make a sound either. They just watched them.

At that point, his father threw him in the car and got in right after him. Without waiting, the old man tore out of the driveway. Short of an actual war with these people, Damon had no doubt they'd never come here again.

Neecy, the last to come in, quietly closed the door. Slowly, she turned and faced her sisters.

Clapping her hands together, she cheered, "What good doggies! Who's a good boy? Who's a good boy?"

The Crows burst out laughing. And they laughed their asses off for the next half-hour.

Yager's eyes didn't stray from the computer screen in front of him as Tye came up behind him.

"What?" Yager learned long ago how to do more than one thing at a time. He had to. It was the only way to manage his life and the Ravens. So he kept working while Tye talked to the back of his head.

"There's a call for you."

"I'm busy. Take a message." He worked code because for him it was mindless and he needed to focus on bigger issues. Like Neecy. Crazy, annoying, sadistic Neecy.

Christ, I am so in love with her.

"It's Didi."

Yager spun his chair around to face his friend and next-in-command. Crow leaders didn't call Raven leaders unless something was wrong.

"What? Why?"

"Don't worry. Nothing's wrong. She just wants to meet with you. Tonight."

And they didn't meet unless something was wrong.

"Then what does she want?"

"She wouldn't say. She just asked that you come to the Bird House tonight. I told her you probably wouldn't mind." Tye grinned. "But that I'd check with you just in case."

Yager turned his chair back around. "Tell her I'll be there."

"Wow. Amazing how I knew that."

Waldgrave walked through his house. An old Westchester, Connecticut mansion that had been in his family for generations. His Hunters, Her disciples, currently lived with him and his many trophies.

Trophies he'd soon be adding to.

He passed the converted family room. Converted into a communications center. They'd been taping the Crow chatter for months. Not hard—they never changed their cell phones. Stupid, stupid females.

Stopping in front of the room filled with top-of-the-line electronics, Waldgrave motioned to the Hunter handling the next phase of this hunt.

"How's it going?"

"Great. I think we almost have what we need. It might even be too easy."

Shaking his head, "Don't get cocky. That'll get you killed faster than anything."

He walked away, heading back to his office. If they were getting close, then he had much work left to do.

Destroying a large group of freaks was a much more time-consuming task than Waldgrave ever imagined.

✧

Arri squealed and ducked.

"Oh, come on! I haven't even touched you yet!"

Arri peeked around her boxing gloves at Janelle. "I was anticipating the worst?"

Janelle took a deep breath and turned to Neecy. "I'm done, Neece. She's driving me nuts."

"Wait!" Arri grabbed Janelle's arm with her gloved hands. "I'm sorry. I just..."

Neecy didn't even look up from her sparring with Katie. "Keep trying, you two." She blocked Katie's fist. "We've got serious hunting coming up and Little Girl needs the training."

Sighing, Janelle turned back to Arri. The girl was practically cowering. She'd seen whipped dogs that looked less frightened.

"Okay, Arri. We're going to take it real slow." Janelle forced a smile, but that seemed to scare her even more, so she stopped. "Now put your fists up again and plant your feet. Good."

Janelle slowly brought her own fists up. "Now, I'm going to swing at you, but real slow. Okay? You'll definitely see me coming. And all I want you to do is to just push my hand out of the way. Okay?"

"Okay."

"Great." Moving in movie-style slow motion, Janelle swung her fist forward. Arri kept her eyes on it until it was about five inches from her, then she squealed and dropped to the ground covering her head.

"That is it!"

"Calm down, Janelle." Neecy and Katie were still at it. Katie was trying her best to get to Neece, but their team leader had some great defensive moves and she was wicked fast. You didn't get to her easily.

"You gotta give her some time."

"Time we don't have."

"I'm sorry," Arri offered from her place on the ground. "Your fist just looks awfully imposing from where I'm standing. Can't we get someone more my size...or just smaller than you?"

Janelle gritted her teeth. She didn't need little Ms. I-can-wear-tank-tops-and-tiny-jeans commenting on her size. All it did was piss her off. "I'm not sure we can find anything that small without following the Yellow Brick Road," Janelle snapped.

"Hey! I'm not *that* small!"

"That's it, you two. Take a break."

"Fine." Janelle reached down and yanked Arri to her feet. For a few moments, they silently watched Neecy and Katie sparring while Janelle seethed.

How come she had to train Arri? The girl was absolutely terrified of her, and Janelle was damn tired of it. She didn't need Minnie Mouse making her feel like the Jolly Green Giant.

Katie tried another attack and Neecy completely blocked her. Nah. Katie didn't have a chance. Neecy was way on. She'd shown up that morning sporting a little attitude. It must be all that Yager love. Janelle couldn't blame her. The man was fine. And he actually made the two of them look small and delicate. She liked that in a man.

The question now was how far would Neecy let their little "thing" go? She'd known Neecy a long time. And Katie was right, Neecy was still trying to make up for something she did years and years ago. And she still hadn't really gotten over what that boyfriend of hers did to her.

Whether Yager was patient enough to wait all that emotional bullshit out, however, was anyone's guess.

Neecy easily blocked another punch from Katie, pushing her arm out of the way. Katie used the momentum to try one of her roundhouse kicks. Neecy saw it coming and prepared herself to block the blow.

At that moment, Delia pushed open the door to the training room. "Hey, Neece. Did you know Yager was here?"

Neecy's head snapped around, allowing Katie to land that kick right at her head. Most likely because she thought Neecy would block it, Katie put a lot of oomph into that one move.

Their team leader went down like a ton of bricks.

Didi stared at the man across the desk from her. Like Neecy, Yager was more than ten years younger than her and a stone-cold fox.

She didn't know what Neecy's problem was, but she needed to get over it. Or some little filly was going to come along and snatch her a Viking stallion.

Yager shook his head. "I can't believe it."

"It's true. I'm done. I've been done for a while now."

"I guess I never thought you'd retire."

"Now, Yager, you know we can't do this forever."

He lifted one big muscled leg and rested his foot on the opposite thigh. "Have you told Neecy?"

"No. I'm informing all the leaders now. And of course Skuld knows. My husband's real excited." Yager frowned and she held her hand up. "Yes! I'm married! Why does everybody keep forgetting?"

"Probably because we never see him. Do *you* ever see him?"

"Don't be a smartass."

Yager smiled. "Okay. Okay." Restlessly, his fingers tapped against the arm of his chair. "So, any idea who's going to take over?"

She knew what worried him. Didi didn't hound her girls. She didn't worry what they were up to when they weren't hunting. But that was her. Some leaders were not nearly as relaxed as she was. Yager wanted to make sure he didn't lose any of his precious Neecy time.

But Didi wouldn't let that happen. The bottom line was, Didi wanted her second-in-command happy before she walked off. It would make her a better, less uptight leader. And she knew Yager was the key. Actually, *all* the Jersey Crows knew that. Only Neecy insisted on playing this "only sex" bullshit. And it was bullshit. The girl *floated* into the house earlier in the day. The man had fucked the cranky right out of her.

"To be very honest, Yager, I want Neecy to take over. But in the end, it's Skuld's decision. Second-in-commands don't automatically get picked to lead. All I could do was recommend her."

Yager leaned back in the seat and Didi was glad she liked good, sturdy wood furniture or he'd destroy the damn thing. "So when are you done?"

"No matter who they choose, the transition will take a few months. Then, of course, a party."

"When don't you guys end something with a party?"

"Now, now. Don't be bitter. But let's face it. A group of crows is 'a Gathering'. While a group of ravens is 'an unkindness'."

Yager threw his head back and laughed. "Oh, I see. Trying to get on my good side, huh?"

"I *am* charming, aren't I?"

"But you guys always seem to forget the 'murder of crows'."

"Well, that would be redundant."

An abrupt knock on her door cut into their conversation. "Yeah?"

Delia stuck her head in. "Uh..." Her eyes strayed to Yager.

"What, Delia?" Delia knew Didi had no patience with long pauses. She hated that. "What is it?"

Delia started chuckling and couldn't seem to stop. "Uh...Neecy...um."

"What about her?"

Delia cleared her throat. "Um...I need that stuff you put on scrapes. She's got kind of a little...uh..." She looked down at the floor and laughed harder.

Embarrassed, Didi glanced at Yager. She bet he never had to deal with giggling Ravens. "Delia?"

Shaking her head, she pointed down the hallway.

"Lord, the shit I put up with." Didi pushed away from her desk and stood up. She walked out of her office, knowing Yager trailed behind her because he only had to hear Neecy's name and the guy's entire body tensed up.

Didi heard them before she even opened the kitchen door. Laughing. Yelling. *Rowdy bitches.*

Pushing the door open, she froze. Neecy held her hand up. "Don't freak out."

"What the fuck happened to your face?"

"Katie nailed her with a roundhouse kick," Janelle said from her seat on top of the kitchen counter. The girl never used a chair if she could help it. "Bam! And she was out."

"You blacked out?"

"Just a little. Nothing to sweat about. I mean, these are just scrapes." Neecy waved at her bloody cheek. "No big deal. I got these when I hit the floor."

"And a juicy-sized knot on the side of her head from Katie's tiny little feet."

Neecy glared at Janelle. "Ya know, you could enjoy this a little less."

Janelle grinned. "You're right. I could."

Neecy glanced around the kitchen for something to chuck at Janelle when she saw him, leaning against the doorframe and staring at her.

Their eyes locked and Neecy felt Yager move all through her body. The way he examined her face, she could almost feel his big fingers brushing the scrapes across her cheek, checking the size of the lump on her head.

So busy devouring everything about Yager, it took Neecy a moment to realize the Crows had gone completely silent. They were staring at her and Yager.

"I'm going to go and...uh..." Christ, when did she start having trouble speaking? She was a professor. She spoke to groups of people every day. But now she was a verbal mess—and she blamed Yager.

Pointing at the ceiling, she said, "Gonna shower." Neecy turned and headed out the other kitchen door that led to the back hallway.

Neecy didn't look at Yager again as she took the backstairs up to the second floor. She walked into her room, closed the door behind her, and stood there for a good two minutes wondering what the hell was wrong with her. This wasn't like her. When she saw Yager all she wanted to do was go to him and let him put his arms around her. She wanted him to take care of the scrapes on her face, kiss the rapidly growing knot on the side of her head. She wanted him to kiss her forehead and tell her she would be okay. He'd make it feel better.

Christ, when did I become such a pussy?

Now thoroughly angry and disgusted with herself, Neecy ripped off her clothes and went to her bathroom. She turned on the shower, adjusted the temperature, and stepped in. She slapped her hands against the cold tile and leaned her head under the showerhead. Closing her eyes, she tried to push out any needy feelings she had about anybody or anything.

She didn't *need* anybody except her sisters. And, hell, they needed her more than the other way around.

Taking a deep soothing breath, Neecy had begun to relax when the shower door slammed open. She spun around, immediately swinging her left fist, but it hit one big palm.

"Goddamn it, Yager!" She pushed wet hair out of her face. "How did you get in here?"

"You didn't lock your door. Besides, Didi said, 'Don't just stand there, go after her.' So I did."

At some point, she really would kill that woman.

"Well, out! As you can see, I'm a little bit indisposed at the moment."

As always, Yager ignored her, instead reaching into the shower and sliding his hand behind the back of her head. He pulled her forward and looked long and hard at her bruised cheek.

"You sure you're okay, baby? Janelle said you took a really bad hit."

"I'm—" she gulped hard so she didn't lose her voice, "—I'm fine, Yager. Thanks."

Still gently but firmly gripping her head, he whispered, "Come home with me."

"Why?"

"Because you said you wouldn't do anything sexual here. So come home with me." He leaned into the shower, completely ignoring the fact that he was getting wet in the process, and brushed his cheek against her unhurt one. So gently, she barely felt it—but she felt it enough. "I promise I'll make you feel better," he whispered against her ear.

Her entire body shook. "Yager—"

"Come home with me, Neecy." His lips barely touched hers—but they touched them enough.

Christ, she shouldn't do this. She knew Yager wanted more than just a sexual relationship. And if she were honest with herself, she was starting to feel that way, too. But she didn't want to want that. It was dangerous. He was dangerous. Her feelings for him were dangerous.

"Yager, if I come with you now, I'll be gone by the time the sun comes up."

He grunted and shrugged, but then he kissed her and she stopped caring.

Yager stared down at the woman sprawled out next to him. Neecy Lawrence could really take over a bed when she slept. But he liked it. One of her legs stretched across his, one arm lay across his waist, and her head rested against his chest, her breath tickling his nipple.

He really didn't know what to do about her. Neecy made it all so difficult.

Brushing her black hair off her face, Yager winced at the bruises on her cheek. He hated to see her in pain. He felt it as surely as if someone had kicked *him* in the head. But he couldn't tell Neecy that.

Anytime he tried to get close, she backed away. Anytime he tried to make this deeper than sex, she ran.

He sighed. He didn't want this anymore. True, he still wanted Neecy, but he wanted her like this. All the time. He wanted to be able to go to sleep and not worry she'd be gone when he woke up. Hell, he wanted a date. To the movies and dinner. Something simple and fun, ending with mind-blowing fucking. It seemed so simple to him, but Neecy made sure nothing was simple. It was like she couldn't help herself.

He wanted to discuss all this with her, but as soon as she even sensed the sun was rising, she'd be gone.

But Yager wouldn't be doing this her way anymore. No more playing by her rules. No more giving her space, hoping she'd come to her senses. No. He was ready to push his hand on this one and she'd simply have to learn to deal with it.

Neecy felt the sun begin to rise. She guessed it was about five-thirty or so. Time to get the hell out before Yager woke up and tried to turn her into some simpering female who couldn't live without him.

Yum. Sunday brunch at the Bird House sounded like a lovely idea after all that sex.

Using every bit of her training, she silently eased out of the bed. Yager was out cold. Snoring, even. Well, that wasn't attractive, but she smiled anyway. Grabbing her sweats and sneakers, Neecy backed toward the door, her eyes locked on Yager. Even snoring like a big bear she found the man gorgeous.

Sighing softly, she steeled herself to leave and turned toward the bedroom door.

Neecy stopped short. Yager stood there. His back against the door, his arms crossed in front of his massive chest. He looked like he'd been standing there for hours, waiting for her.

"Going somewhere, baby?"

"How did you..." She glanced back at the now empty bed. "Where did you..." She growled. *"How the hell do you do that?"*

"I'm really fast." He tilted his head to the side, his hair falling across his face. "Where ya goin'?" He asked it so sweetly, Neecy immediately went on the defensive.

"Home."

"I want you to stay." He took a step toward her and, for the first time in her life, she stepped back. Not because he scared her, but because he didn't.

"That's a bad idea."

"I like it."

Neecy shook her head. *Determined bastard, isn't he?*

"I'm sure you do, but—"

"But what?" Yager now stood in front of her.

"Look, this is getting complicated."

"Complicated? It doesn't seem complicated to me at all."

He'd started walking back toward the bed, forcing Neecy to step back as he stepped forward.

"Maybe you're just making this complicated," he continued.

"I'm not. I'm trying to keep this as simple and uncomplicated as possible."

He took her clothes out of her hand and tossed them to the floor. "Well, you're not doing a good job of that," he offered sadly.

Neecy's eyes narrowed. "I'm not doing a good job of that because of you!" she accused.

"You're blaming this on me? That doesn't seem fair."

The backs of her legs hit the mattress and she stopped. But one good push from Yager on her shoulder and she flopped back on the bed.

"Ya know, Lawrence, I find it really sad I have to go to extremes to get something so simple."

"Extremes?" She really didn't like the sound of that. Nope. Not at all.

He wrapped his hands around her waist and hauled her up into a sitting position, her back against the bed frame.

"Yeah. I had to borrow these from Tye. He has a rather disturbing collection of stuff."

He leaned over her and before she could see what he had, he grasped her wrist. She felt cold metal and heard the click of a lock.

Oh, what an asshole!

"Yager."

He pulled the other cuff through the metal bars and locked up her other wrist.

"Wilhelm Yager," she said calmly, although there was a bit of a giggle there, "this is such bullshit and you know it. Now let me go." She should feel fear. Panic. But she knew, as sure as she knew her own name, she *knew* Yager would never hurt her. He'd never abuse her. She knew it with all her soul...and it terrified her.

"No."

"What do you mean no?" Nope. She wasn't scared, worried, or panicked but she would admit, at least to herself, she *was* a little turned on. Actually she was seriously turned on.

"I mean no," he said. "We need to talk. And we're gonna talk."

She pulled but the cuffs only dug into her wrists. These weren't typical handcuffs either. More like something she could buy at a sex shop. Apparently quiet Tye was the group freak among the Ravens. "We can do that without me being chained up, you idiot."

"No. We really can't. And don't call me names." He walked to his dresser. "I try to talk to you and you run. Or fight. Or something other than talk to me." He grabbed his laptop. "I'm tired of it, Lawrence. So we're going to have this conversation. Like other normal adults."

"We're not normal, Yager." She watched him walk back to the bed. "We have wings and go to parties with gods. *You* take them to strip clubs."

"That was Mike's idea," he snarled through clenched teeth. "Last time I listen to his stupid ass."

"What I'm saying, Yager, is... Don't you dare!"

But he'd taken the sheet they'd knocked to the floor earlier in the night and tossed it over her head.

"That is not funny!"

He chuckled as she gave a quick shake and knocked the sheet back off. He'd already plopped himself down in a chair by the bed. Now he propped his big feet on the mattress, right by her legs, and put his notebook computer on his lap. Then he winced as it hit his cock, re-adjusted, and proceeded to ignore her.

She yanked her wrists. No, she wouldn't be getting out of these without causing herself some serious damage. *Damn kinky people with their damn kinky toys.*

"Let me go, Yager."

He didn't even bother looking up from his computer. "Not till we talk."

Gritting her teeth, she settled her body into the bed. She crossed her legs Indian-style, the fallen sheet covering everything from the waist down. "Talk about what?"

"Next weekend."

Neecy frowned. "What about it?"

"I want you to come with me to my house out on Long Island."

"What for?" Yager's eyes slowly looked up and she cringed. "So we can...date?"

"I like how you say that. Like I asked you to come out to the Island to perform satanic rituals."

He might as well have. This was getting involved. They weren't supposed to be getting involved. She was already in too deep. A weekend away without the normal distractions of the City to get in their way—so not a good thing.

"Forget it, Yager."

He shrugged. "Okay." But instead of letting her go, he went right back to his computer.

"Aren't you going to let me go?"

"No."

"What if I have to take a piss?"

"I've got a bucket."

Neecy turned her head to the window so he couldn't see her laughing. He was kind of a funny, oversized geek.

She cleared her throat. "This is ridiculous, Yager. Just let me go."

After a few moments, he looked up from his computer, but not at her face. Instead his eyes focused on her bare breasts.

"Your nipples are hard."

Damn. She'd hoped he wouldn't notice that. But being all bound and at his disposal was making her crazy with lust.

"So?"

"Is your pussy wet, too?" He raised an eyebrow. "I bet it is."

The not lying thing...kind of in her way here. So, instead of answering, she let out an annoyed sigh and stared at him.

Smiling gently, he placed his computer on the floor by the chair, swung his feet off the bed, and walked toward her.

Neecy tried hard to control her suddenly rapid breathing, but it wasn't easy with that big cock of his bouncing around and practically calling her name.

"Yager."

"Neecy."

"Whatever you're planning—forget it."

"Forget what, Lawrence?" He sat down on the bed beside her. "This?" His right index finger circled around one of her hard nipples.

163

"Or this?" He moved to her other nipple and did the same thing. "Or maybe you mean this." He lowered his head and wrapped his lips around her nipple, sucking hard.

Neecy's back arched as her hands gripped the metal bars behind her. The man didn't play remotely fair. This was not fair. No way.

"Dammit, Yager!"

He released her nipple and leaned forward to lick the skin of her collarbone. "Come to my house, Neecy. I promise we'll have fun. You and me in that big house with so many positions to try."

"This isn't fair."

"Nope."

"This is blackmail."

"Yup."

He pulled away from her and Neecy let out a shuddering breath. She knew he wasn't done; she just had no idea what to expect. For some unknown reason, when it came to her, the man was ruthless. She knew loan sharks less relentless.

She caught her lip between her teeth as Yager slowly pulled the sheet off her lap.

"God, you're beautiful."

Must be all the tattoos and gunshot scars. She tugged again at her bonds.

"Forget it, Lawrence. You're not going anywhere until I let you loose. I hope I remember where I put that key." He shrugged. "Anyway, you might as well relax." He stood up and moved around the bed. She watched as he stretched out next to her, his head propped up with one hand. The other hand completely free to do...whatever.

He stared at her for a long time, then said, "You're trapped here, Lawrence. Bound here. You're helpless and all you can do is rely on me and my good nature. What will I do with you for the next few hours?"

How the hell the man knew those words would turn her into a volcano, she'd never know. And he didn't stop. He just kept going down that darkest-desires path and she hated him for it. Because he made it feel so okay. At least with him.

"Right now you're all mine to do anything I want with. Your body belongs to me." His fingers caressed her breasts, her stomach, her neck, but he didn't go any lower. She wanted to squirm, but she also didn't want to give him the satisfaction of knowing he'd gotten to her.

"Come with me next weekend, Neecy."

"It's...it's—" she let out a long shudder as his fingers squeezed her nipple, "—a really bad idea. And you know it."

Because what if she never wanted to leave? What if she wanted to stay there forever letting Will Yager take care of her while fucking her unconscious? She'd never been one of those please-take-care-of-me women, and she wasn't about to start now.

He sat up. "That's not the response I want, Lawrence." While one hand played with one breast, he lowered his mouth to the other.

Neecy's body shook under the sensual assault.

"Too bad. That's the only one you're getting."

She felt his lips curve into a smile around her hot flesh and he released her breast, kissing his way down her chest and stomach. Gritting her teeth, Neecy watched as Yager slowly pulled her legs apart and hooked them over his shoulders.

He leaned against her thigh, his nose rubbing her crotch. He looked up at her and she gave a short shake of her head. "No."

Just from experience she knew what the man could do with unlimited time, his tongue and her pussy at his disposal. He could easily have her committing to marriage and a garden wedding if she didn't stop him now. At least when he fucked her she rarely spoke. Simply because she was too busy just holding on.

He lowered his mouth to her pussy and Neecy's entire body clenched. *"Wait!"*

Yager stopped and looked up at her.

"Okay, Yager. I'll go. I'll go. But just for the weekend. That's it."

"Good. Now that wasn't so hard, was it?"

Then the son of a bitch went ahead and stuck that amazing tongue inside her pussy anyway. Neecy practically ripped the bed frame apart as her entire body arched right off the mattress.

Yager licked her clit a few times, then suckled it between his lips. Neecy's legs tightened around his neck, her body writhing desperately until he abruptly pulled away. "Sorry about that. Just couldn't help myself."

Neecy opened her eyes as Yager got to his knees. He still had her legs on his shoulders and didn't seem in any rush to remove them. Good thing she was relatively flexible.

He grabbed a condom off the bedside table and quickly rolled it on.

"Tied or loose?"

Neecy looked away from Yager, but only for a moment. She trusted him. With her body, she would always trust him. "Tied."

His cock actually jerked at that. On a shuddering breath, he said, "You got it, baby."

Slipping his hands under her ass, he lifted her a bit until his cock rested at the entrance of her pussy. She stared, fascinated. He did have the most beautiful cock, even when encased in latex.

"Look at me, Neecy."

Grudgingly, she pulled her eyes away from her prize and up to his face. That's when he rammed home. They both gasped as Yager pulled her closer, resting his face against her neck. "Goddamn, Neecy. You're fuckin' drenched."

"Your fault," she gasped.

Yager gave a short laugh while he kissed her neck. "Tell me what you want, baby."

"Move, Yager. Fuck me."

He bit her neck, which caused her to whimper. "You know the magic word, baby. Say it and I'll fuck ya raw."

She licked her lips and tightened her legs against his shoulders. "Will. Fuck me, Will."

He laughed low, his fingers digging deep into her hips and ass. "Good girl," he growled as he slammed into her. Over and over he buried his cock into her. Relentless, brutal...delightful. And being unable to control him and what he did to her, being able to trust someone that much—it drove her insane. Her body shaking and sweating. Her pussy holding on to him with a vicious grip. All of it was sending her over the edge. She was losing herself inside Yager. Again.

His tongue slid around her ear, then in it. "Being inside you, Neecy," he whispered desperately, "it feels fuckin' amazing."

And just like that, she came. Her entire body clenched around him, her pussy snapping around his cock like a vise. Yager groaned but kept going. "You're not going to make me come that easy, Lawrence. We've got all day to fuck just like this...it's Sunday!" he cheered.

If Neecy wasn't still coming, she would have laughed.

✧

Didi stopped by Neecy's room and found she hadn't returned. She didn't bother calling her. She knew the girl was probably pussy-deep in Yager.

Good for her! And a long time coming.

Didi headed toward the stairs. She planned on getting some shopping in before the snow hit. The news kept predicting blizzards or snowstorms or whatever the hell they had in this part of the country any day now. Of course, they'd been saying that since the beginning of January.

Already planning her day's shopping, Didi barely noticed her bedroom door was open. She stopped at the top of the stairs, pausing for a moment. Turning around, she walked back to her room and pushed the door open.

"Banana?"

Crossing her arms over her chest, Didi asked, "Why do you always try to give me fruit?"

"I find it's a nice icebreaker."

Stepping into her room, Didi casually kicked the door closed with her foot.

Exactly how many times would a person find a god lying on their bed, reading their *Penthouse Forum?*

"Comfortable?" While Skuld only communicated with the team leaders by giving them sudden and random information, she insisted on physically visiting The Gathering leaders. Didi just never knew when or how.

"Not really," Skuld complained. "You need a better bed."

"Whiner."

A New York Yankees baseball hat obscured Skuld's face, but Didi knew she smiled. She was the Veiled One, but apparently she'd gotten real tired of those things and had moved onto hats, hooded sweatshirts, whatever. Some days she looked like the Unabomber.

"I'm assuming there's a reason you're here."

"Yes."

Skuld leaned her back against the headboard of Didi's bed and crossed her long legs at the ankles.

Sighing, Didi walked closer to the bed. "And I'm sure you'll tell me what it is before I turn fifty."

"And that's right around the corner, isn't it?"

Officially pissed, Didi glared at the goddess. "It is not!" She still had six years to go before that hell on earth started.

"What is it? Why are you here? Besides your desire to go through my porn collection."

"And a very extensive collection you have, too."

"Skuld."

The goddess laughed. "Okay. Okay. I'm here because of you."

"You are?"

"Aren't I?"

Didi shrugged. "I thought about calling to you, but I figured you'd ignore me. It wouldn't be the first time my pleas went unanswered."

"True, but this time is different, isn't it?"

"I've spoken to all the Clan leaders. They know I'm retiring."

"But?"

"But, they keep asking who will replace me. I'd like to be able to give them an answer."

"It's good to want things, Daughter."

Didi sighed in exasperation. "Is there a problem you have with Neecy I'm not aware of?"

"Her guilt bores me."

"Why? Because she cares about what she did in the past? Because she cares about making it right?" Didi shook her head. "I don't understand you sometimes. You'll never find anyone more loyal to you. She takes her commitment to you more seriously than I ever did."

The goddess pushed her baseball cap back on her head a bit, allowing Didi to see her face. Wow. She was gorgeous. Didi always forgot that.

"I know. But I don't need a slave. I need a leader. A battle chief, in fact."

"Neecy's the best warrior you have and we both know it. She's willing to sacrifice everything to serve you and The Gathering."

"I know. I know. Still...I need to see she can do this. I need it proven to me."

Didi's body tensed as she realized something. "You sent the Hunters after us."

"Of course I didn't!"

"But you didn't cloak the Crows, did you?"

Skuld eased off Didi's bed. A tall and overwhelming female, Skuld once rode with the Original Seven. As tempted as Didi may be to start some shit with the goddess, she knew better.

"No. I didn't cloak them."

"You've put us all at risk for Neecy's Trial?"

"I no longer need a politician, Didi. That's what you are and a damn good one. During peacetime, there's no one else I'd consider to lead the Jersey Crows. But things are about to change. And The Gathering must change with it. I need to know she can handle it. I need to know she'll help my Daughters survive."

So angry she could barely see straight, Didi clenched her hands into tight fists. Skuld walked up to her and leaned down until their faces were barely a few inches apart. "Tell her what's going on, Didi...and I'll make sure all of you regret it."

"But—"

"No. You keep your mouth shut. This is Neecy's Trial. You interfere, and as much as I love you, I'll squash you like a gnat. Understand?"

Didi's eyes narrowed, but before she could say anything, Skuld had her hand around Didi's throat, lifting her off the floor. The goddess also stood to her full height, which meant Didi's drop to the floor would be quite lengthy. "Understand?" she asked again.

Gritting her teeth against her anger, Didi spit out, "Yes."

"Good." Skuld dropped her to the ground. Didi stumbled back, her ass almost hitting the floor, but she didn't want to give the cranky bitch goddess the satisfaction of seeing her sprawled out on the hardwood.

"Now," Skuld said with a smile. "I'm off." She held up the *Penthouse Forum*. "Mind if I take this?"

Chapter Fourteen

The week was fuckin' endless. Every day that passed, Neecy's stomach knotted up more and more. She hadn't seen Yager since their all-Sunday marathon. He'd fucked her witless then put her in a cab and sent her home. "You've got school tomorrow, and if you stay I won't let you sleep."

Considerate motherfucker.

All this time she thought nice guys were dull, predictable...ordinary. Yager was anything but dull, predictable, or ordinary. Still, he was definitely the nicest guy she'd ever met.

In just a few hours, she'd be catching the Long Island Railroad out to some place called Westbury where she'd meet Yager who'd then take her to his house in *Old* Westbury—ugh! She hated leaving the City but if she wanted to get laid, she had no choice.

Neecy piled all her term-paper outlines together, shoved them into her desk drawer, and locked it.

To say she was a horny mess after a week with no Yager truly was an understatement. Every cell of her body demanded his attention. Since Sunday she'd gone to school during the day and hunted at night. She never saw Yager. If any Ravens showed up—and they always did at some point—they came without him. But every night, as soon as she'd fallen into bed for a few hours sleep her phone would ring.

"You okay?" that deep voice of his would ask her when she'd picked up.

"Yeah," she'd respond.

"I miss you. I can't wait to be back inside you."

And Neecy's eyes would slide shut and her whole body would throb desperately.

"Talk to you later, baby." Then he'd hang up. No phone sex. No invite over. Nothing to help alleviate the almost painful ache between her legs. She knew what he was doing, too—ensuring her presence Friday night.

The bitch of it was...she was going to make sure her ass was on that train tonight.

How did she let this happen? How did she let this man get to her? But she did and she had no one to blame but herself.

The only thing she could say with any pride was that at least she hadn't lost her edge in battle. If anything, she was a damn bitch meaner. Apparently abstinence really honed those fighting skills.

She couldn't keep going on like this, though. Her crew had started to give her quite the wide berth lately. Especially Arri. Her and her damn color reading. Arri would take one look at her in the morning and practically run the other way. Actually, just that morning she did run. Like the wind. Neecy didn't know the girl could move that fast. But the previous night had been particularly rough. She dreamed about Yager all night with absolutely no relief.

This weekend, though, she and Yager would get a few things straight...after she fucked the living hell out of the man, of course. Once she did that, she'd settle whatever it was between them. Yager needed to accept the fact that she could never be what he wanted. No matter how much she may want to give in.

Sighing, Neecy stood and grabbed her jacket. The phone on her desk rang and she picked it up.

"Dr. Lawrence."

"Hey, Dr. Lawrence."

She hated the smile that spread across her face at the sound of his voice. "Hi." Christ, even her voice changed when she realized it was him. Lower. Huskier. Just like his.

"You heading out?"

"Yeah. Gotta go to the house first, make sure everybody's doing what they should be doing. And not doing what they shouldn't be doing. Then back to my place to pack."

"Don't worry. You won't need much."

The tip of her boot rubbed the leg of her desk. "That right?"

"Yeah. Just a pair of jeans, sweater, couple changes of panties...if you insist. Don't bother with a bra, I like knowing I can put my hand under your sweater at any time and play with your tits."

"Classy."

"That's me."

She chuckled. "Anything else?"

"Don't be late. I really, *really* need to see you. And then I need to fuck you."

Neecy leaned against the desk. It was the only thing preventing her from dropping to the floor. Well at least she wasn't the only one this out of control. She'd hate that.

"Miss me, did you?"

"Yeah, baby. I missed you. More than I could ever say."

Running her hand through her short hair, Neecy begged, "Stop, Yager."

"Nope. Won't ever stop. Not with you, baby. See you tonight."

Then he hung up and Neecy dropped the phone back into its cradle.

"Was that her?"

Will, his feet up on his coffee table, his hands behind his head, simply smiled.

Morgan sat down next to one of her many "sons". Although, she secretly admitted, Will was her favorite.

"I won't see you all weekend, will I?"

His smile grew wider and Morgan jabbed him with her elbow. "Get control of yourself, boy."

"And what you wanna bet she's going to want to have one of her 'conversations'." Will accented that with lovely air quotes before putting his hands back behind his head.

"Poor thing has no idea what she's gotten herself into with you, does she?"

"Not a clue."

Morgan had been a Valkyrie since she was eighteen. She'd known Ravens for more than thirty years and the one thing she could say about all of them—they were the most determined sons of bitches on the planet. Tough, loyal, warrior alpha males. It took a while for them to find "the one", but once they did...Christ, they didn't give up until they got her.

Her husband of twenty-seven years was an Elder Raven. And even with her sagging ass and tits, her disturbing loss of height, and the grey overtaking her once light brown hair, the man couldn't seem to keep his goddamn hands off her. And she would be forever grateful.

At one time, she'd hoped Will would find himself a nice little Valkyrie to take as his own. But she understood why he'd found a Crow. They both had wings and they were both fierce fighters. Plus, the Valkyries just weren't what they once were. None could fight or train the boys to fight. In fact, buxom strippers were a bit of a distraction to teen boys. Actually, they were a distraction to anything with testosterone.

Really, at fifty-four, Morgan should be able to retire. Except that none of these new bitches had learned any adequate healing skills beyond bandaging basic wounds and wrapping up sprained or twisted ankles or wrists. Not impressive.

But she'd damn near hit a wall with Odin and his bullshit. The two of them had a long history and Morgan was pretty sure she found the next crop of Valkyries who could bring them back to their former glory. Still, first things first. And that meant getting Will Yager happy and settled with his vicious little Crow. She didn't know much about Denise Lawrence but Didi respected her and Morgan respected Didi. So that made Morgan feel better. Because what she didn't need was some little twat coming along and breaking her Will's heart.

She'd stab the little bitch in the face before she let that happen.

"I'm out of here, Will. I can't stand the level of mooning I'm witnessing at the moment."

Will looked at her blankly. "What?"

Oh, he was really lost. That little girl wouldn't even know what hit her.

Arri was halfway down the walkway, thinking she was home free, when Janelle's voice stopped her.

"Where the hell do you think you're going, Arri-girl? Alone?"

Cringing, Arri turned to face the bigger woman. Janelle wasn't as tall as Neecy—who was?—but she was more curvy. And definitely meaner. She'd love to have a body like Janelle's. All lush and womanly. Unlike Arri's. Every day Arri wondered what it was like to have tits that actually needed a bra.

Trailing right behind Janelle was Katie. Crap. Just perfect.

"I'm going to the bus stop, then I'm heading into the City."

Janelle looked truly stunned while Katie merely smirked. "Are you nuts?" Janelle snapped. "It's not remotely safe out there for any of us, but especially not for you."

"Why especially not for me?"

"Come on, Arri, be real. If someone is trying to snatch Crows, you're a prime candidate. You can't fight for shit. Your Magick skills are off the charts. And you can do that aura thing."

Arri opened her mouth to argue but realized she couldn't. Everything Janelle said was true. "I'm a mess. I know."

"I never said that. And that's not what I meant. I meant you're powerful, but until you learn to truly control it, you're vulnerable."

"But I really have to go."

Janelle frowned. "Where?"

"A comic book store."

"Arri, come on! There's tons of comic book stores around here."

"This one is expecting me."

Janelle's frown deepened dramatically. "Why are they expecting you?"

Arri scratched her head and kicked the gravel at her feet. "Um...they're expecting me for a signing."

Blinking in surprise, "You? *You* draw comic books?"

"Uh...yeah."

"Under what name? 'Cause I know it ain't under Arri Chang." After she'd helped to convict her father of attempted murder, she changed her last name back to the one on her Korean birth certificate. She didn't change her first name, though. She loved it.

"I write under Arrianna Days."

Janelle stepped back as Katie spun around to stare at her.

"*You're* Arrianna Days?" Katie demanded. "Who writes Viking Eternal? *That* Arrianna Days?"

Arri didn't expect Janelle and Katie to know that. A lot of the Crows were into anime. But American comic books didn't seem like the Crows' thing and Arri never bothered telling them about her side career. Mostly because none of them seemed to care what she did as long as she stayed out of their way. So that's what she did. She stayed up in her room and worked on her books day and night. The Crows didn't even miss her.

She nodded. "Yeah. That's me."

"Holy shit! I gotta tell Rachel and Sophie!"

Arri grabbed Janelle's arm before she could run off. "No!"

"Why?"

Arri looked at the ground again.

"Christ, Arri. You really need to get over the shy thing…it's gettin' old."

"I'm working on it."

When neither Janelle nor Katie said anything else, she looked up at them. "Please don't tell anybody."

"Okay. Okay." Janelle dug out a set of keys and cell phone from her baggy jeans. She tossed the phone to Katie. "Let 'em know where we're going."

"Huh? Wait. Where are we going?" Arri asked, confused.

"To your signing. You can't miss that and we're not letting you go on your own."

"And," Katie added as she speed-dialed the other Crows, "we better get a first edition of issue one—signed."

Arri grinned as she followed Janelle and Katie to the car.

Neecy leaned out her apartment window, her hands gripping the window frame. Her index finger tapped restlessly against the metal. *Where the hell was that cabbie?*

If she missed this train there would be hell to pay.

The vibration of her cell phone against her hip made her cringe. Probably Yager. She bet he thought she would bail out of this at the last minute. Hence the no-sex rule for the entire week. Still, they needed to get some things straight and it wasn't like she was heading toward Africa. It was Long Island, so it only *felt* a million miles away.

She pulled her phone out of its holster and frowned at the number on caller ID. Flipping it open, "Delia?"

"Neece…" Delia's voice faded and returned. Neecy could barely hear her fellow team leader. But snatches of things kept hitting her. "Your team" and "problem".

Neecy straightened up, thoughts of a wild-sex weekend wiped out in seconds. "What? What problem?"

"Arri…trouble. Janelle…"

"Where, Dee?"

"Village. Sharky's Comics."

Neecy had no idea why Arri and possibly Janelle were at a comic book store, but she didn't care. She knew where Sharky's was and all she needed to hear was Arri's name. Slamming the phone shut, Neecy shoved it back into its holster and tore off her jacket and sweater, leaving just her requisite tank top, jeans, and boots. She stepped through her open window, spread her wings, and took to the air.

Janelle and Katie looked at each other and just as quickly turned away. They had to or they'd explode into laughter. Janelle had never seen anything like it. A line of young boys and men stretched out the door of the big shop. All of them there to see and talk to Arri. Painfully shy, painfully weird Arri.

She signed everything they put in front of her except body parts. And when it looked like one guy was going for his johnson, Janelle moved on him so quick, she scared the guy right out of the store. After that, the rest of them watched her warily. Suddenly she became Arrianna Days' bodyguard. Typical.

Everyone always expected the big girl to protect the tiny woman. No one ever tried to protect her.

She'd do this for Arri, though. She realized she liked the kid more than she thought. Little Long Island princess that Arri was, she was still a good person. And Janelle tried really hard not to compare other people's lives against hers. Especially those she considered the rich ones. Although her family lived in the "wrong" neighborhood and struggled to make ends meet, they still loved each other in their own way. Her father's past did eventually catch up with them all, but not because he was still in the life, but because he'd left it behind at the request of his wife.

The one thing Janelle knew that a lot of these rich kids didn't— her family *did* love her.

Katie motioned to her. "How much longer?" she mouthed at her.

Janelle shrugged and looked at the enormous line still snaking out the door. She sighed. It looked like she was going to be bodyguard chick for a little while longer.

Neecy destroyed a kneecap with one brutal kick while she used one of her blades to slash the throat of the man behind her.

When she landed behind Sharky's shop, she didn't find Arri or Janelle or any other Crow. But before she could even figure out why Delia would send her here for no reason, they'd come out of the shadows. Hunters. Big, older white men who moved around her like a lion they found on the African plains.

A setup. A really good one. They must have been recording the Crows' cell calls for months. And it took nothing to clone a phone number to fool her caller ID. And she'd bet money that Janelle and Arri were around this store somewhere in case Neecy called back at the house to check. A freakin' brilliant plan, but considering her past life as a drug dealer, she still should have known better.

There were a lot of them. Fifteen by her count. A lot, even for her. But now she was pissed. She'd had plans this weekend and they pretty much consisted of having Wilhelm Yager inside her until her eight a.m. Monday morning class. Knowing these assholes got between her and what she, at the moment, considered *her* cock, only enraged her beyond anything she'd felt before.

Without even turning around, she grabbed another one coming up behind her. He would have screamed, she guessed, if her talons hadn't torn through his throat.

She ripped through the men, tearing them apart from groin to neck. A blade in one hand and her talons unleashed on the other. One of them actually had a spear, which she got off him easily and proceeded to impale him with. That was kind of cool, but she was too pissed to even enjoy it.

Now, as she yanked the throat out of the man with the shattered knee, she was down to two. And she planned to get rid of them as quickly as possible, catch the first train she could get out of Grand Central and get to Yager. She knew him. He'd think she stood him up. Changed her mind.

That thought kicked her rage up a notch as she grabbed one of the two and slammed his head into the alley wall—a lot—until it was no more than a pulpy mess.

When she realized she couldn't do any more damage to him, she released what was left of him and turned to the last man. He backed up. She saw the fear in his eyes, but it didn't stop her. Nothing would stop her.

She extended her wings and flew at him, but hands she didn't know were there grabbed hold of her wings and flung her across the alley.

Another had been hiding, waiting for the right moment to kick her ass. It was times like this she wished she had a Shifter's sense of smell. She bet nothing ever snuck up on them.

Neecy landed hard against the dirty concrete, grunting as her body hit the ground. Growling, she scrambled to her feet, but a boot in the back shoved her down.

She fought to get out from under the heavy weight on her back, looking behind her in time to see the ax blade swing at her.

"No!"

But it was too late. The blade, glowing with powerful runes, slammed into the part of her wing connecting it to her back, nearly severing it completely. Pain arced through her as blood flew. An artery severed, Neecy knew she only had minutes left...if that much.

The man raised the ax again and she looked into his face. Christ, some average motherfucker was taking out Neecy Lawrence. Well, she'd never hear the end of this in Valhalla.

Grinning, he lifted the ax that would split her spine in half.

And that's when they attacked. She didn't call them this time. Too stunned by the sudden turn of events, she didn't even think about calling them.

They landed on her attacker with a viciousness she'd never witnessed before. It took them seconds to rip him apart and move on the other one who'd been scrambling for the exit out of the alley.

As blood filled her mouth and her crows surrounded her to escort her to Valhalla, Neecy only had one regret...

Until Yager made it to Valhalla himself, he would always think she stood him up.

Chapter Fifteen

"She totally stood you up."

Tye grabbed hold of Yager's shoulders before he could rip the little pissant apart.

"She didn't stand me up," Yager growled between clenched teeth.

"Was she at the station?"

Yager stared at Mike, in the middle of his living room, and wondered what it would be like to tear one of the bastard kid's arms off and beat him to death with it. Why the hell were these two even out on the Island? Knowing Mike, he probably had a bet with Tye that Neecy wouldn't show up. It looked like he won that bet.

"She stood you up, bro. You need to face it."

Tye stepped between them. "Back off, Mike."

"Neecy isn't like that."

Mike rolled his eyes. "Come on, dude!"

Tye sighed. "She's a Crow. She probably had to work."

"You're not helping!" Mike argued. "You're letting him keep this delusion!"

Yager almost had his hands around the kid's throat when Tye pushed him back.

"Wait. Wait!" Tye looked up. "What's that noise?"

Yager worked to control his breathing and his desire to kick the living shit out of Molinski, but once he did, he heard it, too.

"It sounds like...wings."

Yager pulled away from Tye and walked to the French doors leading to his backyard. He'd just pushed the doors open when Mike grabbed his arm.

"Forget it, Yager. She probably sent those goddamn birds to rip you apart."

And that's when they descended. They looked like a black tornado, spinning, swirling in the moonlit yard.

"Holy shit," Tye breathed.

Then they lifted and left Neecy lying there.

"Jesus!"

Yager reached her first, kneeling down beside her. "Neecy?"

Tye had his fingers against her throat. "There's a pulse. But it's faint."

Yager pushed her hair out of her face. "Call Morgan. Speed-dial three."

Tye ran back into the house as Mike rested back on his haunches. "God, Yager. Her wing. It's like someone hacked through it."

But Yager didn't want to hear that right now. He didn't give a shit about her wing. All he cared about was keeping her alive.

"Neecy? Can you hear me, baby?"

She muttered something he couldn't make out and moved her fingers the tiniest bit. It was just enough to show Yager she was still fighting as only Neecy Lawrence could.

"We need to get her inside." He looked at Mike. "Then we need to call the Crows."

Didi looked up from the television as Arri, Janelle, and Katie walked into the living room. It was a quiet night. No job from their goddess, so they'd all decided to watch movies. As usual, they ended up watching *Aliens*...again. They simply couldn't get enough of Vasquez. Any chick who kicked that much ass was an honorary Crow.

"Where have you bitches been?" Didi snapped.

Katie threw herself into one of the recliners. "Oh that's very nice."

"I'm just trying to get into the New Jersey spirit," Didi laughed.

Janelle sat on the edge of the couch. "Katie told Delia we were hittin' a comic book store."

"Well, as usual, no one tells *me* anything."

"You got my shit?" Rachel asked, her arm no longer bandaged; her body nearly back to normal.

Janelle tossed the paper bag to her. She caught it with both hands and pulled out some comics.

"Yes!" Rachel cheered. She waved the thing at Sherri. "I got Vikings Eternal," she sang to her. Then she stuck her tongue out at the woman. In response, Sherri gave her the finger.

It amazed Didi that the majority of the women in The Jersey Gathering were, in fact, over ten years old. 'Cause they didn't act like it.

Giggling, Rachel looked at the comic. "Oh, my God!" she barked out suddenly. She looked at Janelle. "How the fuck did you get it signed?"

Didi reared back as Sherri leaped over her to get a look at some stupid signature.

Janelle shrugged. "They had a few just lyin' around."

Didi watched Arri turn beet red and wondered what the hell was wrong with her when the phone rang. Delia, having recently gotten involved with a fireman, made a mad dash over her sisters and the couch to reach the phone. Both crashed to the floor and the Crows stared at her for a moment, then turned back to the current conversation.

"Why does our sweet Arri look like she's been up to something?" Didi asked.

Arri blinked in surprise. "Me? What? No!"

Janelle rolled her eyes. "Smooth, Arri. Very smooth."

Didi settled into the couch, ready to torture the little goody two-shoes when Delia stood up, the phone against her ear. One look at her face and a bolt of fear snaked up Didi's spine.

"What, Dee?"

"It's Tye." Didi frowned. Delia looked like she was about to cry and she never cried. Even when she got her hand stuck in the toilet that time.

"What's he want?"

She swallowed. "It's Neece, Didi."

Mike watched as Morgan finished re-attaching Neecy's wing. She'd used black thread and surrounded the bed with powerful runes and three other older Valkyries. All four had made it to Yager's house in record time, which was good. If it hadn't been so cold out, Neecy probably wouldn't have lasted this long.

As Morgan continued to work on Neecy's wing, the other three Valkyries chanted in the old language. The entire time Yager watched; his face hard and expressionless. Mike had never seen him like that. Not even in battle. And he prayed he never saw him like that again.

Morgan cut the black thread she'd used on Neecy's wing and tied a knot.

"Okay, boys," she barked over the chanting. "Now the hard part. I've gotta get her wing back in. It'll need time to heal inside her body." She looked at Yager. "But she's a Crow. She's gonna fight like all hell when that pain kicks in. So I'm gonna need you to hold her down."

Mike stepped forward. "I'll do it."

"No." Yager shook his head. "I will."

"Both of you will."

Leaning over the bed, Yager grasped Neecy's shoulders. He glanced at Morgan and nodded. "Do it."

The older woman straddled Neecy's body. "Get her legs, Mike."

Wishing he were anywhere but here, Mike took firm hold of Neecy's ankles, pushing them into the mattress.

"Okay." Morgan took a deep breath. "Here we go."

She lifted the wing and bent it, angling it into Neecy's body. As soon as she bent it, Neecy screamed, desperately trying to pull out of Yager's grasp.

Mike looked up to see the strain on Yager's face. The absolute pain. Not physical but just as damaging.

"Hold her tight! I've almost got it."

It must have suddenly hurt worse, because Neecy began to fight harder. Morgan hadn't been kidding. Crows really put up a fight. Even half dead and barely conscious.

Mike didn't know how much longer Yager could keep this up, knowing how much pain Neecy was in.

"Just a little more..."

On the verge of telling Morgan to get her ancient ass into gear, he almost dropped in relief when she shouted, "Got it!"

She chanted over the wound and Neecy's skin closed over the wing and she stopped struggling. In fact, she stopped moving altogether.

Morgan blew grey-brown hair out of her face. "Okay. I just need to stitch up this wound near her wing and bandage her up." She slid off Neecy, motioning her Valkyrie sisters away with a wave of her hand. "I'll be able to tell you more once she actually wakes up."

Yager released Neecy's shoulders and stood. "You mean *if* she wakes up."

Morgan sighed and briefly glanced at Mike before focusing on Yager. "Don't get maudlin on me, Will. The fight that Crow just put up? She'll wake. I just don't know when. And her wing...well, that we'll just have to see. But I know how you guys are about your wings. So let's hope for the best." She cracked her neck. "After I'm done bandaging her up, I'll need a break."

"I'll watch her." Yager grabbed a chair and put it down next to the bed. "I won't leave her until she wakes up."

"That may be hours."

He sat down. "I don't care."

"Will—"

"Forget it, Morgan." Mike shook his head. "You're arguing to air."

Morgan shrugged. "Fine." She headed to the bathroom.

Mike rubbed the metal bed frame with one knuckle. "Yager, man—"

"Forget it, Mike."

"Look, I'm sorry. About what I said earlier."

Yager leaned forward. His elbows resting on his knees, his hands clasped together, and his eyes locked on the unconscious woman in his bed. "Don't worry about it, Mike. The Crows will be here soon. You better go help Tye. I don't want 'em all up here at one time."

"You got it."

Mike took another look at his friend, turned, and left him to face this one on his own.

Yager helped Morgan clean the blood off Neecy, stitch up a deep slash on her back, bandage up her wound, and tie her left arm against her chest to help the healing of her wing. They again laid her facedown on the bed and Morgan went to wash the blood off her hands.

Pushing the black hair out of her face, Yager stared at the woman who'd taken his heart.

He wouldn't let her die. He'd waited too long for her. She was his. His wife, his mate, his future.

Leaning down, he kissed her ear. "Sleep for a little while, baby," he whispered. "Then get your ass up. We've got plans to make. I'm thinking someplace warm for the honeymoon. You in a bikini in the Caribbean."

He gave a little smile and kissed her cheek. Neecy Lawrence was going to be okay, because he wouldn't accept anything less.

✧

Didi landed at the same time as the other Crows. She didn't even bother looking at Yager's tidy and huge yard as she strode toward the house. Tye pushed open the French doors and Didi moved past him, the other Crows behind her.

"Where is she?"

"Upstairs. Second floor. Third door on the right. Just cut through the living room. And take the stairs in the hallway."

They made it into the hallway, but Mike Molinski stopped them before they even reached the steps. She briefly wondered if she'd have to kick the living shit out of the kid.

"Morgan just finished with her. She's still out cold. Yager doesn't want a ton of people up there."

Didi could hear the rustling of angry wings behind her, but Yager was right. "Okay. I'll go. And you." She grabbed Arri's arm and dragged her toward the stairs. "You're coming with me."

Marching up the stairs, she ordered to the rest of the Crows, "You guys get warm. I'll be back soon."

As they neared the room Tye directed them to, Didi let Arri know exactly why she wanted her there. "You tell me how bad she is. I wanna know. You understand?"

"Yes."

She didn't care if she was scaring the girl. She didn't care about anything except Neecy.

Didi walked up to the doorway and stopped. Yager sat at Neecy's bedside. His elbows on his knees, his hands clasped together, his head down. Arri stepped in behind her, gave a small gasp, and then backed out of the room.

Frowning, Didi followed her and watched as the girl slid down the wall, her eyes shut.

"Oh, my God...is it that bad?" she demanded in a whisper. "Is she dying?"

Arri shook her head. "I don't know. Didi, there's so much pain...I can't see past it."

"Neecy's pain?"

Arri looked up at Didi, her eyes red-rimmed like she might start crying any second. "Yager's."

Finally, Didi saw Arri's ability as something more than a neat parlor trick to entertain the 'Bama Crows whenever they'd come to visit. It was real and this girl could not only "see" what was inside other people, clearly she could feel as well.

Thoughts of retiring again assaulted Didi. She'd clearly hit that point when she needed to move on. Much more and she would become one of those leaders she always hated. Bitter, unreachable, and evil. No, it was time to go, but not until Neecy was better. Not until her second-in-command was running around protecting her "girls", fighting her lust for Yager and generally controlling the bullshit the crazy Crows could start at the drop of a hat. Until she had that Neecy back, nothing would be okay.

She crouched down next to Arri. "You stay here, hon. I'll check on her."

Arri simply nodded, her arms wrapped around her knees, her small body trembling.

Taking a deep breath, Didi stood and went back into the room with Yager. She walked around to the other side of the bed and looked down at her friend. She lay facedown, one arm tucked up under her because they'd tied it close to her body. Her naked back covered in bandages and her head turned to the side. She wasn't asleep because she didn't move at all. Didi wasn't really even sure she was breathing.

Didi leaned down and kissed the top of her friend's head. "You get your ass better and up, Neecy Lawrence," she whispered. "Or there will be hell to pay. I promise you that."

Looking over at Yager, Didi straightened up. "Yager, I'd like to leave her here, if that's okay with you. I know she'll be safe here."

Yager finally looked up at her. She didn't need to read auras to see the man's pain. "Absolutely. She can stay as long as it takes."

But she knew he meant Neecy Lawrence could stay forever.

Yager didn't even realize Didi had gone or that at least two hours had passed until Morgan came in to check on Neecy. After a few minutes, she walked around to his chair and lovingly ran her hands through his hair.

"Will, hon, ya gotta get some sleep."

"I'm really not tired." And he wasn't leaving Neecy. He'd never leave her.

"Okay. But if you do, lay down next to her." She kissed the top of his head. "Let her know you're here."

Then she left, quietly closing the door behind her.

Again Yager lost track of time. Sitting in the dimly lit room, staring at Neecy's prone body and beautiful face. Eventually, though, his body got the better of him. So, taking Morgan's advice, he stretched out on the bed beside her, stomach-down. He caressed her face with one hand until sleep claimed him.

Chapter Sixteen

Even with her eyes closed, the light was killing her. Christ, why would somebody shine a fuckin' strobe light in her face?

Neecy forced her eyes open and realized it wasn't a strobe light but the early afternoon sun that had been irritating the shit out of her.

And, she realized, she was in bed with Will Yager. Not only that, but she got the feeling the cocksucker had tied her up again. She couldn't move her left arm.

That searing pain, though...where did that come from?

She studied Yager's face. He was frowning in his sleep, but still looked as sexy as ever.

Her right hand was free, so she reached out and slid her fingertips across Yager's furrowed brow and down his nose. She smiled.

He really is a cutie.

That's when his eyes slowly opened. They stared at each other for several long moments. Then Yager smiled. A big, wide, relieved grin that completely turned her insides to mush. Christ, she was turning into such a total wuss because of this guy.

"Hey, baby." His voice was low, scratchy with sleep. Even with the pain in her back it completely made her nipples stand up and offer a big "howdy" to anyone in the room.

"Hey."

"How long you been awake?"

"Not long."

"How do you feel?"

"My back hurts."

"Yeah. It will for a little while."

"Why? I didn't fall off something again, did I?"

His grin turned warm. "No, baby. You didn't. You don't remember?"

"Remember what?"

His fingers brushed her cheek and slid down her neck. "You were in a fight."

"I was?" She didn't remember a fight. She remembered waiting for the cab. The cab to take her to the train and the train that would take her to Yager.

"I'm at your house, right?"

"It's a long story, baby. Don't worry about it for now. I just need you to rest."

She really hated when he got evasive on her. But she wasn't in the mood to fight it. At least, not at the moment. "I've gotta pee."

"Okay." Quick as a cat, Yager jumped out of bed and came around to her side. "Let's get you up, baby."

"I can do it on my own."

"Don't start with me, Neecy Lawrence."

Before she could start anything, Yager pulled back the sheet covering her naked body and slowly turned her, lifting her up into his arms. She sucked her breath between her teeth as the pain in her back tripled.

Yager immediately stopped. "Are you okay?"

Gritting her teeth against the pain, "I'm fine. Really." Not really, but her need to pee overrode any pain she may have.

Of course he didn't remotely believe her, but he was nice enough not to push it.

With her tucked into his big arms, Yager moved easily to the enormous bathroom. Carefully he lowered her onto the toilet. Then he stood back and stared at her.

"Well...go on," he pushed.

Her mouth dropped open in shock, but she quickly recovered. "Have you lost your mind? Get out."

"Come on, Neecy. Aren't we past this?"

The last of her control snapped. *"Out!"*

Chuckling, "Okay. Okay. I'm going." He stepped to the doorway. "And, you know, you can do whatever you need to in here. You don't have to keep it to peeing."

"Yager!"

He laughed a little louder and walked out, closing the door behind him.

Arri tapped Didi lightly on the shoulder and the older woman snapped awake, those dark brown eyes swinging her way.

"I...I brought you coffee?"

The hard look on Didi's face faded. "Thanks, hon."

Somehow Arri had gone from "That Girl" to "hon" in pretty much a nanosecond. She didn't question it too much, but she could read it was a true change. She could see it in Didi's colors.

Didi took the coffee from her as Arri looked around Yager's living room. The Gathering had taken over the poor man's house. Completely and utterly. Add in that most of the Tri-State Ravens also showed up and you had a roomful of winged people waiting around. Everyone spoke quietly. Any loud noise causing quite the stir.

The only ones not there were the teens or Elders with families to care for. A separate group of Elders from both sides took the teens to go stay with the Philly Crows until things settled down and it was safe for them to return. The rest of them stayed up the remainder of the night, playing cards, watching bad, late-night TV, or just staring. Lots of staring.

Around dawn, they'd all fallen asleep except for those who were on watch. Apparently, it'd become the role of the Ravens as well as the Crows to protect Neecy. They all felt responsible for her.

Tye walked into the living room from the backyard. He was on his phone, using it as a walkie-talkie. "Okay. Okay. Got it."

Didi sipped her coffee, then looked up at Tye. "What?"

He smiled. "She's awake. She's already yelled at him. Twice."

As one, the Crows all jumped to their feet. Laughing and cheering, they hugged each other. Arri closed her eyes, the sudden burst of light nearly blinding her. But her sense of relief was so intense, she could barely breathe.

She didn't want to think about life among The Gathering without her friend. Neecy had become her family; she wasn't ready to lose that.

She'd never be ready to lose that.

✧

Yager hovered outside the door. As soon as Morgan came up to check on Neecy, she'd tossed him out. Which he didn't appreciate one damn bit. He didn't like the idea of being too far from her. At least not until he knew Neecy could protect herself. Except for still having a vicious tongue, his woman looked small and weak. Well, as small and weak as a six-foot, one-inch woman could look.

Even bruised, battered, bloody, and cranky, Neecy Lawrence was still the most beautiful woman he'd ever known. And he felt like a total shit, because he didn't just want her to get well for her own sake—he wanted her to get well so that he could have her in his arms again. So he could feel her underneath him, moaning his name as she came. It was one of the few ways Neecy let Yager show her how much he cared.

But that was about to change. He was going to take care of her while she recovered whether she wanted him to or not. He didn't want to hear any shit from her about it either.

"Ow!"

Yager heard Neecy's barked exclamation of pain and he refused to let her or Morgan shut him out any longer. He threw open his bedroom door and both women looked up at him. Morgan had Neecy's hand and seemed to be checking it. Yager worked hard not to think too hard about the fact that Neecy looked damn adorable in his sleeveless Knicks basketball T-shirt. Although she looked even better naked.

"What's wrong?"

Neecy rolled her eyes. "Oh, this is going to get really old."

"I heard you cry out in pain."

"I must have bent my finger back during the fight is all. Morgan was checking it to see how bad it is." The vision of Neecy fighting some unknown enemy all alone made his blood run cold every time. Whereas she acted like it was really no big deal. "So feel free to leave now."

"Forget it, Lawrence. I'm not going anywhere."

"Will Yager!" Morgan dropped Neecy's hand. "I know I raised you better than that!"

"No, you didn't."

Smirking, Morgan turned back to Neecy. "You might as well forget it, honey. I know that determined look in those steely grey eyes."

"Yeah. Me, too," Neecy muttered as she eased herself back against the bed's headboard.

Morgan grabbed her coat from off the foot of the bed. "Your finger's not broken. Maybe a little sprain, but I don't even think it's that bad. Just rest it and try not to mess with it. Try ice if it really starts to hurt."

She tugged on her coat. "Now I know I don't have to tell you not to push yourself, right? As a Crow, you're healing faster than anyone on the planet, but I still want you staying quiet for the next couple of days."

"Yeah, but—"

"No buts, Neecy Lawrence! I don't want to hear it. Didi and the rest of the Crows can handle anything that may come up. You don't need to fight every battle."

"So I'm just supposed to sit here? Doing nothing?"

"Wow. You *do* understand me." Morgan headed toward the door. "But I'm sure this man right here—" she patted Yager's shoulder as she walked past, "—will be more than happy to keep you occupied for a little while. Right, Will?"

Morgan walked out, the door slamming behind her.

Yager looked up to find Neecy staring at him with narrowed eyes.

"I didn't tell her to say that, ya know. So get that look off your face."

"Is there anyone here that doesn't know we're fucking?"

"Is that really all we're doing, Lawrence? Just fucking?"

She tried to fold her arms across her chest, but quickly remembered the left arm tied tight against her body, her fingers close to her throat. She growled in frustration.

"This is going to make me nuts!"

He'd never seen Neecy so openly agitated before. He had to admit—he kind of enjoyed it.

"You leave your arm alone." He strode to the bed. "It's to help your wing heal."

Neecy looked away from him so quickly, he almost didn't catch the look in her eye. Panic?

"What is it, baby?"

"Stop calling me that!"

Grunting in annoyance, Yager got onto the bed next to her.

"Look, let's get some things straight, okay? I'm going to call you baby, because I like it. And you like it, too, you just keep being difficult."

Her head snapped around to glare at him. "How the fuck do you know I like it?"

"Because when I'm inside you and call you baby, your pussy practically turns into a river. That's how I know."

Neecy stared at him for several seconds, then shook her head. "Jesus, Yager. I was hit in the back with an ax. I look like utter shit. I'm covered in frickin' bruises and scrapes and open wounds. And you still..."

"Want you? Yeah, baby. I still want you. Which is why I need you to get better." He brought his hand up to cup her chin, forcing her to keep looking at him. "You rock my universe, Dr. Lawrence. And I almost lost you."

"Yager..." He gripped her chin tighter as she tried to turn away.

"I'm not letting you avoid this, Neecy. Avoid *us*. I've let you get away with it this long, but not anymore. Life's too short, baby. So get over your bullshit."

She opened her mouth to probably yell at him or tell him to get away from her. But before she got the chance, he kissed her. He'd been wanting to since she woke up, but he knew it had to wait. Now, though, he saw she needed a little reminder of what they did to each other. What they'd always do to each other—drive each other crazy.

His tongue swept inside her startled mouth and she moaned, her head tipping to the side so that their mouths fit together better. Her free hand lay across his chest, her fingers digging into his T-shirt and muscle. Their kiss went from sweet and warm to hot and wet in seconds, and his inner voice kept yelling at him to stop. She was still recovering. Not ready for him to throw her down on the bed and fuck her until she agreed to marry him. His body, however, just wasn't listening, and neither was hers.

But Tye and Didi walking into the room? Well, that stopped it. Especially when Didi yelled, "Good Lord, Yager! How about waiting until she's off the freakin' critical list before groping her like a hooker!"

How exactly did the man keep doing this to her? With only a kiss he could make her all wet and needy. It was shameful.

She yanked away from him. So fast, she caused a shock of pain to race down her back. But she refused to let it show because Yager and Didi would be all over that.

"Well, you seem to be doing well, Neecy."

Neecy looked at Tye. Not bothering to hide her sarcasm, "Much better, thanks, Tye."

His low chuckle made her want to slap his face. Christ, what was wrong with her? She actually liked Tye...usually.

"So, what do you want?"

"You are the worst patient." Didi sat on the bed. "You going to keep being this miserable?"

"Yes. Any other questions?"

"Oh, man. You're in for a time, Yager. Sure you don't want us to take her cranky fat ass—"

"Watch it."

"—back to the Bird House?"

Suddenly fear he may send her back to Jersey filled her system and she hated herself for it. She couldn't stay here and let this man take care of her. It was one thing for her sisters to care for her, they did it for each other. She'd nursed many of them through things as simple as summer colds to the more complex open wounds following knife fights. But, no. She couldn't stay and take advantage of the man's hospitality any long—

"Not on your life, Didi. She stays here."

Neecy's head snapped around. Yager sounded so adamant. Like he was willing to fight Didi on this, and few people fought Didi on much these days.

"Okay. Okay. Calm yourself. Just trying to let you off the hook. I know how difficult and evil she can be."

"I like her difficult and evil."

"Ya know I'm right here," she snapped.

They both looked at her and then back to each other. "Look, Yager, you wanna keep the evil heifer, be my guest," Didi joked while standing. If she were any closer Neecy would wrap her hand around the woman's throat. She didn't care her leader was kidding. Calling her "heifer" and talking about her fat ass in front of Yager, however, was not cool.

"Okay. I'll keep her. I mean, you don't want her back or anything, right?"

"Nah. Keep her."

Now they were just playing with the piranha. *Pricks.*

"By the way, Yager, the Crows have made themselves kind of at home. Until our little Neecy can walk herself out of here, we plan on sticking around. Hope that's okay."

"Sure. You guys are always welcome."

"Come on, Tye. Let's leave these two alone."

"You sure that's okay? I mean, she's supposed to be recovering, not getting herself all worked up."

Neecy felt raw embarrassment as Tye and Didi left.

"I hate them."

"He's right, though. I need to leave you alone until you get better."

She didn't like the sound of that either, even though he was right.

"Whatever." She yawned and rubbed her eyes.

Yager reached down and pulled the comforter up, covering them both. "Snuggle down, baby."

She hesitated for a moment, but her last forty-five minutes of activity was catching up with her. Morgan warned her she'd find herself getting tired quickly, at least for a little while, so she decided not to fight it.

She slid down and turned on her right side.

Yager moved up behind her. "Tell me if this hurts." Then he spooned her. His arm around her waist, his legs pushed against the back of her thighs, and his nose nuzzling the back of her neck.

The last thing she felt at the moment was pain.

So she didn't say anything and, instead, went to sleep.

Feeling safe and...loved.

Waldgrave took the ax from his disciple's hand.

Without any prompting, the disciple offered, "He fought well. They all did."

"Is this all that's left?"

"Yes. Those birds of hers came. They ripped him apart in seconds."

Too bad. No proper funeral rites for him.

"And her?"

"Dead. He split her wing at the base."

"And her body?"

"The birds took her."

Back to her other females. Good. The sight of her torn body would have them mad with bloodlust—making the rest easy.

✧

Mike stared up at the trees, barely noticing Tye when he pushed his shoulder then handed him a cup of coffee. "Am I the only one freaked out by them?"

Tye looked up. "As long as we're taking care of her, we'll be fine."

Mike wasn't so sure. He found hundreds of crows and ravens watching them a little bit unnerving. Especially when the one woman who controlled them was still recovering. Morgan said she'd be sleeping a lot. What if they decided to go wild while she was sleeping?

"This is not good."

"Don't be a pussy, Molinski."

Of course Tye wasn't afraid. Tye who had friends many would consider much less than human.

En masse, the birds suddenly took flight—and headed right into Yager's bedroom.

"Bro!"

Now Tye frowned. "Uh...we better go check."

They walked past the women and other Ravens who were eating, talking, or sleeping. Mike liked the fact The Gathering didn't seem distracted by him in the least. He liked a good challenge. To be honest, the Valkyries were way easy.

Getting to Yager's room was simple. But getting inside was another matter altogether.

"Should we knock?" Mike asked.

Tye shrugged. "I don't know. I don't want to startle anybody, if ya know what I mean."

He knew exactly what Tye meant. So, silently, Mike eased Yager's bedroom door open.

Then he stared. So did Tye.

They were everywhere. Just sitting there. Yager was out cold in his bed, but Neecy sat by the window. One enormous crow on her shoulder rubbing her head against Neecy's cheek. A giant raven on her knee. Neecy reached over and rubbed her index finger over the bird's head.

Mike and Tye looked at each other. After a moment, they turned to Yager. They waited and, suddenly, he snapped awake. They knew Yager would sense their presence. It was part of their training.

Yager's eyes immediately focused on them and, a few seconds later, the birds that had invaded his room.

His eyes grew wide as he surveyed his room while slowly sitting up.

"Uh...baby? Is everything okay?"

She nodded without looking at him. "Sure. I was just thinking I wanted to see them, to thank them. And they came." She smiled. "Like they always do."

"That's great, baby." Yager slid off the bed, very careful of where he placed his big feet. "Neecy. I'll be back in a sec."

She nodded as the raven gripped her index finger with its talons.

Stepping very carefully, Yager walked across his bedroom and followed Mike and Tye out into the hallway. He closed the door behind him and then all three men let out huge breaths.

"That didn't happen. And we're never discussing it again."

"Good plan," Mike choked out.

"What ya got there, princess?"

Arri, kneeling on the living room floor, gasped in surprise as Liar-Mike Molinski snatched Neecy's cell phone out of her hand. She'd pulled it from Neecy's torn and blood-encrusted jeans, going through the last incoming and outgoing calls, when Molinski took it from her.

He dropped onto Yager's couch, his inhumanly large feet up on the fine leather.

Growling, Arri reached over and tried to grab the phone back. Without much effort, Molinski held it from her grasp simply by holding it over his head and moving it around.

"Come on, sweet cheeks. Tell me what's going on."

"Give it!"

To her utter horror, Molinski held the phone in one hand—and still out of reach—while he used his other hand to hold Arri at bay—by pushing back on her forehead.

Suddenly she felt eight years old again and the school bully had once again singled her out.

"Tell me what you're doing and I'll give it back to you."

"I don't have to tell you anything!" She tried to force Molinski's hand off her head, but it was useless. Not surprisingly, he was seriously strong.

Seconds away from bursting into frustrated tears, another hand reached over her and snatched the phone from Molinski's grasp. Arri looked up in time to see Janelle ball up her fist and punch Molinski over and over again in his stomach. By the sixth hit, she pulled away then suddenly swung back again, nailing Molinski right in the groin.

"Ow! You Amazon bitch!" He doubled over and turned away from both women, his head buried in the couch cushions.

"Here." Janelle tossed her the phone and Arri caught it, almost dropped it, caught it, dropped it, and crawled after it as it skipped across the floor.

She didn't even have to look at Janelle to know the woman probably rewarded her with one of her patented headshakes. She seemed to save those only for Arri.

When she finally got her hands on the phone, Arri found herself kneeling in front of Delia.

"Whatcha doin'?" Delia asked.

Arri took a deep breath, working really hard to put those frustration tears right back where they belonged. She'd cried enough in front of these women. "I found Neecy's phone in her clothes. I was checking the incoming and outgoing messages from Friday night. Thought it might tell us something."

Delia stared at her in surprise. "Good move, Arri-girl. Find anything?"

"Yeah. You called her."

Delia blinked in surprise and glanced between Arri and Janelle. "That night? No, I didn't." She shrugged at Janelle. "I was waitin' for the fireman to call."

Janelle shook her head. "You and your thing for firemen."

"Hello? They're hot."

Arri opened the phone, found the last incoming message in Neecy's caller ID, and handed the device to Delia. "Isn't that your number?"

Delia stared at it. "I don't get it. I didn't call her. Really."

Janelle walked up behind Arri, grasped her under her arms, and easily lifted her to her feet. "Then how does her phone have you calling at that time?"

"How the hell should I know?"

197

Arri had a good idea, but before she could say it, Molinski barked from his huddled position on the couch, "They cloned it, you idiots!"

"Shut up!" Janelle screamed it so loudly, her voice even dropping a few octaves, Arri was ready to bolt out of the room. But when she turned back around Janelle had the prettiest grin on her face. She winked at Arri and said to Delia, "You know what? I bet they cloned it, Dee."

Delia grinned right back, both of them thoroughly enjoying torturing Molinski. "You're absolutely right, Janelle. You're so smart."

"Bitches," Molinski muttered from the couch.

Janelle gave Arri a quick affectionate head scratch before stepping away from her. "And if they could clone your number—"

"They've been listening to us for months...at least," Delia finished.

The realization of what had been going on for quite some time hit both women hard. Their smiles faded as Janelle's head dropped slightly. "Holy shit."

Delia closed the phone with an angry snap. "We are such dumbasses."

Arri folded her arms in front of her chest. "We didn't know."

"Didn't know what?"

Tye walked into the room and Arri watched in fascination as Janelle's punky, tough colors dramatically shifted as soon as Tye appeared. Of course, his did, too, once he realized Janelle was standing there. Their colors swirled near and around each other, still testing but, unlike Neecy and Yager's, they hadn't quite begun to flow together. Still, Arri knew it was only a matter of time.

Delia, unaware of the growing tension between Tye and Janelle, held up Neecy's phone. "The Hunters, we think they've been monitoring our calls. Cloning our numbers."

Tye shrugged his enormous shoulders. "Makes sense. But don't worry about it. I know somebody who can get all of you new phones, new numbers by tonight. I just need a list."

Nodding, Delia tossed Neecy's phone back to Arri. She almost had it, but it slipped out of her hands, flew across the room, and binged Molinski right in the forehead as he sat up.

"Ow!"

As habit, Arri immediately went to apologize, but Tye's giant hand gently covered her mouth. "Why do I bet he somehow deserved that?" he muttered softly into her ear.

Arri looked up at him and nodded.

✧

"I don't want any more soup. And if you don't make a move, I'm going to chop all your pieces in half."

Yager looked up from the chessboard sitting between them on the bed. "Don't rush me. When I play chess I take my time. I savor the game."

Growling out, "Again with the savoring? What is it with you?"

Rolling those gorgeous steel grey eyes, Yager looked back at the chessboard—and stared.

She glared at the top of his head. She'd been staring at the top of his head for fifteen minutes now.

No. If she looked at the top of his head much longer, she was going to start ripping his hair out. And she really liked his hair.

Neecy allowed her gaze to wander around Yager's bedroom. So far, the only part of the house she'd actually seen. Yager wouldn't let her leave. He brought her food, water, magazines, books. Anything she wanted, he made sure she got. He only let Morgan, Didi, and a few of the Crows at a time in to visit her. He insisted on shoveling soup down her throat like it was some kind of cure-all.

Yager's bedroom in his Long Island home was as beautiful as his City apartment. And just like his other bed, the frame was big, stainless steel, and perfect for fucking in. But, no. Yager wouldn't touch her except to hold her when she slept. She'd initially thought maybe he'd lost interest, seeing as her entire body resembled one big, bloody bruise. Then she'd realized he kept disappearing into the bathroom to take showers. Lots and lots of showers. He had to be the cleanest man on the planet.

She had the distinct feeling those showers were mighty cold.

As Yager contemplated the chessboard like the Rosetta Stone, Neecy looked at the bedroom doorway and freedom. That's when she saw it.

Silently, Mike Molinski ran down the hallway, a wet towel in his hand. Tearing after him a few seconds later was a very wet and extremely naked Janelle.

Yager's hand rose over the chessboard, but he shook his head and lowered it again.

Mike came tearing back, still swinging that towel over his head.

Yager clucked his tongue against his teeth, but didn't lift his head.

Janelle leaped past the doorway. A few seconds later, she and Mike reappeared. She had Mike in a headlock, but he wasn't giving up that towel. Both were still completely silent, even as Janelle repeatedly and brutally punched Molinski in the face.

If Neecy couldn't hear Yager's geeky "thinking" sounds, she would have assumed she'd gone deaf.

The struggling pair stumbled out of Neecy's line of sight.

"You're trying to box me in, Dr. Lawrence." Yager flashed her a gorgeous grin. "But I'm not falling for it."

His head dropped down and Janelle came back into sight. She held one end of the towel and desperately tried to yank it away from Mike, who had the other end. She dragged him across the hallway floor, but he still wouldn't let it go. And Neecy knew that grin of his would set Janelle's hair on fire.

"Aha! I got it!" Yager made a move, but Neecy had completely lost interest now that Tye had suddenly appeared. He picked Mike up and disappeared with him. She knew what he did with him, though, as the muffled sounds of someone tossed down a flight of stairs made it into the bedroom.

The towel in his hand, Tye walked up to a shivering, visibly raging Janelle. He held out the towel to her and she snatched it from him, storming off. Too much dignity to bother wrapping it around herself.

Tye watched her walk away. Actually, that was a little tame. It was more like he absorbed every detail of Janelle's dimpled ass walking back down the hallway. When one of the many bathroom doors slammed closed, Tye flashed Neecy a delicious grin. He shrugged, wiggled his eyebrows, and walked away.

Yager leaned back, his palms flat on the mattress, his arms propping him up. "Checkmate, baby."

He looked so hurt when she burst out laughing and couldn't stop.

Yager gratefully took the cup of coffee Delia handed him and walked over to the glass doors leading from his kitchen to his backyard. Quietly he stood next to Tye.

"She doing okay?" Tye finally asked.

"Yeah. So far."

"Her mood getting any better?"

"Hey, cut her some slack. I'd love to see how well you'd take an ax to the back."

"I don't have a problem with it. I'm just not used to seeing Neecy Lawrence expressing an actual..."

"Emotion?" Yager helpfully offered when Tye seemed at a loss.

"Yeah. Exactly."

"She's too exhausted and drained to have her usual walls up."

"Which you're not minding one bit."

"Nope. Not really."

Delia came up behind Yager. "I'm making her a grilled cheese sandwich. I'm afraid if you bring her soup again, she'll hurt you."

Watching Mike walk across the backyard, Yager said, "Soup is good for her."

"Okay, okay. I'll give her both. Grilled cheese sandwich and tomato soup. Happy now?"

"Very."

The trio stopped speaking as one of Neecy's crows suddenly dive-bombed Mike.

"Whoa!" Delia stepped closer as Mike swung his arms to get the bird away from him. "Yager, I thought you said Neecy was asleep."

"She is asleep. She was out cold when I came down here."

Two more crows dived at Mike, freaking the poor kid out. Then six more.

"Then what the..."

Tye sipped his coffee as Mike did his best to keep the birds away from him. "It's not Neecy," he offered casually. "It's that meat and birdseed I put in his pockets."

Delia covered her mouth in surprise, but she couldn't stifle the laughter.

Yager shook his head. "Why?"

They watched as Mike ran to the doors, trying to get in. But, apparently, Tye had locked them and seemed in no rush to unlock them.

"He knows why."

Mike slammed his fist against the thick glass and pointed at Tye while the growing number of birds steadily attacked his coat and therefore him.

"You motherfucker!"

"See?" Tye took another sip of his coffee. "Told you he knows why."

Neecy stared out Yager's bedroom window at the Crows and Ravens hanging around in his backyard. She didn't even know anyone was in the room with her until she felt a small hand on her shoulder.

She smiled down into Arri's concerned face. "Hey, kid."

"You okay, Neece?" She knew Arri'd read her colors and already knew she wasn't okay.

Neecy shrugged with one shoulder. "I'm breathing."

"Is that good enough?"

"Better than I had a right to hope."

"You're worried about your wings." It wasn't a question.

"It sounds so stupid when you say it out loud."

"Why? Those wings have been a part of you for years."

"Yeah. But it seems awfully petty to worry about my wings when I could easily be having this discussion in Valhalla with Odin."

"But you're not. You're here. And you're still a Crow, Neecy. You'll always be a Crow."

"Yeah. A maimed, useless Crow."

"Neece—"

Before Arri could finish her thought, Yager walked into the room with a pile of books and DVDs for Neecy. He looked at both women and immediately frowned.

"What's wrong?"

Neecy didn't lie, but that didn't mean she wouldn't let others lie for her. She glanced at Arri and immediately the girl said, "Oh, I'm just whining. Mike is being such a...a..."

"Asshole?"

"Schmuck?"

"Fucker?"

"Spastic colon?"

Arri giggled but turned her face away. She was even shy about laughing.

"Yeah. All of the above," she practically whispered.

Yager dropped his pile of stuff on the bed. "Well, I wouldn't sweat it, Arri. I think he'll be mellow for at least a few hours."

Neecy's eyes narrowed. "Okay. What did you guys do to him?"

Yager blinked innocently. "Baby, we didn't do anything to Mike."

"You leave him alone, Wilhelm Yager." Now both Arri and Yager stared at her. "What? I like Mike. He's funny."

Disgusted, Arri walked out while Yager continued to stare at her.

"*What?*" Neecy asked again.

After four full days of bedrest, Neecy couldn't take it anymore. She was bored beyond anything and tired of sitting or lying around. So, when Yager left the room to get her something to drink, she slipped out of bed and slowly made her way downstairs.

As she carefully walked, her free hand against the wall to keep her steady, she marveled at the rest of Yager's house. She'd felt like his apartment was luxurious even with all that manly steel. But his house was just astounding. Tasteful, comfortable, inviting. She could easily see herself spending time here.

Dammit. She'd been afraid this would happen. Afraid she'd get comfortable. Afraid she'd let Yager in. And dammit, she had. He'd barely left her side for four days and he had yet to get cranky about it. She moved, he was up asking her what she needed. She sighed, he rubbed the back of her neck. She burped from all that damn soup, and he chuckled.

His treatment of her should annoy the living hell out of her, but it didn't. Actually, she liked it. A lot. It almost made her forget what she was really scared about.

Neecy made it down the stairs without Yager catching her, but as she reached the last step Mike stepped around the corner. He looked at her with one raised eyebrow. "What are you doing out of bed, young lady?"

"Don't you start, Molinski. I couldn't take it anymore. So I'm making a break for it. And what happened to your face? Did something peck you?"

"I'm not discussing it." His adorable blue eyes strayed to her hand gripping the handrail. Yeah, getting to the living room wouldn't be easy, but she was willing to take it one slow step at a time.

Mike moved up close to her. "I swear, Lawrence. You spoiled chicks."

"Yeah. Catholic orphanages are known for the way they spoil their kids."

He smiled as he reached down, wrapped his arms around her waist, and lifted her up. He carefully avoided touching her major wounds and didn't jostle her tied arm.

"Well aren't you gallant for a boy from the 'hood," she joked, relieved she wouldn't have to make that walk to the living room.

"Don't make me drop you, sweetie."

The pair walked into the living room and right into Yager. He had her requested juice box in his hand and the deepest frown possible on his face. Glaring, he watched the two.

Mike didn't hesitate. "Take her." He practically threw Neecy into Yager's arms, then grabbed the juice box and walked away.

"Don't look at me like that. I couldn't stand another second trapped in that room."

"Fine."

Yager walked her over to the couch and sat her down. Shoved the television remote into her hand and a book on the lives of computer hackers in her lap.

"Happy now?"

She smiled up at him, knowing it would annoy him. "Ecstatic."

With a grunt, he headed back to the kitchen. A minute later, he came back out and handed her another juice box. Then he stretched out on the couch, laid his head in her lap—after pushing the book out of his way—and went to sleep.

Yager woke up when it was dark outside. His head was still in Neecy's lap, but the Crows now filled the room. Not the birds— thankfully. The women. They spoke and laughed in whispers and he realized they were trying not to wake him up.

Yawning, he turned on his back and looked up into Neecy's battered but beautiful face.

"Hey."

"Hey. Sleep okay?"

"Yup. I had your sweet scent to keep me company."

"Awww," all the Crows sighed out.

"Shut up or I'm calling my birds," Neecy barked.

"Someone's bitchy," one of the Crows laughed, then the sound on the television went up as did The Gathering's conversation. He glanced over and realized that yes, they were actually watching reruns of *Buffy the Vampire Slayer.*

Neecy's free hand slid through his hair. He closed his eyes and sighed. Man, he could easily get used to this. She fit perfectly into his world—even injured and cranky as all hell—the same way she fit in his arms when asleep.

Neecy was perfect. Perfect for him. And he wanted her healthy and well and living with him forever.

"They're getting ready to order some Chinese food. Want any?" she asked.

"Yeah. I'm starving."

Janelle walked in from the backyard. "You put your hands on me again, Molinski, and you'll be scratching those tiny balls with a claw."

Yager winced as Janelle stormed into the room, leaving the doors wide open. *Goddamn Mike.* Of course, one look at the big blonde girl's face and Yager was sure she could handle herself quite nicely, but still, no touching without permission. Especially when it came to the Crows. "We're going to need a credit card," she announced to the room. "The Ravens ordered half the menu. You'd think they'd never eaten before."

"Didi's got a card," Katie offered as she lounged in one of his massage recliners. She had it going full blast and appeared to be enjoying herself.

"Then where the hell is Didi?" When no one answered, "*Didi!*"

Now Neecy winced. "Yo! Janelle! Could you act like ya got a little class?"

"Could you—" Janelle mimicked back to Neecy, "—back the fuck off?"

Neecy glanced at Yager, and he suddenly realized she was embarrassed. He didn't know why, though. Especially when Mike ran backward into the room through the doors Janelle just came through. Yager could hear Tye yelling, "Go long, bro! Go long!" Then the football hit Mike in the chest. He caught it, but it flipped him over the couch, his head slamming against Yager's two-thousand-dollar coffee table.

"Fuck! Where'd this table come from?"

Now *he* was embarrassed. Did Mike not have any sense at all? Stupid question. Of course he didn't.

Didi stormed into the room, the *National Enquirer* in her hand. "You know what I would love from y'all? If I could take a shit in peace just once in my goddamn life!"

Neecy rubbed her eyes. "Oh, my God. This is spiraling," she muttered low so only he could hear.

Yager turned on his side, facing her, and whispered, "Now that you're getting better, they're getting comfortable."

"God, I'm sorry, Yager."

"About what?"

She glanced around the room. They were all talking at once. A bunch of loud, noisy birds. "For them getting so fucking 'comfortable'."

"There's nothing to apologize for." He motioned to Mike. "Really. There's nothing."

Neecy looked over and they both watched as Mike—who recovered quite nicely from his dance with the coffee table and now stood by the couch—decided to rest his forearm on the top of Arri's head. She had been standing quietly by him waiting to put in her food order, Yager guessed, based on the fact she held the menu in her hand. Painfully shy, she probably hated that Mike had just made her the center of attention.

"Hey! Get off me!" She slapped at his hands.

"Oh, come on. Like you've never been used as a stool before."

Gasping in indignation, Arri jumped away from him. "You...you..."

"Say it, Arri," Janelle urged.

Apparently that was all the prompting little Arri needed. "You a-hole!"

The room grew quiet. Everyone staring at Arri.

"What?" she finally asked.

Janelle sighed. "Katie."

Without relinquishing her chair, and therefore her massage, "Mike Molinski. You put your motherfuckin' hands on me again and I'll cut off your nipples and make them into a fashionable headband."

Janelle nodded. "That's what you say."

Shaking her head, Arri stuttered, "I...I can't say that."

"What's the matter, princess?" Mike pushed, although Yager had no idea why. "You gonna cry—again?"

Dark brown eyes turned on Mike like two lasers. Her eyes swept from his head to his feet and back again. Then she said the strangest thing. "Your colors are sad and lonely and desperate. And I hope you drown in them."

With that, she handed the menu to Tye, who'd just walked into the room. "Get me the shrimp lo mein." Then she stormed out.

Janelle shook her head. "Damn. That was some cold shit from our little Arri."

"What the hell did that even mean?"

Katie smiled, her eyes closed as she enjoyed the massage. "It means get used to the idea of being a lonely, bitter old man one day, Molinski. Sort of like how you're a lonely bitter young man right now."

Would it really kill her sisters to act like they didn't just roll up from the local bar? As with most Crows, they'd made themselves at home in Yager's gorgeous house. Normally, Neecy wouldn't complain, but she didn't like the idea of them taking advantage of Yager.

He didn't have to do this. Didn't they realize that? He was letting them stay here out of the kindness of his giant geek heart. She wouldn't let anyone abuse that. Even The Gathering.

"You know," Mike began casually. "We are starting to run out of food. Perhaps you lovely ladies could do a little grocery shopping while you're out."

Yager settled his head more comfortably into Neecy's lap as Janelle's arms crossed in front of her chest. Uh-oh. Her "you're pissing me off" stance. This couldn't be good.

"Why don't you got the fuckin' food?"

"Aren't you more comfortable getting the food...cooking the meals..." Mike smiled. "Washing the clothes?"

It was like the kid had a death wish or something.

"Why would I do that when clearly you're much more comfortable being a whorish bitch than the rest of us?"

Mike opened his mouth to say something, but Tye slapped him in the back of the head. "Stop it." He walked over to the couch and climbed up so that his butt rested on the back of it, while his feet were on the seat. Yager didn't seem remotely annoyed that his buddy's enormous feet were resting on his expensive leather couch. "And you're going. I'm sure the ladies could use a big strong Viking like yourself to tote that barge and lift that bale."

"Yeah, but—"

"Go to the kitchen and see what we need," Tye ordered.

Looking like the kid she always thought he was, Mike headed toward the kitchen. Janelle smirked; about to say something that she knew would piss Mike off.

"Cut it, Janelle," Neecy warned.

Janelle didn't bother hiding her smile as she winked at Neecy. *What a bonehead. I'm surrounded by boneheads.*

Tye held the menu between two big fingers. "So, what are we doing, exactly?"

Janelle dropped to one knee and laced up her sneaker. "Getting dinner and I guess groceries now."

Staring straight at Janelle, Tye grinned. Neecy'd seen that same grin on Yager's face more than once. Usually right before he put his tongue in her pussy.

"In other words you're asking me what I'd like to eat tonight?"

Neecy glanced down at Yager, then they both turned away before they started laughing. As it was, Neecy still sort of snorted.

"Yeah." Janelle stood up, completely oblivious. "That's why you have the menu." Confusion on her face, she walked off into the kitchen. Tye looked at Neecy.

She shrugged. "We're not real good with subtle."

"I'm startin' to see that."

Stomach-down on his bed, Yager hugged his pillow and wiped his tears with his thumb while Neecy laughed hysterically from under the covers.

"That had to be the most bizarre dinner I've *ever* experienced."

They spoke in tight whispers since they didn't know who might be outside Yager's door, but it wasn't easy.

"And," Neecy choked from beneath the covers, "it just kept getting worse as the night wore on."

Yager was still shocked no one had come to blows. Although it didn't all start at the dinner. It started at the grocery store. Apparently Mike and Janelle argued about what to buy since it would be going on Yager's account. According to the Crows, it got so bad, eventually Mike called Janelle "Bigfoot". Which prompted him to ask about her actual foot size. This seemed to be a sore point for Janelle, who placed Mike in a headlock and repeatedly slammed him into the glass doors of the frozen food section. Katie separated them by punching both of them in the back of the head.

Picking up the Chinese food seemed to go without incident, the Crows and Ravens even working together to set up the table and lay out the food. All went fine—until they started eating.

Mike decided to hit on one of the girls. Normal behavior for Mike when he was slightly bored. But Mike wasn't used to having a Greek chorus made up of a tiny Asian girl who continually told the entire table, "He's lying, ya know? He is *such* a liar."

For once, Mike had no idea how to handle this. True. He *was* lying. But that wasn't exactly new for Mike. He lied to women all the time. Prided himself on it, in fact. The only people he didn't lie to were his Raven brothers. Of course, that usually meant they heard details about his conquests they could have done without. But even Yager could see having someone call him out every thirty seconds began to wear on Mike. Plus the fact that the Crows seemed to believe Arri didn't really help either.

Then there was Tye, who decided staring at Janelle was a good idea. Tye was what Yager referred to as a "watcher". He didn't say much because he spent most of his time watching what everyone else was up to. Normally not a problem, but Janelle came from a place where staring was a very, very bad thing. Tye may have thought he was making his intentions clear by staring at Janelle like a piece of rib-eye steak fresh off the grill, but Janelle felt threatened. And she let him know that when she threw one of her chopsticks at him, aiming right for Tye's eye. Any other girl, it wouldn't have been a big deal. But Crows were infamous at turning everything around them into a weapon. Thankfully, Ravens were infamous at defending themselves from any weapon. So, Tye simply caught the chopstick in midair and, to Janelle's eternal annoyance, grinned.

All that, though, merely the activities on the main stage. All around them, antics abounded between the Ravens and the Crows.

Yager kept waiting for knives to be drawn. Or at least to see a few talons. But most of it was merely verbal. Lots of yelling, swearing, threatening, and quite a few slap fights. Like he had a house full of ten-year-old first cousins.

To be honest, Yager loved it. Ravens could be a little stoic at times. Stale being the word Tye always used. The Crows, however, knew how to have fun even when they were pissed off. Didi was right. They really were a "Gathering".

"You think we should have left them alone?" Neecy peeked out from the covers. "There might be bloodshed."

"Nah. Didi's down there." The Crow leader kept quiet through the entire dinner, but when they started arguing during dessert in the living room so that she couldn't hear the lines from her favorite movie, *Aliens*, she'd taken everyone firmly in hand. Yager had learned a lot from her in the few days she'd been around.

"Okay." Neecy pulled the covers back over her head.

"Uh...baby? Whatcha doin'?"

"Nothing?"

"Come on, Lawrence. What's the problem?"

"I can't say it."

"Spit it or I'm bringing Didi in here to ask."

The comforter moved just enough so that he could clearly see two beautiful black eyes glare at him.

"Well?" he prompted when she continued to stare at him.

Sighing, she said softly, "I'm funky."

Yager frowned. "You mean musically?"

"No, you geek." She sighed. "I mean...I haven't bathed in a few days 'cause of the stitches, and—"

Yager was off the bed. "Come on, I'll give ya a bath."

"No!"

"Why not?"

"I can take care of myself."

"Ya know, Neecy, if this were a permanent situation, I could totally understand the movie-of-the-week theatrics about independence and all. But you'll be back to your usual dangerously quiet self in a couple of days. So why can't you just relax and enjoy a little Yager care?"

Neecy pulled the covers tighter around her body. "No."

She could be so stubborn. And over the weirdest crap, too. Turning on his heel, Yager walked into the bathroom and ran a bath. He didn't fill the tub all the way up, since he had to make sure her stitches didn't get wet. Once he was satisfied, Yager went back to the bedroom and froze.

The birds were back.

Neecy sat on the bed, the covers still wrapped around her.

"Neecy?"

"I swear I didn't call 'em...they just sort of..." She looked around the room. "Came."

Stupidly, Yager'd left one of the bedroom windows cracked. Well, he wouldn't be doing that again. Good thing he had central air and heat.

Yager took a step forward and an enormous raven moved in front of him. They were protecting her.

"Neecy, you need to stop being freaked out by me. That's what they're responding to."

"I'm not freaked—"

"Neecy."

"Okay. Okay. Sorry." She thought for a moment. "I know. How about you tell me something that will make me feel calmer."

"Nothing I ever say to you makes you feel calmer."

"Well you better think of something."

The raven at his feet moved closer. But so did a raven on each side of him. Uh-oh. The thought of life without his eyes ran through his head. Not good. Desperate, he grabbed on the first thing he could think of.

"One night, me, Tye, and Mike got really drunk and named our cocks."

Neecy studied him before asking, "Excuse me?"

"We named them. We were really drunk."

He saw a smile tug at the corner of her lips. "And what, exactly, did you name them?"

Well, this was awkward. "Mike's was Mr. Lovespussy."

"Of course."

"Tye's was Dangerous Dan."

"I'm not even going to ask why. And yours?"

He scratched the back of his head. "Remember. We were *really* drunk."

"Cough it up, Yager."

With a shrug, "Master and Commander."

When the laughing got so bad she started wheezing, the birds flew back out the window they came in.

Neecy leaned forward, one arm around her knees the other held close to her chest as Yager carefully washed her back and argued with Morgan on the phone.

"Don't yell at me. No, I'm not keeping her awake. No. I'm not getting 'frisky'. And stop calling it that. It's freaking me out. Look, she wanted a bath. I'm being careful of her stitches. How do they look?" Yager leaned over and studied her back while Neecy stared straight ahead and tried not to think too much about his hands all over her body.

The fact that they felt really, *really* good, didn't help. Most of the time she'd been here, Neecy sat around worrying about her wing. She felt certain she'd never fly again. If she couldn't fly, she couldn't remain second-in-command. She'd end up doing administrative work. The thought terrified her, eating away at her like acid. Foolishly she'd taken her wings for granted.

But for just a few minutes, Yager helped wipe her fears away simply by distracting her with those amazing hands of his. They were so big and she'd seen him do much damage with them, but when he touched her it wasn't merely gentle. It was more than that. It was…reverent. Like his hands were worshipping her flesh.

"Yeah. The stitches look fine. You want me to *what*? No. Forget it. Yeah, the wound looks completely healed, but no. Uh-huh. Uh-huh. Good."

He released her long enough to turn off his cordless phone, then his hands were right back, stroking her, caring for her.

"Morgan's coming by tomorrow."

"I hope that means I can get rid of the sling." Yager insisted she keep her arm in the same position it was in when tied against her body. He refused to risk her healing process, even though she felt like there was no hope. The first day, there was so much pain and movement around the area where her wing was. But now there was nothing. She knew Morgan might have to take her wing and the thought sickened her.

"That's my hope." He poured a palm full of expensive shampoo on her hair. The kind one could only buy at a spa. She normally used stuff from the local pharmacy. Two-for-one deals were her favorite. "She wanted me to take those stitches out myself. I told her no way."

"Why?"

"You're not Mike, ya know. I'd actually care if I left you fucked up."

Neecy grinned. "That's very sweet, in a Nordic sort of way."

She closed her eyes as Yager's hands massaged her scalp. Man, what a delicious feeling.

"Look, I know my limits. I don't do medical stuff. I leave that to the professionals."

She wouldn't exactly call Morgan a "professional", but as a healer the woman rocked. Hell, Neecy was still breathing, wasn't she?

"As it is," he continued, "I hate anything medical."

He rinsed out her hair and then put more shampoo in.

"You're a big pussy when you go to the doctor, aren't you?"

"No. I just don't like needles. And no sane person should."

"What about vaccinations and stuff like that?"

Yager shrugged. "My doc's an Elder. When he knows he has to give me a shot, he calls Mike and Tye. They hold me down."

Neecy laughed hysterically as Yager again rinsed her hair. "I can't believe," she spit out, "you're admitting this to me."

He put his expensive conditioner on her hair and finger-combed it through. *Well...that's one way to come.*

"I figure you should know all my major flaws up front."

"Why?"

Yager sat on the floor beside the tub. "We gotta leave that in for three minutes. And what d'ya mean why?"

"I mean why do I have to know about your flaws?"

He shook his head. "We are not having this conversation now. We'll wait until you're better."

"Have what conversation?"

"The conversation I was going to have with you last weekend when you came over. After I'd fucked ya passive, of course."

"Oh, of course." Neecy looked up to find Yager staring at her. "What?"

"Do you have any idea how hard it's been to..." He shook his head. "Forget it."

"How hard it's been to what?"

Taking a deep breath, "Keep my hands off you."

"Oh."

"But that's not the priority right now."

"It's not?"

"No. It's not. First we get you better. Then I fuck ya senseless. Then we'll track down the motherfuckers who did this to you, and wipe them from the face of the earth. That's my plan."

With that, Yager got back on his haunches and proceeded to rinse the conditioner out of Neecy's hair. How she kept forgetting this man was a Viking, she'd never know.

"That's a lovely plan, Yager. And I'm all for it to a degree. But the wiping from the face of the earth thing is down to the Crows. And we don't need the Ravens for that."

"Not every crow is a raven. But every raven is a crow."

Neecy stared at Yager. "What does that mean?"

"It means, we're all part of the...same...uh..."

"Bird family?"

"Exactly. All we're missing are the magpies, the blue jays, and the..." He shrugged. "Something else. Besides us, I really don't know birds."

"You know, Yager. You're a unique man."

He leaned back. "Is this your way of saying I'm weird?"

"No. You're not weird. You're unique. There's a difference."

"Do you think I'm boring?"

She snorted. "No. Why?"

"'Cause I'm nice."

"You ain't that nice."

"I'm not?"

"Yager, if you were nice, really nice, I would have scared you off by now. And the whole 'wiping from the face of the earth' thing...really nice people don't say that and mean it."

"Oh. Okay." He stood up and grabbed an enormous towel.

"You are nice to me, though."

"I like being nice to you."

"Yeah." She looked down at her knees. "I'm not really used to that."

"So I noticed." He leaned down and lifted her out of the bath. "I'm hoping you get used to it." Once he had her standing, he began drying her off with the towel.

"It's only—"

"I'm not going to stop being nice to you, Neecy. That's not even an option."

She stared at him as he dried her off. She didn't get him. Didn't understand him. But she really liked the way he treated her. She thought enjoying it would make her weak. Instead she felt stronger every day under his care.

Yager finished drying her off and wrapped the towel around her. He kissed her forehead, then her nose.

He hadn't kissed her properly since the time after Morgan left. She missed him. More than she'd missed anything before in either of her lives.

"Can I ask you a question?" he asked.

Neecy nodded. "Sure."

"I know you don't remember much of what happened that night, the night you were attacked. But..." He took a deep breath. "I still haven't figured out why your birds brought you here. It would have been quicker to take you to the Bird House. Or the Elders who lived downtown. But they brought you here."

Crap. She'd hoped he wouldn't ask her this question, because she wasn't sure she wanted to admit the truth. Then again, Neecy didn't lie.

"I remember being worried you'd think I stood you up. I guess since you were the last thing I thought about before I passed out—they brought me here."

Yager leaned down a bit and placed his forehead against Neecy's. "I like that answer, Lawrence."

Closing her eyes, her cheeks reddening in embarrassment, "Figured you would."

He slid his hand behind the back of her neck, afraid she'd run. "You don't have to be afraid, Neecy. Not of me."

"I'm not."

"Not of us either."

"I'm—" The bedroom door slammed open, cutting Neecy's words off. He'd been so absorbed in Neecy he never heard the arguing right outside his door.

Janelle stormed in, Mike right behind her. They shoved each other as they made their way to the bathroom. They really were like annoying siblings.

"He—" Janelle began.

"She started it," Mike barked over her.

Yager calmly pulled the towel tighter around Neecy, making sure she was covered. From there, he calmly walked over to Mike and Janelle. He grabbed Mike by the hair and shoved him into the doorway.

"Ow!"

Still gripping Mike's hair with one hand, he picked Janelle up with the other. He dragged them both back to the bedroom door and tossed them out into the hallway.

"I swear by all that's holy, if I have to come downstairs tonight, you'll be washing your own blood off the walls come morning."

Yager slammed the door closed and went back to the bathroom. He scooped Neecy up in his arms and took her to the bed, carefully laying her down. She smiled up at him.

"What?"

She shrugged as he pulled the wet towel off her body and tossed it aside. "Still laughing at the 'am I too nice' fear you seem to have."

Tying her arm back against her body, "I don't want anyone upsetting you. You need to relax until you're better."

Yager worked really hard not to notice her breasts, her nipples hard and begging. "I *need* you to get better, Lawrence."

He pulled his MIT sweatshirt over her head. "I feel better *now*, Yager."

Her hand slid down his chest, but he caught it before it could go any lower. He closed his eyes, the fight for control getting harder and harder every day.

"Not until Morgan tells me you're okay."

"But—"

"No." Releasing her hand, Yager pulled the comforter up and over Neecy's body. "I'm not going to risk hurting you."

"Yeah, but—"

"No."

"But Yager—"

"No."

Yager headed toward the bathroom.

"Where are you going?"

"Cold shower. A very cold shower."

"Just so we're clear, I'm gettin' kind of cranky here."

Yager glanced back at the woman of his dreams lying in *his* bed, wearing his clothes, and growled, "That makes two of us, baby."

Then he closed the door and headed to his very cold and very lonely shower.

Chapter Seventeen

Katie flew up higher into the old oak and perched herself on the sturdiest barren branch she could find. She looked again. Yup. Wolves. Thirty of them, by her estimate. She motioned to the Raven in the tree beside her and he dived back to the ground to warn the others.

She had no idea why Shifters were here, but she bet it wasn't to play Parcheesi.

Wilhelm Yager was in a bad mood. A really, really bad mood. A bad enough mood to start playing fetch with the innards of a bunch of dogs. To be honest, the Viking in him was really hoping for a good fight. He was ready to start hurting people.

He really wished he had a good reason to feel this way, but he didn't. No, the only reason he had an overwhelming urge to shove Molinski's head in the toilet or to set fire to Tye's Lamborghini or to chop up another Raven's *Playboy* collection was because he wanted to fuck Neecy Lawrence so bad he couldn't see straight.

All day he'd been waiting for Morgan to get her ass to his house, so she could tell him Neecy was as good as she was going to get so that he could have his dirty way with her. But Morgan had to take care of some other business in the City first. That meant all day he'd avoided Neecy. He had to. He was starting not to care about her goddamn sling or her wounded wings or the stitches in her back. Which meant he really had to stay away from her. The bottom line was, he couldn't promise he'd be gentle with her. In fact, he could actually promise he definitely wouldn't be.

Now he had those freak Shifters on his property. They didn't even come to him as human, but as wolves. Like *that* was normal behavior.

They'd walked slowly toward his house while it was still light out, ensuring they'd all see them. They didn't make any sudden moves or do anything that the Crows or Ravens would consider threatening.

Yager stayed slightly behind Didi as she moved toward their leader. Many of the Crows and Ravens were perched in the trees or on the roof of the house, silently watching. And he'd sent Tye and Mike to keep an eye on Neecy. He'd decided not to tell her and Didi agreed. No way would she stay out of it if she knew the Shifters were here. And with only one arm and her wings still unusable, she'd be more a liability than a help.

Didi walked up to a silver-and-black wolf. She braced her feet apart and crossed her arms in front of her chest.

"So...what do you want?"

The wolf looked Didi over and Yager wondered what it would take to bash the shit out of him. Could he do it by grabbing this mutt's tail and just going slap happy?

Man, I am in a shitty mood.

After a moment's hesitation, the wolf shifted. Right before Yager's eyes a wolf became a man. A big ole naked man.

Didi, startled, glanced at Yager. She was doing her best not to laugh. Apparently being naked wasn't that big a thing for the Shifters. Still...it was a little distracting.

"I'm Danny Lewis. You met with my father and baby brother a couple of weeks ago."

Didi nodded as she tried to avoid staring at the man's package. Not easy. Even Yager had to admit, the guy had nothing to be ashamed of.

"And you wiped my other brother from the face of the earth."

Cool. Fight.

Neecy couldn't believe she was crying. But she was. While watching some business show on CNN, no less. But she hadn't been able to stop crying since she woke up from that dream. The dream where something hacked off both her wings.

When younger, Neecy used to have nightmares where all her hair fell out or all her teeth had been broken. Those had been horrible, scary dreams, but this dream...

She woke crying and hadn't really been able to stop all day. Thankfully, Yager had been avoiding her. Not surprising since he kept getting up the night before to take cold showers. Because of her stitches that hadn't been an option for her. So, instead, she dreamed. At first they were her typical wet dreams about Yager, but then they became darker.

Neecy didn't know why the dream still upset her so. She'd been awake for hours, why hadn't she recovered yet? But, still, she kept crying. She'd hidden herself in Yager's den most of the day, using his big desktop with the three hard drives and four monitors to catch up on email from her students and play computer games. Eventually, she thought she had complete control of herself, so she'd gone into the living room. It was empty, which was good. Because a television ad for cars or something showed a bald eagle soaring through the blue sky and she started crying all over again.

Hearing footsteps heading her way, Neecy quickly wiped her eyes and did her best to stifle any more pathetic girl tears, as she liked to call them.

The footsteps stopped outside the living room entrance and she glanced up to see Tye and Mike staring at her from the archway.

She forced a smile and quickly went back to the fascinating world of stocks and bonds. She thought the men would leave. But, instead, Tye sat on the sofa next to hers and Mike sat down right by her side.

There was a moment of awkward silence, then Mike said, "So you're a professor."

Forcing her voice and herself to remain calm, Neecy said, "Yeah. Of history."

"Cool."

Yeah. Right. She really didn't see Mike I'm-a-proud-liar Molinski being that interested in history of any kind.

"The game we're working on is set in the Middle Ages. Maybe you could take a look at our graphics, make sure the armor and weapons are right."

Neecy shrugged, keeping her eyes on the television. "Sure."

"You'd be amazed how crazy some of these geeks get about accuracy," Tye added.

"Really?"

"Oh, yeah. Especially with RTS games."

"RTS?"

"Real-time strategy games. You know, where you create yourself a kingdom, an army, enemies, whatever. You create your entire world."

Neecy nodded. "That actually sounds kinda cool."

"It's fun, I guess. I think Yager likes those more than we do. I like role-playing and Mike likes to blow shit up."

"I'm really good at that."

Finally, Neecy smiled. "How shocking."

"So—" Mike stretched his arm out over the back of the couch, "—as a professor, I was wondering..."

Neecy looked at the arm behind her and back at Mike. "Wondering what?"

"Well, say I'm in your class. And I'm bad..." He grinned and Neecy understood immediately why so many females had fallen for this gorgeous blond butthead. "How would you punish me?"

Laughing, Neecy looked at Tye who rolled his eyes and turned back to the television.

"I mean would you use corporal punishment to keep me in line, O Professor Lawrence? Because I've been feeling especially naughty lately."

For the first time all day, Neecy completely forgot about her nightmares.

✧

Didi opened the envelope one of the wolves dropped at her feet. She pulled out a thick sheaf of papers and pictures.

"My brother was a lot of things. But he wasn't smart enough to take and successfully use what he had. Then I heard about your second-in-command. That's when I knew something was very wrong. Talked to some other Shifter breeds, found out that Waldgrave was active again...and now it seems he has some disciples."

"Waldgrave? You mean this man?" Didi pointed at the picture of the older man with grey and blond hair.

"Karl Waldgrave. He's very wealthy. Very dangerous. And he likes to hunt, shall we say, difficult game."

"Oh, that's nice."

"But what truly pisses me off is that he used my brother to get to you guys."

"And yet you're just handing him over to us?"

"It was discussed between the Packs. About doing this ourselves. But we're wolves. We'll just go in and kill them." Lewis smiled, if you could call it that. "But the Crows and Ravens are much more...*artful* about this sort of thing."

"Is that right?"

"Let's just say, you guys really enjoy your job. But if we're wrong, let us know." Lewis' hand reached for the papers he'd given them, but Didi slapped her own hand down over them.

"We'll take it."

"Good." Lewis motioned to his wolves with a flick of his head. Slowly, they began moving out. "And you'll make sure they suffer, right?"

Didi looked at the man, her brown eyes cold. Nope. No mercy there. "Oh, yes. They'll suffer."

The Shifter's grin widened and Yager could see fangs moving out from his gums. "Good."

He stepped away from the table and followed after his Pack. As he moved, he shifted, and by the time he hit the trees, he was wolf again.

Then he was gone.

Didi pushed the papers to Delia. "Find out everything you can on this guy."

"Got it."

With that, Didi grabbed Yager's arm and dragged him back into the house. Once in the hallway, she stopped and looked around. Once assured they were alone, Didi leaned in and whispered to Yager, "You can*not* go after Waldgrave yourself."

"Why not?" He'd already begun building his team in his head. He planned to wipe them out that very evening and spend the rest of his time in bed with Neecy if Morgan gave her the go-ahead.

"Because their deaths don't belong to you. They belong to Neecy."

"They belong to Neecy? Why?" Didi didn't answer and Yager felt cold fear grip him around the throat. He stepped away from her. "This? *This* is her Trial?" There wasn't one Crow or Raven who hadn't had a Trial of some sort. The Viking gods loved a good test of spirit and strength. But this one seemed particularly brutal. Even for Skuld.

"I've gotta warn her."

"No!" Didi took a firm grip on his arm. "If you tell her...just trust me on this. She has to do this on her own. Especially now. Especially 'cause he wounded her."

"But—"

"Yager, if you love her, and I know you do, then you'll back off. Don't fuck with Skuld on this."

He'd never seen Didi worried about much, if anything. And he'd definitely never seen her pleading before, and that's exactly what he saw in her eyes even if her words were commands.

He had no idea what Skuld had said to Didi, but it was enough to convince her it was safer *not* telling Neecy the truth.

"Okay. I'll keep my mouth shut for now."

Didi let out a deep breath. "Thank you. But trust me, Yager. I won't let Neece face this completely alone. We just have to play this a little differently."

Hearing that, Yager eased up a bit. "Okay. Good."

"Excuse me."

Yager and Didi looked up at Connie.

"What's up?"

"We're ordering pizza for dinner. Does that work for you two?"

"Yeah. That's fine," Yager said as Didi nodded her consent.

"Great. Um...and I was wondering, since everyone is getting a little antsy, if I could set up my equipment and—"

"Connie," Didi warned.

"What?" Yager asked.

"They wanna throw a party," Didi explained. "Which, if I were you, Yager, I'd say no to."

"I don't mind." Connie was right. Everyone was getting a little antsy. Actually, they were getting a lot antsy. A little house party might safely blow off some steam.

"Are you sure?"

"Yeah. Sure. My closest neighbors are about six miles away and I've never had a party here."

"Yes!" Connie turned and headed back to the kitchen, where the Crows and Ravens had taken to congregating on a regular basis.

Didi followed after her, but not before adding, "I hope you know what you're doing."

The one thing he knew about Crows, they wouldn't be inviting any rowdy outsiders to his house. Crows only allowed other Crows and friends of Crows to their parties because they didn't really "party" unless their wings could come out.

Pushing it out of his mind, Yager went in search of Neecy. He needed to see her, to know she was okay. He would do as Didi promised and not tell her anything about Skuld's plans for her, but he still needed to see her.

Of course, he didn't expect to find her in tears, hysterically laughing, with Mike Molinski draped over her lap, his ass in the air. Thankfully the little bastard wasn't naked.

"All I'm asking for, *Professor*, is a little demonstration."

A grinning Tye was the first to notice Yager. Clearing his throat, he reached over and slapped Mike in the head.

"What?"

He motioned to Yager and Mike's head whipped around. "Oh, uh...hi, bro."

Shaking his head and scowling, Yager turned and walked away.

Neecy followed Yager into his bedroom. "You're being ridiculous."

"*I'm* being ridiculous? You have Michael Molinski on your lap with his ass in your face, but I'm being ridiculous."

"Don't be mad at him."

Yager's grey eyes glared at her from across the room. "So now you're protecting him?"

"Don't bark at me! He was just trying to make me feel better."

"Feel better about what?"

"Forget it." Neecy headed toward the door, but Yager was already standing in front of it. He'd even closed it. She didn't hear it close. *Christ, how does the man do that!*

"Feel better about what, Neecy?"

"I don't wanna have this conversation now. Move."

"Talk to me now. Or stand here forever. I don't give a shit. But you're not leaving until you tell me what's up."

Letting out a short scream of frustration, Neecy moved away from the door. She eyed the window and, realizing that was no longer an option of escape, turned all her rage and fear on Wilhelm Yager.

She spun around. *"You wanna know what's wrong?"* He didn't move as she advanced on him. *"This!"* She pointed at her tied down arm. *"This is bullshit!"*

"What the fuck are you talking about?"

"Everything that meant anything to me is gone! And we both know it!" She hated yelling, but she couldn't help herself. She'd lost it. Panic turning to full-on rage in a heartbeat.

"Neecy—"

"I'm not a warrior! I'm not a Crow! *I'm a fuckin' invalid!"* And the next words were out of her mouth before she could think about stopping them. "Why didn't you just leave me? Why didn't you just...just..."

"What?" he yelled back. *"Let you die?"*

That's exactly what she was about to stupidly say and the thought tore through her like a blade. Christ, how pathetic was she? Letting something like this make her feel inferior. Weak. Vulnerable.

And that's when she burst into tears. Yet she didn't even have to reach for Yager—he was already there. His big arms wrapping around her, holding her close to his warm body. She wrapped her free arm around his waist and held him tight as the tears and fears from the past five days flowed out of her in one horrible torrent.

He should have seen this coming. Should have known she'd be feeling this way...he sure as hell would have.

Sitting himself on the floor, he pulled Neecy onto his lap and let her cry. The physical pain Neecy could always deal with. She was definitely a girl who could take a punch to the face or a knife to the stomach. But for some unknown reason, she felt like The Gathering somehow defined her. Somehow made her worthy of everything she had. But all Skuld did was give her a second chance. It was up to Neecy to actually take that chance. She did, too. And made herself into the woman he'd fallen madly in love with.

After ten minutes, the tears turned to sniffles, but it took another ten for her to finally pull back from him—as he knew she would.

Wiping her eyes, she tried to pull out of his lap, but Yager wouldn't let her go. "Sorry about that, Yager. Um..." She shook her head. "I have no excuse for that little display."

"Ax in the back can do that to a person."

She chuckled. "Yeah. I guess."

Again she tried to pull out of his lap, and again Yager pulled her back.

Smiling shyly, "You know, you can let me go now, Yager."

"I don't want to. I like you here on my lap. Although, all that wiggling is giving me a hard-on." He ran his hand down her cheek.

"Who the fuck am I kidding? I've had a hard-on for you for the past five days."

Using the sleeve of his Giants sweatshirt, Neecy wiped the remainder of her tears. "You sweet-talker, you."

"You're lucky I'm able to speak at all."

"What? You think it's been easy on me?"

"Girls have it easy."

"You *must* be high." She held her free hand up. "I'm startin' to get carpal tunnel."

Yager buried his face in her neck. "I so didn't need that visual."

"What about me? Every time you went into the shower..." She growled. "Yowza."

His arms tightened around her waist. "Don't, Lawrence."

"Come on, Yager. You're killing me here. Besides, I need comfort...I've been crying." For emphasis, she sniffled. Twice.

"Stop it right now, Lawrence. I mean it." He was holding on by a thread. A very thin thread.

She rubbed her cheek against the top of his head. "Yager," she whispered softly. "Will." *Tricky little brat!* She knew that would get him. And she was right. "Fuck me, Will. Now."

Christ, how was he supposed to fight that? So he didn't. Instead, he gripped the back of her neck and kissed her. Deep, long, and hard. Like he'd been wanting to do for days. She relaxed into him, showing no resistance whatsoever.

He could do this. He *would* do this. And he'd be careful...and gentle...and...

"Open the door, Will," Morgan ordered from the other side, completely uncaring as to what she may be interrupting.

Groaning, the pair separated. "No. No. No. No. This isn't happening," he practically whined. He looked at Neecy's face and saw exactly what he was feeling.

"Wilhelm Yager the Fourth, you open this door right now!"

Neecy grinned. "The fourth?"

"Quiet."

He stood, Neecy still in his arms. Gently, he placed her back on her feet. He kissed her forehead, turned, and snatched the door open with one angry move.

"Don't look at me like that." Morgan walked into the room as Neecy finger-combed her hair off her face.

Shaking her head, "I swear. You two." Morgan motioned toward Neecy as she moved to the bathroom. "Come on, you. Let's see if we can get that sling off you."

Neecy locked eyes with Yager and he knew she felt it, too. That heat of longing building up around them. Much more of this and they'd start killing people.

"Let's go, Crow!"

And it looked like Neecy may start with Morgan.

Mike stared at his friend staring at his computer screen. Yager wasn't typing or anything. Just staring.

Connie, or as he liked to call her "The Lesbian", because that was definitely one of his favorite words, walked by again with more equipment in her hand. For the last twenty minutes he'd watched her bring in all her DJ equipment. He could have helped her unload her stuff, but then he wouldn't have been able to watch her tight ass walk back and forth.

He really liked lesbians.

More Crows walked into the room to grab beer out of the fridge and chips out of the pantry. They all wore their white tank tops and jeans, except Didi who wore black. He'd never seen so many wings in one place. He loved it.

Mike had to admit, he was really enjoying himself. The Crows were different but fun. They weren't uptight and they didn't seem to have much of an ulterior motive. They all loved to laugh and were pretty brazen in their "fight or fight" response—there never seemed to be any kind of "flight" with them. Unless they were actually flying.

The only one he didn't get was the little Asian one. Annie? Ashley? Whatever her name was. She glared at him like he'd fucked her mother. Little rich Long Island bitch. Probably thought she was better than him. That's why he liked Neecy and even hard-ass Janelle. Fellow hoodrats, they understood him. The Princess, as he now called her annoying ass, would never understand him. She'd never deign to involve herself with someone like him. And knowing that made him want to fuck her so bad his teeth ached. Christ. What was wrong with him? Why did he insist on going after the mean ones? Even Neecy was only occasionally mean. Other times, he'd discovered, she was a very cool woman with a will of iron. He admired that.

And, to his surprise, Neecy knew how to enjoy herself. That little one wouldn't know how to enjoy herself if she were dressed in a clown suit.

"Are you just going to sit there feeling sorry for yourself?" he finally asked his mentor.

Not even looking up from his laptop, Yager snapped, "Mike, I haven't gotten laid in nine days...do you really want to fuck with me right now?"

Hell, Yager had gone for longer periods without sex. Really, the sentence should be "I haven't fucked Neecy Lawrence in nine days..." That would be much more accurate.

"Not trying to get you all pissed or anything. Just trying to get you to relax. The place is crawling with women. You should partake."

"You should shut up."

The kitchen door swung open and Neecy walked into the room. She barely glanced at Mike, instead walking over to where Yager sat and leaned against the table.

"See anything different?"

Yager glanced up at her, then went back to his computer. "No."

Sighing, she held up both her hands and waved them around. "See anything different now?"

Yager stared at her for a moment, raised his hands, and did the same goofy move back to her. "No, I don't see anything different."

Muttering words she really should be sent to confession for, Neecy walked to the fridge and took out a beer.

She leaned against the counter next to Mike. "You see something different, don't you?"

"Yeah. But what did you expect from him? The man forgets to comb his own hair."

Chuckling, "Good point."

"Hello," Yager growled from the table. "I'm right here."

Morgan leaned into the kitchen. "Okay. I'm out of here." She looked at Neecy. "You call me if you have any problems."

"I will."

"Good." She turned her light blue eyes to Yager. "Walk with me."

Rolling his eyes, he slammed his laptop down on the kitchen table. "Anyone have any more orders for me?"

Then he followed Morgan out of the kitchen.

"See what you do to the man?"

She had it down, he'd give her that. Neecy had that "leader move". The one where they didn't waste time looking surprised by something he said.

Instead, Neecy slowly turned to look at him and said, "I'm sorry, what was that?"

Mike may be reckless, but he wasn't stupid. He knew enough hoodrat girls to know when they were settin' him up for a beat down. "I'm sorry, what was that?" was just another way of saying, "Exactly how many ways do you want me to kick your ass?"

Grinning, Mike shook his head. "Nothin'."

"Oh, that's what she was talking about."

Morgan shook her head. Like all Ravens, Will was brilliant, but he could still be a major bonehead at times.

"Yeah. I took the bandages off. Everything looks fine, but until she unfurls her wings, I'll never know for sure."

"Why can't she?"

"I don't know really. Could be she's simply scared." Actually, Morgan knew the girl was afraid. Afraid she'd never be able to fly again. That she was vulnerable. And that was a woman who didn't like being vulnerable.

Holding up her big coat so she could put it on, Will asked, "What should I do?"

"Wait it out, or..." She stopped as Will helped her on with her coat.

"Or?"

She grinned. "Get her all worked up."

Frowning, "Get her all..." Yager blinked. "Oh." He shook his head and gently shoved her toward the door. "You need to leave now."

"Get her all worked up and maybe her wings will unfurl."

"Stop it."

"Oh, come on. We've known each other long enough to—"

"We'll never know each other long enough for *this* conversation, Morgan. And we both know it."

She laughed as Will pushed her out the door and closed it behind her.

Yager cut through his living room. Neecy was right. The Crows had taken over his house. But that's what Crows did. They made themselves at home and expected a body to deal with it. The fact that it bothered Neecy warmed his heart. Without even realizing it, she was getting protective of him.

He passed Connie and saw that she'd set up her equipment. He felt kind of honored. Connie was an extremely well-known DJ. She worked at some of the hottest clubs in the City when she wasn't out killing someone stupid. The fact that she was gearing up to do what she did best in his house was kind of cool.

Walking through the kitchen door, Yager froze on the threshold. Why the hell was Neecy surrounded by six Ravens? He didn't like it. He didn't like it one goddamn bit.

Moving slowly, he walked over to them as they leaned against the island in the middle of his kitchen. Neecy glanced at him and frowned. Well, what the hell did that mean?

"Yager, are you sure about this?"

"About what?"

"About Connie breaking out the music? I mean...she starts playing and there will be a party here. Whether you want one or not."

Tye smiled. "You Crows do love a good party, don't ya?"

Mike stretched and ran his hands through his hair. "I've gone to a few raves Connie DJ'd at. She's not bad."

"Wow, Mike. Is that like...a compliment?"

Mike smiled as he bumped Neecy with his hip. "I have my moments, ya know."

"Yeah. Sure you do." Neecy took a sip of her beer as Tye passed her a bowl of pretzels.

The first beats of the music started and Yager heard all the Crows in the living room give a cheer.

Neecy shook her head. "My girls."

"How long has she been DJ-ing?" Mike asked as he grabbed another beer from the fridge.

"Since she was seventeen, I think."

"Was it tough for her to get in?"

"Surprisingly, no. What's really funny is that she really didn't give a shit. She only did it 'cause she loves to watch her girlfriend dance."

All the Ravens froze; beers halfway to their lips, pretzels clenched in big fists and hovering near open mouths.

Mike cleared his throat. "That's Fran, right? With the long legs?"

"Yeah. They've been together since they were fifteen or sixteen. They're the sweetest couple."

Tye glanced at Neecy from the corner of his eye. "Does she still dance when Connie DJs?"

"Oh, yeah. If Connie's DJ-ing, Fran's dancing."

Yager reached over and yanked Neecy out of the way as the six men dived over the island and slammed out of the room heading for the living room and the party.

Neecy laughed as she held onto Yager's arm. "What the fuck was that?"

"You tell six horny guys there are hot lesbians dancing in my living room...what did you expect?"

"God, you guys are pathetic."

"Your point being?" Neecy shook her head as she stepped away, but Yager grabbed her around the waist and pulled her into his body. "Where are you going?"

Instead of pulling away as she usually did, she wrapped her arms around his hips, slipping her hands under the waistband of his loose-fitting jeans.

"Got something in mind, Yager?" she asked as she grabbed his ass and squeezed.

"Maybe the question is what do you have in mind?"

"You. Me. Your bedroom. And a locked freakin' door."

Smiling, as he pulled her closer, "I like that idea Lawrence," She tilted her face up, wanting him to kiss her. And now that Morgan had given her a clean bill of health, Neecy and her amazing body were all his.

Yager leaned down, his eyes locked on her lips, when she suddenly jerked up.

"Uh-oh."

"Uh-oh what?"

"Shit. We gotta get out of here."

He didn't need to hear that twice, but for once he was too slow. He'd just grabbed her hand to drag her out of the house and fly her up to his window if necessary when the kitchen door banged open. *C'mon N' Ride It*, one of his favorite party songs from the nineties, blasted in from the other room accompanied by a line of dancing and singing Crows. Apparently they wanted everyone to ride that goddamn train, so they grabbed Neecy and yanked her away from him.

They were so happy to see Neecy healthy they were completely unaware of what they just interrupted. Or they could care less. With the Crows, you just never know.

Neecy tried to pull away from Patty, one of the younger Crows, but the girl had a grip on her like a rodeo rider on a steer. They danced through the house until they got back to the living room. By then Connie changed out the music to some much harder tech, which meant Fran and Janelle would take over the dance floor.

Again Neecy tried to sneak away, but several older Crows she hadn't seen in some time grabbed her. They hugged her and told her how happy they were to see her doing well. That's when Neecy realized this party wasn't just to blow off some steam. It was for her. To celebrate her being well. As much as she wanted to, she couldn't walk away from the party just yet.

With a small sigh of resignation, Neecy took the beer Arri handed her and counted the minutes until she could get away and back to Yager.

Chapter Eighteen

That was exactly the fifth time they'd done it. Every time Yager tried to make his way over to Neecy, one or more of the goddamn Crows jumped in front of him to "chat".

In the last two hours he'd discussed the world economy, the future of rain forests, whether natural gas was truly necessary to the nation's survival, and the differences between narcissists and sociopaths. A conversation he just found disturbing.

Now little Arri stood in front of him, an uncharacteristically sunny grin on her pretty face.

"I was wondering Yager, what's your opinion on the national debt and its impact on the United States' dominance among the other world powers?"

Yager glared down at her. "*Et tu*, Arri?"

Her impossible grin grew impossibly wider. "I don't know what you mean."

Tye watched Janelle's ass move on the makeshift dance floor. It wasn't a small ass and he liked that. A lot. Add in that the girl could dance that ass off and Tye was feeling pretty good about things. He'd stopped watching the dancing lesbian as soon as Janelle stomped past him. She wasn't angry, it just seemed like she stomped everywhere. She was not exactly light of foot.

Still, seeing her dance couldn't quite beat seeing that gorgeous ass naked. True, he'd literally kicked the hell out of Mike to remind him that Crows were not his little sisters to torment. Yet, as much as he hated admitting it, he loved the man for giving him a good look at Janelle. A really, *really* good look.

Connie put on an old sixties song. He loved when she played the weirder, eclectic stuff. Inevitably, Janelle and Neecy did some hilarious dance move, like when they got everyone to do The Bump. Now they were all singing to *Rockin' Robin.*

He could see where this was going. The song mentioned Crows and Ravens...there'd be much yelling at key points. But Tye loved it. He hated how they got here—Neecy getting hurt—but he loved where they ended up. The Crows and Ravens working together as one team. One family of annoying siblings. Loud, competitive, demanding Vikings always looking for a good fight or a good fuck.

And right there, right in front of him—Janelle McKenna. Daughter of a former Westie who left the life and ended up getting gunned down for it.

It no longer mattered, though. Because she'd become one of the Skuld Daughters. And, next to Neecy, one of the goddess' best warriors. Funny, he often forgot Janelle was his age. She looked more like a girl in her twenties. But she knew the words to every Depeche Mode and Adam and the Ants song Connie played, and the sexy Latin lesbian played a lot of those.

Janelle and Neecy were now back to back, singing or, more like screaming, the words to *Rockin' Robin.* The whole time the girls were laughing, especially when the rest of the Crows joined in. That's what the Crows seemed to do a lot of. Laugh. They found more reasons to explode into peals of laughter, and Tye with his big science brain couldn't help but find them all fascinating. They didn't seem to need much to amuse them. Anything was fair game.

Yager moved out of the crowd and walked over to Tye. He thought he came over to talk, but then Tye realized he was in front of the liquor cabinet and Yager wanted in. He pushed Tye out of the way, grabbed a forty-year-old bottle of scotch, poured himself some in a glass, and shot it back like he was at a drinking contest in Mexico.

"Everything okay, bro?"

Yager winced as the scotch went down his throat and shook his head. "Not really. Just trying to stay in some control here."

He poured himself a little more and put the scotch back in the cabinet.

"Just make sure none of the guys do anything stupid." Ah, Yager-speak for "Keep Mike the fuck away from me."

"The mood I'm in," Yager continued, "I will make them cry."

"Don't worry. I'll keep my eye on him." When Janelle wasn't in his line of sight, of course. "Although he seems much more interested in getting laid tonight."

Yager shook his head, finally forced to smile. "He might as well forget it. Every Crow seems to have his number. They're all calling him Liar-Mike. Like it's his name."

Tye laughed. "Good. About time the little fucker learned he can't get over on everything with a pussy."

Tye watched as Yager studied Neecy. She'd grabbed hold of little Arri and pulled her onto the dance floor as the music shifted to some old disco hit. His gaze was so heated, Tye was shocked Neecy hadn't burst into flame.

"You know, Yager, if you want to get away for a bit, I can watch things here. Just take her upstairs."

"Forget it." He took another drink of the scotch. "They won't let me."

"Who won't let you?"

"The Crows. They're keeping us apart."

"What?" Tye glanced around the room. "You're kidding, right?"

"Nope. Every time I try and get near her, they find a way to get between us. It's been going on for two hours. And I'm starting to get goddamn desperate. At some point I'm going to start doing that thing again...ya know...when I get frustrated."

"You mean when you start speaking in two-word sentences. Mostly curses?"

"Yeah. That."

"Why would they get between you two?" The Crows loved Yager. They especially loved him for Neecy.

Yager gave a short, painful laugh. "I think they think it's funny."

He was probably right. The Crows loved torturing each other and anyone else they considered family. Apparently that included Yager. Unfortunately, Yager was too horny to realize the implication.

"You need a distraction."

"Like what?"

Tye put one hand on Yager's shoulder while using the other to dig his cell phone out of his jeans. "Trust me, bro. I've got it covered."

Neecy didn't even know the Valkyries had shown up until Cassie pushed her from behind.

"Oh, sorry, Lawrence. I didn't see you there."

Cranky, horny, a little tipsy, and still wingless, Neecy was the last person Cassie My-knees-have-permanent-rug-burn Bennet should be fucking with.

"What the hell are you doing here?"

"I heard there was a party. And I do love a party."

Janelle stepped up beside Neecy. "Yeah, but we don't have the pole yet. How will you entertain without it?"

Cassie's eyes narrowed. "Oh, look, girls. The mountain speaks."

Neecy felt Janelle tense and knew she'd been hurt. No one hurt her girls. No one.

Neecy slammed both her hands, palms flat, against Cassie's upper chest. The bitch went flying into the group of Valkyries she'd brought with her.

They righted her quickly and Cassie immediately got in Neecy's face.

"Come on, bitch! Ya wanna fight me?"

Neecy would say this much about Cassie Blue...for a girly-girl, she didn't back down from a fight. Although, she really should when it came to the Crows.

Immediately, Neecy stepped up to Cassie. Her girls behind her.

"Wait."

Yager stepped between them. She rolled her eyes. He had to know better than to get between her and her prey...*especially* a Valkyrie prey.

He grabbed Neecy's upper arm. "I'm really sorry to interrupt. But we've gotta fuck. So I'm taking her. Fight somebody else."

With that, he started to walk away, dragging Neecy behind him. Cassie stared after them, astonishment and jealousy written all over her pretty face.

Okay. Even Neecy had to admit that was too cool. But still...middle of a Crow-Valkyrie brawl. Yager should not be interrupting.

"Have you lost your mind?"

"Horny. Must fuck. Now." Yager turned and wrapped his big hands around her waist. Next thing she knew, she was staring at his ass as she hung over his shoulder.

He has got to be kidding.

"Wilhelm Yager, you put me down!"

He stopped. "Fuck here?"

"What? No! Of course not."

He started walking again, heading toward the stairs. "Then shut up."

Neecy forced her head up, her cheeks burning with embarrassment, expecting to see everyone staring at her. And they probably would have been, if Janelle hadn't sucker punched Cassie, dropping the girl like yesterday's garbage.

"And so the mountain speaks!" Janelle sneered seconds before another Valkyrie leaped at her.

Neecy knew she would be missing the fight of the century. The Ravens standing around, not helping, but clearly praying someone would start ripping off clothes.

Yet she already felt her body responding to Yager's lust. Her nipples so hard they hurt. Her clit twitching, demanding the attention of his tongue or finger.

He didn't speak as he carried her upstairs and to his bedroom. He kicked the door open and stepped inside, slamming and locking the door behind them.

Yager put her down, but he didn't look at her once she had her feet firmly planted on his thick bedroom carpet.

"How's your back, baby?" he gritted out as he picked up a straight-back chair.

"Fine."

"Does it hurt? Are you in any pain?" He fit the chair against the doorknob, ensuring only a serious kick would open it.

Still cranky, horny, a little tipsy, and now frustrated she hadn't gotten to kick a stripper's ass, Neecy sighed in annoyance.

"No, Yager. I'm not in *any* pain. At all. Okay?"

"Perfect."

One second she was standing in the middle of the man's bedroom, hands on her hips, irritated beyond all hell. The next he'd shoved her up against the wall beside the bedroom door. His mouth slamming down on hers as his hands gripped her tits and squeezed hard, his fingertips twisting her nipples through Yager's tank top that she wore.

She groaned into his mouth, completely forgetting anything and everything that might be going on outside this room at this moment.

Finally, Yager pulled back, but only to drop to his knees in front of her, yanking at her sweatpants.

"Tell me you're already wet for me, baby. Tell me I don't have to wait."

"Not a goddamn second, Yager." She waited until he'd finished pulling off her sweatpants, then she reached down and tugged at his T-shirt, ripping it up over his head.

"Condom?" she asked.

"Back pocket."

He stood and she reached around him to dig into his jeans. Big, gentle hands caressed her face as she found and removed the foil packet.

"Jeans. Off."

By the time she tore open the foil and had the condom in her hand, Yager stood beautifully naked before her. His cock hard and desperate, pointing to the ceiling.

Neecy rolled the condom on Yager's cock, her mouth watering at the thought of licking the long, hard shaft. But that would have to wait. She wanted him inside her pussy too much.

Stepping back, Neecy pulled off Yager's MIT tank top, throwing it over his shoulder so that it landed on the bed.

Yager's hands slid under her arms, lifting her off the floor effortlessly while she wrapped her arms around his neck and her legs around his waist. He pushed her back into the wall with his body, the head of his cock teasing her clit.

"Don't even think about making me wait, motherfucker."

Yager groaned at her rough order, slamming his cock into her so hard if he hadn't been holding on to her, he might have shoved her head into the ceiling ten feet above them.

Growling, Yager pressed his hips into her, his cock forcing its way inside her again and again. And the entire time, they never looked away from each other. They never stopped staring into each other's eyes, even as Neecy felt that orgasm ripping up her spine, tearing through her limbs. He wouldn't release her. He wouldn't let her go.

She came. Hard. Brutally. Gasping and moaning, still staring into his beautiful eyes. Needing to see him go over. Needing to feel his body come apart in her arms.

He did. His smooth pumping turning jerky, harsher. His entire body shaking as he came and came, his cock twitching inside her.

Yager released a shaky breath, leaning forward to rest his forehead against hers.

"Holy shit."

"Yeah." She smiled even as she gasped for air. "My thinking exactly."

Chapter Nineteen

Neecy woke up and found herself sprawled over Yager like a well-fed puma. The man had an enormous bed and yet she couldn't seem to stay on one side of it. What was wrong with her?

Who was she kidding? She knew what was wrong. She was comfortable. Way too comfortable. She'd only been in his home a few days but Yager treated her like she belonged here.

She stared at his sleeping face, his arm tight around her. At some point, she'd put his tank top back on. He told her he liked seeing her wearing his clothes. And she liked smelling him on her. She liked it a lot.

Somehow sensing her rapt attention, Yager's eyes snapped open and he stared into her face.

"What is it?"

It was only four in the morning, but she figured she might as well get the difficult part over with before he confronted her over breakfast and in front of a roomful of hungover Crows and Ravens.

"Now that I'm better...I should leave."

"Yeah. Back to work, huh?"

Well, he took that better than she thought he would. "Yup. No rest for the followers of gods."

He stretched and his warm body felt so amazing rubbing against hers. "After everybody wakes up tomorrow, we'll head back into the City."

"Good."

Wow. That was *really* easy. Which, she had to admit, kind of hurt her feelings. Could he really let her go that easy? After they'd peeled themselves away from the wall, they'd started up again moments later on his bed. This time slower, but still an amazing fuck. She saw it on his face. The way he looked at her when he was inside of her, the way he choked out her name when he came. He did care about her. She knew he did.

No, no. She was thinking about this the wrong way. He would let her go easy, and...and that was good. That was what she wanted.

"We can move your stuff into my apartment right away."

Dammit! She should have known better.

"Yager, I can't move in with you."

His expression didn't change. "Why?"

"'Cause...we just...can't."

He stared at her and she waited for some explosion of anger. Some kind of argument. Instead, his hands began caressing her body. She frowned in confusion as he gently rolled her onto her back.

His hands kept moving across her flesh, making it tingle and demand satisfaction. He kissed her neck, her chin, her cheek. But it wasn't until he kissed her mouth—long, slow, and deep—that she knew what he was up to.

She tried to say no. Tried to push him off. But she was weak and he felt so good. But this was wrong. They shouldn't be doing this. They should *never* be doing this.

She let him continue, though. Let him kiss her and touch her. At some point, and without her even realizing he'd done it, he slipped on a condom. Then he was inside her and she almost cried. Cried from relief because her body ached to have him inside her all the time now. And cried from anger. Anger at herself for letting this go on.

Neecy pulled away from his kiss, even as her body thrilled to the slow, steady pace of his thrusts. "Yager—"

"You know how I feel about you, Neecy," he cut her off, panting hard.

"No. Don't." She wanted to beg him to stop. She wanted to demand he keep going.

"You mean everything to me."

"No."

"I love you, Neecy. I'll always love you."

"No!" Now she was crying as she wrapped her arms around him. "God, Yager. Please just—"

"If you tell me you don't love me, I'll stop. I'll stop making love to you and fuck you twenty ways to Sunday. But ya gotta tell me you don't love me."

But she couldn't. Neecy didn't lie. She may bullshit and fool around, but she didn't lie.

It was definite now. The not-lying thing...by far her most annoying trait.

If she were a good liar, she could get laid and then head home tomorrow—and spend the rest of her life suffering for something she'd paid for twenty years ago. But she wasn't a liar. She never had been.

She'd paid for her past. Yeah. She was a drug dealer once. A good one. But she'd paid for all that as soon as her boyfriend pulled the trigger.

Now? Now she deserved to be happy. Or to at least try.

"I can't," she sobbed into his neck. "I can't tell you that."

Yager's arms tightened around her body, as he continued to slowly thrust into her. He turned his head, forcing her to look at him. He smiled into her tear-soaked face and kissed her eyes, her nose, her mouth.

"I love you, Neecy. You might as well get used to it. 'Cause I'm not going anywhere, baby. Not without you right by my side."

Neecy thought a fresh wave of tears might suddenly explode out of her, but the orgasm got to her first. She gripped Yager tight and let him take her exactly where he wanted her to go.

Yager held her so tight, he was afraid he'd break her. Especially when he came and he temporarily lost the ability to speak or think straight.

He knew he might scare her off, but it was a risk he was willing to take. He had to do something. The look in those eyes said it all. Come morning, she would leave him...again. He couldn't face that. He couldn't face waking up another morning without Neecy next to him. Not when he'd had her right by his side for days.

And telling her just wasn't enough for Neecy. He had to show her. To be honest, though, he never thought she'd let him. He was terrified she'd pull away or tell him to stop. If she'd told him to stop, he would have, even though it probably would have killed him.

He kissed away her tears as he gently pulled out of her. He tossed the condom in the trash can by the bed and turned back to her, wrapping his arms around her and pulling her into his chest.

Her warm breath tickled the skin of his neck as he used his hands to soothe her shaking.

"I'm never letting you go, Neecy Lawrence. No matter what. Understand?"

She nodded her head but didn't speak.

"As long as we're clear, baby."

When he was sure she finally slept, he closed his eyes and joined her.

Neecy frowned at the sound of birds. Not her crows. These were birds that didn't actually sound frightening. Yager was behind her, spooning her. His big arms wrapped around her waist like he was afraid she'd fly away.

Her naked skin itched and she realized it was because of the grass.

Neecy's eyes snapped open. *Grass?*

She gave herself a moment to focus and quickly realized they were under an enormous tree. Its limbs twisted and turned, leading up toward the stars while its roots led to the bowels of the earth. It took her a good thirty seconds to figure out exactly where she was—beneath the sheltering leaves of *Yggdrasil* or the World Tree. The way station between the different worlds of the Norse gods, including Asgaard, Helheim, Aesiras, as well as a few other worlds Neecy couldn't remember the names of.

In the halls of Asgaard, Neecy would find Valhalla. Being that close to her final resting place until Ragnarok came gave her little comfort.

"Would you like some grapes?"

Neecy glanced up at the woman standing over her wearing a Boston Red Sox baseball cap, black overalls, and a plain white T-shirt.

"What is it with you and fruit?"

Skuld smiled as she sat under the tree. "I find it a wonderful icebreaker." She popped several grapes in her mouth.

"Do you know why you're here, Denise?" she demanded while chewing.

Christ, it was like dealing with a nun. They were the only ones who called her Denise.

"No. And I definitely don't know why he's here." She motioned to the still-sleeping Yager who, even in sleep, gripped her like his life depended on it.

"Well, let's start with him, 'cause he's easy. He refused to let you go."

"What?"

"I tried to pull you away from him to bring you here and the man would not release you. So I had to bring you both. As a leader of the Ravens, I wasn't too concerned about having him here, but talk about some strength. No wonder he's Odin's favorite. I just thought that was because he was the one who actually had the balls to take the big idiot to a strip joint."

Neecy remembered what he told her last night. "I'm never letting you go, Neecy Lawrence. No matter what." Apparently, he wasn't kidding.

"So this is the deal... Didi wants to retire."

Throwing Yager's arm off, Neecy sat up abruptly. "What? Well, you can't let her."

"I have very little choice."

"Since when?"

"Since I've kept the Crows mortal. At some point, if you survive, all of you will need to retire."

Neecy's eyes narrowed. "So what does that have to do with me?"

"I do love the sound of trepidation in your voice...and you know exactly what this means."

"You want *me* to lead The Jersey Gathering?"

"Why do you sound so surprised?"

"I don't know. I guess I never really thought about it."

"Well, no one could ever accuse you of being power hungry."

"Power hungry? I've got too much shit to do."

Skuld laughed and it was a surprisingly soothing sound. "I see why Didi likes you. You're strange."

"I'll try and take that as a compliment."

Neecy glanced over her shoulder as Yager sat up, his mouth open in a wide yawn. He nodded his head at the goddess. "Skuld."

"Wilhelm."

"Why are we here exactly?"

"It's time."

Yager brushed his hand over Neecy's bare arm. A calming move that worked extremely well. "Time for what?"

"For Denise to prove her worth to me."

"I haven't already?"

"As a soldier, you're exemplary. But I need a wartime leader."

"Wartime?"

"This assault from the Hunters, Denise, is just the beginning. They want you gone for the same reason I want you to lead." Skuld ate a few more grapes, turned her head to the right, and yelled, "I told you two I'm in a meeting! So one of you bitches get out here and water this goddamn tree!"

One of the Fates and Skuld's sister, Urd maybe—Neecy didn't know and she wasn't about to ask—stepped out from behind the enormous World Tree and tossed a watering can at her sister. "Water it your damn self!"

Skuld's barely concealed face turned frightening. No wonder many considered her a less-than-approachable god.

"Bitches."

Skuld stood up. She was tall. Much taller than Neecy.

Neecy pushed herself to her feet as Skuld turned her back. Yager now stood behind her, naked as the day he was born. Unlike Neecy, who thankfully had on his MIT tank top that reached midthigh.

When Skuld turned back to face them she held an ax.

Great. More axes.

Neecy had never been a big ax fan when it came to her weapons, and now that she'd actually had one in her back, she'd like to avoid them. Unfortunately, that didn't seem possible at the moment. She knew Skuld would only give it to her because she'd need it.

"This is a powerful weapon. One of the most powerful you'll find." Skuld ran her thumb along the edge. "You'll need it for your Trial."

She may not be an ax fan, but any weapon was better than no weapon. So when Skuld handed it to her, she took it gratefully.

"Any specific directions go along with this?"

"Now where would the fun be in that?"

Neecy sighed. "Of course."

"But if you succeed at this Trial, you'll become leader of The Jersey Gathering."

Holding the weapon in her hand, Neecy felt the weight. It was heavy but filled with powerful Magick. She felt it running through her fingers. "And if I fail?"

"We'll make sure to have a lovely funeral for you...with roses. I heard they were your favorite."

Yager barely bit back his growl. "That's not funny."

Skuld chuckled. "Actually, it kind of is."

Neecy took a few practice swings with her new ax. It was like she was born with it in her hand. "So what's my Trial?"

"Destroy the Hunters. Especially their leader, Waldgrave. But I want them all, Denise. I want them weeping to Hella come dawn."

Yager had no idea how he ended up here with Neecy, but he would be eternally grateful he did. He wouldn't let her face this on her own. One or two Hunters...maybe. But all of them? With no wings and having just recovered from her last fight? No way would his woman be facing this alone.

Battle plans already filled his head. Ways of attack. Who should be on the team from both the Ravens and the Crows. Together, they'd make sure she passed this Trial.

Neecy swung the ax again, her muscles rippling under his tank top. Powerful runes covered the ax blade and its black handle.

"No Valhalla for them?" she asked.

"Sneaky bastards preying on *my* warriors? No. There'll be no Valhalla for them. No Valkyries to lead them home."

Neecy nodded as her index finger slid across the runes on the ax. "Can I ask you a question?"

"You can ask me anything as long as it's not about your death...which may very well be today," Skuld said with a huge grin.

Man, give him Odin any day. This goddess was a bitch!

Neecy, however, seemed unimpressed and continued on. "What exactly was Didi's Trial?"

Shrugging, Skuld picked up her water can and doused the roots of the World Tree.

"She was to get a feather from one of Odin's ravens. You know, his actual birds Huginn and Muninn. But I wasn't very specific...so she drove over to Mountain Creek, met with one of the Elders, and politely asked him for one of his feathers. Considering he couldn't see past the woman's breasts, he gave it over happily and got a date out of the bargain." Skuld smiled. "Tricky little wench."

Yeah, that sounded like Didi.

"You are running out of time, Denise. Do you accept this challenge?"

Neecy shrugged as Yager wrapped his arm around her waist. "Yeah. Sure. Why not?"

Skuld no longer looked at them as she diligently watered the tree. "I need a direct and clear 'yes' on this, Denise. Just like when you took my hand the first time."

"Okay...yes. I accept."

Didi picked up her white knight and was about to move it—and demolish Tye in the process—when she glanced up to find a naked Yager standing in the middle of the living room.

"Yo, Yager man," Mike stated from the couch. "Put on some clothes."

Yager ignored him as he spun in circles. Didi didn't know Yager as well as Neecy now did, but she could sense the panic coming off the man.

"Where is she?"

Didi stood up as the other Crows and Ravens came into the living room. They'd been dressed and ready for battle for hours. She got the feeling Yager didn't realize he and Neecy had been gone since the day before. That's how Didi knew they'd gone to Asgaard to prepare for Neecy's Trial.

Suddenly serious, Mike pushed off the couch. "Where's who?"

Cold rage spread across Yager's face and he spit out through gritted teeth, "Neecy. Where the fuck is Neecy?"

Neecy landed hard in a crouching position. One knee slamming down first, one palm flat against cold stone, the other still gripping the weapon Skuld gave her. She looked like a runner at the starting line.

She gave herself a moment to breathe and then she looked up. The Hunters all surrounded a blood-covered altar. An altar she was on.

Aw, shit.

Chapter Twenty

Waldgrave stared at the woman he thought long dead. Dressed only in an enormous tank top, she looked as stunned as him about her sudden appearance during their religious rites of power. They'd been invoking the goddess in preparation of their final Hunt of the Crows. They hadn't even gotten to the final sacrifice yet.

He found the Crow surprisingly attractive for such a butch female. He preferred his women pliable and fearful. This woman looked like she feared nothing, and that's how she looked when he scouted her out in that store. He wanted to see the woman his goddess wanted dead so badly, and one look at that cold face and powerful body, and he knew she had to go. She'd do anything to protect her fellow warriors. Anything to keep his goddess from getting what She wanted.

And now he knew he'd been right about her. This would be no easy kill. He knew it as soon as she jumped to her big feet on the altar and took up a classic battle-ready pose.

The enormous but plain ax she held firmly in both hands appeared unused. No nicks or marks marred its surface. Waldgrave would bet money she'd never fought with it before.

Smiling, he hefted his own ax. An ax awarded to him by his goddess. With a powerful move of his arms, he swung the ax over his head and brought it down on the solid stone altar.

An explosion of sound filled the room as half the altar crumbled in his ax's wake.

"Fuck!" she snapped as the bit of altar she stood on fell away at her feet. She hit the ground in a cloud of dust.

Not willing to give her time to recover, Waldgrave swung his ax again, aiming for where he'd guess the female's head would be. It came down in a perfect arc, and already he felt her defeat in his heart. But the clang of metal and an agonizing pain tearing up his arms showed him she still had no intention of being an easy kill.

The dust from the altar cleared and he saw the female had put up her own ax, blocking his. It should have crumbled like the altar. But now that she'd used it, he could see the glowing runes along both sides of the blade and on the black handle.

The bitch's protector goddess had given her a weapon of great power, which annoyed him. This insignificant female was not his prize. She was simply in the way of his prize. He needed her gone so that the full-on assault on the rest of those women could begin. Without her, they would be lost. Without her, they'd never be able to protect the one he wanted.

With a vicious snarl, she pushed forward, throwing Waldgrave away from her. She sprang to her feet and swung her ax, once, twice. One acolyte lost his head, the second she split from one hip to the other.

The other Hunters backed away from her, circling her and Waldgrave. Her eyes strayed to the big picture windows of the ballroom. Then to the doors.

"Going to run, little girl?"

She acted like she didn't hear him, her body turning away from him to see all the exits. Then he heard her muttered reply.

"Crows don't run."

He barely brought his ax up in time as the crazy bitch spun and swung her weapon, aiming for his head.

Bobby Anders hefted his M-16 in his arms and sighed. Goddammit, he was cold. Exactly how long was he supposed to stand here anyway? Ever since his fellow brothers took out that one Crow, Waldgrave made sure to have sentries on duty at all times. At first, Bobby was all for it. It made complete sense. But a week later and nothing. Nothing but nearly frostbitten fingers and toes and a good old-fashioned cold.

Yet something was going on. A battle cry from within the house caused half of the sentries to charge back inside. Bobby wouldn't leave his post, though. He was there to ensure no one attacked from the outside and that's exactly what he would do.

But, he realized, no matter how ready he thought he was or how fast with his weapon he might be, he would have never seen this one coming.

Enormous didn't really do the man justice. And for someone his size, especially with those wings stretching big, black, and ominous from his back, he shouldn't be able to move so fast. But the man moved like lightning. One second Bobby stood all alone and the next the big man easily snatched the weapon from his grip.

Still, the hands attached to the chain wrapping around his neck...those were female.

So was the voice in his ear. "Say goodnight, sunshine."

Tye grinned as Janelle released the chain and allowed the Hunter to drop to her feet like a sack of garbage. She'd snapped his neck the way some people break a candy bar in half. And she made Tye so hard he physically hurt.

Unfortunately, he didn't have much time to focus on his little lust muffin. The rest of the Crows and Ravens were silently dropping from the sky, taking out the sentries quickly and quietly. Like the birds themselves, Crows and Ravens were crafty. Why go in screaming and announcing their presence when they could sneak in and kill everyone efficiently? It wasn't logical.

And Tye was all about logic.

The little one landed behind Janelle, nearly falling on her ass as her feet touched solid ground. Tye cringed. Man, what a clumsy little thing. But he found her entertaining because she hated Mike so much. It was like watching big-league wrestling. Personally, he put his money on the runt.

Yager landed beside Tye. There were a lot of things in this universe Tye didn't much like. And the look on Yager's face at the moment was absolutely at the top of his list.

Following behind his leader, he shook his head. Anything not Raven or Crow would not be getting out of here alive tonight.

How any goddess in her right mind could think putting these psychopaths on her ass was a fair Trial, she'd never know. And now that Neecy knew who was truly behind this—who truly wanted her dead—that made this whole thing much more disturbing. She saw the rune on the altar. She knew who these Hunters belonged to. And Skuld was right. A war was coming—a war among gods. And their warriors were merely pawns.

But at this point, Neecy no longer cared about any of that. They could deal with everything else later. Her only goal at the moment was to kill Waldgrave and keep her girls safe. She sensed that without their leader, the rest of the Hunters would be easy pickings for the Crows and Ravens.

And she knew the two Clans were coming. She knew Yager was already here. She could feel his presence like a physical touch.

Neecy studied Waldgrave. She'd seen this man before. In the video store. And even though she'd only seen him for a brief second, the details were completely accurate. A big, wide man, Waldgrave had muscles on top of muscles bulging under his clothes. But she was a bit taller than him and she knew she was faster.

She swung the ax again, aiming for his head. For a moment, Waldgrave was startled but he recovered quickly, blocking her move. He twisted his blade to pull her off balance.

Neecy rolled with it, ending up on the other side of Waldgrave, but with her ax still in her hands. She jumped to her feet and immediately swung again. Again, Waldgrave blocked her, but Neecy moved in close and slammed her foot in his groin. He grimaced and although he didn't double over in pain like most men would, Waldgrave still lost enough momentum for Neecy to pull her ax away and swing. Unfortunately, the weapon had turned in her hands and the blunt end of her ax slammed against Waldgrave's head. But there was enough force behind the move to knock him off balance.

Waldgrave landed facedown. Quickly, Neecy walked over to him and planted her foot in his back, keeping him down. She swung the ax over her head, but before she could split his skull in two, Waldgrave spit out a spell that threw her back and across the room, slamming into several slow-moving Hunters.

Waldgrave smoothly got to his feet. "Did you really think my goddess was going to let some abomination of Skuld's stop *me*?"

Neecy pulled herself up, her eyes glued on the man walking toward her.

"She wants you gone and it's my job to ensure that you go."

Gripping the handle of her ax tight, Neecy felt the power move through it. She knew the runes on it. Knew what they could do. In fact, she knew exactly what she had to do.

But before she could move, glass shattered, a Hunter's carcass tossed through one of the enormous windows.

Janelle grinned at her...and waved. *Crazy fuckin' female.*

Yager stepped through the window, his beautiful face rigid with anger.

Well, no one not Crow or Raven is gettin' outta here tonight.

"Perfect." Waldgrave leered at her as the Crows and Ravens followed Yager into the room. "All the players in one place."

He turned to his men. "Kill them all. Get the girl."

Neecy didn't wait for him to turn back to her. Crows didn't give a "fighting chance" or a "head start". They were Crows. Mean. Smart. And brutal.

She lifted her ax and swung, her muscles screaming from the effort. Waldgrave turned in time to see the blade flying toward him. He raised his own ax, but he wasn't fast enough. Not fast enough to stop a Crow.

Neecy cleaved his head in two and never made a sound.

Yager watched Neecy Lawrence, dressed only in his tank top and covered in dirt and blood, bury her ax in a Hunter's head.

Another Hunter ran toward him. Without turning to face him, Yager snatched him up, wrapping his hand around the idiot's throat and squeezing until he crushed every bone in his neck. He dropped the body at his feet and looked up at the rest of the Hunters.

He didn't know what they saw on his face, but they ran.

Neecy walked toward him, her eyes never leaving his, as she softly spoke to the two warrior Clans.

"None of them leave this house alive. None."

"Yes!" Mike and Janelle cheered at the same time. Then both groups were moving and destroying.

Standing in front of him now, Neecy stared at him. She had fresh cuts and bruises on her bare arms and legs, but he didn't know from what. He didn't care.

"How did you guys get here so fast?"

"Fast? It took us over an hour. Wind was against us."

She smiled as she stepped closer to him. "Skuld helping us out?"

"Or Odin. You know how he is."

She glanced around. "Where's Arri?"

He gently pushed her bangs off her face. "Outside with Tye. Doing me a favor."

Neecy's brow peaked up. "A favor?"

Chapter Twenty-One

They all stood behind Arri as she chanted. On her knees, her eyes closed.

Neecy was freezing in the blanket they'd given her. She wanted to go home, get warm. At this rate she'd catch a cold or the flu. But she wouldn't rush Arri, not when the girl worked some powerful Magick over Karl Waldgrave's family mansion.

Waldgrave's house gave a sickening lurch. Followed by another sound, like a cannon shot, and suddenly the house folded in on itself, sucked through a big enough doorway only Arri had the power to open. With the house went any bodies of the Hunters as well as those who might still live but had successfully hidden from the two Clans.

It took less than thirty seconds for the house and its occupants, living and dead, to disappear through the doorway Arri created. In the end, all that remained was burnt grass where the house once stood.

Then little Arri Chang burst into tears.

Mike turned toward Yager, his face desperate. "Yager, man. She's fuckin' cryin' again!"

Neecy motioned to Katie and Connie. "Get her. And let's make it quick. I'm catchin' my death here."

As if to emphasize the point, Neecy's head slammed back, then forward, a huge sneeze bursting out of her.

And just like that...she was airborne. Her wings snapped out and she flew back twenty feet, slamming into the trunk of an ancient tree.

Connie pulled Arri to her feet as Katie laughed.

"Well," Didi offered dryly, "she got her wings back."

Neecy pushed herself to her feet. "That's it. I'm now officially done for the night."

She walked back to the warriors. "We're out of here. I'm freezing. I'm exhausted. And, is it my imagination—" she glanced at her enormous black and purple wings, "—or are my wings inordinately large?"

"They are bigger." Katie walked around her. "I could be wrong, hon. But I think Morgan gave you Raven's wings."

Neecy let out a huge sigh. "Typical."

"They're bigger than Yager's," Janelle added.

Katie looked at Yager. "Does that make you feel inadequate?"

"Katie!" Neecy pushed the woman's shoulder, then motioned to the rest of The Gathering. "It'll be dawn soon, Crows. Move out."

Wait a minute. She was leaving...*him*!

Yager grabbed her arm. "Neecy?"

Neecy turned toward him and rewarded him with a warm smile. Going up on her toes she leaned in and kissed him.

"Later." She kissed him again. "I promise."

Neecy and The Gathering took off as Neecy's birds descended on the remains of those not taken with the house. The Hunters they'd dealt with before making it inside. The birds would wipe away any evidence the Hunters even existed.

"You ready, bro?" Tye stood next to him. "Like she said, it'll be dawn soon."

Yager shook his head. "I don't get it, Tye. I don't get her."

His friend smiled as he patted him on the back. "And don't even try. She's a Crow."

Tye was right. Yager was not going to bother trying to figure Neecy Lawrence out. No more playing this game on her terms.

This bullshit was over as of now.

"Now, hold still."

"Ow!"

Katie stepped back from Neecy. "I didn't touch you yet."

"I'm projecting into the future."

Arri, her eyes still red from crying, turned to Janelle. "See?"

Disgusted, Janelle walked over to the kitchen counter on the other side of the room. She slid onto the countertop, taking the cup of coffee Delia handed her.

"So what happens now?" she asked before sipping her coffee.

Neecy shrugged as she leaned away from Katie and her Mercurochrome. "Got me."

"Didi says she's out of here soon." Katie sighed and leaned back. "Would you stop acting like a child, so I can clean off these scrapes?"

"So you'll be taking over, right, Neece? I mean you survived and everything."

Neecy looked around the Bird House kitchen at the warriors ready to call her their leader. Which seemed really strange, considering how she was dressed. In her thermal underwear, under aqua blue Snoopy pajama bottoms from Fran, a pink Hello Kitty sweatshirt from Katie, fuzzy green bunny slippers from Janelle, and a purple knit ski cap from Arri, which for some unknown reason had droopy knit balls hanging from the top that kept tickling her nose.

She didn't look like a leader. She looked like the crazy lady in her old neighborhood who used to say Moses was in her bathtub drinking a forty ounce.

"I don't know. I mean, I guess. It's hard to tell with Skuld. I somehow doubt she'll show up to tell me or anything."

"Well, whatever you do make sure you have a big supply of porn on hand."

Neecy looked at Delia. "Huh?"

"*Penthouse Forum* is her favorite."

"No, no, she likes *Penthouse Variations*."

"Whatever. She's a *Penthouse* fan. Just keep that in mind."

"So you're telling me the powerful goddess we worship and serve likes amputee sex?"

Katie shook her head as she finally cleaned out a light wound on Neecy's neck. "Nah. She likes the bondage."

"And she loves ass play."

Delia chuckled. "There's nothin' like a good corn-holin'."

"Okay. I'm done." Neecy pushed Katie away and she chuckled at her idiot sisters. "I'm going to bed. I'm exhausted and still freezing."

Janelle put down her coffee mug. "What about Yager, Neece?"

She shrugged. "I love him."

"Yeah. We got that part. But what are you going to do?"

"I need some time. Lots of life changes in the past couple of weeks."

Delia, busily cutting up apples and cheese, tossed over her shoulder. "He's not going to wait forever, ya know."

Neecy brushed her bangs and the fuzzy little balls off her forehead. "I never asked him to."

"Your colors meld together so beautifully," Arri burst out as fresh tears began flowing again. "*He's so in love with you!*" she finished on a wail.

Janelle's head fell back. "Oh, my God! How long are we going to have to put up with the sobbing?"

Arri turned so fast in her chair she startled everyone as she pointed one small finger at Janelle. "*Hey! You open a portal to Helheim and see how you do!*" Then she burst into another round of tears.

Rolling her eyes, Neecy stood up and gently pulled Arri out of her chair. "Okay. That's it, 'Tear-leen'. Let's get you to bed so you can get some sleep. Otherwise you're gonna drown us all."

Crying too hysterically to answer, Arri simply nodded and allowed Neecy to steer her to the kitchen door. But before they reached it, Connie's voice stopped her.

"Look, Neece. I say this as the one woman here who never cares if you have a dick in you or not..."

Neecy turned to Connie. "Uh...okay."

"But you need to face a cold, hard fact."

"Which is?"

"The Gathering will *never* in this lifetime be as nice to you as Wilhelm Yager. In fact, we'll probably go out of our way to make your life hell because that's what we do. So if I were your dumb ass, I'd grab that shit with both hands."

Neecy took in a deep breath and calmly stated, with none of the emotion she'd been feeling the past week living with Yager, "Ya done?"

Connie glanced around the room and the other Crows nodded. "Yeah. We're done."

"Good. Now listen up. What I do with Yager is my own goddamn business. You little cunts try and get into the middle of it and I'll squash you bitches like flies. Are we clear?" she finished with a warm smile.

"Yeah." Janelle gave a surprised chuckled. "We're clear."

"Wonderful. Good night."

Chapter Twenty-Two

Her first day back at school was surprisingly uneventful. But that could have been because she didn't have to kill a single person with an ax or have anyone sent through a portal to hell.

A good number of her students actually looked glad to see her back, and when she wasn't in class she was in her office talking to all her PhD and master's candidates.

She didn't bother going to her apartment. She had a full night of work ahead of her. So she went back to the Bird House, changed into her standard fighting clothes, and headed out with her crew. They had a full slate this freezing-cold January night.

The first three scumbags they dealt with were just idiots. They hadn't used their items yet, so luckily for them, their blood wasn't necessary. But for fun the Crows scared the living shit out of them.

The last one of the night, however, was a real piece of work. He'd not only opened a doorway by sacrificing some junkie he found, he'd enhanced his strength. He put up quite a fight, too. No Ravens showed up to "help out". And Neecy was confident she didn't need them, even when she ended up in the alleyway Dumpster. Yet she couldn't shake the disappointment of not seeing Yager.

After she dug herself out of the Dumpster, she'd decimated the man with the help of her crows, leaving barely enough to toss into the doorway Arri pulled open.

Once it was sealed, the team surrounded her.

"Wanna come out with us?" Janelle asked as she slid her blades back into her boots and covered up the weapons with her jeans. "We're hittin' a club or two tonight before it starts snowing."

A blizzard was supposed to be heading their way and Neecy had to admit she was looking forward to a few snow days. No school!

"Nah. I'm exhausted. I've been lounging at Yager's too long. It's weakened me."

Connie smiled. "The Ravens may be at one of these clubs. Tye was the one who told me about 'em."

"Then I'm definitely not going. I've got a lot to think about tonight. Don't need any distractions." Especially those Yager-type distractions.

It had only been a day since she last saw Yager, but she missed him. No, tonight she was going to make a decision and stick with it. And tomorrow, she'd talk to Yager.

Then she'd fuck the living hell out of him.

"Okay." Connie spread her wings. "See ya later." She took off, Katie right behind her.

Arri gave an adorable little wave and followed. The doorway she'd opened this night didn't require much power and Arri didn't even sniffle when she was done.

Janelle bumped Neecy with her shoulder. "See ya, Big Wing."

"Stop calling me that." Before she could take off, Neecy grabbed Janelle's arm. "And watch out for her."

"Who? Arri?"

"Yeah."

"You think she needs it?"

"The girl's got more power than is humanly possible and she has no idea how to really use it yet. Not fully. So we need to watch out for her. Remember, it wasn't me they wanted, J."

"You know who's after us, dontcha, Neece?"

She nodded. "I saw the rune on the altar before Waldgrave destroyed it."

"And?"

"It was Hella."

Janelle whistled. "The Queen of the Underworld?" She laughed, until Neecy glared at her. Clearing her throat, "Uh...sorry. So, why use Waldgrave?"

"Her warriors can only be on this plane of existence for a few hours...they're already dead."

"Dust to dust?"

"Dust to dust. She needed someone who could focus on us full-time."

"You going to tell the others?"

Neecy shrugged. "Eventually."

"But you think Hella wants our little Arri?"

"Maybe." Neecy shrugged. "I really don't know. I do know Arri's the weakest of us. The most vulnerable. At least until she's better trained. But to be honest, I don't want to risk any of you guys."

Janelle smirked. "Okay, Mom."

Neecy playfully cuffed Janelle on her shoulder. "Freakin' smartass."

"Would you prefer I was a dumbass?"

"Some days...yeah."

Janelle laughed and followed after the team.

With a deep, tired sigh, Neecy unfurled her new, way-too-big wings and headed home.

The wind was blowing her way, and it took her only ten minutes to make it downtown. She climbed through her window and stumbled into her dark apartment. Somehow she made it to her bathroom in the dark without bumping into anything. She could barely keep her eyes open, so she decided against a shower and just took a quick toilet break. Once done, she stumbled her way in the dark back to her bed, turned, fell back...and hit the floor.

"What the..." Neecy sat up and struggled to see in the dark. She really couldn't make anything out, so she got to her feet and made it across the room. She hit the light switch and turned to find her apartment damn-near empty.

"He...he wouldn't." But she knew he would. She went to her closets. They were empty. As was her bathroom and all her bookshelves. Her bike was still there as was the basketball net.

"*I'll kill him!*" she screeched as her exhaustion faded away, leaving only raw rage.

She went back the way she came in and launched herself from the small ledge, heading uptown to Yager's apartment.

Even with the heavy wind against her, she still made it to his apartment in record time. She was too pissed to let something like nature get in her goddamn way. She flew to the patio. The glass doors leading into the apartment were unlocked and she knew he'd left them unlocked for her. She stormed in only to find the living room deserted.

Growling, she moved through his home, finally tracking his tight ass down in his kitchen. He stood at the counter, his back to her, wearing only a pair of boxers. He ate an enormous sandwich, read the newspaper, and looked goddamn gorgeous doing it.

Just seeing him sent her heart racing. Had it really only been a day since she'd last seen him? It felt like forever. All she wanted to do was lick his spine from one end to the other.

She shook her head. She was pissed...*remember?* And she planned to stay that way until he explained what the fuck he thought he was doing with her shit.

She opened her mouth to speak, but he cut her off. "I was wondering when you'd get here."

Yager turned around and froze. "Christ, baby, what happened to you?"

"Got thrown in a Dumpster," she bit out.

"That's disgusting, Neecy."

"Look, Yager. You and me, we need to talk."

"Uh-huh." He walked up to her, but stopped abruptly. "Baby...you're funky. Let's get you in the shower."

"Wait. We need to talk now."

Yager took her hand. "Okay." He headed toward his bedroom, dragging her behind him.

"I'm serious, Yager."

"I know. So talk."

She growled again. The man was pushing her patience.

"First off, you took all my shit."

"You make it sound like I gave it to gypsies."

"I don't know what you did with it."

"What do you think I did with it?"

She knew exactly what he did with it. Her clothes were in his closet, lined up right next to his. Her books were in his bookshelves, mixed in with his. And all her tampons and soaps were somewhere in his bathroom cabinets. *Bastard.*

"Look, Yager, this isn't fair."

He stopped in the middle of the bedroom and pulled the wool socks off her arms. Tossing them aside, he lifted her tank top over her head, forcing her to raise her arms. "How so?"

"We're talking about major changes in my life. I need time to think. To plan. To strategize. You don't rush into this sort of thing."

Her black jeans hit the floor and she desperately tried to ignore the fact that the man she loved now kneeled in front of her to remove her boots and shuck her pants. "All that bullshit takes too long."

"It's not bullshit, and that's not your call."

"No. It's probably not. But I have no patience and I was tired of arguing."

He dropped her dirty clothes in the hamper. Giving her a quick wink, he again grabbed her hand and dragged her into the bathroom. He released her long enough to turn the shower on and adjust the water temperature.

Neecy wrapped her arms around her body. She was freezing. Not surprising. She was always freezing after hunting in the winter. "I don't care if you were tired of arguing. And I didn't want to argue. I wanted to discuss."

"Yeah, well, I was tired of discussing, too."

He turned around and frowned at her shivering. He moved up close to her and rubbed her arms.

"Look, all I'm saying is this isn't an easy thing for me to do. I need time."

Shit. How did he get her bra and panties off without her even noticing? *Goddamn him!*

"I'm really not in the mood to give you time."

"You're not..." Before she could punch him in the face, he lifted her by the waist and carefully placed her in the shower. By the time she pushed her still-too-long but now thoroughly wet bangs out of her face, Yager had shucked his boxers and stood behind her.

"This isn't about whether *you* want to give me time."

He put that freakin' expensive shampoo on her hair and began massaging her head. She almost came from that alone.

"True. But I warned you I wouldn't play fair, now didn't I?"

"That's not the...the... Oh, that feels good," she sighed.

He gave a little hum in response as he moved close behind her. She could feel his hard cock pressing into the small of her back. His hands felt wonderful on her scalp and the feel of his flesh rubbing against hers was making her sopping wet and crazy.

Dammit! This was why she needed some time alone! Because the man could distract her without even trying.

He finished washing her hair and finger-combed his expensive conditioner through it. While he left that in, he washed the rest of her, taking his time, lingering over her "hot spots".

At this point, she didn't even bother arguing with him. As it was she could barely speak. Once done rinsing her off, she simply took the soap and began washing him. He closed his eyes and let her do what she wanted, a small smile playing on his lips the entire time. When she was ready to wash his hair, she looked up at him.

"I never thought I'd ever be able to say this to a man who wasn't in the NBA, but you're too tall for me to wash your hair."

She waited for him to bend down a bit so she could make his scalp feel as good as hers, but instead he slowly dropped to his knees in front of her.

Steeling herself at how beautiful this six-seven Viking god looked kneeling at her feet, she began washing his hair. As Neecy worked really hard to concentrate on washing his hair from root to ends, she felt Yager's hands slide up the back of her legs. His big fingers gliding over her wet skin, drawing out those intense feelings she never had with anyone else in her life. As she massaged his scalp, his hands gripped her ass and pulled her closer to him.

"Open your legs, Neecy."

Clearing her throat, Neecy tried to get control over her exploding emotions. It wasn't really working, but she still made the attempt. Silently, she braced her feet apart and buried her fingers deeper in his hair.

Yager leaned forward a bit, burying his face between her legs. His tongue took long licks of her pussy as his hands squeezed and massaged her cheeks.

Without meaning too, Neecy let go. She let go of having her ass tossed in a Dumpster, of getting used to her overly large wings, and of taking over leadership of a clan of indescribably rowdy, bitchy women. She let go of anything that didn't have to do with Yager and her snatch. Tomorrow. She'd worry about all the bullshit tomorrow.

As all her stress and worries melted away, Yager's tongue and an interestingly placed finger shot her over the edge. Her head fell back as she gasped out her orgasm, her fingers still buried in Yager's gorgeous hair.

When the shaking simmered down to a gentle trembling, Yager stood up, quickly rinsed his hair, and then lifted her in his arms.

"God, baby. You're exhausted."

"I am. But I can still walk on my own."

"I know. But this is much more fun."

Placing her carefully on the bathroom sink counter, Yager grabbed a towel and dried her off. Once done, he quickly dried himself off and took her back to the bedroom. He pulled the covers back and put her down on the soft bed.

Yager clicked off the light and snuggled up behind her, his arms tight around her middle, his face buried in the back of her neck. This really seemed to be his favorite position.

Feeling Yager's big body surrounding her, Neecy felt safe, content, and home. With that last thought making her smile, she went to sleep.

Yager woke up to find Neecy staring at him. Her arms wrapped around her legs, her knees tucked up under her chin.

He stretched and smiled. "Hey, baby."

"Morning, Yager." She held up her arm, the metal cuff loose around her wrist, the chain attached to the bed frame clinking against itself. "What is this?"

"I wanted to make sure you were here when I woke up."

She blinked. "You're a little crazy, aren't you?"

He shrugged. "I'm not sane."

Sighing, she looked out the window. "Blizzard hit last night. And it's still going."

Well that explained why it was so freakin' bright in the room.

Grinning, "Cool! Snow day!"

She laughed. "God, you're such a geek, Yager."

"Yup." Yager sat up and leaned in, his eyes focused on her breasts. He couldn't wait to get her nipples in his mouth. He couldn't wait to be buried balls-deep inside her. But one brown hand slammed against his chest.

"Hold it."

He growled. "What?"

"Don't growl at me," she snapped. "We need to talk."

"I don't wanna talk. I wanna fuck."

"Fine. Then I'll talk."

"Can't it wait?"

"No."

Yager gave a deep, painful sigh. Sitting back, he dropped against the headboard, wincing as his head hit hard steel.

Clearing her throat to stop herself from laughing, Neecy raised her chained arm. She gestured to it. "Hello?"

"I'll take it off when you're done." There may be a blizzard outside, but he didn't put it past Neecy Lawrence to still try and bolt.

Rolling her eyes, she again wrapped her arms around her legs, successfully blocking her pretty tits from his view. *Dammit.*

"So this is the deal, Yager. Take it or leave it. If I stay—"

"If?"

"*If* I stay, I won't leave. It means we're together. Forever and all that shit. I don't sneak around and I'm too honest to cheat. So if you plan on keeping me, you'd best be prepared that this is the only pussy you'll be getting until Ragnarok comes. If that's a problem for you, then you best call the movers and start moving my shit back."

"I didn't call movers. The Crows brought your stuff here."

"The...they..." She took a deep breath. "I'll deal with that later. Where was I?"

He pointed at her lap. "That'll be the only pussy I'm getting."

"Oh, yeah. Okay. So, make up your mind now. I will keep teaching. I will lead the Crows until Skuld tells me otherwise. I don't know if I want kids or not. It's definitely not a priority. So, if that's a problem for you, say it now." She took another deep breath. "I am *really* cranky in the mornings and no, coffee doesn't help. That's why I don't drink it. Christmas is my favorite time of year and the Crows do Secret Santa since there's so many of us. Although I always give something special to my team. I say we avoid trying the dating thing again, since that seems to lead to mutilation. I don't go out much, except to party with the Crows. To me a fun night is pasta, *Law & Order*, and masturbating. Although if we can switch out the masturbating for sex...I'm okay with that."

Fighting really hard not to smile, he said, "Anything else?"

"Just one. I like that you're nice to me, even though it still weirds me out a little. But if you promise not to stop, I'll promise to work really hard not to get that panicked look on my face when you do something particularly sweet."

Yager couldn't fight it anymore. He grinned. How could he not? She was wonderful. "That'll work."

They stared at each other until Neecy gestured with a flip of her hand. "Your turn."

"I get a turn?"

"Yes."

"Okay. Um...let's see. The only pussy I want or will ever want is yours. So no worries there." He grinned. "It's very tasty!"

"Yager..."

He held his hand up. "Okay. Okay. Um...I don't really have a favorite holiday, but whatever will make you happy is what I'll do. The only thing, Mike comes to Thanksgiving dinner. His other option is his father's and I can't do that to him. Of course, I figure you won't mind since you already had his ass in your face." He glared at her before continuing. "Even though I don't have a favorite holiday, I do love summertime. Um...oh! I spend hours on the computer. *Hours*. Not just for the business, but because I really love it. But I have laptops, so I won't spend all my time in the office. And nothing makes me happier than the thought of sitting next to you on the couch working on my laptop while you watch *Law & Order*." She smiled warmly at his words. "Especially knowing that I can just reach over and start finger-fucking you."

Neecy coughed in surprise.

"I hope you're not a pet fan, 'cause I really don't want a pet. I could care less about kids. And on very rare occasions, Odin may drop by...in bed...with us."

"What?"

"I already told him he shouldn't do that on a regular basis anymore. Ya know...'cause you'll hurt him. I'm not cranky in the mornings, but I do love to fuck when I wake up. Which was one of the reasons I was annoyed you kept leaving." He glared at her again but she only chuckled. "So, cranky or not, be prepared for a regular dose of morning cock, as I like to call it. I'm okay with not dating, but I have every intention of marrying you and I want the full-on honeymoon. Two weeks in the Caribbean. No telephone. No gods. No work."

"Just me in a bikini!" Neecy reared back startled. "Now where the hell did that come from?"

Yager shrugged. "I have no idea."

Suspicious eyes locked with his, but she apparently decided not to pursue it as she asked, "Anything else?"

"Just one."

"This isn't the Will thing again, is it? 'Cause I actually like calling you Yager."

"No."

"The nice thing?"

"No."

"The this-is-the-only-pussy-you-can-ever-have thing?"

"No."

"Then what?"

"Tell me you love me, Neecy."

She blinked, an expression of horror spreading over her face. "I...I didn't? I didn't already say that?"

"No. You didn't."

Neecy smoothly sat up so that she rested on her knees. "Oh God, Yager, I'm so..." She stopped trying to move toward him, the chain halting her. Growling, she held her arm up.

Yager bit back his smile as he grabbed the key from off the bedside table.

"Sorry about that," he chuckled as he unlocked her.

"Where did you get this thing from anyway? It looks fuckin' medieval."

"Tye."

Neecy stared at him for a long moment. "Okay. Keep him away from my girls. Especially Janelle."

Now free, Neecy crawled into Yager's lap. She placed her hands on both sides of his face, stroking his jaw and staring deep into his eyes. He brushed her nipples with the back of his knuckles and when she sighed, her wings unfurled, black and powerful, from her back. He'd never seen anything more beautiful besides Neecy herself.

"I love you, Yager." She leaned forward and kissed him softly. He knew what it took for her to say the words. And he knew she'd only say them if she meant them. "I love you," she whispered against his lips.

He wrapped his arms around her waist. "I love you, baby. I'll always love you."

She gave an uncharacteristically shy smile as she leaned into him. "So what do we do now?"

"That's easy." Yager pulled her tight against him and her wings curled around them as she slid her arms around his neck. "We're going to spend our snow day being nice to each other, Neecy Lawrence. Over and over and over again...until one of us passes out or dies."

Neecy smiled, resting her forehead against his. "Now *that's* the nicest thing anyone's ever said to me."

About the Author

Originally from Long Island, New York, Shelly Laurenston has resigned herself to West Coast living which involves healthy food, mostly sunny days, and lots of guys not wearing shirts when they really should be. These days Shelly spends most of her time writing, reading and, like her heroines, trying to avoid any serious prison time. To find out more about Shelly's books, check out her website at www.shellylaurenston.com.

*How much trouble can one small female be to a modern-day
shapeshifting Viking? Well...it really depends on local gun laws.*

Go Fetch!
© *2007 Shelly Laurenston*

Conall Viga-Feilan, direct descendent of Viking shifters, never
thought he'd meet a female strong enough to be his mate. He especially
didn't think a short, viper-tongued human would ever fit the bill. But
Miki Kendrick isn't some average human. With an IQ off the charts and
a special skill with weapons of all kinds, Miki brings the big blond
pooch to his knees—and keeps him there.

Miki's way too smart to ever believe in love and she knows a guy
like Conall could only want one thing from her. But with the Pack's
enemies on her tail and a few days stuck alone with the one man who
makes her absolutely wild, Miki is about to discover how persistent one
Viking wolf can be.

*Warning, this title contains the following: explicit sex, graphic
language, and strong violence.*

Available now in ebook and print from Samhain Publishing.

Can a powerless witch find happiness with an arrogant, impatient dragon? If the dragon has his way, she sure as hell will.

About a Dragon
The *New York Times* Bestselling Author
© *2008 G.A. Aiken*
Book 2 in the award-winning Dragon Kin series!

Talaith's life has never been easy. A goddess has forced her into servitude. Her husband despises her. And all those in her tiny village fear her. But just when she doesn't think her life can get any worse, she's pulled from her bed one morning to be burned at the stake for being a witch. What she never counted on was a terrifying silver dragon deciding to rescue her.

Briec the Mighty didn't really know what to do with a human female. Especially this one. Chatty and a bit of a complainer, he doesn't understand why she can't simply admit to herself that she wants him. Who wouldn't? He was Briec the Mighty after all. Females fought to spend the night in his arms. But this one tiny woman with her many secrets and her annoying habit of referring to him as "arrogant" has turned his simple dragon life upside down.

This book has been previously published as The Distressing Damsel by Shelly Laurenston and· is available under its new title, in print, from Kensington Books.

Warning: This story contains explicit monogamous sex and graphic violence!

Available now in ebook from Samhain Publishing.

GREAT
CHEAP
FUN

Discover eBooks!

THE FASTEST WAY TO GET THE HOTTEST NAMES

Get your favorite authors on your favorite reader, long before they're
out in print! Ebooks from Samhain go wherever you go, and work with
whatever you carry—Palm, PDF, Mobi, and more.

SAMHAIN
PUBLISHING, LTD

WWW.SAMHAINPUBLISHING.COM